THE CANARIS FRAGMENTS

By the same author

Hammerstrike

The Canaris Fragments

Walter Winward

Heywood Books

© Walter Winward 1982

First published in Great Britain
by Hamish Hamilton Ltd 1982

ISBN 1 85481 017 0

This edition published in 1989 by
Heywood Books Limited
55 Clissold Crescent
London N16 9AR

Printed in Great Britain by
Cox & Wyman Ltd, Reading

For Vix and John, with love

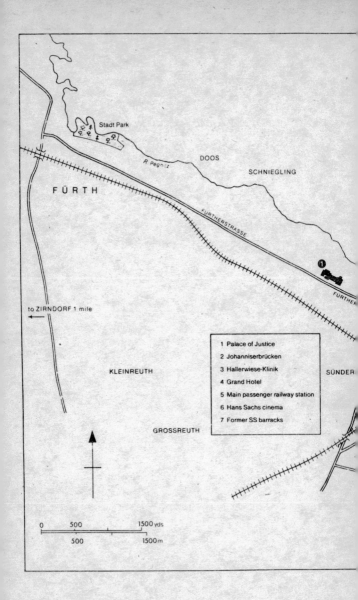

Stadt Park

R. Pegnitz

DOOS

SCHNIEGLING

FÜRTH

FURTHERSTRASSE

FURTHER

to ZIRNDORF 1 mile

KLEINREUTH

SÜNDER

1 Palace of Justice
2 Johanniserbrücken
3 Hallerwiese-Klinik
4 Grand Hotel
5 Main passenger railway station
6 Hans Sachs cinema
7 Former SS barracks

GROSSREUTH

0	500	1500 yds
	500	1500 m

Prologue

Somewhere in Germany – 1943

Beautiful, beautiful.

The two SS officers walked the length of the warehouse, stopping occasionally to discuss the object of their admiration. It had to be admitted, they both agreed, that although the conception of the scheme was brilliant, its execution had surpassed their wildest expectations. It had taken a long time but it was all going to be worth it.

'What about the men who worked on the project?' asked the elder of the pair. He was also the senior of the two and had arrived from Berlin only an hour earlier in response to a telephone call from his subordinate.

'Waiting to be dismissed, paid off.'

'Then perhaps we'd better see to that before proceeding.'

The senior SS officer counted fourteen men huddled against the far wall of the courtyard. He knew that some of them were German, some French, a couple Belgian. Strange, he thought, that women had no skills in this field.

To a man the fourteen were ill at ease. They knew the job was finished; they did not trust the SS. They had been promised their freedom in exchange for their talents, but they had all had experience of SS promises. It was therefore with considerable anxiety that they saw the massive gates swing open and a lorry reverse in.

The two Belgians were quicker than their companions in recognizing betrayal. Even so, they were not quick enough.

At a shouted command from the junior SS officer, the lorry's tailboard dropped, the canvas curtain was pulled aside from within, and the ugly snout of a belt-fed heavy machine gun appeared.

The machine gun crew was commanded by an Oberscharfuehrer. At a signal from him they opened fire, raking the far

1

side of the courtyard, not stopping when all fourteen men opposite were either dead or dying, hosing the supine bodies until the belt was exhausted.

Afterwards the Oberscharfuehrer delivered the *coup de grâce* to each of them, even where the man was obviously already dead. A single shot in the back of the head. He had to reload his Walther pistol twice.

When it was over he marched smartly across to the two officers and snapped up his right arm in the Nazi salute.

'All finished, Herr Standartenfuehrer,' he barked.

'Burn the corpses,' ordered the senior officer, 'then report back to me. There is still much to be done.'

One

German/Danish border – May 1945

Leaving Kupfermühle, a tiny hamlet near the port of Flensburg, he changed his mind about walking in the woods and instead made for the hill overlooking Wassersleben, where he had a fine view of the harbour. The earlier quarrel with his wife had left a nasty taste in his mouth, but he knew it wouldn't be long before she came after him, expecting to find him at their usual spot among the trees. For the moment, however, he needed to be alone.

Although on official documents he invariably gave his height as five feet six or seven, he was a couple of inches shorter than that. He had reached his fortieth birthday a month before, but he looked much older, partly due to undernourishment, partly because the shabby civilian clothes he wore had been tailored for someone else. The ugly scar which ran from the lower right-hand corner of his mouth to below his right ear was an old wound, but when he was anxious, as he was now, it turned pink and appeared fresh. Many of his companions of the last six years believed the scar honourably earned in a duel, but it was, in fact, a legacy from a razor fight in 1924.

He smiled grimly. 1924 was also the year another man the world had yet to hear from was writing *Mein Kampf* in a Bavarian prison.

In an inside pocket he carried a passport made out to Wilhelm Hansen, occupation teacher, resident of Hamburg. To avoid it appearing suspiciously new the issuing date was given as November 3, 1944, though he had not known of its existence until April. He also carried a *Wehrpass* in his real name, one that every German knew. The Hamburg Gestapo had insisted on this, to prevent summary execution if he were picked up by the *Feldjägerkorps*, military police, as a deserter.

3

Not that there was any danger of that now, as neither the FJK nor the Gestapo existed any more. It was May 28 and the war had officially ended three weeks ago. Hitler was dead – heroically leading his troops, the communiqué had stated – as was Goebbels. The Propaganda Minister had promised to protect him, the man with the scar; protect his wife also. He had seen the teletype from the Ministry with his own eyes: *At all costs they must be kept out of Allied hands.*

That was on April 7 and he had to admit that the security services of the Third Reich had done their best, even after all was lost and the Minister dead. He would stay free as long as possible, but it could only be a matter of time.

Still, he was no war criminal. Under international law as he understood it, neither he nor Margaret was a criminal of any description. His greatest fear was that he would be executed out of hand when captured, that he would not be permitted the luxury of a trial in which to plead his cause.

A noise behind him made him start, but it was only an emaciated dog. He snapped his fingers, beckoned it towards him. It backed away snarling, hackles raised. So, even the dogs, he thought, faintly amused.

He got to his feet dusting himself down. He had been away long enough and by now Margaret would be anxious. After taking a final look at the harbour – something told him he would never see it again – he set off down the hill.

He was still half a mile from where he expected to meet his wife when, up ahead in a clearing, he saw two men in the uniform of British army officers. He was not alarmed. He had had several brushes with the Occupation Forces in the last few days, but so far no one had recognized him or even stopped him to ask for papers. He could, in any case, avoid the Tommies by a slight detour. They were gathering wood for a fire and seemed oblivious to anything other than the task at hand. But for some reason he could never later fathom he continued towards the two men. Captain Adrian Lickorish and Lieutenant Perry, both of the Reconnaissance Regiment, Royal Armoured Corps, looked up as he approached. They heard him say, in French: 'Here are a few more pieces.' A moment later he repeated the sentence in English. Then he walked on.

Perry was a German Jewish refugee, an interpreter. Like

many Jews serving in the British Forces against Germany he had taken the advice to change his name for fear of brutality if captured. The sound of the scarred man's voice meant nothing to him. But Captain Lickorish had heard it too many times since the outbreak of war not to suspect the true identity of its owner. Even so, it seemed hardly credible that the man whose name was synonymous with treachery in the Allied camp should be casually walking through the woods as if on a hike, and Lickorish wasted valuable seconds relaying his supicions to Perry.

The interpreter was first to act. With Lickorish hard on his heels he raced after the disappearing figure, who turned and smiled nervously on hearing running footsteps behind him.

Perry glanced at Lickorish, who nodded.

'You wouldn't happen to be William Joyce would you?' asked the interpreter.

At the Old Bailey trial which began on September 17 1945, the Attorney General, Sir Hartley Shawcross, asked Lickorish what happened when the prisoner was challenged. Lickorish answered: 'He went to put his hand in his pocket, and Perry fired his revolver.'

Accustomed as he would be to living under the Gestapo, in 1945 the immediate response of any European when his identity was questioned was to produce documentation. It was for his German passport in the name of Hansen that Joyce was reaching when Perry, thinking that what might appear in his hand was a pistol, shot him. The single bullet passed through both Joyce's thighs, causing two entry and two exit wounds. As he fell to the ground he shouted: 'My name is Fritz Hansen.'

He was so confused or terror-stricken he could not even remember that his adopted forename was Wilhelm. Not that it would have made any difference. A rapid body search not only revealed the Hansen passport but the *Wehrpass* in the name of William Joyce.

Lickorish could scarcely believe his good fortune. Outside the remnants of the Nazi hierarchy and senior officers in the SS, the one man the Allies wanted in custody above all was Joyce, otherwise known as Lord Haw-Haw, he of the sneering voice who had taunted the British with his nightly radio broadcasts for five years, who had warned every man, woman

5

and child in the United Kingdom that their days were numbered, their island doomed, their stubborn resistance futile. William Joyce: who knew, it was reputed, when clocks in English villages stopped and at what time, who preached the wisdom of surrender to the oncoming Wehrmacht, who attempted to spread defeatism, who set neighbour against neighbour, who broadcast lists of the dead after Luftwaffe raids before, it seemed, even relatives knew the fate of their loved ones; who would later claim he was not British at all but American, and above all a naturalized German citizen *before* the United States entered the war, and how dare anyone accuse *him* of treason.

No one who lived in the United Kingdom during the dark days of 1940, when invasion seemed imminent, would ever forget Joyce's preamble to his nightly programme *Views on the News* from Rundfunkhaus, Masurenallee, Berlin: 'Jairmany calling, Jairmany calling.' Radio and stage comedians imitated his voice and intonation; 'Jairmany calling' echoed across bomb-sites and schoolyards, shouted by small scruffy children who knew not what they said. But deep in every British heart it was whistling in the dark. Lord Haw-Haw was no joke and twenty million adult Britons would willingly have knotted the noose and slipped the trapdoor that sent him to eternity.

Which was uppermost in Joyce's mind when Perry and Lickorish handed him over to the nearest frontier post. The RAC officers had treated his wounds with field dressings and, although unable to walk and in a state of semi-shock, Joyce was fully conscious. He had no doubt he could survive a trial by jury, but what worried him now was the possibility of a kangaroo court followed by immediate execution. There were a dozen men in the guardroom including two officers, and their expressions were anything but friendly.

The senior of the officers, Major Quinlan, was a freelance journalist prior to call-up but now served on the Intelligence staff of General Sir Miles Dempsey's Second Army. A visitor to the frontier post on the scrounge for a cup of tea when Joyce was brought in, Quinlan was quick to realize he was sitting on top of one of the major news stories of the moment. He would not be allowed to write it and byline it, of course, but in his Intelligence capacity it was certainly permissible to do a little preliminary interrogation. It wouldn't do his future career any harm to be known in Fleet Street as the first man to get a statement from Lord Haw-Haw – preferably with no one else around. He was wondering how to get Joyce alone when the problem resolved itself.

Far from having thoughts of a drumhead trial and a lynching party, the guard commander, a young lieutenant, was less interested for now in who Joyce was than where he had materialized from. In these first weeks after the war's end rumours abounded that Hitler was not dead but on the run, and the ports of North Germany (where the erstwhile Fuehrer could be spirited away via a small craft to a waiting U-boat and thence to South America) were being close watched. It was not a week since SS Reichsfuehrer Himmler, wearing an eyepatch and using the name Heinrich Hitzinger, had been picked up at Meinstedt. Two days later he was dead, having bitten on a cyanide capsule when challenged regarding his true identity.

Joyce was only too anxious to ingratiate himself with his captors. After complaining that he was in pain and receiving an assurance that an army doctor was on the way, he revealed the location of the house where he and his wife had been staying for the last few days. His main concern was for Margaret Joyce to be told of his whereabouts, and his denial that anyone of importance was at the Kupfermühle address was ignored by the guard commander, who bundled almost his entire detachment into two Bren-carriers and a 3-tonner and raced off for the hamlet. Fearful of missing out on what could be a remarkable coup, Perry and Lickorish went with the raiding party, leaving Quinlan, who volunteered with alacrity, and a Welsh lance-corporal to look after Joyce.

Quinlan estimated he didn't have long. The nearest medical centre was only minutes away and doubtless the MO would arrive with half his staff in tow, all of them itching to get a look at the infamous Lord Haw-Haw. He had a thousand questions he wanted to ask but no time to organize them into some order of priority. They came off the top of his head. Why had Joyce done what he had, broadcast for the Germans throughout the war? When had he left Berlin? Had he seen Hitler recently? And Goebbels? Were they genuinely dead or in hiding?

Joyce was reluctant to say anything. Now that the majority

of the soldiers and one of the officers had disappeared he felt more secure.

Quinlan pressed him. How had he got this far? Had he received help? He must have had assistance. Apart from the Kupfermühle house, were there any other hamlets in the vicinity sheltering fugitives?

'I have nothing to say at this time,' replied Joyce haughtily, as though that settled the matter.

As well it might have done if the Welsh lance-corporal had not dealt himself a hand.

'I don't know why you're bothering with the little bastard,' he said in his singsong voice. 'I don't know why we don't take him outside and shoot him. I lost a sister and my brother-in-law in the Coventry raids,' he added by way of explanation, fingering his Lee-Enfield.

Quinlan was about to tell him to shut up and mind his own damned business when he registered the flicker of panic in Joyce's eyes. After a moment he recalled the collaborator speaking from Berlin during the evening of November 15, 1940, while Coventry was still burning, his voice jubilant at the destruction and death the Luftwaffe had meted out. It was one of his most talked-about broadcasts. He had detailed streets and buildings that were either damaged or destroyed and even the names of some families who had died. It had given rise to the rumour that he had a battalion of fifth-columnists all over England, men and women with short-wave radios in direct contact with Berlin.

'Maybe you're right,' said Quinlan slowly, nodding at the Welshman. 'We can always say he tried to make a run for it.'

Joyce was lying prone on a stretcher. He levered himself up on his elbows, spluttering with indignation and fear.

'You would not be believed,' he stammered. 'A man with bullet wounds in both legs can hardly escape.'

'Then we'll think of something else,' said Quinlan lightly. 'One thing's for certain: you're no use to us if you won't answer questions.'

'I can't tell you what I don't know,' protested Joyce.

Quinlan turned away from him.

'Do you have a round up the spout, Corporal?' he asked.

The Welshman confirmed he did by bringing his rifle to his waist, flicking off the safety as he did so. Neither Quinlan nor

Joyce had any doubt that, given the word, the lance-corporal would send Joyce to meet his Maker.

'Wait!' shouted Joyce. He was sweating now. After almost six years in the Third Reich he was accustomed to summary executions.

He broke into German, establishing first that Quinlan understood the language and guessing correctly that the Welshman did not.

Quinlan had trouble following the avalanche of words. He had a good working knowledge of German, was almost fluent, but some of the more obscure and lengthy compounds defeated him. He understood Joyce to say that he had never met Hitler and had only talked with Goebbels on rare occasions, that he sincerely believed them to be dead. He was no more than a minor member of the Propaganda Ministry, he pleaded, and knew nothing about the former political and military leaders of the Third Reich with the exception of Admiral Canaris and Oberstleutnant (Lieutenant Colonel) Manfred Langenhain.

Quinlan pricked up his ears. The name Langenhain meant nothing to him but Canaris was the one-time head of the Abwehr, Military Intelligence. There was some confusion about what had happened to him. Rumour had it that he was hounded out of office in 1944, his entire organization taken over by the SS. But his fate remained unknown. If he was still alive and Joyce knew his whereabouts, however...

Quinlan had no opportunity to pursue the question. As Joyce finished speaking the door to the guardroom was flung open and an RAMC colonel lumbered in, followed by half a dozen more junior officers.

The colonel pulled rank, quoted Hippocrates, and took over. While Quinlan was not asked to leave – Joyce was still a prisoner and the medicos were unarmed – it was made quite clear that no further questioning of the 'patient' would be tolerated for the present. The Welsh lance-corporal's expression was one of a child who's had his favourite toy confiscated.

Joyce dictated his first formal statement to Captain William Scarden of the Intelligence Corps on May 31 at Lüneburg military hospital. After much string-pulling Quinlan contrived to be present, but Joyce, now confident he

9

would not be executed out of hand, denied ever mentioning Canaris or an officer named Langenhain. Major Quinlan must have misunderstood.

Quinlan knew he had been conned, realized why Joyce, buying time until the medicos arrived, had dropped into German. The Welsh lance-corporal, the only other witness, did not speak the language, leaving Joyce to repudiate, as he was doing now, the tenor of the entire conversation.

It was probably all bull anyway. Joyce would have said anything at that precise moment to keep the Welshman's finger off the trigger.

Quinlan decided to forget it. It mattered little. In a few months the traitor would have his neck stretched and that would be an end to it.

He was not to know then that he was destined to meet Joyce again and, via him, become involved in an intrigue so bizarre that all written records of it were destroyed by order of the highest authority and all surviving participants warned of the direst consequences should they ever find the urge to talk irresistible.

Two

Nuremberg – November 29, 1945.

There was not much left to suggest that the city had once been the shrine of Nazism. If it was born in Munich, it grew up here, orchestrated by the brilliant Speer and later by Goebbels. It was Speer who, after the Roehm purge – The

Night of the Long Knives in 1934 – stage-managed the Party Congress in September of that year, when surviving Roehm supporters were threatening to split the Nazis. Speer took over the huge Zeppelin Field south-east of the Old Town and erected a massive stone structure 1,300 feet long and 80 feet high. Crowning the stadium was a gigantic eagle with a 100-foot wing-spread and on all sides there hung thousands of swastika banners, 20,000 in all. At intervals around the auditorium he positioned 130 searchlights each with a range of five miles. When Goering complained at losing so much candle-power to propaganda purposes, Hitler backed Speer. 'If we can use such numbers for a gathering like this, the rest of the world will think we're swimming in searchlights.'

Two hundred thousand Party faithful crowded into the stadium that September evening. Leni Riefenstahl, the multi-talented actress and director, filmed the entire occasion using a dozen cameras. She called her documentary *The Triumph of the Will*, and it was universally recognized as an outstanding achievement. Certainly everyone who saw it, supporters of the régime as well as implacable enemies, believed thereafter that Hitler's promise of a Thousand Year Reich was no idle boast. And just as certainly no one would have credited then that in a dozen short years it would all be over, Zeppelin Field along with much of the rest of Nuremberg a ruin.

With very few exceptions there was neither electric light nor heat in the majority of private houses and apartment buildings, which were, in any case, mostly bombed-out shells and low on the list of priorities for renovation. Whole families huddled together in any room that still had four walls. Tarpaulins, sheets of corrugated iron and sometimes cardboard covered gaps in the roofs. Sanitation was at its most primitive and there was the ever-present danger of water-borne diseases. The shops that still existed contained the barest rations – courtesy of the Allied transport system – and most of those had to be queued for for hours and eaten cold. Fresh water was obtained from standpipes at specific times or from bowsers when the conduits broke down. Luxuries such as cigarettes and chocolate were impossible to obtain outside the black market. Fraternization between the occupying troops and the indigenous population was strictly forbidden, but it went on nevertheless. For a packet of cigarettes, a bar of chocolate or a pair of stockings, a man could buy whatever took his fancy in the way of women.

Nuremberg was in the American Zone of Occupied Germany and in spite of the fact that no GI had much sympathy with members of the defeated nation (who, it was felt, had brought their present misery upon themselves), US engineering battalions worked round the clock to get the basic utilities back to something near normal. But it was a task that would take much longer than the few months they'd had, particularly as most of Germany's major cities were in a similar state of desolation. Apart from that, since July the engineers had been otherwise occupied getting the facilities in the Palace of Justice up to scratch, for there, on November 20, the International Military Tribunal (IMT) had opened shop, its object to try twenty-one leading Nazis for war crimes. Until October 25 the men in the dock had numbered twenty-two, but on that date Dr Robert Ley hanged himself in his cell using a wet towel. Ley was the former head of the German Labour Front, which is a polite way of saying he ran the slave labour programme in which tens of thousands were worked to death.

Martin Bormann and Gustav Krupp were to be tried *in absentia*, the first because he could not be found, the second because he was reputed to be crazy.

Of the remainder the most important were Reichsmarschall Hermann Goering, ex-Deputy Fuehrer Rudolf Hess, Foreign Minister von Ribbentrop, and SS Obergruppenfuehrer Ernst Kaltenbrunner, since Heydrich's assassination chief of the RSHA, the SS security services which included the Gestapo. Each of the twenty-one had pleaded Not Guilty to the charges contained in the indictment, but none had yet entered the witness box. These were early days; it was reckoned the prosecutors would take six to eight weeks outlining the case against the defendants.

And what a case it was, thought Otis Quinlan, hurrying towards the comparative sanity of the Grand Hotel in Bahnhofstrasse, shuddering at what he had witnessed in the courtroom that afternoon. In future years the world would become more or less immune through over-exposure to the conditions in concentration camps filmed by American and British troops as they overran Germany in the early months of 1945, but in November of that year few people had seen what had happened in Belsen, Dachau, Buchenwald and elsewhere. The press 'stills' shown in newspapers were mild stuff compared to what the court saw on November 29: the hideous piles of skeletal corpses unburied in open pits, the crematoria, the gas chambers. Perhaps worst of all was footage of those who had remained alive through some effort of will: their immense eyes, seemingly far too large for their shrunken, starving faces, their pathetic unbelieving smiles at being liberated from hell, the agonizingly slow pace at which they walked – or crawled. At more than one point in the darkened chamber men and women were heard to gasp and sob openly as a British officer, calmly and methodically, described what he had seen when he stood among the dead and the dying in Belsen.

While the films were being shown, those in the dock, for security reasons, were picked out by spotlamps. Few of the accused could watch every reel. One defendant, Dr Hjalmar Schacht, Hitler's financial wizard who had personal experience of a concentration camp, having been tossed in one for his alleged part in the July Plot, sat with his back to the screen, refusing to look at all. Hess protested loudly that he did not understand what was going on. Only Julius Streicher, the one-time Gauleiter of Franconia with his power base in Nuremberg, and Goering watched everything, though it was said in private by people who should have known better that the Reichsmarschall kept his eyes on the screen because he genuinely could not believe what he was seeing.

Quinlan was inclined to take that sentiment with a very large pinch of salt. There were many, far too many, middle-ranking Allied officers who felt that Goering should not be in the same dock with men like Streicher and Kaltenbrunner, thugs of the first water. They remembered his record from World War I when he commanded the famous Richthofen squadron and was awarded the Pour le Mérite, the German equivalent of the Victoria Cross or the Congressional Medal of Honor. They conveniently forgot that he was also the founder of the Gestapo, that he had looted Europe of many of its art treasures, and that he had joined the Nazis, giving

13

their street-fighter image a tinge of respectability, for no other reason than that he was on the make.

The British were less sympathetic to the former head of the Luftwaffe than the Americans. The British remembered only too well those bleak days in 1940 when Goering's bombers attempted to annihilate English cities and murder their population. They remembered also the brutal executions of fifty RAF officers recaptured after the mass escape from Stalagluft 111 at Sagan. Later Goering would profess not to have known anything of this until it was too late, that, when apprised, he had protested strongly to Hitler. But, like much else the Reichsmarschall said, this too required all but the most gullible to reach for the salt cellar.

Not having a vehicle of his own as yet, Quinlan was forced to hike the mile and three-quarters from the Palace of Justice to the Grand. He could have hung around the courtyard and easily bummed a ride, but for the moment he didn't want company. It was dark now and strictly speaking Allied officers in full uniform were not encouraged to walk the streets alone. There was a dusk to dawn curfew in operation for the inhabitants of Nuremberg, but neither the occupiers nor the occupied paid it much attention. Neither was there usually any trouble, though in two cases to Quinlan's knowledge a captain and a major in totally unrelated incidents had disappeared from the face of the earth, presumably dispatched by Germans unwilling to accept that the war was over. Not that that worried Quinlan. He was young and fit and his Webley service revolver was a powerful and trusted friend. It was going to take more than a truculent Nazi with an unresolved grievance to sell him a one-way ticket.

He had arrived in Nuremberg from Schleswig-Holstein a fortnight ago, four days before the IMT officially set out its stall. It had taken powers of rhetoric he had not known he possessed to get him as far as the city, for he was on the list to be rotated home. Now that hostilities were well and truly over the British Army was trying to reduce its wage bill. It was not keen on paying non-essential majors for the privilege of doing little more than prop up the Mess bar.

Seeing his name on the list and doing a little elementary arithmetic, Quinlan had calculated that he would certainly be back in England before Christmas, a prospect he viewed with dismay. Two hundred and fifty miles down the road from Second Army HQ the most momentous court case in history was at the starting blocks. While he was still on the active strength of Second Army there was little he could do, but now they no longer needed him – well, that was a different matter. If he went home he wouldn't stand a snowball in hell's chance of witnessing the trial. He'd just be another unwanted journalist among scores of others. The staff men would cover it for the major newspapers, press agencies and radio networks. An outsider without a proven track record of war reporting would not even get a sniff at a seat in the press gallery.

Emboldened by half a bottle of good brandy he went straight to the top, to General Dempsey himself, finagling his way past battalion and divisional commanders in a manner that made him a few enemies and left more than one senior officer vowing to have young Quinlan's head for a paper-weight.

The Second Army was being forgotten, he told Dempsey. It was stuck in this north German backwater while the real action was taking place down south. God knows, what was happening in Nuremberg was as much the concern of Second Army as anyone else's, but all they were going to receive were second-hand newspaper and radio reports. It really wasn't good enough and what he, Quinlan, was suggesting was that General Dempsey have a personal representative on the spot, reporting daily or weekly to Army HQ in the form of a bulletin which could be distributed to all ranks. That way, the troops who had fought their way from the Normandy beaches to the Danish border would not feel they were being overlooked. It would be a marvellous morale booster, having their own man *in situ*, especially for those ranks who were to remain for the time being as part of the Army of Occupation.

Did Major Quinlan have anyone in mind?

Well, it would be preferable to send an officer with journalistic experience – someone like himself, say.

Dempsey admired Quinlan's impudence. The proposition also had a certain appeal. Montgomery's 21st Army Group, of which the Second Army was part, had been rather shunted out of the spotlight since the Supreme Commander, Eisenhower, had made it clear in the early months of 1945 that

15

Berlin was not the prime strategic objective, that the Anglo/French/American forces would stop at the River Elbe, leaving the Russians to take the capital of the Third Reich. Montgomery's counter-argument that his tanks could scythe their way across the North German Plain and be in Berlin by mid-April cut no ice with Ike. Occupy Schleswig-Holstein, take Hamburg and the ports of Lübeck and Kiel and hold tight; those were the orders. It was a decision that had driven every Second Army senior commander mad with frustration. While George Patton and Alexander Patch were taking town after town down south and grabbing the headlines, the 21st Army Group was left cooling its heels. There were many who thought Ike had political ambitions and that it would do a future campaign platform no good at all to allow Monty to grab the lion's share of the glory.

It was also a fact that since VE Day the French and British Occupation Zones had taken something of a back seat to the American, and while it was right and proper that Nuremberg (in the US Zone), as the cradle of Nazism, should host the trial, there was no doubt that certain transatlantic senior officers looked upon the whole business as *their* Tribunal. The British, French and Russians were there on sufferance.

So it was agreed that Major Quinlan could go to Nuremberg and remain there on full pay for as long as General Dempsey could swing it. Comprehensive bulletins would be expected weekly, though a seat in the press gallery from which to witness the proceedings might be difficult to obtain, places there requiring a slightly higher order of wizardry than feeding the five thousand. However, Dempsey would see what he could do, and twenty-four hours later it was done. If Quinlan would make his way to Nuremberg and seek out Colonel Eugene Masterson he should find his needs met.

Masterson was an old friend of Dempsey's from the days before D-Day and currently a senior G-2 (Intelligence) officer with Patton's Third Army, part of which was the occupying force in Nuremberg alongside units of Patch's Seventh Army and members of the Counter Intelligence Corps (CIC). The colonel passed Quinlan down the line to his senior deputy, Major Ben Hadleigh, who had a well-deserved reputation as a Mr Fixit. If what you wanted was humanly possible to obtain, Hadleigh would see you got it. Although his job had nothing to do with the Tribunal or the defendants, he had connections in all kinds of places. If he liked your face the sky was the limit. If he didn't – and no amount of money could persuade him otherwise even though he was known to dabble in the black market – you might as well strike your tent and steal away.

Fortunately he and Quinlan got along like ham and eggs instantly, partly because Quinlan had an American grandmother who, it transpired, had been raised not a dozen blocks from Hadleigh's Chicago stamping ground. (It was this same grandmother who had insisted that her only grandson's first forename be Otis; not because of the elevator company but after the town in New Brunswick where she had honeymooned before the turn of the century. It was either Otis, or her daughter and her daughter's English husband need not bother to attend the will-reading. The name had involved Quinlan in many a fistfight during his school years, but gradually he got to like it.)

Quinlan was a rangy 29-year-old with what an ex-lady friend had once called a studious if licentious face, like a medieval painting of a saint who had not quite made up his mind whether he wouldn't be better off running a bar. He was a handy cross-country runner and had done some boxing at middleweight while at university, where he had taken a degree in English. Before heading via a couple of provincial newspapers for the cauldron that was freelance journalism he spent close on a year in Germany where he witnessed first-hand the adolescence of National Socialism.

He had some money of his own and his general background was what he liked to describe as genteel chintzy-on-the-cheap Anglo/American with about a fifth of Bushmill's Irish thrown in three or four generations ago, which accounted not only for his near-black hair, for some reason going prematurely grey at the temples, but for a temper whose flashpoint could be measured in single figures. He was not a hard man but he reckoned he could look after himself when the chips were down. Since the invasion of Europe he had seen a dozen battles from a distance and a few more at much closer range. He considered himself neither especially brave nor crazy, but on more than one occasion he had picked up the nearest –

17

Lee-Enfield and fought his way through hedgerows and villages. Being in Intelligence usually meant he was away from the bulk of the fighting, but there was a book to be written about this war, a good big novel, and he thought he'd better find out what it was like at the sharp end before committing pen to paper.

Hadleigh was regular army, coming up 31 years of age and commissioned from the ranks. He didn't talk much about his early years, but Quinlan got the impression his boyhood in Chicago had been tough. He was an inch taller than Quinlan at just under six feet and was rarely seen without a six-inch Havana cigar in his mouth, though they were supposed to be as rare as gold dust. Wide enough across the shoulders to deter any but the most foolhardy into reducing a verbal argument to fisticuffs, he had a ready broad smile and was always immaculately groomed. Quinlan could confirm the whispered rumour that he kept a couple of girls over in the Sündersbühl district, south of the Ludwigs-Donau-Main Canal, for his own use and that of his special friends.

Hadleigh's primary function, in conjunction with CIC, was to seek out Nazis on the mandatory arrest list – SS, SD, Gestapo, and members of other criminal organizations – and turn them over for trial to the competent authorities. To this end he had let it be known throughout Nuremberg and its environs that his door was open day and night to anyone who wanted to talk, perhaps turn state's evidence in the hope of a lighter sentence themselves. Apart from a handful of sprats, so far he had not been conspicuously successful. Which puzzled him. Exact figures were naturally hard to come by, but Germany must have had several million people who were members of the Party, the SS, and so on. Of that number many would be dead, but many more had to be in hiding. It was therefore odd that there were so few turncoats, odder still that it was a rare occasion when an innocent citizen came forward to report something suspicious, even if for no other reason than to gain a pack of Luckies or a jar of coffee.

Many hated the conquerors, of course, but many more were obviously just plain scared, which tended to support Gene Masterson's hypothesis that the Nazis, the remnants of the hard core, were far from beaten yet; they were around in their funkholes, waiting for another tilt at the ring. They might be – though there was no guarantee of this – disorganized, but there were far too few Standartenfuehrers – SS colonels – and above in the bag, too many junior officers and NCOs. There were rumours that many had got out or were on their way out via a top-secret escape route to South America, but to imagine all had gone or were going was not only to subscribe to a logistic impossibility but to completely misunderstand the Nazi mentality. Fanatics did not cut and run when the going got rough.

Still, in Hadleigh's opinion most of them would be caught and strung up one of these bright days. In the meantime, what was left of the war was not too bad. He had it better than most with his girls and his one or two deals on the side to keep him in loose change, and fixing up the press seat for Otis Quinlan had hardly caused him to break sweat.

The oasis that was the Grand loomed up. The US engineering battalions had worked overtime here also, and the hotel was a brightly-lit miracle, officers and civilian equivalents only, in the surrounding desert.

Quinlan mounted the steps and made for the long bar adjoining the Marble Room where, even though it was still early, uniformed men and women were dancing to a small German band which had yet to get the hang of the latest American hit song.

Hadleigh was sitting on a stool halfway down the bar, staring at a glass of bourbon and a beer chaser, smoking the inevitable cigar. Quinlan made for him. It had become something of a ritual for the pair to meet here after close of business for the day. Hadleigh had a first-class top sergeant watching the shop in case anything urgent cropped up.

The G-2 major signalled the barman with two fingers. Set 'em up again, Joe. He waited until Quinlan had thrown down the bourbon before saying: 'Tough day at the office, honey?'

Quinlan grimaced as the sourmash knifed home. Good scotch was hard to come by even for the Americans, and he still wasn't used to bourbon.

'You can say that again. They had the films out – Dachau, Belsen, all points east.'

'How did the animals take it?'

'Some easy, some hard. Schacht wouldn't look at any of them.'

'Schacht's seen it from the inside, don't forget. He'll probably be acquitted.'

'Inside information?'

'Just good guesswork. That's what I hope, anyway. I'm making a heavy book on the outcome. Schacht could cost me money if they deep-six the bastard.'

'Who's favourite to get the chop?'

'Eight'll get you five on Goering, Ribbentrop, Streicher, Frank and Kaltenbrunner. Most of the rest I'm steering clear of until I see how they stand up in the box.'

'Even Hess?'

'Hess was in British custody for four years. It'll probably go in his favour, though not if he spouts some of the crap he used to spout here in the old days. I'll wait and see what kind of an impression he makes.'

'Kaltenbrunner wasn't there again today,' said Quinlan. 'The word is he's suffering from spinal meningitis.'

'Which is the medical way of saying he's paralysed with fear. He's in the 116th General Hospital, did you hear? Used to be an SD headquarters so I guess he'll feel at home.'

'There'll be a few more in hospital before this is all over, I'll wager.'

'Any ideas who?'

'For the book?'

'For the book. You've got to have an edge if you want to come out ahead.'

'Am I that?' asked Quinlan.

Hadleigh laughed. 'No, but it doesn't hurt to get first-hand impressions from the horse's mouth.'

Quinlan thought back to the first day of the trial, when the defendants were asked how they pleaded.

Goering had tried to make a speech, but the President of the Court, Lord Justice Sir Geoffrey Lawrence, later Baron Oaksey, had silenced him, having no intention of allowing the Tribunal to become a propaganda platform for the accused. Sulking, Goering had then stated that he declared himself Not Guilty in terms of the indictment.

Hess had simply said No, and von Ribbentrop parroted Goering's words.

The erstwhile head of the OKW, the High Command of the German Armed Forces, Field Marshal Keitel, was next to plead Not Guilty, and his declaration was followed by a statement from the President that Kaltenbrunner would have the opportunity to plead when he was fit. In the interim, the trial would proceed against him.

In quick succession Rosenberg, the violently anti-semitic Party philosopher, Hans Frank, Governor-General of Poland, Wilhelm Frick, Minister of the Interior, Julius Streicher, Walter Funk, the homosexual economist and Hjalmar Schacht, declared themselves not to be guilty.

The two senior naval officers came next, Karl Dönitz and Erich Raeder. Both announced themselves Not Guilty in clear voices. Baldur von Schirach, ex-Hitler Youth Leader and later Gauleiter of Vienna, echoed the words of Goering and Ribbentrop, while Fritz Sauckel, Gauleiter of Thuringia being one of his many titles, wanted to dot the 'i's' and cross the 't's'. 'I declare myself in the sense of the indictment, before God and the world and particularly before my people, not guilty.'

Generaloberst Alfred Jodl, Hitler's Chief of Staff, also felt a simple plea would not do. 'For what I have done and had to do, I have a pure conscience before God, before history and my people.'

Franz von Papen, known to his captors as the Silver Fox and acting out the noun, Arthur Seyss-Inquart, who had paved the way for Hitler's take-over of Austria and later served as Reichskommissar of Holland, and Albert Speer were content with simple pleas of Not Guilty.

The diplomat von Neurath, Hitler's first Foreign Minister before the outbreak of war and later Reichsprotektor of Bohemia and Moravia, pedantically stated: 'I answer the question in the negative.'

Finally Hans Fritzsche, a member of Goebbels' Propaganda Ministry, had denied his guilt.

There were four counts in the indictment against the defendants. These were:
1. Crimes against peace.
2. War crimes.
3. Crimes against humanity.
4. Being a member of a criminal group or organization.

It was to be no defence under counts 1, 2 and 3 that a defendant was acting under superior orders.

Of those in the dock, Quinlan considered that Frank, Frick, Rosenberg, Sauckel and Funk would probably require some form of medical treatment before the end. Kaltenbrunner was already hospitalized and Hess was saying he recalled nothing. The military and naval men would probably stick it out, while the remainder were anybody's guess.

He gave Hadleigh his opinion, adding: 'Though I'd watch those wagers on Goering, Ribbentrop and the others you mentioned if I were you. Talk is that the lawyers are going to question the validity of the whole thing, argue that it's impossible to have a fair trial when the judges are chosen from one side only, that of the victors. They're also going to submit that, according to international law in 1939, war was not an indictable offence. Neither were the SS, SD, Gestapo and so on criminal organizations. Their clients are being prosecuted under a law that was only created after the fact.'

'How does that theory grab you?' asked Hadleigh.

'Not at all. Personally I'd have had this lot and quite a few more shot on sight, as Churchill apparently wanted to do. Stick 'em up against a wall as you find them and to hell with trials. But that evidently didn't suit your people or the Russians. Stalin particularly wanted a worldwide hearing to justify what he did in Poland and elsewhere. He's no fool, Uncle Joe. He knows damn well no one's forgotten that until the middle of 1941 he was Hitler's ally. The trouble is, if you start buggering about with the law and lawyers it all becomes a matter of the fine print. Hitler himself said somewhere that he wouldn't rest until it became shameful for any German to be a lawyer.'

'Sounds like a guy I used to know who didn't make sixth grade and went back to blow up the school for having lousy teachers,' said Hadleigh.

'Nevertheless,' grunted Quinlan, 'you know and I know what the SS did in the camps, but if you let a lawyer tell the story it'll come out that the Jews and the other poor bastards had to fight their way into the gas chambers while the poor helpless guards tried to keep them out.'

Hadleigh clucked like a mother hen.

'Goodness me, Major, that sounds like cynicism. How's the girl making out, by the way?'

The girl was Frau Gretl Meissner, a pretty mouse-haired widow in her middle thirties who had turned up out of the blue a month earlier and asked Hadleigh for a job, saying she had a 15-year-old son to support. She could, she said, type, take shorthand, answer the phone, and was fluent in French and English. Hadleigh had checked her out, discovered that she had genuinely never had any Nazi sympathies, and hired her on the spot as a kind of general factotum. She worked twice as hard as his Third Army female clerks, and at present was 'on loan' to Quinlan, sitting with him most days in the Palace of Justice press gallery, for which Hadleigh had got her a press card, and filling in for him when he had business elsewhere.

'I let her go early. I don't know whether it was the films, but she seemed to have something on her mind.'

Hadleigh looked at him enquiringly.

'Nothing going on between you two, is there?'

'Not a thing. I make it a rule never to boff the help. Besides, she's too useful to get emotionally entangled. If I was really the stuff of which crooks are made I could spend my days getting drunk and let Gretl do the work. She's that good.'

Quinlan finished his drink and beckoned the barman for refills all round. Before they arrived Hadleigh was called away to the phone by an orderly. When he returned he sank his bourbon in one gulp and pushed away the beer.

'I have to head for the high sierras. That was the office on the horn. One of my informers came through and we've had a round-up of stooges.'

'Anyone on the black list?'

'Not as it stands right now. You know the routine. They are not now, nor have they ever been, a member of the Nazi Party or any affiliated organization. Christ, they've got Elks lodges in Nebraska with bigger memberships.'

Hadleigh thought for a moment.

'You doing anything special for the next couple of hours?' he asked.

'Well, I thought I might get myself a six-course dinner at the nearest five-star restaurant, washed down course by course

23

with Mouton Rothschild and Imperial Tokay. After that, I had a countess in mind who serves '29 Dom Perignon and sleeps in black silk sheets.'

'But apart from that.'

'Apart from that, nothing. Have you got any suggestions?'

'Just thought you'd like to help out over at the ranch. We've roped in half a dozen from what I can gather and it might be interesting. If we get through fast we can go out on what's left of the town. I can't guarantee the champagne or the black silk sheets, but the girls are clean.'

'Lead me to it,' said Quinlan.

Three

Nuremberg – November 29, 1945

Never one to miss a trick, Hadleigh had set up his headquarters in a former SS barracks on Allersbergerstrasse, which coincidentally just happened to be the site the US army in Nuremberg had chosen for its biggest base. While on the outside, except for the privileged and the cunning, conditions might be as rough as a Victorian novel, on the inside it was toyland with a vengeance.

Although Quinlan had a billet on the base, it still amazed him that once through the gates and past the armed guards he was in a different world. Off-duty personnel walked around as though they were back on the main strip of their home town, clutching cans of beer and smoking whatever brand of cigarettes took their fancy. Over in the PX, with a little fast talking a man could buy whatever his pocket would bear, and the black-market activity in Luckies and Camels and canned Budweiser and Schlitz was a cottage industry which would one day put the down-payment on hundreds of homes and businesses. What was truly astonishing, however, was the amount of electric light shining throughout the compound. It was Christmas and the Fourth of July combined. Little wonder that the German men, women and children who, defying curfew, congregated outside the main gates in the hope of a handout felt nothing but bitterness for their conquerors.

Hadleigh skidded the jeep to a halt outside a building which bore the official legend Third Army Intelligence. Underneath some wag had chalked *Lucky Brains Unit*. Where the codenames were, for example, *Master* for the First Army and *Eagle* for the Twelfth Army Group, *Lucky* was General Patton's personal choice for the Third Army. His Battle CP was always known as *Lucky Forward*.

Master Sergeant Max Judd was waiting for them in the guardroom. Beyond this were rooms which served as offices, interrogation cells, and sleeping quarters if it was going to be a long night.

Judd was a battle-hardened New Yorker whose German accent was atrocious but who could both understand and make himself understood and was finally, with Hadleigh's patient help, getting the hang of tenses and gender.

A thick-skinned thirty-year-old man who had joined up as a boy, he was a couple of years older than Hadleigh and looked as though he wrestled bulls for a pastime. Hadleigh had a handful of junior officers in his unit, but it was Judd he relied upon as his 2 i/c. Max had a street intelligence that was more valuable than anything the kids with college degrees could offer. He had served his war with a combat regiment until shortly after D-Day, when Hadleigh, desperate for some high-class assistance to help put through the grinder the thousands of prisoners being rounded up, had sent a flash request to the brass for someone with more moxie than the Ivy Leaguers under his command. Third Army was bagging, among others, tough Waffen SS men, and Hadleigh needed a right hand who could lean on them without worrying about the Geneva Convention or sleepless nights. Judd hadn't been keen to come out of the firing line until Hadleigh pointed out that he could do a hell of a sight more to shorten the war from an interrogation hut than he could leading bayonet charges. Apart from that, G-2 got first crack at any spare broads, booze and souvenirs.

Like Hadleigh, Judd favoured big cigars. He waved the one he was smoking at the door as Hadleigh and Quinlan came in. Quinlan had had a few drinks with him and swapped a few stories. They got along well together – as well, that is, as a Limey with Quinlan's background could with someone who had hustled his first buck on the streets before his milk teeth were through.

'Majors,' he said.

It was generally 'Ben' and it had got as far as 'Otis' with a few beers aboard, but for the present Judd was being formal.

'What's the score, Max?' asked Hadleigh.

'Got five of them in the Trough.' The Trough was Judd's special word for the room where they kept all prisoners prior to in-depth interrogation.

'All together?'

'Shapiro and Kowalski are making sure they don't go into a huddle and exchange game plans.'

'Who came through?'

Judd looked doubtfully at Quinlan.

'Come on, Max,' insisted Hadleigh. 'Major Quinlan's not in the same racket.'

'Schauff.'

Hadleigh nodded. Walter Schauff was a fat 50-year-old who'd once run his own bar and wanted to do so again if he could get a concession from the Americans – something that the occupying forces were allowing more and more now that the dust had settled. But a German wanting a licence had to have a lily-white past and a recommendation from an officer. The price of that recommendation was cooperation.

Schauff had survived Hitler and the Nazis and kept well away from anything that looked like a rifle or a front line by acting as a police stooge, informing the Gestapo about anyone with a loose tongue who did not subscribe to ultimate victory. He was still at it now the war was over. It was something he did well.

'Any possibles?' asked Hadleigh.

Judd shrugged his massive shoulders. It was pretty much pot luck, these days. Every Intelligence outfit hoped to score by capturing a senior SS or Gestapo officer with known crimes against his name, but mostly what cropped up were petty criminals, former soldiers who had no intention of working in labour battalions, and men (and occasionally women) who were living undercover, without registration or ration cards, for reasons best known to themselves. In the main these involved some minor peccadillo from years past and in which the Allies were not the least interested, but such had been Goebbels' propaganda in the closing weeks of the war – when he had broadcast that every male and female over the age of sixteen who had anything to do with the armed forces would be incarcerated for many years if not executed – that hundreds of Germans preferred a starvation existence in cellars and bombed-out buildings rather than register.

Nevertheless, there was always a chance that something good would turn up, though there were few major coups in the Intelligence game. Mostly it was a question of long and arduous routine. The USAAF and the RAF had, in some respects, done the ground forces a disservice by blasting to fragments tons of records. Hadleigh was certain that many a man with a criminal past had slipped through the net solely because there was nothing on paper to prove he was other than who he said he was. It was the easiest thing in the world to discard an SS uniform and don the clothes of a dead Wehrmacht soldier, relieve him of his paybook. Without eyewitnesses, the criminal stood a good chance of getting away with it, because it would have taken the rest of the decade and more manpower than the United States had at its disposal to doublecheck each and every story. Basically, if an arrestee could convince his captors his record was spotless for the first dozen hours, that was an end to it.

Even the old test of examining everyone's upper inside arm for a tattooed bloodgroup, once a sure sign of a fugitive SS man, no longer worked. Many of the senior ranks, with creditable foresight, had never been tattooed; others had found ways of removing the telltale marks. As always it was the upper echelon who managed to do this; the lower ranks did not have the facilities or the connections. But it was, of course, the upper echelon in whom Hadleigh and others like him were mainly interested

'Let's take a look,' said Hadleigh.

Judd hesitated.

'Come on, Max, let's move it,' prompted Hadleigh. 'Major Quinlan and I have places to go if there's nothing here worth sitting up all night for apart from a headache. They didn't give me this bronze leaf to fill in forms.'

Judd glanced from Hadleigh to Quinlan. He was plainly uncomfortable.

'Well, there's a slight problem,' he said. 'I told you we had five in the bag but actually it's six.'

'So you can't count. So what's the problem?'

'It'll be easier if I show you, Major.'

'Any way you want to play it, Max, as long as you get off the pot.'

Apart from the outside door, there were two others in the guardroom. One led to the Trough, offices and interrogation cells; the other to what were, in former days, punishment cells. It was through this door that Judd preceded them.

There were three punishment cells on one side of a short corridor. Each was no bigger than a large pantry and each had a judas-hole in its heavy iron, soundproof door. Judd stood to one side, pointed to the first in line. He indicated that Hadleigh should look inside.

The G-2 major squinted through the spy-hole and stepped back instantly as though stung.

'*Jesus Christ, Max*....'

Quinlan took his place. These days Hadleigh's outfit used the punishment cells as extra storage space for the massive overflow of files Third Army Intelligence was accumulating, but there was still room for the young girl who occupied cell number one.

She was, Quinlan estimated, about seventeen years of age, too thin by about fifteen pounds but pretty enough if you liked skinny teenagers who tied their hair back in bunches. She was sitting on a pile of cardboard boxes, staring at the cell door. In spite of the soundproofing something told her there was someone in the corridor. The naked electric light bulb high on the wall and protected by wire mesh revealed a pale face and deep green eyes.

'What the hell's all this about, Max?' raged Hadleigh. 'Haven't you read the goddam rules about under-age female prisoners? She screams rape and you put us all in the stockade until we're too old to care!'

'Sorry, Major, but blame Shapiro. He came back in the meat-wagon with her, said she wouldn't leave her father, says he's sick or sump'n. We tried tossing her out but she yelled blue murder. She calmed down when I said she could stay until we'd finished with her old man.' He raised his shoulders apologetically. 'It seemed the easiest way out. She's been as quiet as a full-fed cat since we put her in there.'

Hadleigh brought his temper under control. It had happened before – wives, daughters, mistresses of arrestees claiming their husbands, fathers, lovers were guilty of nothing – and doubtless it would happen again. Tossing her back on to the street yelling her head off wouldn't have helped. The time was coming when the occupying powers would be looking for 'good' Germans to take over the business of restoring some form of civil government, and the word from the top was not to rock the boat unnecessarily.

'Okay, Max, okay. You did right. Sorry I yelled. You say her father's in the Trough?'

'Yeah. Middle-aged guy Shapiro picked up in a house on Humboldtstrasse, between the Siemens factory and that burnt-out cinema.'

'What's the good word from Schauff?'

Knowing that the girl and her father signalled trouble, Judd had the story at his fingertips. But he referred to his clipboard anyway.

'He claims – Schauff, that is – the guy's name is Arndt and the girl's got the same name on her papers. He's not sure of his rank but he remembers seeing him around Nuremberg during the war, in uniform. He's got no identification and he's not registered.'

'How did Schauff know where we could pick him up?'

'Said he saw the girl in the street, recognized her and followed her. You know what Schauff's like.'

Hadleigh did. For a fat man Schauff could move like a wisp of smoke. It wasn't unusual; either, for the German to have a decent haul before tipping off Third Army G-2, even though the arrestees might not, probably were not, connected in any way to one another. That was the way Schauff worked. He wanted that licence pretty bad.

'What about the daughter?' asked Hadleigh. 'How does she check out for papers?'

'She's got a full house. Ration book, ID card, Zone pass.' Judd hesitated. 'It looks like she was drawing rations for herself and splitting them with her old man.'

'And that's all?'

Judd knew what Hadleigh meant. There were prostitutes a good deal younger than Fräulein Arndt on the streets, picking up a packet of cigarettes here, a slab of chocolate there.

'Not easy to tell without a thorough medical, but she doesn't look the type to hustle.'

'They never do.'

Quinlan stuck in his two cents' worth. Until a couple of weeks ago he had done a similar sort of job to Ben Hadleigh, and men who had once been in uniform but were now hiding out, unregistered, usually had a damned good reason for doing so. Certainly a father who allowed his young daughter to share her already meagre rations warranted investigation.

'Has Herr Arndt offered any explanation for his lack of cooperation?' he asked Judd.

'Nobody's put the question yet, Major. I was waiting until Major Hadleigh got here.'

'What about the others?' queried Hadleigh.

'*Dreck*,' answered Judd. 'The usual shit Schauff turns up with to make his score-sheet look good. If any of them has got more against his name than running a red light, I'll take up ballet.'

Hadleigh winked at Quinlan.

'What d'you think? The girls'll keep and Herr Arndt could be Martin Bormann.'

Judd was quick to point out how this contravened protocol. With a thirty-year hitch to complete, he wasn't about to buck standing orders.

'Major, with due respect this is Third Army territory. I'm not sure the brass would go for letting outsiders in. No offence intended.'

'None taken, Max,' smiled Quinlan. To Hadleigh he added: 'If you want me to take a walk, that's fine.'

But Hadleigh hadn't make 'his rank from the boondocks because he smiled prettily.

'Crap. Max is just protecting me and taking a closer look at that pension he'll be drawing around 1960. Besides, if Arndt has something under his hat he'd rather keep to himself I'll be glad of the help. Okay, Max?'

'Whatever you say, Major. What about the kid? Seems kind of hard leaving her stuck in there.'

'She'll have to suffer it for the time being. If it looks like lasting all night I'll think again, but if her father's got something to tell us she might get in the way. If he hasn't – or won't – she could be useful later.'

'What about the other four?'

'You're sure they're just Schauff pulling shit?'

'As sure as I'll ever be.'

'Then put them through the machine yourself. Question and answer stuff. Are there any officers on duty tonight?'

'None I'd trust getting change for a nickel.'

Hadleigh chuckled. 'I just wonder what the hell he says about me when my back's turned.'

On the way to the Trough he told Max that he and Quinlan would go into the good guy/bad guy routine.

'I'll be the bad guy. When I'm through I'll come and give you a hand with the others.'

They halted outside the door of the Trough and peered through the glass partition. Without any prompting from Max both Hadleigh and Quinlan identified Arndt without difficulty, a tall thin individual with iron-grey hair and an intelligent expression. He was in his late forties, and although he looked far from being in the best of health he was the only man in the room who could conceivably have worn a uniform with any sort of rank tabs. Max was right about the rest; they were nondescript shit. Hadleigh made a mental note to have a quiet word with Schauff. He wouldn't be getting his liquor licence this way.

Arndt did not seem surprised at being singled out and hurried into the nearest of the interrogation cells. Each of these was much bigger than the punishment cells, with room for a bunk, a wooden table and two upright chairs. There was also a chemical lavatory.

Hadleigh closed the door behind them and indicated that

Arndt should sit on the bunk. The German did so, enquiring anxiously about the whereabouts of his daughter.

Hadleigh ignored the question.

'Do you speak English?' he asked.

Arndt said he did but not much, and Hadleigh opted to converse in German. His accent was not much better than Judd's, but he had done a six-month total immersion course in the language back in the States long before Pearl Harbor was much more than a glint in an oriental eye, and since June '44 had had plenty of practice. Besides, there was always Quinlan if it got sticky.

'Now Herr Arndt,' he began in his best schoolmarmish tone. 'Or should I be addressing you as Sturmbannfuehrer Arndt?'

Sturmbannfuehrer was an SS rank equivalent to major and Arndt did not seem to like the association at all.

'I was not a member of the SS,' he protested quietly.

'That's not the story we've heard.' Hadleigh dropped easily into his role of bad guy. For the moment Quinlan said nothing. His turn would come later. 'We've got an eyewitness who will swear you were an SS officer working out of police headquarters at number 36 Ludwigstrasse.'

'Impossible. There can be no such eyewitness. I repeat, I was never in the SS.'

'Nor the Nazi Party either, I suppose,' sneered Hadleigh.

'Nor that. He's a liar, your eyewitness.'

'I never said it was a he,' said Hadleigh, 'but let's assume it is, for the moment. He's proved pretty reliable in the past. I have no reason to doubt his word this time. There's one sure way of proving him right or wrong, anyhow. If you're not Sturmbannfuehrer Arndt and you were never a Party member, who are you really and what have you been doing for the last six years? If you've got nothing to hide, why haven't you registered? Why have you been skulking undercover, allowing the daughter you seem so concerned about to sell herself on the streets to keep you in food?'

'That's another damned lie …'

Arndt started to his feet angrily. But he was no match for Hadleigh, who planted a fist in his chest and pushed him back on to the bunk.

'Don't raise your voice to me, Herr Sturmbannfuehrer,' he

growled. 'You lost this fucking war and that means you say please and thank you and watch your goddam manners. As for whether your daughter's been on the streets or not, we'll soon have the bottom line on that. I've sent for a doctor to give her a head to toe physical, which includes a Wassermann test. You know what that is? It's the standard test for syphilis.'

'You can't do that! She's only a child, just sixteen. Think what such an examination will do to her.'

'I'm not in the least worried what the examination will do to one more Kraut hooker. What does concern me is how many GIs she infects.'

'You bastard!'

Hadleigh hit him across the face. It wasn't a hard blow, more a dismissive insult, but even so Quinlan looked on uneasily. The G-2 major seemed to be playing his part with more conviction than was necessary.

'Mind you,' said Hadleigh easily, 'there's one sure-fire method of stopping all this before it starts and that's to tell us what you did in the war, Daddy. If you're not Sturmbannfuehrer Arndt and you never worked out of Ludwigstrasse, just what the hell have you been up to since 1939?'

'I have nothing to say,' said Arndt quietly, wiping a speck of blood from his mouth. 'I am guilty of no crime other than being a German. I also wish to point out, for the record, that I have a heart condition.'

Hadleigh glanced at Quinlan. There was a damned sight more here than met the eye. Maybe Schauff had turned up trumps for once because it didn't make any sense at all for Arndt to allow his daughter to be humiliated (he couldn't know the bit about the medical was a bluff) unless he had a hell of a lot to hide.

'Screw your heart condition,' jeered Hadleigh. 'I don't believe one fucking word you're saying. As far as I'm concerned my information is correct and you're a former SS officer with probable crimes against his name. It'll take us a while to run them down, make out a case against you, but we'll do it, make no mistake. Then we'll swing you from a fucking tree. In the meantime you're going to stay here until we've got a few more answers and that daughter of yours is going to have a physical like she was entering the Olympics.

33

If she's diseased she's going to a women's prison and there she's going to stay. If she's clean – well, I've got a couple of boys on my staff who like making it with young girls. Just so's there's no misunderstanding, these boys of mine are not what you'd call White. In fact, their ancestors came over as slaves.'

Arndt sprang to his feet, screaming and cursing, spitting, throwing punches. He moved so fast for a man of his age who probably hadn't seen a square meal for months that Hadleigh and Quinlan were taken unawares. It was several moments before they could subdue him and only that was achieved by wrestling him to the bunk and sitting on him until the fight was gone. When they felt his muscles relax they allowed him to sit up. His face was a pasty grey, his breathing laboured. Maybe, thought Quinlan, his story about a heart condition was the truth.

He beckoned Hadleigh to the far side of the cell.

'For Christ's sake take it easy, Ben,' he hissed in English.

Hadleigh tipped him a big wink. However it might look to an outsider, the American was still playing a game.

They went back to the good guy/bad guy routine.

'For Christ's sake take it easy,' repeated Quinlan, but this time in German. 'This is not going to get us anywhere. Let me have a talk to him. I don't give a damn if he is SS, since when did we start using their methods?'

'Since we saw Dachau and Belsen and Treblinka,' said Hadleigh. 'And to hell with leaving him to you. You'll be feeding him coffee and doughnuts as soon as my back's turned. There's only one thing his sort understands and that's a fist in the gut. Give them some of their own medicine, that's the way to deal with these bastards.'

'Not while I'm around you don't, and if there's any more of this there'll be a report going upstairs.'

'Eat it,' sneered Hadleigh, but he appeared to take the threat seriously. At least there was less venom in his tone when he added: 'You Limeys are all the same, soft as sheep shit.'

'Half an hour,' urged Quinlan. 'Give me half an hour alone with him and hold off with the examination on his daughter for that length of time. If he still refuses to talk after thirty minutes, you can have 'em both.'

Hadleigh pretended to think about it. Finally he nodded.

'Thirty minutes and not a minute more,' he said from the cell door. 'In thirty-one minutes I'll be back here bringing someone with more balls, and you, Major, will be on the first jeep out of Nuremberg. Also in thirty-one minutes the doc will be stripping Fräulein Arndt down to the buff and prodding her with more instruments than you've ever seen outside a laboratory. In sixty minutes, if he gives her a clean bill of health, I'm turning my ex-slaves loose on her.'

Hadleigh went out, slamming the cell door. He would give Max Judd a hand with the others while waiting.

Quinlan passed Arndt a cigarette and lit it for him. The German inhaled deeply and looked up at Quinlan with gratitude.

'Thank you,' he said.

'Don't thank me,' shrugged Quinlan. 'He means what he says. Unless you start talking he'll be back and I won't be able to help you. We're in the US Zone and I'm a visitor. He might not be able to kick me out of Nuremberg but he sure as hell can turf me out of this place. Then you're on your own, you and your daughter. What's her name, by the way?'

'Ilse.'

'Okay, you and Ilse will have to face the music unless you can come up with a satisfactory explanation regarding why you were in hiding and why you didn't register according to the law.'

'Allied law.'

'But the law nevertheless. Come on, Herr Arndt.' Quinlan adopted his most persuasive voice. 'I don't believe you were in the SS but my beliefs don't count for much around here. If you've got nothing to hide you can at least tell me your rank and service arm.'

'I never said I was in the services.'

'You didn't have to. I've been in long enough myself to recognize a soldier when I see one.'

'You may think what you wish, Herr Major.'

Quinlan made a performance of checking his wristwatch. He pulled up one of the wooden chairs and reversed it, sitting with his arms resting against the back.

'Look,' he said, 'I'm trying to help but I need your cooperation. Consider it from Major Hadleigh's point of view. Whatever you might think of Allied law, you're in

35

Nuremberg illegally because you didn't register. Add to that the fact that you refuse to tell us your former rank or service and you can see why Hadleigh is suspicious. About all we're sure of is that your name is Arndt.'

'Not necessarily. Ilse's papers could be forged or stolen.'

'We're not relying solely on Ilse's papers. Don't you understand yet, Herr Arndt? You were informed on. How the devil do you think the Americans found you?'

'That is not possible. I have hardly been out of the house in months.'

'Nevertheless, you were informed on. Believe me, we *do* have a witness who remembers you from before the war's end.'

Arndt's eyes widened in dismay when he realized Quinlan was speaking the truth.

'That could not possibly be...'

'It could possibly be and is. It may take us longer to trace your background via him, but it will be done.'

There was a tiny sigh of relief, it seemed, when Quinlan confirmed the informer to be male. It meant nothing to him at the time, but he was to remember it later.

Quinlan tried a different tack. That Arndt knew something he wanted to keep secret could no longer be in doubt, but it seemed likely he would hold out for ever unless the gloves came off. He was undernourished, far from the first flush of youth and possibly sick, but he possessed a determination that was almost admirable. The weak link was Ilse.

'The war is over, Arndt,' said Quinlan softly. 'None of us liked it and things were done by the Germans which should never have been done. Any decent man will see them as a crime and want the perpetrators punished regardless of nationality. Only those who committed the crimes or paid lip-service to the criminals will wish there to be no retribution. I don't believe you fall into either of those categories.

'Let me tell you something about Major Hadleigh. He has seen Buchenwald and Dachau, and he is a man in a rage. He believes the whole German nation to be guilty because without the compliance of the people there could have been no Hitler, no SS. Those who now call themselves guiltless turned their heads when Jews were bundled off to concentration camps in the Thirties. Many of you had Jewish neighbours and friends and didn't consider them lesser beings or stateless citizens until Hitler made it official policy. Then you let happen what did. The pictures from the camps are not faked, Herr Arndt. The corpses are real, the deaths unavenged. That is how Major Hadleigh sees it. The fate of one teenage German girl matters little to him if he can catch and see hanged some of the criminals who committed the atrocities.'

Quinlan could see that his words were having no effect. He needed an extra gear. He found it and engaged it.

'Let me tell you what will happen to your daughter,' he said. 'Let me tell you what will happen to sixteen-year-old Ilse in twenty-two minutes if Major Hadleigh does not get some acceptable answers. She will indeed be examined by a doctor and pronounced clean. I know she'll be pronounced free from disease because I've seen her. I very much doubt she's been anywhere near a man. I would suspect her to be a virgin, which will make it worse.

'After what Major Hadleigh has seen in the camps, after what the guards did to women there, the violation of Ilse will mean nothing to him, not if he suspects her father possesses information which he needs to do his job. Ilse will be taken to one of the larger cells – possibly the one next door to this, where you will be able to listen. Then any man who wants to will be permitted to do what he likes with her. I don't have to tell you that there are some appetites and tastes for the bizarre that not even a grown woman could survive, let alone a young child. Neither do I have to remind you that her unwillingness and fear will merely add spice to the occasion. Long before it's all over she'll be out of her mind – because her father was stubborn.'

'The Americans do not do such things,' said Arndt dully.

His complexion had taken on a bluish tinge and his breathing was becoming laboured. Quinlan hoped to God he wasn't overdoing it. He experienced only the mildest tremor of guilt when he saw the fight go out of the German, his shoulders droop, his features crumple. Nothing was going to happen to Ilse Arndt, but if it took threats to make her father talk, so be it. The memory of the afternoon's films was fresh in his mind, and Quinlan was more than willing to live with his conscience.

'I'm sick,' mumbled Arndt, massaging his chest.

'You're also wasting time. You'll be given medical attention as soon as I have your full name, rank and unit.'

'And that's all?' Just getting the words out seemed to take an immense effort.

He wasn't stalling or faking, Quinlan was certain. But if he was allowed to see a doctor before he talked, the last fifteen minutes could be written off as a complete waste of time. He would be given treatment, pills, an injection. He would recover his strength and with it, possibly, his will to resist. Six months earlier on the German/Danish border Quinlan had been unable to complete an interrogation because of doctors. It wouldn't happen again.

'To start with.'

Quinlan made notes in the back of his diary. Twice he had to ask Arndt to speak up or repeat a sentence.

'My full name is Heinrich Adolf Arndt. My rank is – was – that of Hauptmann – captain. Since 1940 I have worked as a cryptanalyst for the Abwehr. Until this year, that is.' In spite of his obvious pain he managed a feeble joke. 'Since May I have been unemployed.'

'The Abwehr? You worked for Canaris?'

The reply was a long time coming.

'I knew Canaris, yes.'

Arndt also suspected he was dying. He could barely see his interrogator now through the thick curtain of red mist that eroded his vision. He thought his chest was about to burst, his heart explode, felt that organ flutter wildly like a thousand butterflies trapped in a killing jar. There was a terrible noise in his head, a fierce buzzing that was growing louder and louder.

Quinlan tried a shot in the dark. For him the name Canaris would be for ever linked with that other name William Joyce had denied giving him all those months ago outside Flensburg.

'And your immediate superior was Oberstleutnant Manfred Langenhain, I believe.'

My God, they knew of Langenhain! How was that possible?

'Yes, Langenhain.' Arndt's voice was scarcely audible. 'Please, I must have a doctor.'

'In a moment, a moment.'

'No...' Using all that remained of his strength Arndt got to his feet. '*Ilse*...'

Quinlan caught him before he hit the stone floor, knocking over the chair and dropping his diary in the process. He screamed at the top of his voice for Hadleigh and Max Judd. Arndt heard none of it.

The official verdict would be a massive coronary brought on by extreme stress. It could have happened at any time. A healthier man might have withstood it and recovered, but an autopsy would later show that Arndt was forty pounds underweight for his build and that his body contained less than seventy per cent of the minerals necessary to sustain life.

Four

Nuremberg – November 29-30, 1945

The medical officer had been and gone, the body taken to the morgue, and a fifth of bourbon dispatched before Quinlan got round to telling Hadleigh and Max Judd what had transpired in the interrogation cell. In his own mind there was no doubt that the threats against Ilse had caused Arndt's death, but it wouldn't do to dwell on it. Talking would help. That and the bourbon.

Quinlan believed in the laws of probability as much as anyone, but he could not accept as mere coincidence that the name given to him by Joyce, now languishing in the death cell of Wandsworth Prison, London, was the same as Arndt's immediate superior.

Hadleigh topped up his coffee cup from a round-bellied iron pot.

'It's interesting enough,' he said finally, puffing away at his cigar, 'but it's asking a lot to make a connection between Arndt and Joyce and Langenhain and Joyce. You've probably got as nice a case of happenstance as I've ever come across, but no more than that.'

Quinlan didn't buy it. Hadleigh could call it instinct or spinach, but there was more to this than chance.

'I mean, what the hell *was* Arndt doing hiding out six months after the war's over?' he demanded. 'Why did we have to go through that entire performance before he'd even give me his full name? Christ, the Abwehr aren't war criminals. We want to interrogate them, sure, because as Intelligence officers they can maybe fill in a few blanks, but I haven't come across any of them playing coy before. They were serving soldiers, same as the rest of us in this racket.'

Judd tried to say something, but Quinlan waved him irritably to silence.

'Then there's Langenhain. It's a name I haven't seen in any file, yet this is the second time it's come to my attention in six months. So who is he? And what the hell was Arndt's big secret? He said he'd hardly been out of the house since May. Why? They were both living on the daughter's rations. Why? It doesn't make any kind of sense.'

'It does to me.' This time Judd insisted on saying his piece. 'Okay, we're not going to stick the majority of Abwehr officers in the dock, but we are going to intern them until we're sure all they've been doing since 1939 is a little Intelligence work. Who'd look after the girl if we'd put Arndt in the bucket? I haven't heard anyone mention a mother up to now. Maybe he stayed undercover to look after the kid.'

'It seems to me it was the other way round,' retorted Quinlan. 'Ilse was looking after him.'

'Talking of which,' said Hadleigh, 'she'll have to be told.'

She would also have to be taken care of until it was decided what to do with her.

Hadleigh had no female personnel on his staff apart from army clerks and Gretl Meissner, but the Counter Intelligence

Corps did and there was little doubt in any of their minds that Fräulein Arndt was going to need a woman's companionship this night. The G-2 major wasn't at all happy at bringing in CIC, letting it become common knowledge that a death had taken place on Third Army property, but there was nothing else for it.

While he placed the call, Quinlan took it upon his own shoulders to talk to the girl.

They left him alone with her in one of the offices. Now that Quinlan could see her better she seemed much younger than he had thought earlier; hardly a sixteen-year-old at all, more thirteen or fourteen. Green saucer eyes dominated a pale, pretty face, and she appeared to know what he was going to tell her long before he hesitantly found the words. Perhaps she was half-expecting it. She must have witnessed her father's gradual deterioration over the past six months and mentally prepared herself.

There were no hysterics. She cried a little while Quinlan looked on helplessly, wanting to reach out and comfort her but not knowing how. When the tears were over and she had wiped her eyes, he saw her make a conscious effort to regain her equilibrium. For an adult it would have taken a tremendous effort of will; for a young girl it was a magnificent feat.

He had not, of course, told her the entire truth. He mumbled something about a sudden heart attack and she accepted it without demur. The facts would come out later. Somewhere along the line there would have to be an enquiry, and then she would know. But tonight was not the night. She did ask if she could see him, but Quinlan managed to persuade her to leave that until tomorrow. He didn't add that Arndt was not a pretty sight and that it would be better to allow the morticians to work some cosmetic wizardry before viewing the body.

He asked her where her mother was.

'She was killed in an air raid in 1944.'

'Do you have any other relatives in Nuremberg?'

'There was an uncle and aunt in Fürth.'

'Who looked after you while your father was away?'

'Yes.'

The professional in Quinlan wanted to pursue this, not the

41

uncle and aunt but Heinrich Arndt's absences. If the girl could remember dates and perhaps snatches of conversation, they might all be a little closer to discovering the reason when he had elected to remain more or less close-mouthed.

But the human being in Quinlan rejected the notion. Tomorrow or the next day would be time enough for detailed questions.

'If you'll give their name and address I'll see you're taken there tonight.'

'You misunderstood me, Herr Major. I used the past tense. You see, they too are now dead. The terror fliers dropped their bombs with great accuracy. Of course, there's always my father's mistress. Her name is Hannah Wolz. When she's not with my father or whoring for the Americans, she sings in a place on Scheurlstrasse that used to be the Hans-Sachs cinema. But she wouldn't want me. She only used to visit my father when I was out. She didn't like me and I didn't like her. There's no one else.'

They were terrifyingly bald words from a youngster who had just been orphaned, but he detected no sarcasm or irony, nor any symptoms of delayed shock. Nevertheless, he would recommend she saw the doctor before leaving the compound.

'Besides,' she added in the same flat voice, 'I should like to go home.'

Quinlan searched his memory for the address where Judd had said Arndt and his daughter were picked up.

'To Humboldtstrasse?'

'Yes.'

The telephone on the desk rang. It was Hadleigh on the other end.

'Did you tell her?'

'Yes. The quick brown fox jumps over the lazy dog.'

'Whaat?'

Quinlan glanced at the girl but there was nothing in her expression which told him she understood.

'Just checking if she speaks English.'

'How did she take it?' asked Hadleigh.

'Too quietly. I reckon a doctor had better take a look at her.'

'I'll lay it on. I've explained the situation to CIC and they're sending across one of their female operatives. She should be here any time. We'll rig up a couple of cots someplace and…'

'She says she wants to go home. To Humboldtstrasse.'

'Well, Christ – I don't know that's such a great idea.'

'It's what she wants, Ben. If the CIC woman will go along with it I think it might be best.'

There was a short silence.

'Well, okay,' agreed Hadleigh. 'I don't suppose it can do any harm. Will you stay with her until CIC arrive?'

'I'd rather not. Send someone down here, will you.'

When the GI came in Quinlan told him to keep an eye on the girl and make sure she didn't do anything stupid. Then he rejoined Hadleigh and Judd in the guardroom. The ever-alert master sergeant had a mug of coffee and a glass of bourbon at the ready.

'Thanks, Max.'

'Rough, Major?'

'It's not something I'd like to do every day.'

The mug of coffee was down to the dregs before the guardroom door opened and a very attractive dark-haired woman in her late twenties came in. Like many CIC operatives she was dressed in civilian clothes, in her case a tailored two-piece which set off her trim figure to perfection. She gave her name as Angela Salvatini and produced her ID. Hadleigh examined it perfunctorily and handed it back.

'Where's the patient and what do you want me to do?' she asked.

Hadleigh introduced Quinlan and passed the floor to him. The G-2 major had already given the bald facts to CIC on the telephone. All Quinlan had to do was explain that Ilse Arndt might need medical attention and wanted to spend the night in her own home.

'I don't know what sort of condition it's in,' he added apologetically.

'Don't worry about it. Or about a doctor. I've had some nursing training and I've handled these cases before. A sleeping pill is probably all she needs. If it looks like anything more serious I'll get back to you.'

'What about transport?'

'I've got my own plus driver outside.'

'They're starting to attract a better class of recruit to CIC,' cracked Hadleigh. 'Beautiful trained nurses with their own wheels.'

Angela Salvatini wasn't buying the come-on. She flashed him a dazzling smile.

'I guess it was inevitable, considering how often we have to bale out Third Army Intelligence.'

Hadleigh winced.

'Can I see the girl?'

'I'll take you along,' offered Judd.

'I wonder where the bastards have been hiding her,' muttered Hadleigh after the door had closed. 'She makes my clerks look like Sumo wrestlers.'

When Quinlan did not respond Hadleigh clapped him on the shoulder.

'Come on, Major, snap out of it. It's done now and there's not a damned thing you can do about it.'

He checked the time. It was not yet 10 p.m.

'What say we blow our minds, forget the whole fucking thing? It'll look better in the morning. Max can watch the store. I could use a diversion and I'm damned sure you could.'

'What about the other four you picked up? Shouldn't you be doing something about them?'

'Routine. There's nothing there. They were still filling out questionnaires when I last checked, but they'll be back on the streets before midnight. Come on, what d'you say? If those girls of mine over in Sündersbühl haven't gone into business for themselves tonight – which Christ help them if they do – they should be just about right for plucking.'

Quinlan wasn't keen, but he knew he wouldn't be able to sleep for hours yet and allowed Hadleigh to persuade him that what he needed was a couple more drinks and the body of a compliant, experienced Fräulein.

As an exercise in mind-blowing it was an unmitigated disaster. On the Richter scale of excitement levels it registered roughly on a par with pissing in your own boot as far as Quinlan was concerned. His partner for the session was one he'd had a couple of times before – Ingrid, a sexy little dumpling who acted as though she'd seen it all at least once and done most of it twice. She tried everything she knew to

44

please Major 'Otters', going down on him with considerable skill and energy when all else failed, but between Hadleigh grunting away on the far side of the only habitable bedroom in the house and his own private thoughts, Quinlan was unable to get it together. He was more than relieved when dawn came. It was about the only thing that was going to that night.

Wrapped in a short silk robe (doubtless from one of Hadleigh's black-market sources) which left just enough to the imagination and which ordinarily would have had Quinlan straining at the leash, Ingrid took him into the kitchen and made him a pot of coffee on a portable burner, anxious in case he should put in an adverse report about her to 'Major Ben', who by this time was snoring his head off, arms and legs akimbo. Helga, his bedmate, had given up the unequal fight for a share of the covers and was on the floor, scrunched up in a raincoat.

After reassuring Ingrid that it wasn't her fault the past few hours were unlikely to figure in her memoirs and promising to give her Alpha-plus when Hadleigh recovered consciousness, Quinlan stepped out of the house into the cold Nuremberg morning, his mouth like the inside of a sewerman's boot and thinking that there was only one thing worse than a bombed city by night and that was a bombed city at first light.

It was not quite 8 a.m. and there was a damp chill in the air which suggested snow was on the way. It was going to be a hard winter, this first one after the war's end.

Because it was not only a indictable offence but the height of insanity to leave an unattended vehicle on the streets overnight if you wanted to find it with wheels and tyres the next morning, Hadleigh had had them driven over the previous evening. As far as Quinlan remembered, the parting instructions were for a duty driver to pick them up around nine, but come nine Quinlan expected to be washed, shaved and changed and on his way to the Palace of Justice.

The Sündersbühl district was a good two and a half miles from the Allersbergerstrasse barracks where Hadleigh had fixed him up with a billet for as long as he cared to stay, and while he could probably have thumbed a lift if he'd tried he didn't want strangers seeing him unshaven and unshowered. Apart from that, on foot he would have to cross Humboldtstrasse, and on impulse he decided to see how Angela Salvatini and Ilse Arndt had passed the night. He did not, he realized, know the number of the house, but he recalled it was between the Siemens factory and a burnt-out cinema. It shouldn't be hard to find. He had a tongue. He could ask if anyone knew the Arndts. Even if no one had seen (or was willing to admit having seen) Hauptmann Arndt, they would surely know Ilse.

As it turned out he had no need to ask. When level with the eastern extremity of the Siemens buildings, where Tafelfeldstrasse emptied into Humboldtstrasse, he saw, with a sinking feeling in the pit of his stomach, the two MP jeeps and the military ambulance a short distance up ahead. No one had to tell him they were standing outside the house where Ilse Arndt and Angela Salvatini had spent the night.

A US Army MP tried to bar his way and might have succeeded or suffered a broken jaw in the trying if Quinlan had not recognized Master Sergeant Judd among the knot of figures in the street. He shouted to get his attention and Judd indicated that it was okay for the British major to come through. Judd was the senior NCO present, but there were also two men in plain clothes by his side. There were no prizes for guessing they were CIC.

'What the hell's happened?' demanded Quinlan.

'Where's Ben.... Where's Major Hadleigh?' responded Judd. He pulled Quinlan to one side, out of earshot of the civilians. 'Where the fuck's Ben?' he repeated. 'I sent transport for the pair of you.'

Quinlan explained that he'd left the Sündersbühl house around thirty-five minutes ago.

Judd nodded. 'That figures. I only got here myself ten minutes back. When I saw what had happened I sent the jeep straight over. I guess the Major will be here any time now.'

'What's he going to find, Max?'

'You'd better see for yourself. And take a deep breath. It ain't pretty.'

Judd led the way inside and up the creaking stairs, ignoring the questioning glances from the CIC representatives.

It was actually a first-floor apartment above a bicycle shop where the Arndts had lived. (Quinlan already found himself

46

thinking in the past tense.) At one time there had been two more floors, but in trying to put Siemens-Schuckertwerke A.G.'s electric motors division out of action, the USAAF and the RAF had bracketed the target and many of the buildings on all sides of the factory complex were either completely in ruin or damaged extensively. The bicycle shop itself was boarded up, out of business for good by the look of things. Floors two and three were little more than gaping masonry and no longer occupied.

Before someone had torn the place apart Ilse Arndt and her father had evidently done their best with what remained to them – two rooms, a kitchen and a bathroom from whose taps no water ever came. There was no glass in any of the windows; they were covered with planks of wood and tarpaulin. Illumination was obtained from oil lamps, of which there were eight or ten burning away, the majority, if not all, of them apparently brought in by two tough-looking MPs who were standing by the bedroom door.

Quinlan looked around the living-room in shocked bewilderment. Practically every stick of furniture was smashed, every item of clothing torn, every drawer upturned, every cupboard ransacked. Cushions had been slashed, the stuffing scattered in all directions.

'We got an anonymous phone call just before eight,' said Judd in a quiet voice. 'Or rather the MPs did. A woman said she'd heard screams coming from this address in the middle of the night, and hung up.' He shrugged. 'It's not unusual. If you've lived in Nazi Germany for a few years you learn to mind your own business.

'The MPs came over, saw what had happened, and hit the panic button for CIC. CIC called us, because it was to us they'd loaned Angela Salvatini. Hang on to your stomach.'

Judd waved the two MPs to one side and preceded Quinlan through the bedroom door. There were more oil lamps in here, giving the youngish uniformed doctor plenty of light with which to work.

Quinlan would remember the scene for the rest of his life. He had seen some of the camps for himself and many more of the atrocities committed there on film, but this, macabrely lit by the flickering lamps, was something straight out of hell.

Like the other room, the bedroom was a wreck, mattresses

47

ripped apart, bedding torn, drawers upended. Ilse Arndt and Angela Salvatini were both naked and very much dead. It required no stretch of the imagination to deduce they had been raped, brutally and many times. The position of each body gave that away. But whoever had killed them had not settled for sexual assault followed by swift dispatch. Both torsos were covered with cigarette burns, dozens of them. Both women (if Ilse Arndt qualified in that category) had been severely beaten about the face, and both throats were cut. Both pairs of hands were nailed to the floor.

It was one of these six-inch nails that the doctor was trying to remove when Quinlan ran out and was instantly and violently sick in the passage outside the living-room. Somewhere below he heard the sound of Ben Hadleigh's voice.

Five

Nuremberg – November 30, 1945

The remainder of the morning developed into a blazing row between CIC and Third Army Intelligence in the person of Ben Hadleigh, with Quinlan an uneasy spectator. A call to Allersbergerstrasse had ensured that Gretl Meissner would fill in for him at the Palace of Justice.

CIC had all the questions and Hadleigh few of the answers – none he was willing to discuss in depth at this time, at any rate. *Sotto voce*, he advised Quinlan to keep his trap shut also. This wasn't the moment to be voicing half-baked theories about Arndt, an unknown Abwehr lieutenant colonel called Langenhain, and the traitor Joyce.

Why, demanded the senior CIC officer, who turned out to be a light colonel fond of pulling rank, were they not told that Angela Salvatini was wanted for more than a routine overnight child-minding job?

What were the full circumstances surrounding the death of Heinrich Arndt?

What had Arndt said?

What had taken place between the German and this British major?

Who the hell *was* this British major?

Why was he allowed to interrogate a Third Army arrestee?

Who, where, why, what, when, how.

It went on and on and would doubtless have continued all day had not Hadleigh suddenly declared himself sick and tired of the whole lousy business and called in his boss, Colonel Masterson.

This was the first Masterson had heard of any of it, though somewhere on the way to him through channels was a medical report on the death of Hauptmann Arndt. The colonel knew, however, how to protect his own, and after a short, sharp argument on the telephone CIC were on their way, their spokesman vowing that Third Army had not heard the last of it.

Hadleigh gave their retreating figures the finger and held a rapid conversation with Masterson before hanging up. He shook his head wearily when Quinlan seemed keen to continue their discussion of the previous night's horrifying events in private. One way or another it had been a rough twelve or fifteen hours for all concerned. There was much to talk about that it was better CIC did not overhear, true, but they'd achieve more with clear heads. Some sack time was called for. They would all meet in Hadleigh's office this evening at 7.30.

'If I'm not in the stockade by then,' said the G-2 major with a long sigh. 'Right after I'm cleaned up I've got a date with the old man. I don't think he's very happy with me.'

Shaved and rested and wearing fresh linen, Quinlan was a

49

few minutes early. Even so, Hadleigh and Judd were already there, the coffee pot on the boil, a small mountain of sandwiches on the desk.

Though spruced up, Hadleigh had evidently been put through the wringer by Colonel Masterson. Gesturing Quinlan to help himself to food and drink, he briefed him on how the meeting had gone.

'As expected, he chewed my balls, telling me that CIC would have a field day over this. Maybe you don't understand how it works in this man's army, Otis, but CIC and regular Intelligence don't exactly hit it off. Half of them are bucking for jobs in this new organization Dulles is forming, the CIA, and they reckon they're the pros and we're the amateurs. When the solids hit the air conditioning it usually flies our way.'

Quinlan had come across similar problems himself with the British Army's SIB, the Special Investigation Branch, the military version of Special Branch. He said he understood.

'Good,' grunted Hadleigh, 'because what I'm going to say next involves you specifically. Before we get down to cases, before we go over what happened – or what we think happened and why – last night, there's something you and I have to get sorted out.'

Quinlan glanced across at Judd, puzzled, but the master sergeant was busy mustarding a sandwich.

'I don't know what the hell to make of the connection between Arndt, Langenhain and William Joyce,' went on Hadleigh, 'even if there's anything to be made of it at all. Neither does Gene Masterson. If there *is* anything in it, maybe you're the only one who knows what it is or can put two and two together. Only you spoke to Joyce and you were the last man to speak to Arndt. In other words, if this investigation – assuming there's something to investigate – is to remain in our hands and not CIC's, and if my career and maybe Max's too aren't to go down the tubes, we're all going to need your help.'

Quinlan started to say something, but Hadleigh held up his hand.

'Let me finish, Major. You can have your two cents' worth in a minute.

'While you were in dreamland this afternoon I got Gene

50

Masterson to do the reverse of what happened when you first came down here. That is, ask General Dempsey a favour, ask him if we could borrow you for a week or two or as long as it takes. By we, I mean Third Army Intelligence. More specifically, me. Your General said we could providing you agreed. Apparently you were due to be rotated home but finagled your way down to Nuremberg to cover the Trials. Dempsey wasn't too sure you'd be willing to give up covering them. He still wants the bulletins you promised him as often as you can get in court, but your head won't roll if they're not there every week. He said he'd leave the final decision in your hands.'

There was really nothing to decide. It was true he wanted to be sitting in the press gallery when Goering and the others were called to testify, but the way things were going the Allies would still be presenting the prosecution case up to and beyond the Christmas recess. It was equally true that he wouldn't be here now were it not for Gene Masterson and Ben Hadleigh. Gretl Meissner could take verbatim notes of the proceedings. He would type up a résumé as and when he found time.

Besides, it had become a personal matter. He was indirectly responsible for Arndt's death and, because of that, young Ilse's. He wasn't going to tell Hadleigh this, but Third Army would have had to boot him physically out of Nuremberg before he gave up trying to find a few answers.

'You don't have to ask me, Ben,' he said. 'As long as I can have Frau Meissner on permanent loan, if you want me here, here's where I'm staying.'

'Consider her yours. We can sort it out with her tomorrow.'

Keeping their coffee cups filled but taking it easy on the bourbon in case it turned out to be another long night, they went over what they knew.

One: Hauptmann Arndt, for reasons best known to himself, had remained in hiding since the end of the war.

Two: Arndt had served in the Abwehr under Oberstleutnant Manfred Langenhain, about whom nothing more was known.

Three: William Joyce had also known, or known of, Langenhain.

Four: Ilse Arndt and Angela Salvatini had been raped,

51

tortured and killed and the Arndt apartment ransacked.

Conclusion to Four: Some group – all the signs pointed to more than one or two – believed something to be hidden in the Arndt household and that Ilse and/or Angela knew of its whereabouts.

'It's the only possible inference,' said Quinlan finally. 'We all saw what happened to them. This wasn't any ordinary rape or burglary. They were tortured for information. The rape was incidental.'

Hadleigh fumbled through his in-tray before coming up with the document he wanted.

'I can give you an up-date on that. The medicos won't know all the answers until they've performed a full autopsy, but first indications are that the burns and the rape took place several hours before the killing.' He tossed the report on to his desk. 'Don't ask me how they figure these things out, but I guess we take their word for it. Which still leaves us asking who did it and what were they looking for.'

'And if they found it,' put in Quinlan.

'It also leaves another question,' said Max Judd. 'Why did they choose last night? Arndt was in hiding for six months, presumably in the same place.'

'Maybe they didn't know where he was until last night,' said Quinlan. 'Nobody else did.'

'So how did they suddenly find out?' asked Hadleigh.

Judd had a possible answer. 'Schauff?'

Hadleigh shook his head.

'I don't think so. I'll have him picked up, but I don't think so. No, I think they – whoever it is we're talking about – have been watching the main gates of the barracks. Remember, there's always a crew of people out there day and night, regardless of the curfew. Remember too that Ilse Arndt came in with her father and kicked up hell when Max tried to toss her out. That would have attracted someone's attention. Am I making any sense?'

'Keep talking,' encouraged Quinlan.

'Let's figure it this way. Some group is looking for Arndt. They know he's in Nuremberg but don't know where. We've made the assumption up to now that Arndt was hiding out from us, but what if he was hiding from this unknown group? They can't find him but they figure sooner or later we will.

What the hell have they got to lose by watching the gates anyway? Maybe they're not just looking for Arndt. Maybe they're looking for others too. They see Arndt and his daughter brought in but only the daughter and Angela Salvatini leave. They follow them, see Miss Salvatini's driver head for home, and move in. The way they tore the place apart, maybe they didn't want Arndt himself but something he had on him or hidden. Yeah, that's a reasonable deduction because it would take around ten seconds for guys with their methods to find out from Ilse that her father was dead. Yet they still ransacked the entire joint. Any takers for that theory?'

Quinlan nodded, but it was left to Judd to frame another question no one had yet bothered to ask.

'We keep talking about "they", but don't we mean the SS or some part of it? Everything about those killings bears an SS hallmark.'

Hadleigh and Quinlan agreed.

'Okay,' Hadleigh said, 'let's say it's the SS. Christ, there are still plenty of them around, we know that much. If we had them all in the pen I could go back to Chicago where the mobsters are civilized.' He put a match to the stub of his cigar. 'Arndt had something this SS group wants and they're willing to kill for it. But we still don't know what or why.'

'But we are back to Canaris and Langenhain again,' said Quinlan. 'And maybe Joyce too. Right, let's forget Langenhain and Joyce for the moment because we can't find one and the other's due to swing before long. But there's a definite tie-in between Canaris and the SS.'

Six months after the end of the war the facts concerning Canaris's fate were not fully known, and would not be known for many years. All that the Allies had established was that the ex-chief of the Abwehr had fallen from grace around the time of the July Plot to assassinate Hitler, though whether he was part of the conspiracy remained a mystery. He was, however, purged for being less than loyal to National Socialism when the SS absorbed the Abwehr, and at the beginning of April 1945 executed in the SS concentration camp at Flossenburg on the German-Czech border. The order for his execution could only have come from one of three people: Hitler, Himmler, or the former head of the RSHA,

Ernst Kaltenbrunner. Himmler was definitely dead, Hitler almost certainly so, and Kaltenbrunner on trial for his life in Nuremberg. Or rather he was suffering from spinal meningitis and at present in a military hospital in the city.

'Not that he'd tell us anything even if we were allowed to talk to him,' said Hadleigh. 'The friggin' judges – the *Allied* judges – are so anxious to do everything nice and legal that if anyone in the dock as much as *sneezes* there are a dozen guys rushing towards them with the Kleenex. Apart from that, I hear Kaltenbrunner's denying everything. According to his deposition he never even *heard* of the fucking SS and much less was he deputy head of it, second banana under Himmler.'

'Maybe they'd let me talk to Joyce,' mused Quinlan. 'He clammed up as soon as he knew he was safe back in May and later claimed I'd misunderstood him, but now it's his neck he might sing a different song.'

'If there's anything to sing,' said Judd.

Quinlan grimaced. 'We're back to the coincidence factor again, which we either believe in or we don't. Joyce, Canaris, Langenhain, Arndt, the murder of Ilse and Angela Salvatini. Even if it is coincidence it doesn't explain why the two women were killed or what their killers were looking for.'

'Or whether they found it,' said Hadleigh.

'Or whether "it" was there at all,' added Judd. 'Whether we're not trying to make two and two add up to five when it's really four. Arndt could have been a black marketeer with a corner in – Christ, I don't know – medical supplies or tobacco, and his killers wanted in. He could have sneaked off with a safe full of somebody else's loot before the war ended and was waiting 'til the dust settled to spend it. There are a hundred reasons why somebody could've wanted his balls in the grinder, and low on my list is some sort of loony conspiracy involving Canaris.'

'Maybe you're right,' said Quinlan. He thought for a moment. 'And maybe the answer lies somewhere in Arndt's apartment, which is where we should be now instead of sitting around here.'

'Not me.' Hadleigh shook his head emphatically. He was tired and it was beginning to show. While Quinlan and Max had had their heads down, he was being carpeted by Gene Masterson. 'Include me out. If there was anything there it's been found. You saw what was done to the joint. Either it was found or it wasn't there.'

'Maybe.'

'Maybe, schmaybe. Christ, you don't even know what you're looking for. You haven't got a clue whether it's a document or a telephone number or a sackful of doubloons. You play detective if you want to. Perhaps I'll join you when my mind's back in gear, around nineteen fifty.'

'Me neither,' said Judd. 'I've got a couple of cubic yards of paperwork to catch up on.'

Quinlan was in no way fazed at having to go it alone.

'Can I borrow a vehicle?' he asked.

'Sure,' said Hadleigh. 'Help yourself from the pool. I'll call through when you leave to tell 'em it's okay.' He fished a buff card, three inches by two, from his tunic pocket and tossed it across the desk. 'You'll need this also.'

Quinlan picked it up and examined it. It was a laissez-passer authorized by Masterson himself. It entitled the named bearer, in this case Major Otis Nicholas Quinlan, to go anywhere in the US Zone without hindrance and demand unqualified assistance from any member of the US Armed Forces, regardless of rank. There was a space for the bearer's signature at the foot.

'I can just about start World War Three with this.'

'I took a chance you'd want to stay on the team and had Masterson okay it this afternoon. You'll need it at the bicycle shop. There are a couple of MPs on guard outside in case last night's visitors are considering a return match. They can watch the jeep so you won't need a driver. Unless you find Martin Bormann under the floorboards, don't bother to call. As of five minutes from now I'm not available until Gabriel toots his horn.'

It was close on 10 p.m. before Quinlan arrived at the bicycle shop in Humboldtstrasse. The MPs on guard in the street were the pair he had seen earlier in the day outside the bedroom door. Although they recognized him they insisted on seeing his pass.

'Sorry, Major,' apologized one, handing it back and throwing a salute that was nearer a royal wave than anything from a drill manual, 'but previous orders were that no one goes inside.'

'No problem,' smiled Quinlan. 'Make sure nobody takes off with the wheels.'

The oil lamps were still there but extinguished and Quinlan spent five minutes going from each to the next, lighting them all. The bodies of little Ilse Arndt and Angela Salvatini were gone, of course, and a fatigues party had made a reasonable job of cleaning the blood from the floor and walls. But the smell of death remained in the air.

Quinlan put it all from his mind and began to look around. Optimistically he had brought his briefcase, but in under a quarter of an hour he was willing to concede he'd find nothing to put in it. He prodded among the blood-stained cushions, chairs and bedding and examined spare clothing and cupboards. He even prised off a couple of feet of wainscot, but by 10.30 he was ready to admit defeat. Ben Hadleigh was right; he hadn't a clue what he was looking for. Dousing each of the lamps he returned to the street.

The snow which had threatened all day had now started to fall, small flakes that looked as though they would stick. It was no night to be driving around in an open jeep. After saying good night to the MPs, now shivering and cursing in the shop doorway, he flicked his headlights to full beam and headed for home.

All but the most insignificant side streets had long ago been cleared of bomb debris by German labour gangs, and the quickest route from the bicycle shop to his billet in the barracks was down Horst Wesselstrasse to where it became Katzwangerstrasse then a hard left into Frankenstrasse opposite the M.A.N. heavy engineering works. Total mileage around one and a half; total journey time four or five minutes depending upon other traffic and the weather. At least that was the theory.

Quinlan was still in third gear and had covered only a few hundred yards when he became aware that he was being followed. The driver of the trailing vehicle was making no attempt to disguise his intentions. He had tucked himself in on Quinlan's tail and there he was staying, headlights up. At first Quinlan thought it might be a patrol jeep curious to know what kind of lunatic was driving around late at night in a snowfall, but when he slowed opposite Kopernikusplatz, the car behind slowed also.

The density of the snow increased, restricting vision and

compelling Quinlan to drive at under 20 mph. He asked himself why the pursuing vehicle made no attempt to overtake, ram him into the pavement if the object was to make him stop, but found no logical answer until he was level with the Gudrunstrasse intersection and a second vehicle shot out from his left, causing him to wrench the steering wheel to the right in order to avoid a collision.

Partly because of road conditions and partly because his lack of familiarity with left-hand drives made him slow to compensate, he went into a tail-wheel skid, slewed across the street, and stalled the jeep. Before he could restart the engine the following car ground to a halt and three men piled out, running towards him. From the second car a further two figures emerged. It was hard to tell in the snow but they seemed to be carrying clubs. Or rifles. In German they called to each other to hurry.

His heart thumping at the suddenness of it all, he was trying to climb out of the jeep and either face his attackers or make a dash for it when they were on him. Something hard and heavy smashed against his temple, but before lapsing into unconsciousness he heard, with a jolt that hit him like an electric shock, the German voices joined by another which said, in English with a broad northern accent: 'Nail the bastard!'

In the distance he was vaguely aware of a car horn blaring and flashing lights. Then there was nothing but blackness.

When he came to he was sitting in the passenger seat of the jeep, his head thrown back, the snow wonderfully cool on his face. Ben Hadleigh was saying: 'He'll have a mother of a headache in the morning, but he'll live.'

It took several more minutes before he felt fit enough to talk. Coughing over the brandy that Max was trying to force down his throat, he managed: 'What the hell happened?'

'You tell us.'

Quinlan shook his head to clear it. The jeep was where he had stalled it but there was no sign of the other two cars or their occupants. Neither was his briefcase on the back seat.

He told Hadleigh and Judd what he remembered.

'It all proves one thing, anyway,' he concluded. 'Whoever's looking for whatever it is hasn't found it. They must have thought I had – in the briefcase.'

'But you didn't?'

'There was nothing more in there than a couple of out-of-date maps.' He concentrated to bring his mind into focus. 'How come you two turned up when you did?' he asked. 'Don't think I'm not grateful, but how come?'

'You can thank Max for that,' said Hadleigh. 'I'd just about got to the bit where Ingrid Bergman is inviting me for a long weekend in Acapulco, her treat, when he woke me up with the notion that if I was bright enough to post a couple of guards on the off-chance last night's visitors would come back, they could be watching the Arndt place. That being a possibility, you were putting your head in a noose. We just hoped to God you'd take the obvious route home.'

For the first time Quinlan noticed that Hadleigh was wearing only an army-issue raincoat over his pyjamas and that his shoes were unlaced.

'Thanks, Max,' he said. 'I thought you didn't believe in two and two making five.'

'Still don't a hundred per cent,' grunted Judd, 'but we can't have you getting dusted in our Zone.'

'Did you get a look at any of them?' asked Quinlan.

'Naw.' Hadleigh pulled his raincoat more tightly about him. 'Even with the snow we could see what was happening a hundred yards off, so Max hit the horn and made like the Fifth Cavalry. They took off in a hurry east along Gudrunstrasse. It was a toss-up between following them and seeing if you were okay.' He grinned. 'Apart from that, there seemed to be a hell of a lot more of them than there were of us.'

Quinlan told them about the English voice he'd heard among the German ones. Hadleigh whistled.

'Now what the hell do you make of that?'

Quinlan didn't know. Hadleigh saw he was shivering, part cold, part shock. It was no night for a man in his pyjamas to be on the streets, either.

'Better get you back and have the sawbones look at that head. The amount of trade we're giving him we should be on discount rates. Then a couple of days in bed if you've got any sense.'

'Not me. If you'll fill me with coffee and lend me a phone, I'm going to pull a few high-level strings and see if I can't have a word with Lord Haw-Haw before they top him.'

Six

London was cold and wet, but even postwar austerity and rationing could do nothing to dampen British spirits. The islanders were nearing their first Christmas at peace for six years and they were going to enjoy it. There might not be much on the table but it could be eaten and drunk without worrying where the next bomb or V-2 rocket would fall or whether that knock on the door was a War Ministry telegram announcing the death in action of a loved one.

William Joyce was in the condemned cell, where he was prisoner number 3229 though he referred to himself in letters to his wife, incarcerated in Holloway Prison for Women, as Wandsworth William (as opposed to Wormwood Will after Wormwood Scrubs, where he was held while his Wandsworth cell was being prepared). His trial at the Old Bailey had begun on September 17 and, despite a spirited defence by his leading counsel, Mr G. O. Slade, K.C., had ended on September 19 with a unanimous verdict of Guilty. Prosecuting counsel was Sir Hartley Shawcross, at present leading the British contingent in Nuremberg.

There were many who argued then (and who still argue) that Joyce was convicted on a flimsy technicality. At one time bookmakers were offering 6-4 on an acquittal, and at the close of the first day of the hearing Shawcross had asked an eminent constitutional lawyer, Professor J. H. Morgan, whether the prosecution had any chance. Morgan replied: 'No, not unless the judge is prepared to make new law.'

The points of law which emerged during the trial were obscure to the layman, but, crystallized, hinged on whether Joyce, as the holder of a British passport (no matter how obtained) at the time of his defection to the enemy, owed allegiance to the British Crown. If so, in broadcasting for

59

Germany had he violated that allegiance? The jury decided he had. So did the Court of Appeal on November 7. He was guilty of high treason under the Treason Act of 1351 and the fact that he was the son of a naturalized American citizen or that he later adopted German nationality was not going to help him. He had joined Sir Oswald Mosley's British Union of Fascists, had claimed on the application form for his passport that he was a British subject by birth, born in Galway, Ireland, and had always thought of himself as British, even in his broadcasts, until it became inconvenient. All he could hope for now was that the House of Lords, due to sit on December 10, would overturn the Appeal Court's confirmation of the original verdict, and there was little chance of that. Joyce had cocked a snook at beleaguered Britain during its darkest hours, and it was not only the man in the street who wanted his head.

Realizing how hard it would be even to get permission to go to England, let alone see Joyce, Quinlan had enlisted Hadleigh's aid, beginning in the small hours of December 1. The G-2 major was destined not to keep his date with Ingrid Bergman, not this night. He hoped Miss Bergman would understand.

As a regular army man of considerable experience, Hadleigh knew that the worst way to approach any problem was head-on. That was poor military thinking, though he hoped to God old Blood and Guts Patton never heard him say so. If the second step was to get General Dempsey to make a few top-level phone calls to his political friends and the last step to obtain the British Home Secretary's fiat to visit Joyce, then the first step was to acquire some clout.

In tandem, Hadleigh contacted Colonel Masterson and CIC. The story he told each was the same: that a possible clue to the identity of the killers of Angela Salvatini might be found in Wandsworth Prison.

Masterson was more than willing to talk to his friend, the commanding general of the British Second Army, but CIC proved awkward to begin with. They wanted in on the act and were only persuaded that as yet there was no act to get in on by a lot of fast talking from Hadleigh. When and if there was, they would be the first to know. In the meantime, would they be kind enough to make waves?

By mid-afternoon on December 1 Quinlan was making a direct appeal by telephone to General Dempsey, who was by now accustomed to peculiar requests involving his subordinate and who had, in any case, received several similar entreaties from American sources before he had finished his second cup of breakfast coffee. Dempsey was revered by those who served under him for his policy of either trust and delegate, or fire, and he thought a lot of Otis Quinlan. He promised to do his utmost to help.

It was not incumbent upon the Home Secretary to allow anyone outside immediate family to see a condemned man (and Joyce was that all bar the shouting), but in the peculiar tradition of British jurisprudence most individuals due to be executed were granted a far greater latitude facing death than, for the most part, they had ever had, or given others, in life. It was as if the Law was saying: We're going to stretch your neck because those are the rules, but until it's stretched we'll be nice to you.

The only real obstacle might be Joyce himself, who could refuse a visit from anyone. Fortunately he remembered the British major from Flensburg and with the sardonic humour for which he was noted (he referred to Sir Hartley Shawcross as Hotcross and his trial at the Old Bailey as 'a business trip to the City') agreed to see the man who had threatened to have him shot six months earlier.

After that, wheels turned, strings were pulled, lines buzzed, cogs meshed, and Quinlan found himself on a plane for England, not at all sure what he intended saying to Joyce.

He was permitted to interview the former Lord Haw-Haw in an anteroom well away from the condemned cell, though the prison Governor insisted on two warders being present for security reasons. There was to be no smoking, nothing was to change hands, and the conversation would be conducted exclusively in English. Any infraction of these conditions and the warders had instructions to terminate the dialogue.

Quinlan was already seated on one side of a long wooden table when Joyce was brought in, dwarfed by the warders either side of him. For some reason he was never later able to fathom, Quinlan stood up. Evidently amused and delighted by this involuntary gesture, Joyce said: 'Sit down, my dear chap. Never stand in the presence of the dead.'

The circumstances were vastly different from their Flensburg encounter, and Quinlan experienced a sense of unreality. It was hard to credit that he was face to face with the man whose bullying, arrogant tone he had heard so often during the war years.

He was plumper than Quinlan remembered and looked reasonably fit, though it was difficult to tell if he was carrying excess weight, dressed as he was in the shapeless grey prison suit. His pale blue eyes were alert, eager even, and Quinlan reflected on Doctor Johnson's words: 'Depend upon it, sir, when a man knows he is to be hanged in a fortnight, it concentrates his mind wonderfully.'

Quinlan tried to recall how old he was; forty if memory served him, though he looked older. His hair was cut short in the prison fashion, but someone had made a neat job of it. The scar on his right cheek was barely noticeable under the unshielded electric light.

Joyce took his seat on the opposite side of the table and clasped his hands while the warders retreated discreetly to the far end of the anteroom.

'Well, and what can I do for Major Quinlan? I see you *are* still a major. Promotion must be exceedingly slow now there is no war to eliminate those at the head of the queue.'

If Joyce was trying to bait him, Quinlan was unaware of it. The journalist in him bellowed for attention. There were a thousand questions he wanted to ask that would give him an exclusive story anywhere in the world if he could bypass the Official Secrets Act, and it was with difficulty that he brought his mind back to the present.

He reminded Joyce of their first meeting, how he had said he knew nothing of former leaders of the Third Reich with the exception of Oberstleutnant Manfred Langenhain and Admiral Canaris.

'Did I really say that? I can't imagine why unless it was because of the rifle that little Welsh corporal was pointing in my direction. He was Welsh, was he not? I seem to recall a malevolence in him reminiscent of all our cousins beyond Offa's Dyke. Of course, I had bullet wounds in both legs so I was perhaps slightly delirious. In any event, I did not mean it the way you apparently took it. I did of course meet many of Germany's leaders, notably Doctor Goebbels. I really cannot say why I singled out those two gentlemen for mention apart from the fact, as I said a moment ago, I judged your leek-eating underling's intentions to be less than friendly.'

He had always had that curiously stilted way of talking, like someone with a thesaurus constantly at his elbow, and prison had evidently done nothing to diminish it.

Quinlan was conscious that the interview could get wildly out of hand if he allowed Joyce to dictate the pace. The little man was obviously quite proud of his facility with the English language and would have small opportunity to exercise it here.

Quinlan had conducted interrogations before and was conversant with the theory and practice of selective memory. Equally, he understood that, no matter how calm and superior Joyce might appear on the surface, deep inside him was the knowledge that he was shortly going to die. He would have to be handled with kid gloves if anything was to be gained.

Keeping his voice as neutral as he knew how he told Joyce what, to the best of his recollection, his precise words were in the border guardroom.

'You didn't exactly say you had never met anyone else. What you did say was that you *knew nothing about* former military and political leaders of Germany with the exception of Langenhain and Canaris.'

'The implication being I had intelligence on their recent whereabouts and activities?'

'Yes.'

'Hmmm.'

Always keep your subject off balance was the golden rule of every interrogator, but in this instance Quinlan disobeyed it. Joyce was not someone dragged in off the streets who could be browbeaten. He was a man with nothing to lose. At the flick of a finger, on a whim, he could close the interview. Quinlan's one hope was to keep him interested, allow him his vanity, encourage what was evidently a prodigious memory, make him *like* the man on the opposite side of the table.

But the traitor's next statement floored him.

'As I recall,' said Joyce, 'you asked the Welsh corporal if he had a round up the spout. You also implied that if I was shot you could always say I had tried to make a run for it, and

63

who would question the word of a British officer, especially when the cadaver was the infamous Lord Haw-Haw.'

Quinlan's heart sank. He had feared all along that, if Joyce could remember mentioning Langenhain and Canaris, he would also remember the circumstances. He considered briefly trying to bluff it out, calling his words those said in the heat of the moment, but something told him to play it straight. At the back of his mind he recalled a piece he had read in the *Manchester Guardian* or *The Times* at the time of the Old Bailey trial. The commentator had written that the impression he got was of Joyce wanting to be thought of as British through and through. Never mind what the excellent Mr Slade was pleading for the defence, Joyce was as British as village greens, pints of dark ale, the thud of leather against willow, red London buses, smog and hot chestnuts from a brazier. Had he been allowed in the witness box there was little doubt (in this commentator's opinion) that Joyce would ever have denied for a moment broadcasting for Germany. He would have said yes, certainly he had, to reaffirm to the British people his belief that their true friends were in the Reich, their real enemies amongst them and in government. He was a man who would hope to see in his obituary the sentiment that he had played with a straight bat.

Quinlan took a chance.

'You're right,' he said. 'Your memory does you credit. I can't say at this distance whether I would have allowed the Welshman to shoot you, but yes, it was in my mind.'

There was a short silence before a flicker of a smile crossed Joyce's face.

'Good,' he murmured. 'That's the only answer I would have accepted.' He paused. 'May I ask you the purpose of your visit and the reasons for your interest in Canaris and Langenhain?'

'I'm afraid not.'

'I'm not likely to shout it from the rooftops, you know,' teased Joyce.

'Nevertheless....' said Quinlan.

Joyce glanced across at the warders who were listening with total fascination. This was heady stuff. What a story they'd have for the pubs and the family, a British Army officer wearing green Intelligence flashes asking the most notorious prisoner in the land about Hitler's chief spymaster.

'Canaris is dead, I believe.'

It was a statement but Quinlan chose to answer it anyway.

'So we understand.'

'And Langenhain?'

'That's for you to tell me.'

'I'm not at all sure, Major Quinlan, that I have much to tell. I never met either of them, you know, but it was around the beginning of April this year I heard them being discussed. In Berlin.'

Berlin – April 1945

Word came from on high that the Reichsrundfunk English Language Service was to move out. Berlin was too dangerous for men and women who still had a useful propaganda function to perform. The city was on the verge of becoming a smoking ruin. Even though it would take Soviet ground forces several more weeks to get within artillery range, the Allied bombers were over night and day. The firemen were barely able to control one lot of fires before another conflagration started elsewhere, and the TENO platoons (*Technische Nothilfe* or Technical Emergency Help) were stretched to breaking. Everywhere Berliners looked, buildings which had been standing unscathed the day or week before were now tableaux of yawning masonry. The Fuehrer kept on encouraging them not to desert him, to remain and fight the Mongolian hordes from the east, but there was little fight left in them. There was none at all in the majority of the English language broadcasters.

Herr Winkelnkemper, the Foreign Service Director, first suggested Dresden as the new base of operations, and Gauleiter Mutschmann conducted one of Winkelnkemper's representatives over every available building in the city. But the February raids by the combined forces of the USAAF and the RAF had virtually destroyed the capital of Saxony and the idea had to be abandoned.

It was finally decided that Büro Concordia, as the English Language Service was known, would be moved to Apen, a town midway between Bremen and the Dutch frontier. Most of the staff were keen to go and face the consequences of falling into Anglo/American hands rather than be taken by the Russians. The lone voice pleading to be allowed to stay, fight to the death if it came to it, was that of William Joyce.

Now a *Volkssturmmann*, a member of the Home Guard comprising the very old and the very young and those not fit enough to fight with a front-line regiment, Joyce had a violent argument with his wife Margaret in their Kastanienallee apartment the morning before they were due to leave.

He was drinking brandy straight from the bottle and, as always when the real world did not accord with his fantasies (he had once thought he would return to England with the victorious Wehrmacht as Gauleiter of London), he became irrational.

'The troops can't run away and neither can the aged and infirm,' he shouted, 'so why should I? You go if you want to. I'm staying.'

His wife tried to reason with him. Although as dedicated a supporter of National Socialism as her husband, the former Margaret Cairns White, daughter of a Lancashire businessman of Irish lineage, was frightened of her husband's rages, the more so when he was drinking.

There was nothing for it but to go, she argued gently. He was employed by Reichsrundfunk and if he did not do what Toni Winkelnkemper said he would soon be unemployed. It would then be back to the old days when they first arrived in Berlin, living hand to mouth.

Joyce refused to see reason, but he was beyond that stage of drunkenness where he wanted to lash out. Taking the bottle of brandy with him, he retired to the bedroom and fell asleep in his clothes.

When he awoke it was mid-afternoon and his wife had gone. A hand-written note on the dressing-table told him that she was visiting friends and would be back later.

In spite of the picture depicted of him in the British press, Joyce was no physical coward. He genuinely wanted to remain in Berlin until, and if, it was overrun. But Margaret was right. If he disobeyed Winkelnkemper's orders to go to Apen with the others, not only would his contract with Reichsrundfunk be terminated but he might soon receive a visit from the Gestapo. The Third Reich was battling for its ife; it would give short shrift to individuals who could not do what they were told. The only man who could possibly grant him authorization to stay was Doctor Goebbels.

After washing and shaving and putting on a clean shirt, he made his way across town to the Propaganda Ministry in the Wilhelmstrasse, taking trams where they were running and walking where they were not.

The huge building which faced the eastern windows of the Reich Chancellery had received several direct hits during the previous night's air raid and there was dust and debris everywhere in the massive entrance lobby, but its personnel were still functioning. The official behind the desk where all visitors were obliged to report was less than helpful. He knew Joyce by sight, of course, as did every member of the Propaganda Ministry and most Berliners of any rank.

'Impossible, Herr Joyce,' snapped the official. 'The Reichminister does not see anyone without an appointment. If you care to send in a written request I will see it's forwarded via proper channels, but other than that I cannot help.'

'It's a personal matter which cannot be delayed,' tried Joyce.

The official sighed wearily.

'There are three million Berliners who all have personal business which cannot be delayed. You are merely three million and one.' Smiling slyly, for Joyce's fondness for the bottle was well known, he added: 'I suggest you decamp to the nearest bar and write your request there.'

Outside, Joyce considered the virtues of the idea. His mouth was dry and he needed a drink, and a short walk away was the Adlon Hotel, famous before the war as an international watering-hole for the rich and influential and even now a meeting-place of the powerful. He would kill two birds with one stone, quench his thirst and hope to bump into someone who could help him attain his ambition to remain in Berlin.

Miraculously, the Adlon was untouched by bombs. Its windows were filigreed with tar paper and the entrance was sandbagged to the second floor, but it was still there.

Inside the great hallway with its priceless tapestries and crystal chandeliers, he paused for a moment, faced with a sea of uniforms representing all the services and an equal number of civilians. Many of the latter were with women who could only be their wives, but scattered among the uniforms were pretty little blonde creatures, laughing, giggling, as anxious as the men they accompanied to make hay while the sun still shone. Liveried waiters hurried from group to group bearing trays. The drinks were almost exclusively champagne.

Feeling mightily underdressed in his shabby suit, Joyce searched the lobby for someone he recognized, his gaze at last alighting on a trio of men huddled deep in earnest conversation. Two of the men, senior SS officers in full uniform, were unfamiliar to him, but the third, in plain clothes, he knew well. All three had their backs to him as he sidled up in time to hear the older of the officers say: 'Canaris is finished, but it's that bastard Manfred Langenhain who bothers me. He skipped before we could pick him up and he's dropped right out of sight. If we don't find him we're in trouble.'

'You can leave Oberstleutnant Langenhain to my people,' said the second officer confidently. 'He can't remain in hiding for ever.'

'It's not for ever I'm worried about. It's the next few months. He could pass on what he knows to dozens of others. We could finish up not knowing who the hell to look for.'

It was at this point that the third man, conscious of someone behind them, turned and saw Joyce. His eyes widened in dismay and he greeted Joyce's ingratiating smile with a scowl.

The two officers turned also. The older of the pair recognized Joyce.

'Well, well,' he grinned, 'the celebrated Lord Haw-Haw, I believe. I thought you people had moved out.'

'Not yet,' said Joyce. 'In fact, I'm rather hoping not to go at all.'

'Determined to die for the Reich, eh? Admirable, admirable.'

The third man whispered anxiously to the older SS officer who seemed unconcerned.

'I don't think Herr Joyce heard anything of major importance, did you, Herr Joyce?'

'Nothing,' lied Joyce.

'I thought not. Even if he had, he has his own neck to worry about now.'

'I'm not in the least worried about my own neck,' blustered
Joyce.

'Again admirable – if unique.' The older officer glanced
pointedly at his wristwatch, a beautiful creation in twenty-
four-carat gold. 'I would invite you to join us, Herr Joyce, but
I'm afraid we have much to discuss. If you will therefore
excuse us....'

London: Wandsworth Prison – December 3, 1945

'.... As you know,' concluded Joyce,' I didn't stay in
Berlin. I went with the others to Apen.'

'And that's all?' Quinlan was unable to disguise his
disappointment. 'That's all you heard?'

'I'm afraid so.'

'Did you learn the names of the two SS officers?'

'No.'

'But the third man, the one in civilian clothes. You said
you knew him.'

'So I did.'

'Who was it?'

Joyce shrugged. 'It can be of no importance now.'

'It might be to me.'

'I think not.'

Quinlan knew that Joyce had said all he was going to, and
little enough it was. He was no further forward than
yesterday. Two SS officers and a third man had been
planning the capture (and presumably the execution) of
Oberstleutnant Langenhain, who apparently possessed information they preferred kept secret. What the information was
would probably remain a mystery, as would Langenhain's
fate. With Arndt dead and Joyce unable or unwilling to fill
in the gaps he might never learn who had killed the
Abwehr captain's daughter and Angela Salvatini or who
was responsible for the attack on himself three days ago.
The chain had run out of links unless there was something in the Arndt apartment everyone had overlooked and
unless....

He almost snapped the pencil with which he was taking notes in his excitement. Of course it wasn't over yet. What

a damned fool he was! With all the drama of the past seventy-two hours he had completely forgotten...

He packed his notebook and pencils into a brand-new briefcase, courtesy of the Third Army. There must be words for situations like this, he thought grimly, but I don't know them.

But apart from that, Mrs Lincoln, how did you enjoy the play?

'I'd like to thank you for your cooperation,' he offered lamely.

'Think nothing of it, Major Quinlan. I've enjoyed our talk. It would be pleasant to think we might meet again, but I doubt that.'

Quinlan stood up awkwardly. He was wondering, in spite of everything, whether he should offer to shake hands when Joyce solved the problem for him by abruptly getting to his feet and indicating to the warders that he wished to return to his cell. It was not until much later that Quinlan realized Joyce had perceived his dilemma and purposely left the table quickly to save him embarrassment.

From the door the condemned man called over his shoulder: 'I trust your head will be fully healed soon. Be careful of the world, Major Quinlan. It can be a very dangerous place.'

Unconsciously Quinlan put a hand to the bruise on his temple.

Nuremberg – December 7, 1945

He was left cooling his heels in London for three days before his number came up for a return flight and even that was delayed by a dozen hours due to a real pea-souper of a fog. With money in his pocket, seventy-two hours in the capital would normally have delighted him, but he was anxious to get back on the job. He managed to contact an old girl friend who happily was between affairs, have a decent dinner at the Ritz and get laid, but his mind was in Germany.

He arranged with an RAF acquaintance for a signal to be sent to Third Army when he was airborne, and Hadleigh was at the military airfield to greet him on the afternoon of the th with the news that Schauff, his informer, had been found dead two days ago, his throat cut. Hadleigh had also sent in a specialist team to tear the Arndt apartment to shreds, but they'd come up with nothing. When he was able to get a word in Quinlan told him about Arndt's mistress, the woman who had not got along with Ilse: Hannah Wolz.

Seven

Nuremberg – December 8-26, 1945

But of Fräulein Wolz there was nary a whisker nor a feather to be found. The manager of the Hans-Sachs cinema in Scheurlstrasse confirmed that she sang there, but she had not turned up for work last Friday week and he had not seen her since. These girls, his tone implied, who could trust them? Not like us men, eh, German, American or British?

On hearing the date Quinlan experienced a sense of dread. Last Friday week was November 30. During the small hours of the 29th-30th Ilse Arndt and Angela Salvatini had been killed.

The Hans-Sachs cinema no longer showed films. The projection equipment had been damaged in an air raid and replacements were impossible to come by. Besides, there was more money to be earned by converting the building into a club. Ignoring the fraternization prohibition and the need for a licence, the enterprising owner had ripped out the tip-up seats, installed a bar and a small stage, and let it be known he

had the finest singers and strippers in the entire Zone. H
obviously carried some hefty clout somewhere, because whe
Quinlan and Hadleigh visited the place beer and hard liquo
were flowing like there was no tomorrow, while on-stage
young redhead a few pounds underweight was peeling off he
clothes to music from a hand-cranked gramophone an
raucous shouts and whistles from the audience.

As a demonstration of the erotic it matched watching th
grass grow, but as the spectators had not, for the most par
been anywhere near a woman outside a quick knee-tremble
in a back alley for as long as they could remember, it wa
Marlene Dietrich in *The Blue Angel* in spades.

The majority of the clientele were enlisted men, but her
and there was a sprinkling of officers fed up with the actio
elsewhere. Hadleigh recognized many of them. Scheurlstrass
was a mere five-minute drive from the Allersbergerstrass
barracks and just across the main railway line from the Gran
Hotel. It was ideally situated for men tired of their billets an
getting drunk with each other.

The manager had introduced himself as Herr Lorenz. H
was a small worried-looking Pickwickian character, the sort t
be kept well away from a Party rally or uniform for fear o
tarnishing the *Ubermensch* image of National Socialism. H
had, he claimed, run the cinema for a quarter of a century
had tried to keep its standards of the highest 'even during th
unpleasantness of the last few years'. It was of cours
lamentable that projection equipment could not be obtained
If it could, he seemed to be inferring, the cinema would a
once revert to showing movies. Circumstances being wha
they were, however, one had to make a living as best on
could, and if the two officers would be his guests he would b
pleased to seat them at the best table and serve them th
finest brandy. It was also not impossible that two of th
prettier performers would join them after their acts.

By some trick of inflexion he managed to make this las
statement both salacious and prudish simultaneously, like
clergyman telling blue jokes apologetically to keep hi
congregation in church. Hadleigh guessed afterwards that h
was the proprietor as well as the manager but was keeping hi
ownership quiet for fear of trouble with the authorities, whe
he could plead he was only an employee.

72

They declined refreshment and entertainment. What they wanted was Fräulein Wolz's home address. Presumably Herr Lorenz could provide that.

Herr Lorenz was reluctant until Hadleigh threatened to have the MPs here in thirty minutes and the whole joint closed down for good within the hour. Besides, it seemed to Lorenz that the Allied majors wanted nothing more than to conduct a little private business with his star attraction. They did not want to arrest her or persuade her to join a rival establishment.

Hannah Wolz had a room on the second floor of a boarding house in the northern suburb of Weigelshof, close to the orphanage. Aerial bombing was not an exact science, but evidently the RAF and the USAAF had known of the orphanage and steered well clear of it. In any event, few of the buildings in the vicinity were damaged and the windows of the boarding house were all intact. There was also electricity in this part of Nuremberg, a rare luxury for private houses.

The landlady had not seen her tenant for a week or so, she confessed. Fräulein Wolz kept strange hours but was clean and quiet, did not receive men in her room, and the rent was paid until the end of December. She had no objection to the two officers looking over the room. The Allies had won the war, hadn't they? They could do what they wished.

She was on the point of leading the way when Quinlan held out his hand for the pass key, making it clear they did not require company, just directions.

Hannah Wolz was as clean as her landlady had intimated. Her lodgings were small, no more than a bed-sitter, but the bed was neatly made, the tiny table covered with a bright yellow cloth. In a free-standing wardrobe under whose front legs were wedged pieces of newspaper to balance it there hung several dresses and skirts on hangers. There was underwear, handkerchiefs and the like in a chest of drawers. It was apparent that Fräulein Wolz had not packed and left for good, but a quick search of her belongings told them nothing more.

'She's probably dead,' surmised Hadleigh. 'A woman in present-day Germany doesn't leave her clothes behind through choice.'

Quinlan disagreed.

'How would they know who she was or where to find her? They didn't know where Arndt lived until the night he died. The landlady says she never entertained men and Ilse, I seem to recall, said something about her father's mistress only visiting him when she, Ilse, was out. She might have told her killers about the Hans-Sachs cinema, but I doubt she knew the existence of this place.'

Hadleigh shrugged. 'Have it your own way, but these guys seem to be a jump ahead of us all along the route. Anyway, she's not here so what's the next move?'

'Hope she turns up, I guess. We can ask the landlady and Herr Lorenz to contact us if she comes back, but apart from that I haven't a clue.'

'So in the meantime we forget it?'

'I don't see what else we can do. I'd better see what Gretl Meissner's up to and reacquaint myself with the Palace of Justice anyway.'

'I'll second that. I'm still on Third Army payroll and if I don't start earning my per diem by clearing my desk someone upstairs might conclude I'd make a good civilian.'

As it happened, Third Army had more to think about than one G-2 major before twenty-four hours had elapsed, for on December 9, while driving between Frankfurt and Mannheim with his Chief of Staff, 'Hap' Gay, General George S. Patton was seriously injured when the Cadillac in which he was riding was in collision with a military truck. Gay, the driver of the truck, and Patton's driver, Pfc Woodring, were unhurt, but Patton was hurled into the windshield.

Although he had formally handed over command of the Third Army to General Lucian K. Truscott as long ago as October 7, to the officers and men who had served under him since Normandy Patton *was* the Third Army. The news of his injuries, head wounds and what appeared to be partial paralysis, shocked everyone.

He was taken to a hospital in Heidelberg and there it was ascertained, during surgery, that his neck was broken. Bulletins were posted daily on notice boards down to company level concerning his progress and within a few days he seemed to be making a full recovery. There were sighs of relief all round. Old Blood and Guts was going to make it. The indestructible would not be destroyed.

Quinlan and Hadleigh saw each other regularly during the middle weeks of December, but there was still no sign of Hannah Wolz and gradually both their lives returned to something near normal. They sank a few drinks in the Grand Hotel, paid a couple of visits to Hadleigh's girls over in Sündersbühl (Quinlan's performance on both occasions being up to scratch, much to the relief of Ingrid who suspected she was losing her touch), and generally got on with the business of being serving soldiers.

In the Palace of Justice it was the situation as before, with the prosecution evidence still being laid before the Tribunal. It had become such a catalogue of horror that by now it was no longer making the front pages of newspapers. Indeed, many of the journalists rarely bothered to attend every session, relying upon borrowing colleagues' notes for their daily or weekly pieces. The defendants were not due to take the witness stand for several weeks, perhaps more, and to hear Sir Hartley Shawcross and Sir David Maxwell-Fyfe and Chief Justice Jackson, leading counsel for the US, recite long lists of atrocities had become tedious. Like sex, blood and gore needs counterpoint, lows to balance the highs. In their anxiety to give a fair trial to the defendants and to ensure that the entire chronicle of Nazi crimes was officially documented for history, the Allied prosecutors had succeeded in making the Tribunal, for the moment, a non-event.

The only interesting snippet of information to circulate – and it was not given in evidence but somehow leaked from the prison – was that Doctor G. M. Gilbert, a psychologist, had given each of the defendants an intelligence test. In descending order their IQs were:

1.	Schacht	143
2.	Seyss-Inquart	140
3.	Goering	138
4.	Dönitz	138
5.	Von Papen	134
6.	Raeder	134
7.	Frank	130
8.	Fritzsche	130
9.	Von Schirach	130

10.	Von Ribbentrop	129
11.	Keitel	129
12.	Speer	128
13.	Jodl	127
14.	Rosenberg	127
15.	Von Neurath	125
16.	Funk	124
17.	Frick	124
18.	Hess	120
19.	Sauckel	118
20.	Kaltenbrunner	113
21.	Streicher	106

It has never been (quite the reverse) a hard and fast rule in any age or in any state that political and military leaders have to be highly intelligent, but on the basis of Gilbert's test only Schacht and Seyss-Inquart would have obtained an honours degree from a modern-day major university. Goering down to Speer would probably receive some sort of academic laurel, while the others would be fortunate to matriculate.

Not unexpectedly, Streicher's score was only six points above the average, a fact that he scarcely had the grey matter to comprehend. Goering was reportedly delighted with his own showing, though why a man on trial for his life should be at all interested in his IQ only the former Reichsmarschall could have said, and he didn't.

On December 18 William Joyce was told that his Appeal to the House of Lords had failed, though their Lordships' reasons were not to be given until a later date. It was the final irony. Joyce's execution was set for January 3 and he knew he would never learn the grounds for the dismissal.

After the Governor had left his cell, Joyce thought briefly of Major Quinlan and the identity of the third man in the Adlon Hotel. He would reveal it to Quinlan but not yet. In a couple of days, that would be time enough.

The International Military Tribunal adjourned for the Christmas recess on December 20. One of the last pieces of evidence to be presented by counsel for the United States was, from Buchenwald, a large piece of tattooed human skin which one of the overseers had fashioned into a lampshade.

After such a horror the gathered journalists, radio commentators, film cameramen, judges, counsel, interpreters and military personnel were relieved to quit the courtroom. For those who drank it was a moment to anaesthetize their senses; for those who did not it was a time to wish they did.

The build-up to the festivities had hardly begun when the news flashed around Nuremberg that Patton hadn't made it. Since December 19 he had been experiencing difficulty with his breathing, but the doctors thought they had it under control. At a few minutes before 6 p.m. on the 21st, however, he died of acute heart failure. His last words were reputed to be: 'This is a hell of a way for a soldier to go.'

A seemingly endless procession of GIs came to pay their respects while he lay in state in the Villa Reiner, Heidelberg, and after a funeral service on the 23rd at Christ Church in the same town, he was buried in the US Military Cemetery at Hamm in Luxembourg, where he joined 6,000 other men of the Third Army.

Those members of codename Lucky who survived him went on a gigantic binge. Old Blood and Guts would not have wanted a small thing like his death to spoil their Christmas, and neither did it. Beginning the evening of the 23rd, booze flowed like water.

Among those who didn't draw a sober breath between the 23rd and the 26th were Quinlan, Hadleigh, Master Sergeant Max Judd, and a Soviet Intelligence colonel they all knew and had got to like, Yuri Petrov. Across in the Sündersbühl house for something like eighty hours, in the company of Ingrid, Helga and two other girls imported by Hadleigh for the occasion for Judd and Petrov, they fornicated and drank, pausing only occasionally to eat and sleep and bathe.

On December 28 Hannah Wolz turned up for work.

Eight

Herr Lorenz's clout (the source of which Ben Hadleigh was determined to discover before another week was out) extended to having a telephone where few private lines existed any longer. He called shortly after 8 p.m. and announced that Fräulein Wolz had walked in ten minutes ago and started changing for work.

'Of course, in the old days she would not have been given her job back,' intoned Herr Lorenz pompously, 'but these are difficult times and my customers have missed her.'

'Did she say where she's been for the last four weeks?'

'No, Herr Major. I asked for an explanation, naturally, but she said it was none of my business.'

'And you didn't tell her we were enquiring after her?'

'Not a word. I called you instantly, as instructed.'

Hadleigh couldn't resist it.

'Who supplies your booze and protection, Lorenz?'

There was what sounded like a mild coronary at the other end of the line.

'Herr Major?' Lorenz managed eventually.

'Skip it. Act as if nothing has happened. What time does she go on?'

'Almost immediately.'

'Don't let her leave if she finishes before we arrive.'

'There will be no danger of that. She does several more spots later in the evening.'

'We'll be there in fifteen minutes.'

Nursing fat heads all round, thought Hadleigh, wearily replacing the receiver. He was getting too old to go on three-day benders. It took him a further seventy-two hours to get over them.

He was about to ring through for Max when he remembered

78

the master sergeant was away overnight in Tübingen, just
across the demarcation line in the French Zone, delivering a
truckload of Lucky Strikes which Hadleigh had bought under
the table for a tidy sum. In exchange, Max would pick up
several crates of perfume from their contact there, perhaps
some lipsticks too. Cigarettes, booze and cosmetics were
worth their weight in gold in the Zones of Occupation, but
while quantities of the first two were readily available, at a
price, in and around Nuremberg, the French had cornered
the market in scent and the various paraphernalia women
seemed lost without.

Wheel and deal, sell and buy, give some, take some. That
was what made the world go round. The only items Hadleigh
refused to deal in were narcotics and medical supplies. Ah
well, perhaps he'd never be rich.

Quinlan was in his billet when Hadleigh arrived in the
jeep, typing up on a portable (mostly from Gretl Meissner's
notes) a résumé of the trial to date for onward transmission to
Second Army HQ. He should have done it before Christmas,
but the Sündersbühl sirens had got in the way. His head was
still throbbing from the excesses of the last few days and he
needed no arm-twisting to abandon the Olivetti, not when he
learned that Hannah Wolz was no longer on the missing list.

Lorenz was waiting for them at the entrance. It had
occurred to him since calling Hadleigh that the Allied majors
were just a little too keen to get in touch with Fräulein Wolz,
that maybe she had contravened some law and was about to
be taken away for interrogation or worse. Business had
dropped off alarmingly during her absence. A few illicit clubs
like his could provide liquor and strippers, but there was only
one Hannah.

Quinlan reassured him that, as far as they knew, the
Fräulein had committed no offence.

'I have reserved a table for you near the front, gentlemen.'

'Forget it,' said Hadleigh. 'We'll find our own way round.'

'I think you might change your mind,' murmured Lorenz
slyly.

Apart from a pianist and a bass player in the wings,
Hannah Wolz was alone on stage, sitting on a high stool and
bathed in a soft pink spot emanating from what had once
been the cinema's projection booth. She was as natural an ash

blonde as anyone could wish to meet, a welcome guest in any fantasy. Her hair was straight, parted in the middle, and cut to the shoulder. She was dressed in a figure-hugging full-length black evening gown, *décolleté* and slit to mid-thigh on one side. On her feet she wore high heels with ankle straps.

She would be in her early twenties, perhaps twenty-three, and at full stretch without her heels around five feet four inches tall. She was slim not because of inadequate rations but because that was how she was naturally built. Her face was a near-perfect heart, her cheekbones high, her lips full. Although it was impossible to tell from the distance, Quinlan and Hadleigh would find out later that her eyes were blue-grey.

She was wearing long self-supporting dark stockings. One leg was on the lower crossbar of the stool, the other, revealing a glimpse of pale thigh which took the breath away, on a second, higher bar. Her hands were clasped around the upper leg.

Without the aid of a microphone and in German, which it was doubtful many of her audience understood with any degree of fluency, she was singing a universal song about a soldier and his lost love. It was not a big voice. Her vocal chords were never going to set Broadway or the West End of London ablaze, but there was something in her delivery which convinced every listener that her words were for him alone.

There were several hundred men in the auditorium – at the bar, at tables and standing – and they gave her their silent, undivided attention. There were no catcalls, none of the ribaldry which greeted the strippers. Save for the muted clinking of glasses there was scarcely any sound at all until she finished. Then the audience erupted, whistling, shouting, stomping, appealing for more.

She accepted the adulation with a dip of her head and a slight sad smile, not part of the act as Quinlan and Hadleigh were to discover.

'Jesus Christ,' muttered the American, 'that has to be the horniest thing I've seen since Jean Harlow jumped out of a cake wearing nothing but skin.'

She sang three more songs before, in a broken English accent that was a delight, thanking the men for their kindness and promising to return later. When she left the stage via the wings and a big-breasted stripper came on with her bump-and-grind act, it was back to business as usual.

They sought out Lorenz and asked to be directed to Hannah Wolz's dressing-room, which turned out to be a converted office and hers exclusively. The strippers shared an adjacent one.

Not really knowing where to begin Hadleigh kept it simple, telling her of Arndt's death, the murders of Ilse and a US security agent. Her name, he added, was given to Major Quinlan by Ilse.

Close up, her eyes were more grey than blue, the colour of exhaled cigarette smoke. They also had a quality of vulnerability not really noticeable from a distance. It was this defencelessness she somehow injected into her songs. Her male audience might lust after her but they also wanted to protect her from whatever harshness she had suffered.

She knew, she told them quietly, of Herr Arndt's death and that his daughter and another woman had been murdered. She was about to call on Herr Arndt on the afternoon of November 30 when she saw the Military Police outside the bicycle shop. She asked one of the civilian by-standers what had happened and in the manner of such things the crowd knew almost as much as the authorities. When she learned of Arndt's death and the murders, the thought uppermost in her mind was to get as far away as possible. She had been staying with friends in nearby Fürth since the 30th and had only returned today because money was short and she needed to earn her living.

Quinlan found her actions most odd. He said as much in a tone which surprised Hadleigh by its severity. Her lover dies and his daughter (with whom admittedly she did not get along) is killed, and she calmly goes to stay with friends. Instead of doing what most women would have done – breaking down or at least waiting around for the funerals – she disappears.

'My ... Herr Arndt made me promise on many occasions to go away instantly if—'she hesitated— 'if anything happened to him.'

Quinlan seized on this.

'Does that mean he was expecting something to happen?'

'I ... I don't know. I think he always considered the possibility, though he never spoke of his fears. But he rarely went out. He was also such a proud man. I have a good job and a legitimate ration book, but he would never let me take him as much as a loaf of bread. He and Ilse lived on her rations.'

'That doesn't sound like pride to me,' said Quinlan sharply, 'taking the food out of a sixteen-year-old girl's mouth because he's too frightened to register with the authorities.'

'That's because you didn't know him, Herr Major.'

Her voice was unsteady. Quinlan felt a bastard for asking his questions and making his statements without a spark of compassion. When he examined his motives later he came to the conclusion he had overreacted because of her loveliness. She produced a gut feeling within him he didn't understand and didn't like, and Otis Quinlan, wonder boy reporter, was not going to be sucker-punched by a Kraut girl's distress.

On the way across in the jeep he and Hadleigh had debated how much to tell her and decided it would have to be most, if not all, of the little they themselves knew. The killers of Ilse Arndt and Angela Salvatini would not hesitate to torture and murder Hauptmann Arndt's mistress if they knew of her existence and whereabouts, if they thought she had the information they seemed to be looking for.

Not really sure – it seemed a most peculiar relationship – how close she and Arndt had been, Quinlan brusquely expressed his regrets at the former Abwehr captain's demise but reminded himself silently that there was still unresolved business to be dealt with and that it was possible Hannah Wolz was the key.

'Have you been back to your lodgings yet?'

'No. I came directly here from Fürth.'

She indicated a small suitcase in the corner of the dressing-room.

'Am I to be told why you're asking all these questions?'

Hadleigh took over. Quinlan was being too heavy-handed and that wasn't the way to handle this girl.

'We believe Herr Arndt possessed information or documents of great value,' he said. 'His daughter and the United States security agent were murdered because the killers thought that Ilse, at least, knew what the information was or where the documents were. It seems they were mistaken.'

'But you think I might have this information, these documents?'

'According to Ilse you were ... er ... close to Herr Arndt,' said Hadleigh delicately.

Her big eyes looked at him enquiringly.

'Ilse told you I was her father's mistress.'

It was a statement and Hadleigh elected not to beat about the bush.

'Exactly that.'

This was getting them nowhere and Quinlan came in again.

'You knew Herr Arndt held the rank of Hauptmann in the Abwehr during the war, did you not?'

'Of course, though he spoke little of his work.'

'But you do know the Abwehr was the Intelligence arm of the Wehrmacht?'

'So I understand, though it's not something a German girl pays much attention to. Any more, I suppose,' she added with a surprising toughness in her tone, 'than an English or an American girl would care about the spy services of her own country.'

Hadleigh suppressed a grin – fifteen-love to the Fräulein – but the comment washed over Quinlan.

'What we're trying to establish, Fräulein Wolz,' he went on, 'is whether Arndt said anything to you or gave you anything for safe keeping that could possibly explain why his daughter was killed. I should add that if you do know anything it would be advisable to tell us. Ilse's murderers will undoubtedly find out sooner or later of your existence and your one chance is to help us get to them before they get to you.'

'You're saying my life is in danger?'

'It could be. It very well could be.'

She spent upwards of thirty seconds in thought, studying each of them in turn, before abruptly coming to a decision. Walking over to her suitcase she knelt and opened it. Rummaging through the contents she took out an ordinary buff commercial envelope, eight inches by five. She held it to her breast.

'He gave me this,' she said, 'with instructions to keep it with me at all times. If anything happened to him I was to hold on to it until Oberstleutnant Langenhain....'

'Wait a minute, wait a minute,' interrupted Quinlan. 'Oberstleutnant *Manfred* Langenhain? You know him, you've met him?'

'Of course. Several times right here in Nuremberg. Before the end of the war, that is. I haven't seen him since.'

She appeared to have lost her train of thought.

'Please continue,' encouraged Quinlan.

'I don't suppose it matters now,' she went on. 'The envelope was sealed but I opened it when I learned Herr Arndt was dead. It may be what you're looking for. I don't know. It certainly seems to have no value.'

She hesitated for a moment before handing the envelope to Quinlan, who could barely disguise his disappointment when he saw what it contained.

It was a torn fragment of colour photograph measuring some two inches by two and depicting an irregular section of island or islands with sea on three sides. The fourth side was hard against one edge of the photograph and would evidently have shown the rest, or another part, of the island or island group had the picture been entire.

It seemed to have been taken with a powerful camera – at least the definition was perfect – from an ordinary atlas, but there was no way of telling what or where the island was. The photographer had erased all distinguishing marks such as towns, as he had the lines of longitude and latitude.

Whoever had mutilated the picture had also made certain that the remaining outline would furnish no clues to the island's whereabouts by reference to a world map. For that matter, what was shown did not even have to be an island, though that was the impression given. But it could equally have been the coastline of a country or a continent. As was presumably the intention, without the missing pieces it meant absolutely nothing.

Flicking over the photograph Quinlan saw the word KIKA handwritten in ink on the reverse side. But that too meant nothing.

He handed the fragment to Hadleigh.

'And this is all Arndt gave you?' he asked Hannah.

Again there was a moment's hesitation before she answered.

'Not quite all,' she said finally 'There was also an address, which he asked me to keep separate from the photograph. If something happened to Herr Arndt and Oberstleutnant Langenhain did not appear after a reasonable period, I was to contact a Herr Helmut Bachmann in Munich and give the envelope to him.'

'*Herr* Bachmann?' queried Quinlan. 'No rank?'

'I was never told a rank.'

'Where in Munich?' asked Hadleigh.

'I don't remember the exact address. It was written down for me. It's on a piece of paper I use to prop up one leg of the wardrobe in my lodgings, inside an old newspaper.'

They remembered the wedges of newspaper and cursed themselves for making such a perfunctory search of the room. Not that the name and address would have meant anything to them at the time.

'There's one other thing,' said Hannah. 'No, perhaps two. Herr Arndt told me not to worry if Oberstleutnant Langenhain never turned up or if I could not trace Herr Bachmann. After January 10, he said, it wouldn't matter. He never explained what he meant by that.'

'January 10 next year, nineteen forty-six, in less than a fortnight?' said Hadleigh.

'Yes.'

'And the second thing?' asked Quinlan.

'I was never Herr Arndt's mistress,' she said after a long pause. 'Like Ilse, I was his daughter.'

Nine

The silence in the dressing-room was broken by Hannah reaching for a cigarette from a packet on the table. Hadleigh leaned forward to light for her. It was, he observed, an American brand, a Camel. But Hannah Wolz would have many admirers more than willing to give her cigarettes and much else.

'You might as well tell us the rest,' he said. 'As Arndt's mistress you might have been in danger. As his daughter you certainly are.'

'I was what you would call a love child,' she began. 'My father was already married to Ilse's mother when I was conceived and, though Ilse was not of course born at the time, there was no question of a divorce.

'I didn't know of my father's existence until late in 1944 when my own mother died. I had always been led to believe he was killed in a road accident when I was very small. That there were no formal photographs of them together around the house she answered by saying they were destroyed in a fire. She had a couple of snapshots of herself and Herr ... I mean my father, but they could have been of any young man. All I'm telling you I learned from him, of course. It was a different era, the early Twenties. I suppose my mother was in some way ashamed I was illegitimate.

'She never told him she was pregnant. They had a brief affair in the autumn of 1922, and then it was over as these matters frequently are. It wouldn't have stood the test of time anyway, but he was a handsome man in his youth and she was a beautiful woman.'

There could be little doubt of that, thought Quinlan. Like mother, like daughter.

'When she died,' Hannah went on, 'I had to go through her

papers. I had never had any need for my birth certificate before, but there it was. Mother Gerda Wolz, father Heinrich Arndt. I wasn't shocked, more disappointed that I'd had a father all these years without knowing it. Neither did I know whether he was still alive, but of course he was and living, when on leave, right here in Nuremberg, not six kilometres from my mother's house in Fürth. It's no longer standing, my mother's house. It was destroyed by an *Ami* bomb, which is why I live where I do.'

She said this without a trace of bitterness.

'It took me a little while to track him down,' she continued, 'but I did so earlier this year. I judged he would be in the military and contacted the authorities. They were reluctant to cooperate at first, but finally they gave me his address and after that it was just a question of waiting until he came home on leave.'

'They gave you his Humboldtstrasse address?' asked Quinlan.

'No. At the time he was living in the Gibitzenhof district. He and Ilse didn't move into the apartment above the bicycle shop until March this year. He kept on the Gibitzenhof house but lived mainly in Humboldtstrasse.'

Quinlan nodded. That figured. A man in hiding would have one address for the official records and another up his sleeve. What Hannah Wolz could find out from the authorities so could anyone else.

'Did he ever mention where he was stationed, where his base was?' asked Hadleigh.

'He never spoke of his work at all, not even when the war was over. Neither did he tell me why he rarely went out. He said it was better I didn't know.' She sighed deeply. 'I suppose I thought he was wanted for war crimes. Once that idea was in my head I decided it was better not to press him. I'd only just found him. I didn't want to lose him again to an Allied court.' She looked at them anxiously. 'He wasn't a war criminal, was he? He had nothing to do with those dreadful camps we read about?'

'Not as far as we know,' answered Hadleigh. 'In fact, I'd say it was almost a certainty.'

'I didn't think so,' said Hannah, but it was clear the thought had crossed her mind more than once.

Quinlan had a question. It was the obvious one and he

wasn't sure how relevant it was, but he couldn't help asking out of curiosity.

'I don't understand the reason for the subterfuge. Why didn't Arndt acknowledge you as his daughter and tell Ilse she had a half-sister? Why allow her to believe you were his mistress?'

Hannah stubbed out her cigarette in an ashtray.

'You didn't know Ilse,' she explained. 'She was going through a difficult time. Her own mother was killed in an air raid shortly before mine died. She was insanely possessive with our father. At least, that's what he believed. He never told her I was his mistress, of course. That was a deduction she made for herself. It might seem odd, but while she was willing to accept her father receiving visits from another woman while she was out, a half-sister with whom she would be compelled to share her father's love – that's how she would have phrased it – would be too much to take.'

Thinking it over, Quinlan concluded there was more to it than that. Hannah had been entrusted with the photographic fragment and Bachmann's address, which were of vital importance to Arndt no matter how trivial they might seem to anyone else. If anything happened to him, Ilse could become a potential target. There was no getting around that; his enemies would know he had a daughter. But what she didn't know she couldn't reveal. It must have worried him sick wondering if he should try to get her away, get her out of it, but that was easier said than done under the Occupation Laws. Freedom of movement was restricted. While adults could, and did, flout the rules almost at will, it was asking a lot of a sixteen-year-old girl to go to a different town or district and fend for herself. Arndt was doubtless hoping that, if he kept his head down, no one would find him or Ilse until it didn't matter.

Except: until what didn't matter?

Apart from the killers God alone knew what had taken place in the Humboldtstrasse apartment before Angela Salvatini and Ilse had mercifully died. The CIC agent could have told her attackers nothing because she knew nothing, but Ilse, Arndt may have reasoned, would probably have revealed the existence of a half-sister under torture. She might not have said anything about a mistress.

On the other hand, there was no evidence to suggest she hadn't. Hannah had disappeared very quickly the following day. It was possible the killers knew of her but were unable to trace her. If that was so, she was in grave danger.

Quinlan examined the fragment of photograph again, willing it to give up its secret. Could it really be part of something so important that it had already to his knowledge cost three lives? With his own a fourth if Hadleigh and Max had not intervened.

There was a timid knock on the dressing-room door. Herr Lorenz enquired from the corridor when Fräulein Wolz would be ready to go on again. The men had missed her and were demanding more.

Hadleigh told him to go away and come back in five minutes. He added to Hannah: 'You mentioned you'd met Langenhain several times. When was the last?'

She had to think about it.

'It was before the end of hostilities and before, I believe, they moved more or less permanently into Humboldtstrasse. Around the end of March.'

'Did you hear what he and your father discussed?'

'No. On each occasion it was made clear they wanted to talk in private.'

'Did Langenhain know of the true relationship between you and Herr Arndt?' asked Quinlan.

'I very much doubt it.'

'Or your Weigelshof address or where you worked during the war? I presume it wasn't here.'

'It wasn't. No, to the best of my knowledge Oberstleutnant Langenhain knew nothing more about me than my given name.'

'But your instructions were to hand over the envelope to Langenhain if anything happened to your father.'

'Either that or contact Herr Bachmann, yes.'

'But how could you,' demanded Quinlan, 'if he knew nothing more than your first name? How would he find you or you him?'

'I've really no idea. Perhaps I've misled you. It wasn't as though my father was saying that the *moment* something happened to him I must both leave my job and seek out Herr Langenhain. It was more a question of holding on to the envelope *in case* Herr Langenhain contacted me or I could get to Munich to see Herr Bachmann. He was a sick man but I don't really think he expected to die before he saw Herr Langenhain again.'

And perhaps he wouldn't have done, thought Quinlan, if I hadn't put him through the hoop.

Hadleigh sensed Quinlan's discomfort and came to the rescue.

'But he never did see Langenhain after March?'

'No.'

'How can you be so sure?'

'I knew my father well even on such short acquaintance. He was always agitated for several days after a meeting with the Oberstleutnant. I noticed no such agitation after March.'

Quinlan held out the fragment of photograph.

'When did he give you this, before or after March?'

'Oh, a long time after. Not until this past autumn.'

'So it could have come from Langenhain in the first place?'

'I expect it could. It never occurred to me.'

Lorenz was still outside in the corridor. He tapped again on the dressing-room door.

'*Please*, Fräulein,' he begged.

'May I continue my act?' she asked.

Hadleigh nodded. 'But come back here when you're through.'

'Am I under arrest?'

'No, but we may have more questions for you.'

She swished out of the room. In her heels she was almost as tall as Quinlan.

A moment or two later they heard a distant roar of approval from the auditorium.

Hadleigh bit the end of a fresh cigar and put a match to it. When it was well and truly alight he said: 'Curiouser and curiouser. But what's the bottom line?'

'For the moment keeping her out of the morgue. You'll have to take her in or she could wind up like her half-sister.'

'Forget it.' Hadleigh shook his head. 'Where the hell would I put her in Allersbergerstrasse? Half the guys out front are billeted there. If they got to hear she was in the barracks I'd have a riot on my hands.'

'You can't let her go back to Weigelshof.'

'Not even if I detail you as a twenty-four hour guard?' Hadleigh grinned.

'Not even then, much though the idea appeals. I wouldn't find her presence hard to get used to.'

'Me neither. Okay, I'll give it some thought. In the meantime, let's get down to cases. There's something about this whole business that's puzzling the hell out of me.'

'Just one something?'

'One more than all the rest. Her father was a serving officer in the Abwehr, right? So was Langenhain. Now furloughs are hard enough to come by in peacetime, for Christ's sake, but at that stage of the war leave would be cancelled all round. Yet here we have Arndt and Langenhain having cosy little meetings in Nuremberg just a few days before the Third and Seventh Armies overran the city. Arndt lived here, fair enough, but we've heard nothing to say he was based here. But from what Fräulein Wolz said he was more or less a permanent fixture in Gibitzenhof or Humboldtstrasse from February onwards. He seems to have had an awful lot of freedom for a lousy captain. Langenhain was in and out like a bridegroom's cock and in any case he was a light colonel. But Arndt I can't figure.'

Quinlan thought he could.

'Remember what Joyce told me about the meeting in the Adlon, that the SS officers were worried because Langenhain had dropped out of sight? It's my guess Arndt did the same, took French leave. They were up to something, the pair of them, something that was bothering the hell out of the SS.'

'More than just the pair of them would be my guess,' Hadleigh conjectured. 'That piece of photograph you're holding has to have brothers and sisters some place. It's hard to tell, but it looks like a quarter of the original, perhaps a sixth. There are three or five other fragments somewhere.'

'And together they'd add up to what? A picture of an island or islands or a section of mainland? A place where the SS have stashed some loot or documents? And what about this word KIKA on the reverse? What's that, part of a code, the name of a person, the name of the island or a town?'

Hadleigh frowned at the end of his cigar.

'You're asking me questions I can't answer, but there's one

I can. Until you spoke to Joyce we were only guessing that the SS were in on this. Sure, the killings of the two women had SS written all over them, but it was still guesswork. Now it's not. Now we can be as near as dammit certain that a bunch of them are up to their greasy necks in something, probably not a dozen miles from where we're standing.'

'Which makes it imperative we put Hannah Wolz out of their reach. They'd have a field-day with her long before they killed her. We'd better check with Lorenz to see if anyone made enquiries about her during her absence.'

Lorenz confirmed that there had been many, many enquiries.

'Dozens of them, daily.'

Hadleigh explained that that was not what they meant. They were not interested in horny GIs who wanted to know when their favourite piece of fantasy tail would be back on the circuit.

'Any Germans or anyone you didn't recognize as a regular customer?'

'No Germans, but there was one man who spoke the language fluently if with an accent I couldn't place. I thought at first he was English, but his pronunciation was like nothing I'd heard before.'

Quinlan recalled the broad northern voice saying 'nail the bastard' on the road back from Humboldtstrasse that night, and gave a passable impression of a Yorkshireman asking the time of day in German.

'Yes,' said Lorenz, 'something like that. He was also capless but wearing a uniform, though over it he had a civilian raincoat. I couldn't see any marks of rank, just his khaki trousers.'

'What precisely did he say?' asked Quinlan.

'And when was it?' added Hadleigh.

Lorenz's brow furrowed as he tried to remember. He wished this American and this Britisher would go away and leave him in peace, leave him to get on with the business of making a living. How could he possibly have known when he voted for Hitler back in the Thirties that he would end up running little more than a brothel for foreigners?

'Herr Lorenz,' prompted Quinlan.

'Yes, yes, I'm thinking. It was, I believe, the first evening

Fräulein Wolz did not appear for work. Yes, I'm sure it was. I didn't pay him much attention at the time, apart from his strange accent. Many others were also enquiring why she wasn't singing. When I told him I had no idea where she was he asked me if I knew where she lived. I said I did not. My customers frequently tried to find out Fräulein Wolz's address, but I never gave it.'

'You gave it to us,' accused Quinlan.

'Only because the Herr Major threatened to close me down. Besides, you were obviously on official business.'

And equally obvious, thought Hadleigh and Quinlan simultaneously, was the fact that Ilse Arndt, before she died, had told her killers of Hannah Wolz's existence and where she worked. She could not have given them her address. Heinrich Arndt would have made sure she never knew it. If he could not protect one daughter because she was too young to send away, he could protect the other.

'And you never saw him again?'

'Never.'

'Which doesn't mean to say he or they haven't got this place under surveillance,' Hadleigh speculated when they left Lorenz and went into the auditorium. To the customary hush Hannah was singing about a rose which died a little each day her lover was away. It should have been corny, but it wasn't.

He jerked his head in the direction of the stage.

'You're right about putting her out of reach. It doesn't bear thinking about, what they'd do to her. One of us had better spend the night with her up in Weigelshof – and I mean that in the purest possible way – until we can come up with something better.' He sighed a long sigh. 'It'll have to be you. *No todos los dias son dias de fiesta.*'

Quinlan's command of Spanish extended only to asking for the men's room and whether the dark-eyed señorita would care for another drink.

'Which means?'

'Not every day can be a party. I've got to watch the store. Don't forget to pick up Bachmann's Munich address.'

In spite of Lorenz wanting his leading lady to do the midnight spot, as she always did, they insisted she quit after her second session. It was then close to eleven o'clock.

They repeated to Hannah that they believed her life to be

93

in danger and urged her to agree to Quinlan staying with her until morning. Tomorrow they would try to find her somewhere safer to stay, though where that would be neither of them had any notion. She was in the public eye; that was her job. Short of keeping her under wraps in protective custody until the entire business was sorted out (but until *what* entire business was sorted out? they asked themselves), there was little they could do to prevent someone determined enough getting to her. Hadleigh hadn't got the manpower to give her round-the-clock protection. Nor could he justify it to Gene Masterson even if he had. So far it was guesswork.

Hannah accepted the arrangement with only the mildest protest, and they stood in the corridor while she changed into her street clothes: low-heeled black pumps, a skirt and sweater which had seen better days but which were clean, a hooded grey cloak covering the whole ensemble. The latter reminded Quinlan of the outer garment some nurses wore back in England and she confirmed that she had spent much of the war in the DRK, the German Red Cross, her base being the Hallerwiese-Klinik.

'But at school I always wanted to be an entertainer, a singer. Then the war came along and spoilt it all. I'll never get further than Herr Lorenz's now.'

Outside it was snowing lightly and the jeep's driver was stamping his feet to keep warm, and cursing. He had had the good sense to put the top up, but a jeep wasn't a Cadillac.

'Second item on the agenda is to get myself a decent set of wheels,' muttered Hadleigh, shivering at the sudden drop in temperature.

The first item was for Quinlan to draw from the Allersbergerstrasse armoury something that packed more of a punch than his Webley.

'Just in case,' said Hadleigh.

Unnoticed by them their departure was observed by two men on the far side of Scheurlstrasse, sitting in a stationary unmarked Opel sedan. They made no attempt to follow the jeep, however. They had other things on their mind.

The armoury was locked and it took Hadleigh forty minutes to raise someone with a key.

Quinlan chose a Thompson .45 submachine-gun, Mark

M1A1. This was the box-fed model manufactured by the Savage Arms Corporation of Utica, New York. It was shorter and lighter than the familiar drum-fed version used in early commando raids and was less liable to jam due to the introduction of a firing-pin in place of a hammer. Quinlan also helped himself to three 30-round clips of ACP ammunition.

Hadleigh remained behind while the driver took Quinlan and Hannah to her boarding-house. The Pfc at the wheel did not know the route and because the snow had thickened even Hannah found it difficult to recognize familiar landmarks.

North of the River Pegnitz they got lost several times and it was coming up to 1 a.m. before the jeep dropped them outside the house. The Pfc roared off while the return route was fresh in his head. He had had more than enough for one evening, though from what he had seen of the Fräulein he judged the British major to be one lucky son of a bitch.

Hannah had a key to the front door. Frau Schrieber, the landlady, was accustomed to her peculiar hours, but she was something of an insomniac as well as a nosy parker and invariably opened the door to her own rooms, ground floor back, when she heard someone enter.

'To make sure I'm not bringing a man in,' said Hannah with a hint of mischief.

But she didn't on this occasion. While the rest of the house was in darkness there was a light shining through a crack under Frau Schrieber's door. But it remained closed.

Quinlan felt the hairs on the back of his neck stiffen. He'd had the same feeling a dozen times since June 1944, in the hedgerows of Normandy, the narrow streets of German towns. Frau Schrieber could be in the lavatory or boiling a kettle and not have heard the key in the lock, but he didn't think so. Something was wrong.

It was near enough pitch-black in the hallway but his eyes were rapidly becoming accustomed to the darkness and he remembered the lay-out of the house from his previous visit.

Directly opposite the front door were the stairs which led to the upper floors. Right of the stairs, where he and Hannah were now standing, was a narrow corridor which ran the length of the house to Frau Schrieber's rooms. There were no other apartments on the ground floor.

He passed Hannah her suitcase and cocked the Thompson.

'Keep your head down by the stairs and don't move a muscle until I tell you,' he whispered.

To her credit she did as she was told without question.

From the stairs to Frau Schrieber's door was a distance of some thirty feet. Keeping flat against the right-hand wall, he moved slowly along the corridor. He was thinking he was going to look a mite foolish if the old woman suddenly appeared in her nightgown when her door was flung open and a man's voice shouted, in German: 'For Christ's sake don't shoot the girl!'

It was their reluctance to risk harming Hannah before she could tell them what she knew, he realized later, which saved his life.

Blinded by the light from Frau Schrieber's rooms Quinlan's instincts took over. He dropped into a crouch and squeezed the Thompson's trigger.

Within the narrow confines of the corridor the noise was deafening. Above it all he heard answering shots coming from the doorway, a man's shriek of agony and Hannah screaming behind him.

Half a clip had gone before he released the trigger. It now became a question of either moving backwards to the safety of the stairs, or forwards. He chose the latter, covering what remained of the thirty feet in a couple of strides, jumping over the prone and bloody figure of the man blocking the doorway as he did so.

Frau Schrieber was bound to a chair, and gagged. She was fully conscious and her eyes were wide with terror. Edging swiftly towards her, sideways on, intending to use her as cover, a thick-set fair-haired man was waving an automatic pistol in Quinlan's direction. He loosed off a couple of shots which missed their target by several feet before Quinlan pumped a short burst into his upper torso.

Then the lights went out, literally and figuratively. One moment the room was flooded with electricity, the next it wasn't. But, even as Quinlan turned on hearing footsteps behind him, something very hard hit him across the back of the head.

He recovered consciousness to find Ben Hadleigh standing over him and the room full of heavily-armed GIs, a sergeant in command.

'This,' he managed, 'is becoming a habit. What the hell hit me?'

Frau Schrieber was sobbing in a corner, drinking greedily from a GI flask which obviously contained anything but regulation water. Close by, eyes averted, Hannah was standing amid the ruins of her suitcase. One of its metal corners was dented.

'She did and that did,' said Hadleigh.

'I'm sorry, Herr Major,' the girl apologised. 'When the shooting stopped I switched off the lights from the mains by the front door and hit out at the first thing I saw.'

It was a gutsy performance from someone who had been screaming a few seconds earlier and who could just as easily have run into the street. Quinlan nodded his acceptance of her apology.

'What brought you here?' he asked Hadleigh.

'Herr Lorenz. Twenty minutes after you left I had him on the horn. He said he'd been beaten up and left unconscious by a couple of Germans – these two, I presume, but we'll get a formal identification later – who forced him to give them Fräulein Wolz's address. They would have killed him from what I can gather but a couple of the strippers heard the ruckus and started singing soprano. They watched us leave is my guess and what with all the screwing around at the armoury got here before you. They're both dead, by the way. I didn't tell you to start World War Three.'

Quinlan struggled to his feet, holding his head.

'Who are they?'

The sergeant answered that. He and a couple of GIs had dragged the corpses into the corridor for examination.

'SS, Major. Blood-group tattoos under their armpits. No other ID on them.'

'Which just about settles for good and all who the bad guys are,' said Hadleigh. 'Come on, we'll leave the sergeant to clean up here, pick up Bachmann's address from Fräulein Wolz's room, and make tracks.'

'Changed your mind about putting her up in the barracks?'

'No, she'd still be raw meat to hungry lions there, but if she doesn't mind sharing a house with a couple of hookers, Sündersbühl is probably the safest bet. I'll put a guard on the joint for the night.'

They were speaking in English and Hannah, although she understood hardly a word, realized her immediate future was under discussion.

'What about tomorrow and the next day?' asked Quinlan.

'Tomorrow – later today rather – we'll pay a visit on Herr Helmut Bachmann in Munich. The Fräulein goes with us. For all we know Bachmann is Langenhain in another hat and only Fräulein Wolz is in a position to recognize him. Besides, I'd like to get the pair of you out of Nuremberg. Together you're more lethal than Bonnie Parker and Clyde Barrow. Sleep as long as you like. I want to take Max along in case we run into more trouble and he won't be back before noon.'

But Quinlan was destined to be awakened at 10 a.m. by Hadleigh. The US major had a signal flimsy in his hand.

'Sorry to rouse you from your beauty sleep but this is important. It's come the long way round and because of Christmas it's been held up right down the line, but it started with William Joyce. Should I read it? It's addressed to you via Third Army.'

Quinlan struggled to full consciousness

'Go ahead.'

'It's bylined your Home Office and states that in a private conversation with the Governor of Wandsworth Prison Joyce revealed the identity of the third man in the Adlon Hotel to be John Amery.'

Quinlan was suddenly wide awake. Son of Leo Amery, Churchill's wartime Secretary of State for India, John Amery was the founder of The Legion of St George, later known as the British Free Corps, whose volunteers, recruited from POW camps in Germany and Occupied Europe, had been controlled by and fought with the Waffen SS.

Then he remembered something else.

'Oh, Christ!'

'Right,' said Hadleigh. 'I recalled the name even if I didn't know all the details of his cockamamie outfit, and I checked the newspaper files for the date before I came over. They hanged Amery at Wandsworth on December 19.'

Ten

Max drove the Mercedes staff car Hadleigh had comman-
deered from the pound of captured vehicles. It had once
belonged to Panzer Generaloberst Heinz Guderian, and
Captain Jim Pepper, the officer i/c the compound, had
pronounced it on the fritz, never likely to run again, good
only as a museum piece. Hadleigh knew different. Jim
Pepper had his own beady eyes on it and was keeping
all-comers at arm's length until he figured out a way to ship it
back to the States. It would cause a sensation in Poughkeep-
sie.

Hadleigh made him a deal: a dozen bottles of the perfume
Max had brought back from Tübingen in exchange for a loan
of the Merc. Pepper thought of the tail twelve bottles of scent
would buy him and quite suddenly the car was in perfect
running order.

'But make sure I get the damned thing back in one piece.'

Sure Jim.

'And take it easy on the gas pedal between fifty and eighty
kays.'

Right, Jim.

'She's a bit sticky on her steering above a hundred and fifty
kays.'

Okay, Jim.

'For Chrissake let's get out of here before he gives us advice
on how to burp it,' moaned Hadleigh.

They were late leaving Nuremberg. Max had not returned
from the French Zone until 2.30 and then it had taken time
to bargain for the Merc and stash the remainder of the scent
where no bastard would find it. With the hood up and light
snow falling, it was therefore close on dusk when Max left
Reichsstrasse 8 and joined the Berlin-Munich Autobahn,

99

which wasn't quite the magnificent piece of civil engineering Hitler had opened in the Thirties. But Wehrmacht labour gangs had repaired much of the bomb and artillery damage and travelling at speed was now permitted, even at night.

Quinlan had spent most of the morning and early afternoon looking through old Third Army newspaper files and on the telephone, refreshing his memory on the subject of the British Free Corps and its founder. He related his findings in German so that Hannah, sitting next to him in the back, would also understand. Hadleigh passed the journey in the front passenger seat, translating the more obscure nouns for Max and filling the massive interior of the Merc with cigar smoke.

A month ago, on November 28, Amery's trial at the Old Bailey had lasted a mere eight minutes. At the earlier Bow Street committal proceedings he had pleaded Not Guilty to the charge of high treason by virtue of the fact that he was a Spanish citizen, naturalized during the Spanish Civil War. But moments before his Old Bailey trial was due to begin he called his defence counsel, once again the excellent Mr Slade, down to the cells and said he was changing his plea to Guilty, which gave him no recourse of appeal to a higher court as had happened with Joyce. Before passing sentence of death Mr Justice Humphreys asked Mr Slade if his client fully understood the implications of his plea. Slade said he did. The reason for the change of heart was never publicly established, but it was presumed to be to save his distinguished family the agony of a prolonged hearing and the attendant publicity. If that was so, it was a remarkable volte-face, as Amery had caused his parents nothing but trouble for most of his life, which had ended ten days ago at the age of thirty-three.

Nine years earlier he had been made bankrupt to the tune of £5,000 with assets nil, and this time his family refused to bail him out. He left England for Spain, where he ran guns during the Civil War for Franco's Falangists.

At the outbreak of World War II he quit his San Sebastian base and went to France, where he joined up with the Cagoulards, the French Fascists, and also formed a relationship with a lovely young Frenchwoman, Jeannine Barde. Throughout the whole of 1941 and much of 1942 he offered his services to the Nazis, who, at first ignoring his entreaties,

100

relented in October of that year and invited him to Berlin, where he suggested over dinner at the Hotel Kaiserhof with a high-ranking official of the German Foreign Office and Dr Friedrich Hansen, a member of Hitler's personal staff, that he raise a force of British POWs to fight the Russians at the side of the Wehrmacht. He also wanted to do some propaganda broadcasting, and on November 19, 1942 he was permitted to do so.

Introduced as the son of a British Cabinet Minister, he made a long speech which, encapsulized, beseeched the British to form an alliance with Germany to fight the 'twin enemies' of Judaism and Communism. In another speech a while later he said it could never be treason, in wartime or any other time, ardently to love one's country – which would have put paid to any claim to Spanish citizenship had he elected to defend his life.

Eventually he quarrelled with Hansen, partly because he was broadcasting to the British on one note while William Joyce was sneering at the other end of the scale, and partly because he ran up huge accounts in Berlin, the stores, restaurants and hotels always being told 'to send the bills to Dr Hansen'.

Accompanied by Mlle Barde, he returned to France, to Paris, where, encouraged by the French collaborator Jacques Doriot, he rehashed his ideas for the Legion of St George.

By the beginning of April 1943, with defeats at El Alamein and Stalingrad to stomach, Berlin was willing to listen and approved a brigade of 1,500. Around this time Jeannine Barde, a hopeless alcoholic, died after a heavy drinking spree, choking on her own vomit. Amery was apparently distraught, but while taking Mlle Barde's cremated ashes back to her birthplace by train he met another young Frenchwoman, Michèle Thomas. Before the journey was over he had proposed they set up house together.

On April 21, 1943, the day after Hitler's fifty-fourth birthday, Amery began his first recruiting drive at the St Denis internment camp outside Paris. It was less than successful. Most of the inmates shouted him down and hurled any handy missile at him. At the end of the session he had attracted three converts.

He was bitterly disappointed. The prophet was without

101

honour even outside his own country, and he quickly lost interest in his brainchild. He dropped out of sight. Apart from several more broadcasts, little was heard of him until he was captured by partisans on the road between Milan and Como at the end of April 1945.

But the Legion of St George, soon to become the British Free Corps, was an established fact. It continued to attract recruits though other men were doing the recruiting. Until late in the war it was part of the Wehrmacht, but eventually control passed to the SS, whose field-grey combat uniforms it wore with the addition of collar patches depicting three leopards and a Union Jack on the upper left sleeve. A cuff-band bearing the words British Free Corps in Gothic letters was also worn.

'There were never very many of them, nothing like the fifteen hundred Berlin envisaged,' Quinlan concluded as the huge Mercedes ate up the hundred-odd miles between Nuremberg and Munich. 'A couple of hundred tops would be my guess, mainly on the Eastern Front, those who hadn't decided the jig was up anyway and elected to go back to their POW camps.' He smirked at Hadleigh. 'And you can take that superior look off your face. The unit wasn't exclusively British in spite of its title. There was at least one American among them, probably more.'

'Probably more is right,' nodded Hadleigh. 'I remember the one we netted, a guy named Hale from Michigan. Got ten years a while back. But there were other names we haven't accounted for, guys who were taken out of their POW cages for reasons other than the usual treatment from the Gestapo and who were never heard from again. Anyway, it solves the problem of the guy who visited Lorenz and the English accent you heard the night they tried to dust you on the way back from Humboldtstrasse.'

Quinlan agreed, adding that he would give a lot to meet up with the owner of that voice again. What it didn't explain was how remnants of the BFC and the SS were tied in together, nor what the two SS officers and John Amery were talking about in the Adlon Hotel back in the spring. And it was too late to ask Amery in person about the connection.

Damn Joyce for being so secretive! What had he gained by concealing Amery's identity? Nothing except, knowing the ttle man's vanity, he would have hated to think that a ritish Army officer was visiting Wandsworth Prison to see omeone other than himself.

By all accounts Amery was top dog with Berlin, swanning round Europe unrestrained, living high off the hog, while oyce was stuck with Büro Concordia. That probably explained ;, that and Joyce's envy of Amery's aristocratic connections. The former Lord Haw-Haw had grown up with a huge chip on is shoulder. Even in the old, prewar days, when it was quite ashionable for the British upper classes to flirt with Fascism, he vas never accepted by the more blue-blooded of the Mosleyites. He was always that funny little man with the scarred face. Vell, in Wandsworth Prison he was king. The other inmates poke of William Joyce, not of John Amery, and he was going o make sure it remained like that. He was the man British ntelligence thought could help them, not Amery.

Hannah was bewildered by it all. Englishmen fighting with he SS and somehow, now, a threat to her. She had never leard of such a thing, she said, though she knew about the Dutch and Flemish SS divisions, the Estonian and the Norwegian.

'Munich in fifteen minutes,' grunted Max from the wheel, purring with pleasure at the response he was getting from the Mercedes.

Quinlan told Hannah that neither had many other people leard of the British SS unit.

'It's not something we brag about. In any case,' he added to Hadleigh, 'although I'm obviously wrong I thought they were ll dead or in the bag.'

One who was emphatically not in the bag had watched their departure from the Allersbergerstrasse barracks before walking the mile and a half to the Grand, his head huddled deep inside the turned-up collar of his British officer's greatcoat to keep out the bitter wind and the snow. He had ransport elsewhere in the city but it wasn't due to pick him up for at least an hour yet.

It took him twenty minutes to reach the hotel, where he lad to queue for a further fifteen to use one of the phones. He asked the operator for the number and, when connected, gave he name he wanted.

Thirty seconds elapsed before a voice at the other end said 'Yes?'

The man in the greatcoat did not identify himself.

'The Grand in thirty minutes,' he said curtly.

'I'm not sure I can make that.'

'Be there,' said the caller, and hung up.

He left his greatcoat, cap and swagger-stick in the cloak room, brushed an imaginary speck of lint from his rank insignia, and walked into the bar. The barman had seen him around but did not know his name.

'What can I get you, Captain?' he enquired.

'A small beer, please..'

Once served, he left the area of the bar and sat at a table near the door. In a room filled mostly with Americans he felt unnervingly conspicuous in his British uniform, but with his accent he couldn't get by in US rig. He knew he stood out like a sore thumb and it was with difficulty a few minutes later he convinced an RAF squadron leader looking for a friendly face that he was waiting for someone and did not require company.

Born William John Riordan in Halifax, Yorkshire, on October 31, 1918, the papers in his pocket belonged to the original owner of the uniform, Captain Eric Spencer. They were for emergencies only, however. Dead to Riordan's certain knowledge, Spencer would be on someone's AWOL sheet and there was always a possibility an alert MP would recognize the name.

Riordan was not, therefore, entitled to the uniform he presently wore, nor had he the right to wear the rank tabs of any officer. Prior to his capture by Rommel's forces in North Africa in 1942 he was a sergeant with the 51st Highland Division. Nor should he have been at liberty, for Riordan was one of the first to succumb to the temptations of an easier life by enlisting in the British Free Corps. Others who had done the same had lived to regret it. Now incarcerated in British prisons or waiting to come to trial, they doubtless wondered why they hadn't stuck it out. Riordan didn't. He was as far from a believer in National Socialism as it was possible to be, but the BFC and the SS had offered him a route out of the dreary discipline of a POW camp and promised him more. They still did.

104

His contact was five minutes late and looked around anxiously before spotting Riordan. This was no place to be seen with a fake British officer.

They got straight down to business, keeping their voices low.

'Where have they gone?' demanded Riordan. 'I saw Quinlan, the Americans and what I take to be the Wolz woman leave in a Mercedes.'

'Munich.'

'We should have been informed.'

'It wasn't possible. I didn't know myself until a short while ago. I'm not told everything.'

'Where in Munich?'

'I don't know.'

'That isn't an answer I accept.'

'It's nevertheless the only one I can give. I know who they hope to see but not where.'

'Who then? Who?' he repeated when a response was not immediately forthcoming. 'You know the consequences if you hold anything back.'

'A man called Bachmann. I think his given name is Helmut.'

'But no address.'

'None that I heard. You don't understand how difficult it is.'

'If you're lying…'

'I'm not, I swear it. There's something else I can tell you to prove it. Quinlan was in a gun battle last night, over in Weigelshof. I didn't hear it all but two men were killed, two Germans.'

'Their names?' asked Riordan, though he was fairly certain he could supply the answer to that himself.

'No names. From what I overheard they carried no identification papers.'

'And what is the significance of Weigelshof?'

'I believe it's where Hannah Wolz lived.'

'Lived?'

'You saw yourself, she went with them.'

'But she has to live somewhere when they return.'

'Of course but I don't know where.'

Riordan elected not to pursue the matter. It was of no

105

importance now, in any case. It was perfectly obvious that Hannah Wolz had had Arndt's fragment all along. She would by this time have handed it over to Quinlan and the Americans. Why else would they be going to Munich? Bachmann had to be the second link in the chain.

'You will have to do better than this,' he said coldly. 'We won't be strung along with things you believe or think or assume – or things you don't know. We have to have hard intelligence before the event, not afterwards. Bear that in mind.'

'I can't leave as and when I choose. I don't have that much freedom.'

'Then make it. Remember the alternative.'

'I'll try to let you know when they return.'

'I need to know more than that. I need reports on their conversations, their attitudes, if they're elated or depressed.'

'If only I knew what you were really looking for it would be easier. I could ask Quinlan. He's the most trusting of the three.'

'You'll do nothing of the kind,' said Riordan. 'There will be no direct questioning. You know the conditions. If you're suspected or arrested it's the same as if you betray us.'

Riordan glanced furtively around the bar. His voice had risen an octave and he was aware of it. Besides, they had been sitting there too long.

'Go now,' he said quietly, 'but remember what I said. It's the boy's life.'

Frau Gretl Meissner got to her feet and smoothed her skirt.

'Please,' she asked, 'may I see him?'

'You know that's not possible. He's in good hands and healthy. He'll remain healthy as long as you do as you're told. It won't be for much longer, either way. Now leave.'

She answered Riordan's smile with a forced one of her own. Anyone watching would have assumed that a British officer and his lady friend were making arrangements for later.

She went down the steps and into the street, hating herself for betraying Quinlan and Major Hadleigh but knowing there was no other option. Unless she did as she was told Riordan and his SS friends would murder Willi.

Riordan gave her five minutes to clear the building before

collecting his greatcoat, cap and swagger-stick, and following.

Outside he walked south along Frauentorgraben, looking over his shoulder every so often until a jeep carrying Third Army markings pulled up alongside and a cheerful American voice called, loud enough for anyone in the vicinity to hear: 'Give you a ride some place, Captain?'

'Thanks,' said Riordan. 'I'd appreciate that.'

Once aboard and under way he added: 'Kramer and Wildehopf are dead. They must have picked up the Wolz woman's trail last night and followed her home. Unfortunately Quinlan was with her and they were killed in some sort of shoot-out. Quinlan, the Americans and Hannah Wolz are now on their way to Munich to see a man named Bachmann. Have you heard him mentioned before?'

'No,' answered the driver.

'Maybe one of the Krauts knows him.'

The driver grinned. 'Don't let the Krauts hear you call them Krauts.'

'Fuck 'em. They don't bother me.'

At the wheel, Frank Hallam, who was rising twenty-five but looked older, wondered if that was the truth. Riordan was tough enough, he'd seen that with his own eyes, but the Krauts were also hard men.

Late of Milwaukee and formerly a corporal with the 2nd Canadian Division, from which he had been separated during the abortive raid on Dieppe in August 1942 and later made a POW, Hallam took a left turn at the wooden markers and headed south-west for Grossreuth, a fifteen-minute trip.

'If they've gone to Munich, does that mean we go to Munich?'

'Someone, maybe,' answered Riordan, 'but not us.'

'What if this guy Bachmann has another fragment and they get it?'

'So they get it. By the looks of things they've got Arndt's already.'

'We don't have much time. What is it, ten, twelve days tops?'

'Much less. We have to move well before January 10. But, if we don't have much time, neither do they. Assuming they get it all together they've still got to decipher what it means. They don't stand a chance.'

Hallam acknowledged a wave from an MP in oilskins at a junction.

'Bet I make it Stateside before you do!' he yelled.

'Don't push your luck,' cautioned Riordan.

Hallam shrugged over the wheel. 'What the hell. I'm as American as he is.'

'I meant about the jeep.'

'Same thing. When I was in England in 'forty-two we used to lose around a dozen vehicles a week from 2nd Division. You know, guys going out on the town and forgetting where they parked the fucking thing. My guess is it's the same round here. Worse. Remember how we picked this one up – and the other stuff? Nobody gives a fuck. Uncle Sam's paying and you can bet your ass two-star generals and above have got a whole fleet of Caddies sold off to the Krauts and the money in a Swiss bank.'

'Nevertheless,' said Riordan, 'no point in taking chances.'

Hallam tossed a glance at him to see if he was kidding. He wasn't. Dumb Limey son of a bitch. He was right, though. Too close to blow it.

'Do you ever think of the old days?' he asked, out of the blue.

'Never.'

'Never? Sometimes I have a hankering for them.'

'In the States?'

'No, in the mob, with the rest of the guys before the war was over. Christ, we had some times.'

Eleven

Once they understood they would get few recruits for the
Legion of St George by propaganda, the German brass came
up with a different idea: the special camp. Commandants of
regular POW camps were invited to select non-troublemakers
for a fortnight's stay in a camp where all discipline would be
relaxed, extra rations provided and, perhaps most important
of all, brothels established. There were two camps, one for
officers, one for enlisted men. The former was known as
Special Detachment 999 and was based in a villa in
Zehlendorf, a south-west suburb of Berlin. There the incom-
ing officers were greeted by the commandant, Herr Doktor
Falkner, and told that the facilities available in 999 were
simply Germany's way of giving POWs a rest from the rigours
of normal camp life. The inmates were provided with recent
copies of British newspapers and taken on sightseeing tours of
Berlin. There was no attempt to indoctrinate them with the
virtues of National Socialism, but they were frequently
lectured on the threat the Soviet Union posed to all 'civilized'
nations.

The Senior British Officer in 999 was not amused and
warned his subordinates against being taken in by this
display of Nazi generosity. When the question of joining the
Legion eventually cropped up, there were few takers. The
half-dozen who succumbed finally agreed to do no more than
a little broadcasting.

In the autumn of 1943, due to increased Allied air force
activity over Berlin, Special Detachment 999 was moved
away from Zehlendorf to a wired-off section of Stalag 111A at
Luckenwalde, twenty miles south, where it was safe from
bombers because the RAF knew of the POW camp there.
Later it was transferred to Küstrin on the River Oder, and

at the end of September closed altogether due to lack of success.

The special camp for NCOs and enlisted men was, first, attached to Stalag 111D at Steglitz, another southern suburb of Berlin, but in June 1943 found a new home in Genshagen, south-west of the capital. Here there was accommodation for almost three hundred POWs in three large huts; a fourth hut was used as kitchens and a dining-hall. Set in a pleasant country estate, by mid-July it was almost full. Many of the internees were ex-members of Mosley's British Union of Fascists and almost as pro-German as their captors. Others were simply men looking for a good time away from the POW cages.

Recruiting for the Legion did not seriously begin for another month. When it did, many of the men signed on the dotted line because they were unwilling to give up this new-found luxury, some because they believed the Allies would lose the war, and a handful because they were terrorized into doing so by stronger personalities. They were a mixed bag, mostly British but with a sprinkling of Commonwealth troops and Americans.

Once committed, they were taken to a house in the suburb of Grünewald, where they remained while formalities were completed and their Allied battledress changed for civilian clothing. All volunteers had to sign a declaration that they had no Jewish blood and were assured they would never be called upon to face their own countrymen. The Legion was being formed to fight Bolshevism, no more.

From Grünewald they were sent to a permanent base in Pankow. Here there was a canteen which served beer and spirits. A portrait of the Duke of Windsor when he was King Edward VIII dominated one wall. Discipline was maintained at a minimum by the Germans. It was enough if the recruits kept themselves clean and tidy, did not cause trouble when drunk – and did not catch clap. This wasn't easy to avoid, for there was never a lack of willing German girls, not all of them paid whores, and it was the promise of an active sex life which attracted most volunteers.

Towards the end of 1943 a meeting was held between the OKW (the German High Command), the SS and the German Foreign Office to decide what was to be done with

110

the fledgling Legion. Present were some of the original recruits, among them Bill Riordan and Frank Hallam, who had met up at Genshagen. Also there were two other Britishers who could be regarded as founder members, ex-corporal Tom Granger, a hard 26-year-old tankman captured at El Alamein, and ex-corporal Harry Laidlaw, a 30-year-old dour Scot taken prisoner in the early North African fighting. This quartet could reliably be described as the hard core of the Legion, something which an SS Sturmbannfuehrer took note of during the discussions.

The first gripe Riordan and the others had was John Amery. Although no longer interested in his creation, on paper he was the Legion's nominal leader and they wanted him out. This was left in abeyance though it was all but agreed in principle.

Next came the question of a unit title. Granger had noted in Pankow and elsewhere that the Germans frequently referred to them as the British Legion, which would not do at all in view of the ex-servicemen's organization in Britain of the same name. Nor were any of the turncoats keen on the Legion of St George. Apart from St George being exclusively the patron saint of England, which could well deter potential recruits from Wales, Ireland and Scotland, the Legion of St George was Amery's idea. The British Free Corps was much more acceptable, and they were allowed, via channels, to petition Hitler to be called that.

The formal document read:

> We, the true soldiers of Britain,
> wish to swear allegiance to the Fuehrer and to the German Reich. We volunteer to fight side by side with the Germans against the enemies of Europe. For this purpose, the undersigned make application for the corps to be called the British Free Corps.

The only non-Briton at the meeting, Frank Hallam, had no objections. It didn't matter to him what the hell they were called.

Penultimately, the subject of uniform was raised. They did not want khaki. Riordan had no hesitation in pointing out that by reverting to their own battledress there might be a temptation to use them in an intelligence capacity in the west, when the Allies invaded Europe. (He sugared the pill by adding that only an unscrupulous commander would consider such a notion, but his statement was nevertheless greeted with stony silence. It was not part of official German thinking even to contemplate the Allies on European soil.) If it was genuinely intended for the Corps to face no one but the Red Army, surely field-grey was the answer.

This was accepted, the Waffen SS representative present undertaking to supply regulation breeches and tunics, the latter minus SS runes. In place of these, it was agreed after discussion, three leopards would be used as collar patch insignia. The brassard would be a Union Jack shield on the upper left sleeve.

It was also proposed that, as the Corps was to fight alongside Waffen SS troops, its members should have their blood groups tattooed under the armpit in the customary manner. There was not a chance of this motion being carried, nor was it. If the war went the other way and the Allies won, it would mean a firing squad or the rope for anyone burdened with physical evidence of having campaigned with SS formations.

The last item on the agenda was that of a Corps commander. As no officers from Special Detachment 999 had been tempted into doing more than propaganda broadcasts, Riordan, though only a sergeant in the British Army, was hoping for this job himself. But the SS insisted that the CO be German and someone of their own choosing. They opted for Hauptsturmfuehrer Johannes Roggenfeld of the SS Panzer Division Viking in January 1944.

The most pressing need in the opening months of that year was for more volunteers. The Corps was a corps in name alone and still too small to be allowed anywhere near a battlefield. The recruiting drives should have been led by the Big Four (as Riordan, Hallam, Granger and Laidlaw were now known), but using a combination of cunning and brute force they persuaded others to do the job for them. It was a dangerous pastime, canvassing POW camps.

As Corps headquarters Roggenfeld was given St Michael's monastery at Hildesheim, twenty miles south of Hanover. Formerly (some might say aptly) a lunatic asylum and later an SS hospital, in 1943 Reichsfuehrer Himmler had taken it

112

over as a centre for maintaining cultural bonds between the Nordic nations and rechristened it Haus Germanien. The BFC moved there in February 1944.

While Roggenfeld concerned himself with the massive administrative problems engendered by the formation of any new unit, the Big Four took over the business of licking the recruits into shape. Discipline tightened. Where before it was fags, food, fluid (alcoholic) and fornication with a seemingly endless supply of flaxen-haired maidens, now it was on parade at 8 a.m., inspection, physical training and lectures. Many newcomers thought to hell with it and applied to be returned to their POW camps. They were generally quickly replaced, but the Corps' combat strength never rose beyond fifty or sixty during this period.

In April their uniforms arrived and pay was regularized to one Reichsmark per day regardless of rank, with a further thirty RMs a month from a separate SS account. But they had yet to hear a shot fired in anger and there was not even a whisper of them being sent to the Russian Front.

The dedicated anti-Soviets blamed Roggenfeld for this, though it was not his fault. In reality the Waffen SS (the field commanders as opposed to the desk-bound political officers) could find no use for the Corps. In spite of everything it was still too small, and the men truly gifted with leadership qualities and golden tongues, the Big Four especially, always had some plausible excuse for going nowhere near a recruiting drive. Those who did take the chance (or were bullied into doing so) of being lynched by their one-time fellow Kriegies (*Kriegsgefangenen* or POWs) invariably threw in their hands at the first sign of determined opposition and ended up drunk and incapable in some brothel or other. That the Germans, the SS and Gestapo in particular, should allow this sort of behaviour was not so incredible as it appears at first sight. After the Allied invasion of Normandy in June 1944, those with their eyes on the future were already making 'travel arrangements'. They could not have cared less what the handful of BFC renegades did.

By August Roggenfeld was thoroughly disenchanted with the whole conception of the Corps. After all the trumpeting and ballyhoo to start with and a predicted brigade of 1,500, his command was still around company strength. He had several titanic rows with his seniors over the telephone and was eventually summoned to Berlin and peremptorily dismissed. His replacement as CO was Hauptsturmfuehrer Erich Jupp, who had lost a leg in Russia fighting with the crack Waffen SS Division Das Reich. A few days after he took over, orders came through for the Corps to move base from Hildesheim to Dresden, where they arrived at the beginning of September.

The SS were very proud of the Dresden barracks. Begun in 1936, all the buildings were centrally heated and the enlisted men's quarters were close to luxurious. As was the food. All ranks received grade one-alpha rations, the highest food scale in the German Armed Forces.

But a change of environment did not mean a change of habits. Liquor became more readily available than at Hildesheim and the other basic soldier's need was present in abundance, to such an extent that three of the Corps went down with gonorrhoea within a fortnight.

Towards the end of the year, after a long hard look at the BFC, Reichsfuehrer Himmler concluded that the game was not worth the candle and proposed disbanding the Corps. He was persuaded otherwise only after a series of long and bitter arguments, partly with senior SS officers and partly with the Foreign Ministry, who convinced the Reichsfuehrer that dissolution would be a major propaganda defeat.

Riordan and his immediate circle offered up a quiet prayer of thanks when the news came through. If Himmler had decided otherwise it would have meant either a return to a POW camp (with all that entailed) or absorption into a Waffen SS line regiment with the ritual blood-group tattooing and no guarantee their outfit would not be sent to the west or come up against Anglo-American forces at some point.

But if disbandment was taken off the agenda, it was merely postponing the inevitable. During the opening weeks of 1945 the Allied advance across Europe proved to even the most intransigent that the writing was on the wall for the Third Reich. The propaganda services could pump out promises until they were blue in the face that 'wonder weapons' would shortly be available to turn what seemed like defeat into victory, but few believed the stories.

Towards the end of January Riordan held a secret meeting with his three principal henchmen, the tenor of which was that it could only be a matter of time before the whole lousy house of cards fell in around their ears. The BFC had never been much but it was now in tatters. Half a dozen corpsmen had already tried to desert, being picked up in Czechoslovakia by the Gestapo, making for the Russian lines. Another dozen had volunteered for the Waffen SS, some as combat troops, some as medics. And the US Eighth Air Force raid on Dresden on January 16 was a forerunner of worse to come. For whatever reasons, Dresden was no longer a desirable place to be nor continued membership of the BFC an attractive proposition.

The trouble was, their options were virtually nil. Going AWOL did not appeal, as being on the run without friends and legitimate travel documents would inevitably put them in the hands of the Gestapo. The Gestapo couldn't last for ever, but when it was a thing of the past they would be taken by either the Russians or the Anglo-Americans. The Russians would kill them, no matter what the fools who had earlier deserted thought, and the Anglo-Americans would put them in prison for the remainder of their lives or execute them with the full support of the law and to the applause of the citizens.

Riordan considered himself to be a hard and practical man and flight without purpose or objective was not something that appealed to him. Neither did staying put, waiting to be overrun. It was a conundrum which seemed insoluble until the first week in February, when fate dealt itself a hand in the game.

There appeared in Dresden on February 6, bright and shiny in an immaculate uniform with SD (SS Security Service) sleeve patches, the same Sturmbannfuehrer who had sat in on the December 1943 meeting and who had taken note of the BFC ringleaders' names. He was not in the city by chance. His name was Heinrich Scharper and he had full authority to take Riordan to Berlin, if the ex-sergeant wanted to go. There was to be no coercion. Neither would there be any explanation until he got there.

Riordan held a consultation with Hallam, Granger and Laidlaw. The last two were of the opinion that Sturmbannfuehrer Scharper, Germany's war situation being what it was, wanted Riordan to organize the remnants of the BFC for some kind of death-or-glory mission on behalf of the Reich. Hallam was more concerned that Riordan was being offered a solo way out.

It was finally agreed that he should go, but not before Scharper had taken great pains to reassure them all that he would be back, possibly with something encouraging to report. They were not to mention this conversation to any of the others, however. This – whatever 'this' was – was for the Big Four only. If anyone asked, Riordan was being taken by the SS to face a disciplinary charge. It would all be squared with Hauptsturmfuehrer Jupp at a later date.

They went by road – Allied fighters by this time were able to maraud over German air space almost at will – and arrived in Berlin on the evening of the 6th.

Scharper's driver took them directly to the Adlon, where the Sturmbannfuehrer ushered Riordan up to a suite on the third floor, a Wehrmacht greatcoat covering his BFC uniform to avoid exciting attention. Inside, he was introduced to Standartenfuehrer (SS Colonel) Hugo Sternberg and re-acquainted with John Amery.

Riordan and Amery had never got along, the former believing the latter to be a milksop dilettante who lacked balls. He was fully prepared to dissociate himself from any scheme which had the Cabinet Minister's son as a leading participant, but it soon became apparent that Amery wasn't staying, had no wish to. After he had gone and the champagne was poured (Riordan would have preferred whisky but there didn't seem to be any), Sternberg explained that Amery was not involved.

'It was he who jogged Scharper's memory when it was realized we would require English-speaking personnel who could be trusted absolutely, but other than that he knows nothing of why you were brought here.'

'I wouldn't have thought he'd have recommended me for whatever you've got in mind,' grunted Riordan. 'He hates my guts.'

'He didn't recommend you. Quite the reverse. Which is why we concluded you might be the man we want.' Sternberg smiled as though he was the sole possessor of a mildly funny

116

story. 'Sooner or later Amery plans to return to Italy. I think he believes it will go better for him if he is captured there.'

He put an American cigarette in a long ebony holder and patted his pockets. Scharper supplied the light.

'What I am about to tell you involves my taking a great risk,' Sternberg said to Riordan, 'and you should fully understand that once told you are committed. In other words, I am asking you to pledge yourself before hearing what I have to say. You will be responsible for the others in your group also.' He referred to a type-written document. 'Hallam, Granger and Laidlaw.'

After two and a half years in captivity and twenty months with the BFC, receiving orders and passing them down the line, Riordan's command of German was fluent if accented, and it was in this language they conversed.

'I don't know if I can speak for them,' he said roughly, deliberately omitting Sternberg's rank.

'Let me put it another way,' murmured Sternberg, ignoring the discourtesy. 'If what I have to tell you appeals, I leave it to you whether or not you pass it on to Hallam, Granger and Laidlaw – or any other three you trust. But we have calculated we are going to need four genuine English-speaking men. Fewer will give us no back-up should anything go wrong and more will make us top-heavy. Bear in mind that you are all, you British Free Corps people, now in something of a cleft stick. You will either be killed in the fighting to come or taken prisoner by the Allies, regardless of who tells you the war can still be won with new weapons. Either option seems somewhat limited.'

Sternberg was right, of course, which was why he, Riordan, was in Berlin.

'Let's hear what you have to say.'

'You understand you will not leave this building alive if, having heard, you decline to participate?'

'I understand.'

For over an hour Sternberg and occasionally Scharper talked while Riordan listened. The two SS officers outlined a scheme of such staggering proportions and imagination that, had Riordan not known for certain the SS did not indulge in flights of fancy, he would have thought the pair opposite candidates for an asylum.

117

By 10 p.m. when the meeting ended Riordan was so full of enthusiasm for the project that he wanted to return to Dresden immediately and put it to the others. Scharper persuaded him to stay in Berlin overnight and for his pleasure provided a smaller suite along the corridor, a dinner the like of which Riordan had only seen in films, two bottles of malt whisky and the services of a Swedish countess whose sexual appetite left Riordan exhausted. She was evidently accustomed to 'entertaining' at the Adlon, for when the air-raid sirens went at 2 a.m. she refused to disentwine herself from Riordan's embrace, murmuring some crap about the Adlon never being hit. Riordan allowed himself to be convinced, but he had the peculiar notion that the countess's enduring fantasy was being killed by a bomb as she was climaxing.

With the same driver at the wheel, he and Scharper drove back to Dresden the following afternoon. During the small hours of February 8 the Big Four left Dresden for good – not too soon, as it turned out, for on the 13th-14th of that month the RAF and the USAAF levelled much of the city. The estimated death toll was 150,000. Without leadership, surviving corpsmen were drafted into the Waffen SS with no argument. The great majority of them were killed in the final days' fighting in Berlin.

Their uniforms replaced by civilian clothes of good quality, the BFC quartet were driven to Austria, where they were installed in a country villa outside Salzburg, owned by a titled Austrian who, with the full backing of the SS for just such an emergency, had managed to convey to everyone who knew him that he was and always had been an anti-Nazi. To support the stratagem the SS had, on several occasions throughout the war, taken him into custody.

It was most unlikely, according to the general opinion, that the villa would ever be subjected to more than casual scrutiny when the Allies overran Salzburg, but if it was there was a well-concealed underground bunker on the estate, which was not the only bolthole in the Third Reich. For many years, especially in Bavaria and Austria, the SS had prepared similar 'safe' houses, many apparently owned by implacable enemies of the regime.

From time to time Sternberg and Scharper put in an appearance, and around the second week in April two names

118

started to dominate their whispered conversations: Canaris and Langenhain. A few days later, after an overnight drive from Berlin, Amery was mentioned. Fearing that the man he loathed, in spite of earlier promises, would turn up in Salzburg and become part of the group, Riordan challenged Sternberg, who assured him that that was not the case. They had simply arranged a meeting with Amery in the Adlon because the original founder of the Legion of St George knew Langenhain, and the SS very much wanted to meet up with the Oberstleutnant. As it happened, Amery could not help them, but there was no question of his coming to Salzburg. Nor, for the moment, was it explained why Canaris and Langenhain were so important, though Riordan and his confederates would learn the reason in due course.

During the third week of April Sternberg and Scharper more or less took up residence at the villa. There was no further mention of Canaris and Langenhain, and Riordan got the impression the problem no longer existed.

They were joined about this time by two SS NCOs, Oberscharfuehrer Oskar Flisk and Unterscharfuehrer Kurt Zander, both, from what Riordan could gather, connected somehow with a concentration camp called Flossenburg. Later still, SS Sergeants Kramer and Wildehopf became fixtures.

Throughout the rest of April there were others too. They did not stay long. It was all very secretive, but it seemed to Riordan that the transients were heading for Italy, for Genoa and Rome. Sternberg confirmed that the villa was not for the exclusive use of their group, that it was a staging-post in an SS escape line. But that was nothing to do with their business, he stressed.

The last few days of April and the beginning of May were anxious ones for the villa's permanent occupants. It was learnt via the SS grapevine that on April 25 John Amery had been captured in Italy by partisans. Although he knew nothing of the plan discussed in the Adlon suite, there was always the possibility he would mention during his interrogation his part in bringing together members of the SS and the British Free Corps. Sternberg thought it unlikely.

On May 1 over Radio Hamburg came the news that Hitler had died the previous day. No one believed the propaganda story that he was killed leading his troops against Bolshevism, and none of the Germans seemed much distressed by his death. He was the past.

In any event, they had their own worries, for Patton's Third Army was now occupying Salzburg. As predicted, however, the reputation of the titled gentleman who owned the villa had preceded him. His property was to remain untouched. Situated as it was among trees at the head of a two-kilometre drive from the gatehouse, ample warning was given for the illicit houseguests to retreat to the underground bunker when the first US troops were spotted.

They did not stay on the premises long. The villa and its owner were on a list of people and places not to be harassed or used as billets, and that was an end to it. It was all too ridiculously simple, though Riordan was to reflect later that Sternberg had chosen the funkhole with great care.

A few miles east of Salzburg were the salt mines at Alt Aussee where, as even the man in the street knew, a vast storehouse of looted art treasures was kept. Once German resistance in Salzburg was overcome, the MFA & A (Monuments, Fine Arts and Archives) detachment with the Third Army went hell for leather, spearheaded by tanks, for the mines, fearful that the SS had orders to destroy the lot as an act of vengeance. They made it just ahead of the advancing Soviet troops. The villa's owner joined the celebrations which followed the news that the Americans and the Ivans were already squabbling over who owned what. He judged, wrongly, that his guests were jubilant because the *Amis* would be far more concerned about removing the booty before the Russians claimed their part, than in hunting fugitives.

The official end to the war in Europe came with the signing of the unconditional surrender document by General-oberst Jodl at 2.41 a.m. on May 7, calling for a complete cessation of hostilities at 11.01 p.m. Central European Time the following day.

On hearing this over the radio and from the loudspeaker vans which toured the centre and outskirts of Salzburg, the villa's occupants felt a sense of relief. They were all on the mandatory arrest list, of course, and doubtless, when things calmed down, there would be a massive manhunt for the thousands of individuals not yet in captivity. But at least the

120

shooting had stopped and the strategy outlined in the Adlon was a step closer to beginning.

Riordan wanted to know when, but Sternberg was in no hurry. They were not yet a full complement. It could take months before the time was right. In the interim they had everything they wanted here, did they not? Their host had black-market contacts, there was as much food as they could eat and alcohol as they could drink. Lack of women was a problem, naturally, but it would not be wise to ferry in whores for the present. Women were talkative bitches.

To move prematurely would not only be risky but could prove counter-productive. Their plans had been laid with great care several years ago, their existence known only to a few, all evidence destroyed. Patience was the order of the day.

And might well have remained so had word not filtered through to the villa early in June that one of the men for whom they were waiting was in custody.

Twelve

Nuremberg – December 29, 1945

Not as large or as sumptuous as the Salzburg villa, the house nevertheless stood in its own grounds midway between the south-west suburbs of Grossreuth and Kleinreuth, an area which had escaped much of the heaviest bombing. It was shielded from the main road and surrounded on three sides by a high hedge. The fourth side backed on to open fields and the nearest neighbours were half a mile away.

The SS had owned it (and back-up houses in Fürth and Zirndorf) since 1937, though the name on the title deeds was Frau Elke Niemeyer, a woman in her fifties whose husband was at present under arrest in the Russian Zone accused of war crimes while on the staff of Mauthausen concentration camp, crimes he had undoubtedly committed. Although it was his private opinion that ex-Hauptsturmfuehrer Niemeyer would have his neck stretched before too long, Sternberg had promised on arrival to look into ways of either freeing or defending the man. In the meantime, Frau Niemeyer would kindly keep to the small gardener's cottage, ignore the comings and goings at the main house and not enter it unless invited. She was not to leave the grounds without permission and casual visitors were to be discouraged.

The latter would not be a problem, Frau Niemeyer had informed Sternberg when the SS colonel first appeared towards the end of September. Since the war's end her so-called friends had shunned her, wanting nothing to do with a woman whose husband was connected with 'those terrible camps'.

'Though they were willing to sit at his table and beg favours in the earlier years.'

Sternberg had clucked sympathetically, told her not to worry about rations (which he could easily obtain on the black market with the funds at his disposal), and had hardly set eyes on her since. He or one of the others checked on her from time to time, but as long as she was fed and supplied with booze she was more than happy. She would be sorry to see them go, though as 1945 drew to a close they did not seem in any hurry to do so.

The house was a three-storey structure containing six bedrooms spread equally between the upper two storeys. In one of these fifteen-year-old Willi Meissner was handcuffed to a heavy iron bed. A consensus had wanted to kill him, to save them the trouble of having to supervise and feed him, but Sternberg vetoed that. If Gretl Meissner ever became difficult or uncooperative she might need a gentle reminder, such as a high-pitched scream over a telephone as one of her son's fingers was removed, to bring her back into line. Willi Meissner was more useful alive than dead at present and, besides, it wouldn't be for much longer.

On the ground floor were three living-rooms, the largest serving as a common-room for the occupants. It was towards this that Riordan and Hallam headed after the latter had parked the jeep, alongside two others carrying Third Army markings, in the garage and secured the lock. There was always someone patrolling the grounds at night – in this instance Tom Granger, who saw them arrive and called a soft greeting from the shrubbery – but it paid to be cautious.

The common-room was illuminated by oil-lamps and Riordan saw at once that everyone was present. Apart from Harry Laidlaw the rest of the group were Germans. Having lived in their company for eight months Riordan knew them as well as he knew himself, and there wasn't one he would trust further than he could spit. They needed the Big Four for the foreseeable future, but they would all be advised to watch their backs when that need ended.

At the head of the long oak table sat Sternberg, an impressive-looking individual even out of uniform. Tall, lithe and silver-haired, he belied his forty-odd years. On his right Heinrich Scharper was cradling a goblet of brandy, to judge by his eyes and past experience not his first of the night though he could hold his liquor. Somewhere in his late twenties he was a heavy-set man who would one day have a weight problem – if he lived that long.

Over by the curtained window Oskar Flisk was buffing his nails with a handkerchief. A few years older than Scharper, Flisk looked mild enough, but Riordan knew him to have been part of the team which had executed Canaris. As had Kurt Zander, who smiled a lot when there was little to smile about and who was, in Riordan's private nomenclature, a psychopath looking for a victim.

It was a rare occasion when the pair who made up the German contingent were not in each other's company, though there was nothing sinister or homosexual in their relationship. Formerly tank drivers with the SS Panzer Division Totenkopf, Hans-Dieter Kleemann and Anton Isken were not only the youngest of the Germans but also the last to join the group. They had been on their way down the escape line to Italy when Sternberg picked them out, after it became obvious that two others who were supposed to make the Salzburg villa rendezvous were either dead or in captivity somewhere. Both in their early twenties and alike enough in Aryan good looks to be taken for brothers, they were generally sent elsewhere when something important was being discussed. It did not seem to bother them. Their blue eyes shone with fanaticism and they dropped their voices whenever discussing the late Fuehrer. They would willingly have died, if Riordan was any judge of character, protecting the life of the Third Reich's founder.

Harry Laidlaw made up the septet, his expression showing relief that Riordan and Hallam were back. A willing and rugged fighter, his command of German was least adequate of the Big Four and he felt uncomfortable being only able to catch the meaning of two words out of three.

Riordan helped himself to a brandy from the bottle at Scharper's elbow.

'Kramer and Wildehopf are dead,' he announced without preamble. 'According to Gretl Meissner there was some sort of shooting match last night and they bought it. Quinlan and the others are on their way to Munich with Hannah Wolz in tow. They're going to find a man called Bachmann, given name probably Helmut.'

Scharper's eyes betrayed his alarm.

'Were they carrying anything to connect them with us or this house?'

'According to Frau Meissner, no.'

'Damn it,' said Sternberg mildly. It was apparent from his tone that he was less concerned about the deaths of Kramer and Wildehopf than the loss of two able-bodied men. It was going to make everything that much harder. 'Where did all this happen?'

'Over in Weigelshof, which was evidently where Hannah Wolz lived.'

'What about the Opel Kramer was driving?' asked Flisk.

'We have to assume the Americans have it.' Riordan tossed back his brandy. 'If they haven't it will be stripped into a thousand pieces by now. In either event, it's lost to us.'

'Stupid bastards,' cursed Scharper. 'What the hell could they have been playing at?'

'They must have picked up Hannah Wolz's trail somehow or found out where she lived. Unfortunately she had an escort.'

'Bachmann, Bachmann,' murmured Sternberg. 'He holds the second fragment, presumably. Does the name mean anything to anyone?'

It did not.

'But we can take it for granted he's another one of Canaris's damned Abwehr,' said Scharper. 'I hope the man rots in hell. He's been dead for eight months and he still haunts us.'

'I think we can also take for granted the fact that Langenhain did not know the second name,' added Sternberg. 'Either that or he was a braver man and a better liar than we thought.'

Kurt Zander remembered the day they had finally caught up with Langenhain in mid-April, how long it had taken him to die.

'No, he did not have the second name,' he said slowly. 'Believe me, if he'd known of Bachmann he would have told me. He'd have fucked his own grandmother if I'd asked him in the end.'

There was a unified burst of laughter from Kleemann and Isken. Sternberg glared at them. The sooner he no longer had to deal with gutter rats like Zander, the better. But he concurred that Langenhain had known only of Arndt.

'Does someone go to Munich?' asked Flisk.

'Someone does not go to Munich,' asnwered Sternberg. 'It would be far too dangerous. We don't know where this Bachmann is or even whether he's alive. And we have nothing to gain. Without the first fragment the others are useless and the Americans must have obtained the first from Hannah Wolz or they would not know the whereabouts of the second.'

'What if they find Bachmann and he gives them the second fragment?' Scharper wanted to know.

'That still leaves two others and a long way for them to go. Even if they find the last pair they have to work out what it all means. We have twice as much information as they do but I'd wager we wouldn't solve the riddle overnight. Canaris was very clever. Or Unterscharfuehrer Zander not so persuasive with the old man as he was with Langenhain.'

125

'That's not true,' muttered Zander. 'You know very well the circumstances were different. If I'd been allowed a free hand we would not be sitting here now.'

'Perhaps,' said Sternberg. 'In any case it is of no consequence now. It would however be an advantage to learn when Major Hadleigh and the rest return from Munich and also where Fräulein Wolz is to be kept. We can presumably rely upon Frau Meissner to provide us with that information.'

'I'll make sure of it,' growled Riordan.

'Then in the meantime, gentlemen, I suggest we concentrate on our own business. There is still much to be done. It goes without saying that I should like to bring the date forward, but as you all realize that does not depend upon us. We can only hope it is fully understood in other quarters that it must be done well before January 10. I'm rather hoping for the 3rd or 4th, but at the very outside it must be Monday the 7th.'

Thirteen

Munich – December 29-31, 1945

They drove into Munich from the north, down through the Schwabing district via Schleissheimerstrasse where, at number 34, Adolf Hitler had first lived above a tailor's shop on arriving in the Bavarian capital as a student in May 1913. In number 106 an earlier revolutionary, registered as Meyer, had spent a year at the turn of the century studying Marx. His given name was Vladimir Ilyich Ulyanov, but the world would later know him better as Lenin. Anyone given to irony could scarcely find a better example.

There was not much left of the Eleven Executioners, the notorious cabaret where Franz Wedekind had shocked and titillated audiences with his songs about sexual depravity in the Thirties, though the famous Löwenbräu brewery and Löwenbräukeller seemed back in business. Hadleigh cracked that if the fliers of the RAF and USAAF had known what they were hitting, they'd have lynched the bomb-aimers.

They had to ask their way opposite the technical school in Elizabethplatz, where Hitler had done his basic military training with the 2nd Bavarian Infantry Regiment in August 1914. Although Max had had the foresight to pack an army-issue street map, it was way out of date and some of the roads and buildings listed were no longer recognizable.

The MP who gave them directions after referring to a typewritten sheet said that Sedanstrasse, where they hoped to find Helmut Bachmann, was on the other side of the River Isar but that all the bridges were open to light traffic. To get there, he added chattily in his best guidebook manner, they should follow the signs for Haidhausen. En route they would pass Thierschstrasse 41, where old Adolf had lived during his rise to power, a few doors away from what was later to become the offices of the Nazi Party Press Chief.

Once across the river they should turn left at the massive Bürgerbräukeller in Rosenheimerstrasse, from where Hitler had launched his Beer Hall Putsch in 1923. First on the left was Steinstrasse, which was open, and at the end of that Sedanstrasse. They couldn't miss it.

Nor would they have had there been anything of it to miss, but as they cruised down it, the Merc's headlights blazing, they saw that every block in the street was a ruin, most of them razed to the ground. There was nothing left of Sedanstrasse, certainly nowhere for anyone to live.

Quinlan was sick with disappointment. It was a trip wasted. If they'd picked up a telephone or used the wireless they'd have known in a moment that Sedanstrasse was no longer anything but vast mounds of snow-covered rubble.

'I don't know what I was expecting,' he said disconsolately. 'Probably for Bachmann to be waiting for us with a glass of schnapps. Well, that's that.'

But Hadleigh had different ideas. If Bachmann was sitting in his house when the bombs landed they were going to be out of luck. On the other hand he could be a prisoner, having surrendered or been captured when Patch's Seventh Army stormed the city. In which case he'd be on file somewhere.

'No reason why he should be,' muttered Quinlan. 'Arndt kept his head down for six months. Maybe Bachmann did too and is still doing it.'

'Well, Jesus H. Christ!' exploded Hadleigh. 'If that's the postwar bulldog spirit, you're not going to keep the empire. Arndt had the SS on his tail and Ilse and Hannah to worry about. Anyway, what the hell can we lose by checking? We've got to report in and find somewhere to bunk down for the night.'

They re-crossed the Isar and stopped a mobile jeep patrol comprising a corporal and a Pfc. Hadleigh flashed his credentials and asked to be directed to his opposite number in Seventh Army G-2. The corporal wasn't sure where Intelligence had their HQ, but his sidekick got on the radio and had the answer within minutes.

'It's Major McLusky you want, Major, and he's based over at the infantry barracks south of Oberwiesenfeld airfield.' They knew where the airfield was; they had passed it on the way in. 'But he isn't there right now,' added the Pfc. 'His office says your best bet is the Bavaria Hotel at this time of night.' It was coming up to 8 p.m. 'They've got that pretty well organized now.'

The Pfc told them to follow the road they were on, Bayerstrasse, until they reached the Hauptbahnhof, the main railway station. The Bavaria Hotel was a couple of hundred yards off to the left but there were Seventh Army signposts at the station.

'The 3rd, 42nd and 45th Divisions have got some of their brass living there. Just follow the markers.'

It seemed to all of them that Munich was much brighter and more full of life than Nuremberg. Although it was bitterly cold there were hundreds of people on the streets, German civilians as well as armed troops. Max offered the opinion that it had something to do with Christmas just being over and New Year round the corner, but Hadleigh begged to differ.

128

'No, things are changing fast. In a couple of days we'll be talking about the war that ended *last* year. Whatever any of us might think about the Germans' – he was still speaking in English and Hannah wasn't following him – 'we've got to help them rebuild the country we knocked down before some clever bastard in the Kremlin decides these are ideal conditions for a revolution. It's only in Nuremberg, because of the IMT, and maybe Berlin where people aren't going to forget in a hurry.'

The forecourt of the Bavaria was crowded with vehicles, civilian as well as military, but Max found a vacant slot for the Mercedes. He and Hannah stayed with the car. It was really too cold to be hanging around outside, but Hadleigh didn't want to tread on anyone's corns by inviting a German girl inside, beautiful though she was, until he knew the lie of the land. From the stencilled signs on the wall at the entrance, the Bavaria now functioned as part hotel, part command post.

They asked a Seventh Army staff sergeant, who stood behind a desk beneath a notice reading ALL PERSONNEL ON OFFICIAL BUSINESS REPORT HERE, for Major McLusky, and a dogface was sent to fetch him. While waiting, Hadleigh confessed that a little of his earlier optimism about tracing Bachmann was fading. By the looks of things Sedanstrasse was a ruin long before Arndt told Hannah that she would find Bachmann there. Which must mean, at the very least, that Arndt hadn't seen Bachmann or Munich for some months prior to the end of the war.

McLusky turned out to be a beefy individual in his late thirties. Over a much-needed drink in the bar, Hadleigh explained their business in Munich.

'This guy Bachmann got a rank or a record?' asked McLusky. 'Any strikes against him?'

'Not as far as we know. It's only a guess but he could have been Abwehr. Probably a middle-ranking officer, but that's a guess too.'

'Well, it narrows the field – if we've got him or had him and if he confessed to being Abwehr.'

'No reason why he shouldn't,' said Quinlan. 'They were clean enough.'

McLusky looked at him curiously.

129

'What's the British interest in this? For that matter, what's the tie-in between the British and Third Army?'

They decided to lay it on the line, tell McLusky about Arndt, the murder of Arndt's younger daughter and Angela Salvatini, the fragment of photograph, Quinlan's shoot-out with a couple of unidentified SS men, the probability that remnants of the SS and the British Free Corps were working together.

It sounded like science fiction, but fortunately McLusky was an old hand and accustomed to the weird. They were also fortunate he was the cooperative type.

The Seventh Army major scratched his head.

'Well, there's no easy way of doing this. All I can suggest is that you go over all the records I have back at the office. I say office, but what I mean is they're stored in a room the size of a conference hall. It's going to be a helluva long job. We must have processed twenty or thirty thousand individuals in and around Munich alone, most of them in the few weeks right after the war when we were all a bit keener, when we expected to find Himmler, Bormann, Gestapo Mueller, maybe Hitler himself right under our noses. We've slackened off a bit in recent months.' He shrugged apologetically. 'Inevitable, I guess. Anyway, that's the first problem, the sheer volume of names.

'The second problem,' he went on, 'is that not all the Krauts gave us their real John Hancocks to start with. You wouldn't believe the number of guys we came across who claimed to have "lost" their ID.'

'I believe it,' said Hadleigh.

McLusky grinned amiably. 'Yeah, I guess you would at that. Anyway, some of them gave us phoney names because they had something to hide and some because they wanted to make it as hard as they could for us to introduce a form of military government. The trouble is, if a joker gave us the name of Schmidt to begin with and later we discovered his name was Braun, it only takes one dogface with a hangover to say, fuck it, I'm not hunting through that stack of files to find the original Schmidt and change it, and you're left with a Braun *and* a Schmidt, two guys that are really one.'

'What happened to all the people you processed?' asked Hadleigh. 'The individuals, I mean, not their files.'

He knew how it worked with Third Army but each outfit had its own way of doing things.

'Those with three strikes against them we put in the bucket to await trial,' McLusky explained. 'To listen to the radio and read the newspapers you'd think the only trial that matters is going on in Nuremberg. But the smaller fry – if you can call any of those bastards small – are being tried up and down the country right now, or about to be. That's the first category.

'The second category are those we're still not sure about, guys who've changed their stories a dozen times or claim they spent the whole of the war in the fire service or issuing ration cards. There are more of those than you might think. Even if we know almost one hundred per cent that one of them was a camp guard or a senior Nazi official, we still have to hunt down witnesses to verify it. That's not easy. Anyway, those we've got locked up in the Oberwiesenfeld pound. It's surrounded by dogs and armed guards, but it gives me the shakes to think what might happen if they decided to bust out one dark night and to hell with the consequences. We can shoot them "trying to escape", sure, but then the Germans are going to turn round and ask us what the hell's so different between our lot and the Nazis. Anyway, if Bachmann was Abwehr it's unlikely he's in the first two categories. Sadly, the last two are the biggest.'

The third category, McLusky told them, consisted of military personnel who had fought only as soldiers and could prove it.

'Those we put in labour battalions to clear up the mess the air forces and artillery made, though that's more or less finished now. It's skilled people we need today, not muscle. Guys who can drive bulldozers and cranes, man telephone exchanges, repair fuel and water conduits, staff power stations, fight fires, run schools and colleges, maintain generators. I know the late Georgie Patton got it in the neck from the newspapers back home and from some of the brass here for allowing proven Nazis to occupy key posts, but what the hell was he supposed to do? We may not like it, but it remains a fact that many of the better educated and skilled Krauts joined the Party. If we don't let them get on with the business of running Germany we'll be here 'til 1990, and the US taxpayer's going to have something to say about that. So is

Mrs Horowitz from Omaha, Nebraska, who's wondering when her little boy's coming home to apple pie and icecream. There's a lot of talk about making Germany pay reparations, but what the hell are they going to pay with if they haven't got any industry?

'The last category, military and civilian personnel who had nothing against them, we sent packing if they were too sick or worn out to be any use in a labour battalion. Back to their civilian jobs if they still existed or to bum around the streets if they didn't.'

Hadleigh remembered a fifth category from his own experience.

'And there were those who, for one reason or another, were never picked up and processed at all. Not war criminals as such but guys who can get along by hustling, who don't need ration cards or who're in the rackets.'

McLusky looked at him shrewdly.

'Yeah, there are those,' he agreed. 'I guesss most of us have done a little black marketeering from time to time, but small stuff – stockings, French perfume, booze, cigarettes. The Kraut heavies deal in currency, medical supplies, forged papers, vehicles and gasoline. Anyhow, let's not be negative about it. If Bachmann passed through our hands under his own name, we'll have a record of him somewhere.'

Quinlan shook his head in dismay at the thought of having to plough through twenty or thirty thousand names, but McLusky said it was not as bad as it first appeared.

'We've got them classified under various headings, those we were able to pin down, that is. General SS, Waffen SS, Wehrmacht, Police, SA, Todt Organization, Party members. And so on. While we're far from able to say for certain that everyone we cleared as not being part of a criminal organization is as pure as the driven snow, I think we can assume that anyone not in the SS, the SA and so forth would hardly claim that distinction. So that takes care of thirty or forty per cent of the dossiers. We've got a section on Abwehr personnel also, which I suppose it would be wise to try first.'

'How is everything filed?' asked Quinlan.

'By job and organization as far as possible, but within the sub-sections it's pretty random. We tried alphabetical order, but with guys coming along and taking files and adding to them I wouldn't lay money that Bachmann's not with the zees. Neither would I trust the card index, though it's a place to start.'

And the sooner they got on with it, the better, said Quinlan.

'Now?' asked McLusky incredulously.

'Why not? Neither Major Hadleigh nor myself can stay in Munich more than a couple of days. The quicker we start, the quicker we'll find out.'

'How big's your team?'

Hadleigh explained that apart from the two of them, there was only a senior G-2 non-com and a German girl.

'She speaks almost no English, but as all we're looking for is a name on a dossier she should be able to pull her weight there. We'll need accommodation for the four of us and victuals. We'll sleep where we work and the favour's returnable any time you're in Nuremberg.'

'Which God Almighty forbid,' intoned McLusky. 'I can maybe lend you a couple of my boys,' he offered, 'but a couple is tops.' He pulled a long face. 'Christ, I don't think you know what you're letting yourselves in for.'

'We'll take our chances.'

'I guess you will at that.'

McLusky came to a decision.

'Okay, if you're determined to do it we'd better break up this *kaffeeklatsch*. So much for the evening I had lined up.'

'There's no need to drag you into this,' protested Hadleigh.

'You're going to need someone to show you the ropes and set the ball rolling for you, maybe lend a hand. Yessir, three guys and a Kraut Fräulein who doesn't speak English are going to need all the help they can get. I'll bet she's a middle-aged dog, too, huh?'

Hadleigh and Quinlan grinned at each other.

McLusky cancelled his own transport and travelled in the Mercedes with them to the Oberwiesenfeld barracks. His eyes damn near popped out of his head when he saw Hannah, and he whistled softly between his teeth. He had a few Kraut beauties working under him as clerks and translators but nothing like this.

The Oberwiesenfeld military training ground and barracks, separated from the airfield of the same name by the

Nymphenburger Canal, was ten times the size of the Allers-bergerstrasse barracks in Nuremberg and had at one time housed infantry, reconnaissance, observer, anti-tank and signals regiments, SS as well as Wehrmacht. The building where Seventh Army interrogation records were kept was as big as a small warehouse. Olive-green filing cabinets stood row after row, separated by narrow corridors. Quinlan groaned inwardly when he realized fully the magnitude of the task facing them.

First things first, McLusky set them up with bunks in two anterooms adjacent to a washroom and shower. Rather than expose Hannah to what would undoubtedly be a stream of ribald comments in the general mess area, he arranged to have meals sent across three times a day, beginning immediately. As an extra, he also had sent over half a dozen bottles of bourbon, a case of beer, and a coffee machine. Two Pfcs, Martin and Toogood, were assigned to help, unwillingly at first until they saw Hannah Wolz.

It was 2230 before they got down to it, starting with the card index, which produced seven Bachmanns but no Helmut. Four were designated as SS, two were women, and the last a major-general in the Luftwaffe. McLusky took the airman's dossier to check it out. He returned around midnight with the news that Wilhelm Bachmann was hardly the man they were looking for. His wartime job was senior Luftwaffe liaison officer with the *Hauptamt für Kriegsopfer* – the Main Office for War Victims. He was currently in a military hospital, slightly out of his head. At sixty-eight years old he still seemed unaware that the war was over. According to the doctors his conversation, even in his more lucid moments, comprised telling anyone who would listen that the Fuehrer was coming to Munich and they must do all they could to see that his visit was a pleasant one. There was nothing in his dossier to indicate he had ever lived anywhere near Sedanstrasse, and it seemed most unlikely he would have been trusted with anything that required a cool head and steady nerves. He was a desk man, a World War I flier who had kept his nose clean and been rewarded with regular promotions and non-sensitive jobs. They would give his record a thorough going over if no Helmut Bachmann materialized, but everyone agreed that this could hardly be the man Arndt had told Hannah to contact.

134

The Abwehr dossiers produced no Bachmanns, not even a name which, in transcription, could have been misspelled. The gods of fortune were not going to assist. It was going to be a long job.

As suggested by McLusky they ignored the sections which dealt with the SS, SA, Police and so forth, working on the assumption that Bachmann would not be a member of a hard-core Nazi organization, nor claim to be. Standing at the filing cabinets they concentrated on the remainder, working their way from drawer to drawer, from front to back. Because they each had different rest requirements and tiredness was their worst enemy, it was agreed early on that whenever anyone felt weary they could hit the sack, no questions asked. It was also agreed with McLusky that they could put a white chalkmark on each cabinet that was finished with, so that effort would not be duplicated and no one have to be woken up and asked if cabinet X in row Y was completed.

Time passed, food arrived, coffee and bourbon were consumed, bunks occupied. December 30 came and went and so did most of December 31 without any sign of Helmut Bachmann's name appearing on the cover of a dossier.

By 10.30 p.m. on the evening of the 31st there were only half a dozen cabinets, a few hundred files, remaining.

It transpired quite by accident that Hadleigh and Judd tended to be asleep or resting while Quinlan and Hannah were awake, and vice versa; and so it was at 10.32 when Quinlan slammed shut the bottom drawer of a cabinet with his foot, stood up and flexed his muscles. A few feet away Hannah smiled sympathetically at his frustration.

'Time for a break, I think,' said Quinlan.

Hannah finished with her own cabinet, marked it with chalk, and joined him at the centre table, on which a pot of coffee was regularly filled.

Pfc Martin was in his bunk somewhere, but Toogood was still at it. He glanced enviously across at the British major, watching Quinlan pour a cup of coffee and light a cigarette for the German girl. She was a beauty but she was also, by the looks of things, spoken for.

Quinlan didn't quite see it that way; nor was he sure he wanted to. There was something there between them, something tenuous, unacknowledged, but it might be no more than guards being dropped because they were both close to exhaustion. They were on first name terms now and were also, it seemed to him, very aware of each other physically. They had talked quite extensively during the last forty-eight hours, told each other something of their prewar backgrounds. There was little doubt in his mind that they could get to know each other a lot, lot better were it not for Arndt's death, the father she had lost after such a short acquaintanceship.

She did not know the full story. She accepted that he'd suffered a heart attack in the Allersbergerstrasse barracks, but she was unaware it was brought on by Quinlan's fierce interrogation, his threats against Ilse. Part of him wanted to tell her the truth before she found it out elsewhere; the other part accused him of being a romantic fool. Let sleeping dogs lie, it cautioned. He was not sure he could.

'We've almost finished,' she said, cutting into his thoughts.

'Yes. It looks as though we've wasted our time.'

'There are still a few hundred files to be examined.'

'I doubt we'll find Bachmann's name among them.'

'But it would be the height of irony if his was the last dossier, would it not?'

'Also the height of coincidence, which I'm afraid I don't believe in.' Quinlan sipped his coffee. 'Herr Bachmann's either buried in an unmarked grave or elsewhere in Germany.'

'Then we return to Nuremberg tomorrow?'

'I expect so, though we'll have to find somewhere other than the rooming house in Weigelshof for you to stay. Nor would I advise you to return to Herr Lorenz.'

'I have to earn my living. As for somewhere to live, the girls in Sündersbühl were very nice to me.'

Her eyes twinkled mischievously. It was pretty obvious she knew how 'the girls' made their daily crust and it was logical for her to assume, if Ingrid hadn't told her straight out, that he had shared one of their beds. To get her off the subject he asked her if she was quite sure her father had given her nothing more than Bachmann's name and address.

'No rank or branch of service that might help us?'

'I wish he had,' said Hannah sincerely. 'I wish I could tell you more. I've been racking my brains for several days now, trying to recall if he said anything about Herr Bachmann when he gave me the slip of paper bearing his address. If he did I've forgotten it. If only....'

She left the obvious comment unspoken.

There would never come a better time than right now, thought Quinlan, taking a deep breath. Quite quietly, stumbling over a word or two, he told Hannah the full circumstances of Heinrich Arndt's death, sparing himself nothing. After he finished there was a long, long silence.

'I see,' she said eventually. 'I wondered if it might be something like that.'

Whether she would have said any more, become bitter or sullen or accusatory, he was never to find out, for at that moment the door leading from their sleeping quarters was flung open with a crash and, from the far end of the records warehouse, Hadleigh and Judd appeared.

'For Christ's sake,' shouted the G-2 major, 'it's almost New Year's. Were you two going to let us sleep through it? How far have we got to go?'

Not knowing whether to curse or bless the interruption, Quinlan pointed to the half-dozen filing cabinets left.

'Then let's run through the damned things as quick as we can and tie one on,' said Hadleigh.

There was still no sign of Helmut Bachmann's name when McLusky rolled up with a canvas holdall full of champagne, just as they were finishing. Pfc Toogood was anxious to get to where his own action was, and McLusky dismissed him: It was then 11.40.

'No luck?' he enquired.

Quinlan told him no, no luck.

'We've seen everything, have we?'

'Everything bar the criminal organizations' dossiers. And the morgue file,' he added as an afterthought.

Hadleigh and Quinlan turned on him.

'The morgue file?' they chorused.

'Yeah, the stiffs. Guys who've died in captivity from accidents, illness, malnutrition, fights, guys repaying old debts. There are only a couple of hundred.'

'But they're not here, not in the warehouse?' accused Quinlan.

'Well, no,' admitted McLusky hesitantly. 'You see, if

someone croaks on us we pull his file and keep it separately over in the morgue building. Oh, Christ,' he groaned, 'you don't think Bachmann's one of those?'

'It's possible,' said Quinlan grimly. 'Let's hope so anyway,' he added in a lighter tone, seeing McLusky's downcast expression.

The morgue was on the far side of the main compound. They drove there in the Mercedes, McLusky at the wheel, the windshield wipers just about holding their own against the newly falling snow.

McLusky spoke to the non-com i/c the morgue, who directed them to a tiny anteroom containing just two filing cabinets, the dossiers in alphabetical order. The fifth name they came to was Helmut Bachmann, rank Hauptmann, branch of service Abwehr, condition deceased.

McLusky read aloud as he flicked through it. Bachmann was picked up in Munich on May 10, seriously ill with pneumonia aggravated by malnutrition. He was taken to a military hospital where, on May 16, he died and was cremated. There had been no formal interrogation as he was too ill to answer questions. The dossier details were taken from papers found on him.

'What happened to those papers, his personal effects?' demanded Quinlan.

'They're kept here, Major,' answered the non-com.

'SOP,' said McLusky. 'Non-sensitive material such as photographs, letters, personal diaries and stuff we retain, after examination, in case a relative turns up to claim them one day. It's part of some bright PR guy's hearts and minds campaign, to show the Krauts the US Army and government are not like their bunch.'

Hadleigh said Third Army did the same, mentally kicking himself for not having thought of it earlier.

Bachmann's effects were in an adjacent room, in a US Army-issue tin box the size of a bank deposit box, numbered and tagged alongside several hundred identical boxes. The contents comprised letters, Bachmann's paybook and Abwehr pass, a gun-metal cigarette case and lighter, a few hundred now-useless Reichsmarks, a leather wallet containing a picture of a smiling Bachmann next to a young woman holding a small, grinning infant. Right at the bottom was a torn fragment of colour photograph, attached by a pin to a piece of paper. The fragment measured approximately two inches by two and depicted an irregular section of island or mainland with sea on three sides. Quinlan had Hannah's fragment in his pocket but there was no need to compare the two pieces. They were obviously from the same original, though, again, there were no distinguishing marks such as towns or bays, no lines of longitude or latitude, no clues to where the island or island group or section of mainland actually was.

On the reverse side of the fragment, handwritten as before, was the word KIKA.

The sheet of notepaper gave a name and address; Klaus Butterweck, Tirpitzufer 72/76, Berlin. They were only guessing but it was a near certainty that Herr Butterweck had, or used to have, the third fragment.

Not that that knowledge was going to be much use to them. Tirpitzufer 72/76 was almost as well-known an address to Allied Intelligence personnel as the Gestapo HQ in Prinz Albrechtstrasse or the Foreign Office in the Wilhelmstrasse. It was the one-time headquarters of Admiral Canaris's Abwehr and stood a couple of hundred yards on the British side of the border which separated the British Sector from the Soviet. The trouble was, like the Gestapo HQ, it had been flattened by bombs and artillery before the end of the war. It no longer existed.

Even if it had, Hadleigh pointed out, it wouldn't have done them much good. As the original occupiers of Berlin the Russians treated the city as their own, paying scant respect to demarcation lines. They had in any case – long before the official boundaries were drawn up – captured or killed key personnel foolish enough to be in the capital when it fell. If Butterweck was still alive – which had to be considered doubtful – he was in Soviet hands.

'Berlin,' moaned Quinlan. 'It would have to be Berlin.'

'Yuri Petrov might help,' suggested Hadleigh. 'He's a good joe and he owes us something for Christmas. It's worth a try.'

They were brought out of their gloom by the sudden blowing of klaxons outside. It was 1946.

McLusky had had the foresight to bring the canvas holdall

with him and the morgue non-com provided paper cups. When they each had their champagne, McLusky raised his drink in a toast.

'Happy New Year.'

Quinlan looked at Hannah, but her eyes were elsewhere.

'Happy New Year,' he said to no one in particular.

Fourteen

Nuremberg – January 1 1946

When they got back early in the afternoon to the Allersbergerstrasse barracks, Hadleigh was greeted with a sheaf of Most Immediate signals from Gene Masterson.

1: Where the hell had he been for three days? Permission to go to Munich did not include permission to take the scenic route, nor take his own good goddam time about returning to duty. The US Army wasn't paying him to go schlepping around Germany like a tourist. Major Hadleigh was either Army or civilian. If Army he should remember the adage about not trying to buck the system. If he wanted to be a civilian, that could be arranged.

2: The whole outfit had gone to hell in his absence. Five of his enlisted men – their names were appended – had seen the New Year in in style by gatecrashing a bash at the Grand Hotel reserved for officers and their guests only. Four of them had started a fight with a bunch of journalists, laying into them with bottles, ashtrays and stools. The fifth had insulted the ladies present by exposing himself and yelling: 'I'm the easiest lay in town. Come and get it.'

3: Two other enlisted men were AWOL, neither tail nor whisker seen of them since 1800 hours December 31.

4: A Sherman tank and its crew were missing, vanished off the face of the earth. This was not strictly a G-2 problem but all units were being asked to assist and would Hadleigh look into it. They'd had this trouble before, Third Army, with guys joyriding in tanks down the autobahns until the gas ran out of the machine and the booze out of the crew. This time the guilty parties were for the chop, thirty years in the stockade for openers.

5: If discipline was a problem and Major Hadleigh could no longer cut the mustard, perhaps the said Major might like another posting, say in the Aleutians.

There were a six, seven and eight also. Quinlan left Hadleigh muttering something about what they all needed was a brand-new war. These problems never existed during hostilities.

Quinlan drove Hannah across to the Sündersbühl house in the Mercedes, making sure he was not followed. For the time being, they had decided in Hadleigh's office, she should be safe enough there.

Amid some opposition from Hannah they had also decreed she should not return to Herr Lorenz's for a week or so. When she asked whether 'a week or so' meant a week or a fortnight or a month, Quinlan had to confess he couldn't say. Arndt had told her that after January 10 it wouldn't matter – whatever 'it' was and whatever significance January 10 had. She should stay away from the club until then. After that, they would think again.

Short of rescinding her work permit there was no genuinely legal way they could have kept her from singing had she elected to ignore their advice, but fortunately the events in her boarding-house the night before they left for Munich had convinced her to take seriously the threat against her life. There was, however, the question of money; she had to support herself. With her meagre savings she could just about do that for ten days, but after that she would be penniless.

Quinlan wanted to say he would lend her money until she was earning again, but the words stuck in his throat.

Throughout the journey back from Munich she had remained silent, and she was still silent as they drove through Nuremberg. He didn't need two guesses to divine what was occupying her thoughts.

He chose not to bring the subject out into the open for the present. She would either get over learning his part in her father's death or she would not. Time would be the healer, not words. There was nothing he could do about it.

He could, however, keep himself occupied by trying to solve the whole mystery and perhaps remove the people who wished to harm her by tracking down the third fragment. For which he was going to need Yuri Petrov's help.

A red-faced bear of a man in his forties, Lieutenant Colonel (or Podpolkovnik, to give him his official Soviet rank) Yuri Alekseyevich Petrov could be found in the Grand Hotel most evenings, but where his colleagues congregated around the bar, drinking themselves into insensibility, Yuri was generally in the Marble Room, cavorting around the dance floor with any partner who didn't mind his enthusiasm. He had discovered Western-style dancing on his arrival in Nuremberg as second-in-command of the security team which protected the Soviet members of the International Military Tribunal. It had been love at first sight, mainly because it allowed him to get close to scores of women without emotional commitment. He had become quite an expert and he would wear out several partners during the course of an evening. It would normally take something of the order of a personal directive from Stalin to get him off the floor, but for Quinlan he was willing to make an exception. Quinlan was Hadleigh's friend, and Hadleigh supplied him with girls when his needs became more basic and urgent than cheek-to-cheek waltzing.

They retired to the bar, ordered drinks, and had no difficulty in finding an empty table. Most of the serious drinkers were still getting over their New Year's Eve excesses and would not surface for a hair of the dog until later.

Quinlan spoke no Russian and Petrov no English, and it was in German they conversed.

Quinlan kept it short and simple but told Petrov everything he knew. There was no point in holding anything back if he was to enlist the Soviet colonel's help. Petrov might enjoy the high life in the Grand, give the impression of being a hedonist, a *bon viveur*, but he was a professional to his fingertips and as tough as old boots. He would soon detect if he was being told anything less than the whole truth. Besides, Quinlan wanted to intrigue him, capture his interest. Girls or no girls, Petrov would be unlikely to assist unless there was something in it for him.

'So all we can guess,' Quinlan concluded, 'is that Klaus Butterweck's last base was Tirpitzufer. Whether he's dead or alive we have no way of telling. If he's dead, that's probably the end of it. If he's alive, he may have the third fragment and know where the fourth is. The way the picture, literally, is building up, it looks like there's only four.'

'But Tirpitzufer or what remains of it is in the British Sector of Berlin, my friend,' said Petrov.

'The British Sector, like the American and French Sectors, only came into being after your forces had overrun the city. You were there first. If Butterweck was still in Berlin when you occupied it, you'll have him, not us.'

'It's possible, of course, but more than likely he's dead, either killed during the heroic Soviet advance or by the SS. When the SS absorbed the Abwehr they settled a lot of old scores. From what you've told me it seems probable that anyone connected with these fragments was no friend of the SS. Butterweck is in his grave, my friend. Leave it.'

But Quinlan would not.

'You can't be certain of that,' he insisted. 'He could be alive in one of your camps.'

Petrov raised his beetle eyebrows.

'Camps? You're confusing us with the Nazis. I know of no such camps.'

Quinlan bit his tongue at the lapse.

'All right, in protective custody, then. Or being debriefed by your Intelligence people.'

He did not add 'being debriefed prior to being turned'. It was no secret that the Soviets had taken tens of thousands of prisoners back to the Mother country, the major objective being to use them as slave labour. At some future date, to a fanfare of trumpets, they would return many of them as a 'gesture of humanity'. In the meantime of course, hundreds would have gone over to the Soviet cause, either out of genuine conviction or because of threats. The Anglo-

143

Americans would then discover they had a legion of agents in their midst and no real way of ascertaining who was an authentic repatriate and who a spy. The hot war was over, the cold one about to begin, and highly trained ex-Abwehr operatives who knew the ropes of the Intelligence game would be invaluable. There was no doubt in Quinlan's mind that, if Butterweck had survived the war, the Soviets would not have put him up against a wall and shot him. But that very argument, of course, was the one good reason why Petrov could refuse to help. Unless he, Quinlan, could up the stakes a bit.

'I think it's important for all of us to find out what these fragments mean,' he said, 'why elements of the SS and the British Free Corps are willing to kill to get hold of them. We don't know how big the SS contingent is. There could be dozens, even hundreds of them. It's in all our interests to put them out of business permanently at the end of a very long rope.'

Petrov thought about it. As deputy head of the security detail it did little for his peace of mind to be informed that a unit of SS gangsters was roaming around loose in Nuremberg. If Butterweck was alive and in the process of being turned or broken to make him more malleable, it could make no difference if Quinlan saw him. The Abwehr man would have to return to non-Soviet Germany one day and face a grilling by American Intelligence. It could do no harm at all to let Quinlan see him. It might even be insurance for the future, for if Quinlan reported back to his superiors that he had met with Butterweck and that the Abwehr man looked as though he had been ill-treated (and there was no doubt he *would* appear so), that would become part of the written record. Few would suspect Butterweck of working for the Soviet Union if he had suffered while a POW. And, if there was something to be gained from these wretched fragments, so much the better.

Priorities, that was the name of the game. There was an American joke Petrov had heard which he thought funny. One GI says to another, 'What's the first thing you're going to do when you get home?' The other answers, 'First I'm going to take off my boots, then I'm going to fuck my girl friend. Then I'll take off my pack.'

Priorities. It would inconvenience him little to make a few enquiries. If Butterweck was alive, perhaps a meeting could be arranged – carefully monitored, of course.

'These fragments, the ones you already have, would we be given access to them assuming a third can be traced?'

Quinlan had them in his tunic pocket, but he was not about to hand them over or even let the Russian see them until he had some sort of commitment.

'I see no reason why not.'

Petrov grinned, showing teeth yellowed by tobacco.

'British doubletalk,' he said. 'Does that mean yes or no?'

'It means yes, but only if you come up with Butterweck and in the next day or two. None of us has any idea what Arndt meant by January 10, but it was important enough for him to mention it and it's a little over a week off.'

'A day or two is out of the question,' spluttered Petrov. 'Butterweck could be anywhere in our Zone of Occupied Germany or the Soviet Union. Which is not,' he added sarcastically, 'a tiny island like Great Britain. It will take several weeks simply to trace his name.'

'It shouldn't. Let's not beat around the bush, Yuri. Butterweck was Abwehr. Your people will have Abwehr personnel segregated from the run-of-the-mill German. You should be able to find out whether you have Butterweck merely by picking up a telephone.'

'You give us too much credit.'

'I think not. Anyway, I know you'll try. It would be a tragedy if, for example, the SS plan to murder the Tribunal judges, including the Soviet representatives – *especially* the Soviet representatives – on the way to the Palace of Justice some time before January 10. Simply to show us that they're still around. If that happened I wouldn't like to be in your snowboots.'

Petrov shuddered at the thought but considered such an eventuality unlikely.

'The judges are heavily guarded travelling to and from the Palace. Besides, the fragments have been in existence since before the end of the war. Whatever they mean it can hardly be an assassination plot by the SS. No one knew what form the Tribunal would take before the war's end, nor where it would be held. I am more than willing to concede that many

Germans, and not only surviving members of the SS, would drink a toast if the judges were killed, but their deaths would have nothing to do with the fragments.'

'But you'll do what you can as soon as you can?'

'Of course.'

'Beginning now?'

Petrov glanced at his wristwatch, a handsome gold Omega which said a lot about his subscription to the doctrine of from each according to his ability, to each according to his needs.

'Perhaps not quite now. There is a Belgian countess working for a French news agency in the Marble Room. She is a superb exponent of the old-fashioned waltz, as light as a feather. Unfortunately she has an American lover and leaves early each evening. However, I'm working on it. Unless I succeed in the near future, though, I shall be asking you to arrange with Major Hadleigh a further visit to Sünders-bühl.'

Quinlan couldn't resist it.

'I don't know what Uncle Joe would have to say, a Soviet colonel prancing around a dance-floor with European aristocracy.'

'Marshal Stalin knows little of the finer things of life, and if you repeat that I shall deny it. To him, power is an end in itself.'

'Yuri, you're a snob.'

'But a Communist snob.'

From the far end of the long bar Riordan, in his British captain's uniform, watched them leave before making for the lobby and joining the usual queue for the telephone.

Outside, Quinlan debated whether to seek out some action or return to his billet, type up a few notes and have an early night. He elected to do the latter but somehow found the Mercedes pointing its huge bonnet in the direction of Sündersbühl. Approaching the house, however, he decided he was being foolish, stamped on the brakes, and angrily slammed the gears into reverse. Making a U-turn, in the distance, across the canal, he could see the searchlights illuminating the Palace of Justice and the gaol. The Christmas recess was not quite over, the Tribunal not due to reconvene until this coming Thursday, but security was as tight as ever. In passing, he wondered what the defendants were doing, whether any of them were thinking that 1946 could be the year in which their lives ended.

Some were, some were not.

From his cell Goering eyed the GI peering through the grille with distaste and attempted, by a system of mnemonics, to commit to memory everything he wished to say to his defence counsel, Dr Otto Stahmer, when they next met. He would have liked to write it all down, but the Americans were peculiar about pencils, fearing that a sharpened point could be used as a suicide tool. As if the only holder of Reichsmarschall's rank in the Third Reich would contemplate such an unworthy exit from the world!

In the adjacent cell Hess was muttering quietly to himself. The GI at the grille was never sure whether he was genuinely crazy or faking. He doubted if Hess knew the truth most of the time.

Further along the brightly lit corridor there was little doubt, judging by the comings and goings of medical men, that Kaltenbrunner was unwell again, though whether it was blue funk, as many suggested, or really spinal meningitis was open to question. The doctors resolved to take no chances. The trial could and would proceed in his absence and it was decided to transfer Kaltenbrunner as soon as possible. Not to the 116th general hospital on this occasion, where the facilities were inadequate, but to a civilian clinic.

Julius Streicher was convinced, and repeatedly said so in a loud voice, that all the guards – everyone in the prison, for that matter – were Jewish. As far as the Beast of Nuremberg was concerned there were very few people on the planet who were not Jews or working for Jews.

Of the remaining defendants only one was looking forward eagerly to the resumption of the trial: ex-Governor General of Poland, Hans Frank, who was anxious to continue purging himself in public, having told anyone who cared to listen that he regarded the Tribunal as a God-bestowed world court, destined to examine and punish and bring to an end the terrible age of suffering under Adolf Hitler. The same Hans Frank had once gone on record as saying: 'We must not be squeamish when we hear a figure of 17,000 Poles executed.'

147

Curiously enough, Frank's conversion to a disciple of the Almighty was under ribald discussion between Zander and Flisk when Riordan arrived just after 9 p.m. with the news that Quinlan and the others were back from Munich.

'They seem to have found Bachmann's fragment.'

Sternberg was unimpressed.

'They will not find and decipher the others in time.'

'They might. We've heard nothing that tells us we can go for the 3rd or 4th. It will have to be the 7th. That gives them almost a week.'

'You're certain they have Bachmann's piece of photograph?'

'Not certain. The Meissner woman cannot ask direct questions for obvious reasons. She picks up what she can.'

'It would be useful to know,' mused Sternberg.

'There is a way, perhaps,' said Riordan, and told his audience where Hannah Wolz was staying.

Fifteen

Berlin – January 3-6, 1946

Quinlan and Petrov flew to Berlin in a Douglas C-47 troop transport carrying Soviet markings, one of the hundreds sent to Marshal Stalin by the Americans during the war under the Lend-Lease Agreement, which was terminated in September 1945 and supposedly meant the return of unpaid-for hardware to the United States. So far Uncle Sam had not figured out how to persuade Uncle Joe to give back the marbles.

They were not the only passengers. The aircraft was packed with Soviet brass and non-coms sitting side by side against the fuselage and looking decidedly uncomfortable in each other's company. There were also one or two civilians who seemed to be under arrest; at least they were isolated at the for'ard end of the aeroplane, their every movement watched by armed guards. When asked by Quinlan who they were, Petrov shrugged evasively and muttered something about enemies of the state.

The windows were blacked out. Whether this was par for the course or because much of the flight was at low level over Soviet-occupied Germany, Quinlan never discovered. In any event, he saw nothing of the ground until they landed at Tempelhof airfield, strictly speaking in the British Sector but used by the Soviets.

Petrov had moved with remarkable speed in tracing Butterweck. After spending most of January 2 in his billet making a half-hearted stab at completing his résumé, Quinlan had come round to thinking that his conversation in the Grand with the Russian was likely to be the last he heard on the subject. Even if Petrov managed to work up some enthusiasm for the task, it could take days to track down the former Abwehr operative, assuming he was still alive. He was therefore startled to receive a telephone call at 10 a.m. on the 3rd, while still digesting the radio bulletin that William Joyce had been executed at 0800 in Wandsworth Prison, that Butterweck was indeed alive and 'somewhere in the Soviet Union.' Arrangements were being made to fly him as soon as possible to Berlin, where Quinlan would be allowed to interrogate him. His personal effects, those on him when he was captured, would also be made available for scrutiny, though at this moment it was not possible to say whether they included a fragment of photograph.

Petrov made it clear he could not give a precise hour, or even day, when Butterweck would arrive in the capital, but there was a special flight leaving Nuremberg that afternoon and they could both be aboard it if Quinlan wished.

Quinlan had jumped at the opportunity.

They were met at Tempelhof by a uniformed Starshiy Leytenant, or Senior Lieutenant, who ushered them to a waiting Opel staff car which, in spite of a recent paint job,

149

still bore signs of its previous owners. Quinlan began to suspect that Petrov carried more clout than he had previously admitted, for two-star generals were left waiting for their own transport while the Opel sped off towards the distant, ruined city.

The lieutenant drove with Petrov next to him in the passenger seat. Quinlan sat in splendid isolation in the back. After a brief conversation with his subordinate, Petrov swivelled his neck and announced that there might be some delay in getting Butterweck to Berlin.

'How much of a delay?'

'Possibly twenty-four hours, perhaps a couple of days. I apologize but these things happen.'

Speaking no Russian, Quinlan had not followed the dialogue between Petrov and the lieutenant. Had he been able to do so he would have learned that Butterweck was not in a fit state to be seen by outsiders, not yet. In the special camp for former Abwehr officers near Kharkov he was proving a troublesome convert to Soviet-style communism, unlike, in a different camp, ex-members of the SD and the Gestapo, who switched sides with astonishing alacrity (and were accepted with open arms by the Soviets) once it was obvious the jig was up.

Butterweck's softening-up process consisted of periods of solitary confinement and sleeplessness to disorientate him and short rations to break his will to resist. It was having the desired effect, but it would take a day or two to clean him up and fatten him up. As far as Petrov's superiors were concerned, Quinlan's request to see Butterweck could not have come at a more opportune moment. With a full belly and fresh linen the Abwehr man would realize what he had to gain by cooperating, and how reasonable his would-be paymasters could be. Not for a few more years would the technique become known as brainwashing.

Tempelhof was several miles due south of the city centre. Quinlan had never been in Berlin before and was quite unprepared for the destruction the air raids and the Soviet ground assault had inflicted. Munich and Nuremberg looked like landscaped gardens by comparison.

Much of the southern suburbs was wasteland, though the devastation here was small beer compared to the area around

he Brandenburg Gate, the western central extremity of the
Soviet Sector where the Charlottenburger Chaussee in the
British Sector became Unter den Linden in the Soviet. Here
there was scarcely a habitable building in sight and gangs of
German men, women and adolescents were with their bare
hands still clearing, eight months after the war, mountains of
rubble. Quinlan surmised that this was due less to a shortage
of heavy machinery than to punishment ordered by Moscow.

God only knew where the Berliners now lived. Quinlan
didn't care to think about the wretched existence they'd had
and were about to have.

Petrov seemed totally unmoved by it all and chatted away
cheerfully, translating the signs in Cyrillic script for Quinlan's benefit. On the left was what remained of the former
Gestapo headquarters in Prinz Albrechtstrasse. Further up
the Wilhelmstrasse on the right was the Propaganda Ministry, right opposite what remained of the Reich Chancellery
and Hitler's infamous bunker. Separated from the Chancellery by a square was the one-time Nazi Foreign Office, whose
chief incumbent, von Ribbentrop, was now on trial for his life
in Nuremberg. On the corner of Pariserplatz stood the
battered remains of the Adlon Hotel. Over there, just in the
British Sector, was the Reichstag. Further west was the
once-beautiful Tiergarten, most of the animals in its world-
renowned zoo now dead.

After fifteen minutes of similar travelogue, always heading
north-east, the Opel entered the suburb of Weissensee and
cruised up to a relatively unscarred building complex that
had evidently once been a school. Now, however, instead of
children in the grounds there were tanks, lorries and half-
tracks, and on the gates two uniformed sentries who saluted
smartly on seeing Petrov's rank tabs and waved him through.

Bringing the car to a halt, the lieutenant-driver hopped out
and opened the door for Petrov. Quinlan was left to look after
his own exit.

'What is this place?' he asked.

'Part barracks, part interrogation centre, part administra-
tion block for Marshal Zhukov's First Byelorussian Army
Group. It used to be a residential school and we were
fortunate to find the dormitories more or less intact. We have
also converted several other buildings into private sleeping

quarters for high-ranking officers and their guests, which includes you and me. The enlisted men eat in the dining-hall and two of what I believe were called senior common-rooms are now messing areas for officers. There is also a bar and a brothel.'

Quinlan was surprised at the bland manner in which this admission was delivered. He had somehow never connected the great worker state with overt indulgence in anything so base as copulation.

'A brothel?'

'Of course. Two of them, to be exact. One for the enlisted men, another for the officers.' He grinned cynically. 'We don't want the diseases picked up by the rabble to be passed on to their superiors, now do we? Although I must confess there hasn't been a venereal infection on the premises in my time. They're all good, clean German girls willing to give their bodies to the occupiers in exchange for food and shelter.'

'They must be kept busy,' said Quinlan shortly.

He had meant the comment to be ironic, but Petrov took him literally.

'Not at all. Someone should write a paper on it one day, but it's surprising how little interest the girls generate, now they are so readily accessible. The Russian soldier is, perhaps, accustomed to the spice of a little rape, but so far we've been unable to come up with a solution that satisfies his fantasies without damaging the goods. Well, not officially. Unofficially there are one or two girls who seem to enjoy being manhandled. However, that too has its drawbacks as after a beating it takes several weeks before the girl is, shall we say, open for business once more.'

'Are you sure you should be telling me all this?' asked Quinlan, amazed at how frank the Soviet colonel was being.

'Why not? It's only what the democracies think of us anyway. There is little I can tell you that actually happens which is not exaggerated one hundredfold in the lurid imaginations of Americans and Englishmen. If it did not exist it would be necessary to invent it.'

Quinlan preceded Petrov through a door and found himself in a long corridor which immediately brought back memories of his own childhood. Cyrillic script denoting military function on classroom and study doors or not, there was no disguising that this was a school.

'What happens when the students want it back?' he asked.

'Why should they want it back?' Petrov was genuinely puzzled.

'To complete their education.'

The Russian laughed openly.

'My dear comrade, the kind of education the average German child will need in the foreseeable future will not be found in a classroom. It's all around them, among the debris. There they will learn the only lessons worth knowing, about what it's like to be on the receiving end. The sins of the fathers will be visited upon the children unto the third and fourth generation.'

Quinlan was not at all surprised that Petrov could quote from the Second Commandment.

'For now, maybe,' he said, 'but sooner or later that will all change.'

'You think so? If I had my way it would never change. I would leave Berlin exactly as it is today, its citizens scrabbling among the ruins with their bare hands, a permanent reminder to future generations that there is a price to be paid for everything.'

Quinlan shivered involuntarily when he realized Petrov meant every word. This was a totally different individual from the one he had known in Nuremberg. Gone was the lover of good living, the man who spent hours on the dance-floor wooing Belgian countesses. In his place stood a dedicated servant of Moscow.

Petrov recognized the silence for what it was.

'You disapprove? Where is good old Yuri Petrov of Nuremberg, you ask yourself. Well, he's still there, my friend, but so is the other Yuri Petrov, who took part in the retreat to Moscow, who returned when our armies advanced to find the village where he had grown up no longer existed, who identified the bodies of his mother and his sisters among a mountain of rotten corpses, who heard from the few survivors how the SS *Einsatzgruppen* had swept through the village with their flame throwers, burning the men and houses, raping and mutilating the females, even the very old and the very young. Can you imagine the terror a twelve-year-old girl

153

must feel when a fully grown man approaches her with his cock in his hand, when he pushes it inside her, inside an orifice? To be killed outright is better. You in the west sometimes forget just how many lives we lost in the Great Patriotic War. The figure was twenty million dead. Can you conceive of that? *Twenty million*. In battle, by starvation through summary execution, in extermination camps. Half the population of Great Britain. Fifteen per cent of the United States. Almost twice as many men, women and children as there are in the whole of Norway, Sweden and Denmark combined. You are here in Berlin, comrade, because of those twenty million. While a single SS butcher survives, the dead will remain unavenged. If former Abwehr agent Butterweck, however unwittingly, has information which will lead to the apprehension and execution of *just one* SS private, none of us will have wasted our time.'

As if embarrassed by his outburst, Petrov walked Quinlan to his quarters in an annexe without another word. On leaving he said he would return later in the evening, to take Quinlan to the mess hall. In the meantime, it would be appreciated if Quinlan did not wander around the complex.

Quinlan had no intention of doing any such thing. His quarters were far from the last word in luxury, containing nothing more than a large bed, a wash-basin and a hand made wardrobe, but he was tired and fell asleep in his uniform.

He was awoken by Petrov at 7.45. While he shaved, the Russian chirruped away like a blackbird, his earlier saturnine mood forgotten.

Dinner was a sumptuous affair served by liveried flunkies at long linen-covered tables, each seating twenty. Petrov headed one of these and, despite Quinlan's obvious unease at being the only non-Russian in the mess, insisted the British major take the honoured position on his right.

They partook of Beluga caviar served with iced Russian brandy (a combination Quinlan found bizarre but pleasing), wonderful fish soup, fresh trout as the entrée, followed by choice of venison or wild sucking pig. A cornucopia of exotic fruits topped off the meal, Petrov confiding that they were flown in twice weekly from the Middle East. There was little wine but enough vodka to float a fleet with each course. To much for Quinlan who, pleading fatigue, begged to be excused and retired early.

The following morning there was still no word of Butterweck, but Petrov expressed the hope they would hear something before the day was out.

To pass the time Quinlan was given an escorted tour of the barracks and, more from boredom than any other reason, joined Petrov in a marathon drinking session, where his stock rose several points in the Russian's estimation for his ability to keep pace, vodka for vodka. Later, Petrov suggested they pay a visit on the whores, but Quinlan knew he was far too drunk to be much use to a girl or himself.

Still, it seemed that Petrov was not going to let him get away without sampling some of the delights on offer, for in the small hours of January 5, while Quinlan was still asleep, a girl no older than seventeen joined him in bed. In spite of the warning lights flashing in his head that his antics could well end up on film, he thought to hell with it and took full advantage of the lush young body even though for much of the time, in the semi-darkness, the image in his mind's-eye was that of Hannah Wolz.

The girl was gone when he awoke, but his hours with her had done him good. He felt completely relaxed and more than ready to demand of Petrov just where the hell Butterweck was.

As it happened it was unnecessary. Grinning lasciviously and expressing the hope that Quinlan had enjoyed his entertainment, Petrov announced that Butterweck was on his way and would be here at 10.30 a.m.

He was brought into the room set aside for his interrogation under armed guard, a senior lieutenant in command. This officer handed Petrov a dossier, saluted, and left with his men.

Petrov read aloud from the dossier as though Butterweck were not within earshot.

'Klaus Emil Butterweck, born Berlin April 20 – I see he shares his late Fuehrer's birthday – 1915. Which makes him what, thirty. Looks older. Profession before enlistment lawyer. Abwehr rank Oberleutnant. Served with the Brandenburg Division before being seconded to Tirpitzufer – where he

almost certainly had regular contact with Canaris himsel
There's much more,' he said to Quinlan, 'but I don't kno
how relevant his past is. Do you want to see the dossier?'

'Is it in Russian?'

'Yes.'

'Then I don't.'

Butterweck certainly did look older than thirty, though
Quinlan. Hardly surprising after two-thirds of a year i
Soviet hands. There would be no caviar and fresh trout whe
he came from.

He was a smallish man, five feet seven or eight, an
considerably underweight. His fair hair was thinning and h
eyes, though intelligent, were dull, defeated. He looked n
unlike the sort of photograph one sometimes saw i
newspapers of a dead man, one touched up by the polic
artist in an effort to get the public to identify him. He wa
wearing a civilian suit a size too big. In it he resembled
child dressed up in his father's clothes.

Quinlan was wondering how to begin when Petrov antic
pated him by laying the ground rules.

'This interrogation,' he said formally, in a manner whic
suggested the entire interview was being recorded by hidde
microphones, 'must relate solely to relevant matters and is n
to touch upon questions regarding Butterweck's health no
his treatment since he became a legitimate prisoner of wa
You are not to ask where he is currently being held nor t
nature of his life there. Neither will the prisoner – who h
been instructed to cooperate fully otherwise – offer any info
mation that is not directly requested unless it is germane
the matter under consideration. Any contravention of the
conditions will oblige me to bring the interview to a
immediate end. There will be no others. The floor is you
Major Quinlan.'

Quinlan kept it as brief as possible, leaving out Arndt's fa
and also that of Ilse Arndt. Nor did he mention Hannah.
was hardly likely Butterweck knew of her existence. H
simply gave the Abwehr Oberleutnant the names he kne
Langenhain, Arndt and Helmut Bachmann, adding that h
Butterweck's, name had come to light because of a scribble
note attached to the fragment of photograph found amon
Bachmann's belongings.

'Bachmann is dead?' Butterweck's voice was curiously soft, as though he had spent hours talking to no one but himself, which indeed was the case.

'Yes,' answered Quinlan. 'In Munich directly after the war.'

'A pity,' murmured Butterweck. 'He was a good man.'

'Irrelevant,' snapped Petrov. 'Kindly do not make unsolicited comments.'

'Did you know Arndt?' asked Quinlan.

'No, not personally. I had seen him around in Tirpitzufer and elsewhere, of course, but I wouldn't say I knew him. Oberstleutnant Langenhain I knew well, but not in connection with this business.'

'What business?' demanded Quinlan.

'The photograph fragments. I take it that's why I have been brought here. You wouldn't have mentioned Bachmann's otherwise.'

'You will have to speak up,' barked Petrov, removing all doubt that the session was being recorded. 'I can hardly hear you.'

'The photographic fragments,' repeated Butterweck. 'Those Admiral Canaris distributed. At least he gave me nine so I suppose he did likewise with the others.'

Quinlan felt his pulse race with excitement.

'Just begin at the beginning and tell me what you know.'

'There's very little to tell. I didn't know Helmut Bachmann was involved, nor Arndt or Oberstleutnant Langenhain. But that's the way the Admiral would have wanted it.'

'To the point, please,' insisted Quinlan.

Butterweck frowned as he tried to remember.

'It's hard to recall the exact date but it would be somewhere in the spring of 1944. Admiral Canaris called me into his office and told me that the Abwehr was breaking up, that the SS were plotting to take it over and probably imprison, perhaps execute, himself. He gave me the fragment of photograph and told me to take good care of it. If anything happened to him, if he were murdered by the SS, someone would approach me and ask for it. That someone would have further instructions, information that might perhaps be of value to me personally.'

'How would you know this person to be the genuine article?' asked Quinlan.

'Because he would have other fragments. I was to hand over mine to this individual and direct him to the holder of the fourth fragment.'

Quinlan took a deep breath.

'You know who holds the fourth fragment?'

But Petrov interrupted before Butterweck could answer.

'Why did Canaris choose you?'

'Who can tell? I was close to the Admiral, he knew me to be loyal when loyalty was at a premium.'

'Presumably so too were Hauptmann Arndt and Langenhain?' queried Petrov. 'And Bachmann.'

'Arndt I can't answer for but I believe so. Certainly Bachmann was loyal to the Admiral personally and Oberstleutnant Langenhain was a close friend.'

Quinlan tried his original question again.

'And the fourth man, the one who has the fourth fragment – he can be put in the same category?'

'Your tenses are wrong, Herr Major, but yes, Oberleutnant Straub was in that category.'

'What do you mean, my tenses are wrong?' asked Quinlan knowing the answer before it was given.

'Straub was killed in Berlin during the last days.'

'And his fragment?'

'Destroyed with him, I imagine.'

No matter, thought Quinlan. Three was better than two and, like a near-finished jigsaw, it should be possible to build up the whole picture from the three quarters.

'But you still have your own fragment?'

The bottom fell out of Quinlan's dreams with Butterweck's reply.

'I'm afraid not.' A spark of defiance entered the Abwehr officer's voice. 'We lost many things when Berlin was overrun – homes, friends, personal effects. My fragment was in a wallet that was taken from me when I was first captured. It was doubtless consigned to some Russian fire as being of no value.'

'That's enough,' rasped Petrov.

'As you say.' Butterweck meekly lowered his head.

Quinlan tried the only shot left in his locker.

'The word KIKA is handwritten across the back of the fragments in my possession,' he said. 'Does it mean anything to you?'

'Certainly. It was written by Admiral Canaris across the back of my fragment too. Also Straub's. It was to guarantee authenticity. Few outside the Abwehr would know it, but KIKA was the *nom de guerre* adopted by the Admiral when acting as an agent in Spain during the 1914-18 war and between the wars. It was what he termed his yesterday name. He was a man who loved an ironic joke, Admiral Canaris. I suppose it pleased him to use his yesterday name for some future project.'

'But you don't know what that was?' asked Petrov.

'No. My role was simply to be part of the whole. I never learned what the entirety was.'

'But you did see Straub's fragment, didn't you?' probed Quinlan, thinking back to Butterweck's words a moment or two ago. 'You said Canaris had written across the back of it, as he had across yours. Which means you saw it or discussed it.'

'Both,' said Butterweck. 'Although my orders from the Admiral were to speak to no one about the matter until I was contacted, I knew, because he told me, that Straub held the next fragment. The final one.'

'Why final?'

'It's an assumption. Straub did not have a fifth name. I therefore assumed he was the last link in the chain.'

'That's the second time you've implied there were only four fragments. How could you possibly know how many came before yours?' asked Quinlan.

'By comparing mine and Straub's it was obvious the original photograph had been divided into quarters.'

'So you compared them. In spite of your orders from Canaris you discussed the matter with Straub before you yourself were approached.'

'There seemed no reason to do otherwise. The war was almost over.' Butterweck shot a glance at Petrov. 'The Soviets were at the gates of Berlin. There was nothing to be gained by waiting any longer. For all I knew the fragments Straub and I had might save our lives. Don't ask me how. I don't know. Anyway, I spoke to him.'

'And examined each other's fragments?'

'Of course.'

'Then you could draw a rough outline of both of them.'

159

'I can draw you a *precise* outline of both of them, Herr Major. Straub and I looked at them so often, trying to divine what they meant. I could draw them in twenty years' time.'

'For God's sake,' cried Quinlan, half rising from his seat, 'why didn't you say so in the first place!'

'I was instructed at the start of this interview not to offer unsolicited comments,' murmured Butterweck coyly.

Petrov went to the door and called along the corridor.

'Bring pen and paper. Lots of it.'

Butterweck's memory was not quite as good as he claimed or his periods of isolation had affected it. It took him a score or so attempts before he got it right, before he pronounced himself satisfied that to the best of his recollection what Quinlan and Petrov saw before them were facsimiles of the fragments he and Straub had once possessed. They were drawn larger than the pair Quinlan had in his pocket; nor, of course were they in colour. But Quinlan could see that, scaled down, they would dovetail with his own.

'Is there anything else you have omitted to tell us because the question has not been posed?' asked Petrov. 'You may answer freely on this occasion.'

'Nothing except . . . .'

'Carry on'

'It's hardly material.'

'We'll be the judges of that.'

'Well, apart from telling me I would not be contacted unless he was dead, the Admiral also said that I was not to worry if no one *ever* contacted me. After January 10, 1946, he said, it would no longer matter. I regret I do not know whether today's date is before or after January 10 or even whether it is January at all.'

'Enough,' said Petrov, and called for the guard to take Butterweck away. 'He is to remain in the barracks until order otherwise,' he added.

Quinlan could see the pattern now. Langenhain was the link man, Canaris's trusted friend, briefed to contact Arndt if and when the Admiral was executed or otherwise died. Arndt would lead to Bachmann who would lead to Butterweck, and so on. But Langenhain had panicked and decided to jump the gun while Canaris was still alive. Either that or he assumed that once in Flossenburg Canaris was as good as dead.

anyway. Which explained why Arndt would not part with the first fragment.

The outstanding question was why, what did it all mean?

'I think the moment has come to live up to your end of the bargain,' said Petrov, when they were alone.

Quinlan had forgotten the agreement made in the Grand.

'Bargain?'

'You have the drawings of Butterweck's and Straub's fragments. We should now see if they all fit together.'

It took Quinlan twenty minutes to scale down Butterweck's drawings. When he had done so he took the two pieces of photograph from his pocket and assembled the whole. It wasn't a perfect fit. Either Butterweck's originals were inexact or his own cartographic skills inadequate. But it was close enough. It wasn't a section of mainland. What they had was an island; to be precise one large island surrounded by a number of smaller ones. What they did not have were lines of longitude and latitude or any other clue to the whereabouts of the group. Nor, even if they could have pinpointed the spot, did they know what it meant. What had Canaris intended to convey? And what was the significance of January 10, after which it all wouldn't matter?

'It beats me,' said Quinlan eventually. 'I don't know what the hell it all means.'

'Perhaps a large-scale world atlas would help,' suggested Petrov.

Quinlan had his doubts.

'It would be a start, I suppose, but there must be tens of thousands of islands throughout the world, some as big as Cuba, some as small as cays. We'd be looking for a needle in a haystack. Besides, the original photograph seems to have been blown up, magnified, twenty or thirty times. A world atlas showing features on this scale would occupy a building.'

'We might perhaps narrow it down,' proposed Petrov. 'Remember what Butterweck said about Canaris's yesterday name, how he used it in Spain and how he was fond of an ironic joke. I don't speak English as you know, but I have a little knowledge of Spanish from Civil War days. *Islas Canarias* . . . .'

'The Canary Islands,' Quinlan interrupted him. 'It's a

thought. He could have been making a pun on his own name.'

There wasn't a large-scale world map available but, as the complex had formerly been a school, one of Petrov's men unearthed a stack of student's atlases from a cupboard. None of the Canary Islands looked remotely like the montage in front of them.

They flicked from page to page in the hope of stumbling, by chance, on something, but as Quinlan had predicted the needle remained firmly in the haystack.

After a while they concluded they were tackling the problem back to front. They required specialist help, a military cartographer. Quinlan suggested Ben Hadleigh as the man to find them one.

'But you will keep me informed of progress,' said Petrov. 'I would be within my rights to confiscate Butterweck's drawings as they were made by a Soviet prisoner of war on Soviet-occupied territory. However, that would leave each of us with only half a possible answer and a lot of memorizing to do.'

Quinlan agreed that anything Ben Hadleigh's people came up with would be passed on to Petrov.

'Though even if we identify the island,' he added wearily, 'we're still only halfway there. Is it a jumping-off point for SS men on the run? Is something or someone hidden there? Why are the SS involved with the British Free Corps? The permutations are endless. The only people who could give us the answer are Canaris, who's dead, and Langenhain, who's missing, either dead or in a camp somewhere.'

'He's not in our hands,' said Petrov. 'It was one of the first things I checked when enquiring whether or not we held Butterweck.'

'What will happen to him?' asked Quinlan. 'What happens to Butterweck now?'

'Have you finished with him?'

'I can't see how he can help us further.'

'Then he'll be taken back.'

'Back where?'

'You know better than to ask that.'

'But we, the West, will see him again one day, won't we?' said Quinlan mischievously.

'That I couldn't say.' Petrov's expression scolded Quinlan for breaking the rules.

There was no space for them on an aircraft flying out of Berlin that day, and it was not until late afternoon on the 6th that Quinlan and Petrov arrived back in Nuremberg. The Russian had a car waiting for them and dropped Quinlan off at the Allersbergerstrasse barracks before continuing to his own destination.

Thirty seconds after walking into Hadleigh's office Quinlan had forgotten about Canaris, Butterweck, fragments of photograph and much else. Grim-faced, Hadleigh informed him that earlier in the day Hannah Wolz had been abducted from the Sündersbühl house by three German-speaking men.

Sixteen

Nuremberg – January 6, 1946

Quinlan accepted a tumblerful of bourbon from Max and tossed it back. It took a supreme effort but he managed to erase from his mind the image of Hannah in the hands of those who had killed Ilse Arndt.

'Tell me about it.'

There wasn't a lot to tell, Hadleigh informed him. He and Max were catching up on some paperwork in the office when a wireless message came through. It was from a mobile patrol in the Sündersbühl district claiming they had an hysterical young German girl in the jeep. She'd flagged them down in a

163

state of great distress. About all they could get out of her was that she had to talk to Major Hadleigh. At once.

'It was Ingrid,' said Hadleigh. 'I couldn't make much sense out of what she was saying over the radio because she was babbling. But as soon as she mentioned Hannah I knew we were in big trouble.'

Telling the patrol commander to take his directions from the girl and meet them at the Sündersbühl house, he and Max grabbed a car and drove over there as fast as they could.

'They were outside,' continued Hadleigh. 'Ingrid wouldn't go in.'

It did not take them long to discover why.

The other regular occupant of the house, Hadleigh's girl Helga, was lying across the bed, her throat cut. Of Hannah Wolz there was no sign.

'It took us a while to piece it all together,' went on Hadleigh, 'because Ingrid was in no fit state to answer questions until the doc back here gave her a shot to calm her down. When she could talk she told us that around three-thirty or four – she's a bit vague on time – there was a knock on the door. I'd given them all strict instructions to open up to no one without confirmation of identity, but Ingrid looked out of the window and saw a US jeep – yes, a fucking jeep – parked outside and three guys in what seemed to be US or British uniforms. She unlocked the door and in they came.'

Hadleigh shook his head in despair.

'It all gets a bit confused after that, but from what we can gather they identified Hannah quick enough and shut off Helga's screams by killing her. It was round about here that Ingrid made a run for it. She's not sure herself how she got out, but she did and kept on running. The rest we saw for ourselves. Helga dead, Hannah vanished. In spite of the uniforms and the jeep they all spoke German. We might not have found out about it for several days if Ingrid hadn't taken it on the lam.'

'You mean neither you nor Max nor anyone else has been making regular checks while I was in Berlin?' said Quinlan incredulously.

'I've been over there twice, Max not at all.' Hadleigh shrugged in futile apology. 'What the hell difference would it have made if we'd been out there ten hours out of twelve? If they knew where Hannah was they'd only have to wait until we left to make their play.'

'But twice in four days! Christ!'

Hadleigh swallowed his annoyance. It was easy to be wise after the event.

'In the first place,' he explained patiently, 'we've been busy and in the second place we thought it safer. They got to Ilse Arndt and Angela Salvatini easily enough, found out where Hannah worked and where she lived. Frequent visits to the same house would have aroused their suspicions if they've got the barracks under observation and six times a day wouldn't have been enough if they knew where she was from another source.'

'Meaning what?'

'Meaning if they've got inside information.'

'You're kidding me!'

Hadleigh looked at Max uneasily.

'I hope so.'

Quinlan fought down a sudden surge of panic. It was now just after 5 p.m. Hannah had been missing for an hour, perhaps an hour and a half. She might already be dead or undergoing the most terrible suffering at the hands of her captors.

'Where's Ingrid now?' he asked.

'Here. Under sedation in a private room in the women's infirmary. She's got a couple of bruises but mostly she was just terrified out of her wits. The doc' reckons she'll be okay, but he wants to keep her drugged for twenty-four hours. We've spoken to her, Otis. She couldn't tell you any more than she's already told us.'

Quinlan waved away Max's offer of a refill.

'What action have you taken so far?'

'Not a lot,' confessed Hadleigh, explaining that he and Max had only got back to the barracks with Ingrid twenty minutes ago. 'I've put out a general alert for all mobile patrols to stop and hold any jeep carrying three men in Allied uniform and a girl, but it's a long shot. It's Sunday. It's dark outside. They're not going to be in the open now. Wherever they were heading they'll have got there.'

Hadleigh wanted to add that he was almost as much

concerned about the uniforms and the jeep as he was about Hannah, but decided this wasn't the moment. Still, it was a far from comforting thought, knowing that the SS were riding around Nuremberg like they owned it.

Quinlan hammered Hadleigh's desk-top with frustrated rage.

'How?' he asked of no one in particular. 'How the hell did they know where she was? I'll swear to Christ no one followed me when I first took her to Sündersbühl. I was as careful as hell.'

'Me too,' said Hadleigh. 'I made sure there was nothing behind me on both occasions.'

There was a long silence.

'So,' said Quinlan finally, 'they've got someone on the inside.'

But Hadleigh still could not figure out how that was possible.

'Max and I were chewing it over before you arrived. Apart from the three of us no one knew you were taking her to Sündersbühl. We discussed it here in the office, you, me, Max and Hannah. No one came in, no one went out.'

'What about Ingrid and Helga?'

'For Christ's sake,' groaned Hadleigh, 'that's clutching at straws! You're trying to say that a couple of little hookers are somehow wired in to the SS? It won't wash.'

Quinlan knew it. He also knew that every moment they spent talking could be another moment of agony for Hannah.

Unaware that he was clenching his fists until the knuckles whitened, he cast his mind back to the day they returned from Munich. Hadleigh was right; the four of them had debated Hannah's temporary accommodation behind closed doors. To the best of his recollection they had never even mentioned the exact address, merely saying that she should be safe enough for the time being with Ingrid and Helga.

On the way out they had passed Gretl Meissner in the corridor. Knowing he was about to meet Yuri Petrov and that a trip to Berlin could be on the cards, he had sent Hannah on ahead while he briefed Gretl to look after his end of things in the Palace of Justice if he wasn't back before the IMT reconvened on the 3rd. Gretl had asked if he wanted the whole proceedings taken down verbatim or whether, as none of the defendants would as yet have taken the stand, thumbnail sketches of their reactions to the prosecution witnesses would suffice. He had replied: 'Let me think about it. I'll jot down a few notes *when I get back from Sündersbühl.*'

Christ.

'Gretl Meissner knew I was taking Hannah to Sündersbühl,' he said, slowly and painfully relating the circumstances of the encounter. If anything happened to Hannah because of his own stupidity he would never forgive himself. 'Does she know where the house is?'

Hadleigh wasn't sure but thought so.

'I've never made it a big secret that I've got a couple of broads stashed over there. She's probably heard me mention the address one time or another. But it's crazy,' he added plaintively. 'It's not possible she's in touch with the SS. Jesus, she's got a confirmed track record of anti-Nazism. You think I didn't check her out before hiring her? Why would she do it?'

'Maybe she didn't,' said Quinlan, 'but there's only one way to find out for sure. Is she around?'

'It's Sunday. She doesn't work Sundays.'

'I'll go get her,' offered Max.

'We'll all go,' said Quinlan.

Hadleigh did not think that was a good idea. As Quinlan would undoubtedly accept if he were thinking straight, it was always poor tactics to interrogate suspects in their own environment, where they felt secure.

'It's a twenty-minute trip there and back. If she's got anything to hide this is the place to sort it out. You'd better bring her son in also,' he added as Max reached the door. 'If we've gotten round to suspecting Gretl we may as well include her kid.'

While Max was away Hadleigh asked if the Berlin jaunt had proved fruitful. Although Quinlan had never felt less like talking in his life he knew Hadleigh was only trying to take his mind off the waiting. In any case, the fragments in his tunic pocket were somehow tied into Hannah's disappearance.

He spread them across the desk and explained what had transpired during his cross-examination of Butterweck.

'There's a cartographic unit somewhere in Nuremberg,' Hadleigh said eventually, 'working with US Army and Kraut

167

architects to see if this city can in any way be rebuilt to look like it was. Give me a minute.'

He spent six on the telephone while Quinlan paced the office. Finally he hung up.

'They're based over in Fürth but I've told them what we want and they've agreed to go through their files as a matter of urgency.'

'The islands may not be in Germany, may not even be in Europe,' Quinlan cautioned.

'That doesn't matter. These guys travel everywhere with the whole *schmear* on microfilm, the entire box of tricks. Their aerial photographs of Nuremberg and Fürth break down to something the size of a postage stamp. I guess they can put the world into a couple of suitcases. If this island group exists and is not part of Canaris's imagination, they'll find it. They've got gizmos now called computers, electronic gadgets. I don't understand how they work, but you punch a bunch of information in one end and out comes the answer the other. Doubt if they'll ever catch on.'

Hadleigh put the two photo-fragments, Butterweck's original drawings and Quinlan's scaled-down versions into a buff envelope and scribbled a name and address across the flap. He summoned an orderly and told him to take the package over to the dispatch-rider's pool. It was urgent. If the DR stopped for a beer on the way he'd find his ass in a sling.

As the orderly went out Max and Gretl came in. One glance at her face was enough to tell them how the SS had known where to find Hannah.

It came out slowly and tearfully, how one day in the middle of November her fifteen-year-old son Willi had not appeared for his evening meal, how she was approached later that night by a German-speaking foreigner who informed her that Willi was being held hostage as a guarantee of her future cooperation. This man knew she worked in the Allersbergerstrasse barracks, even for whom she worked. He had obviously studied her movements and her companions carefully.

At first all she was asked to do was listen out for the name Arndt. When Arndt died she was told to report anything she overheard concerning a Fräulein Hannah Wolz. While she

168

behaved Willi would live. If she disobeyed orders, he would be killed.

'He is my only son, Herr Major,' she said between sobs to Hadleigh. 'I couldn't let anything happen to him.'

Sitting there weeping, she presented such a pathetic picture that Quinlan had to remind himself that her treachery might well have killed Hannah. Keeping his voice hard, he asked her how she passed on her information.

'If I had anything to tell them I called the Grand Hotel and left a message for Captain Eric Spencer. Although I don't believe it to be his real name, it's the one used by the man I usually meet, an Englishman. He telephones the Grand each evening at six-thirty and asks if there are any messages for Captain Spencer. If there are, he knows to meet me there one hour later.'

'You say Spencer is the man you *usually* meet,' said Quinlan. 'Does that mean you sometimes meet others?'

'Yes and no.' She lowered her eyes, unwilling to face Quinlan. 'It was obviously only safe to meet Captain Spencer in the hotel if neither you nor Major Hadleigh was in Nuremberg. Otherwise, you would become curious at seeing me with a man in British uniform.'

'He wears the uniform of a British Army captain, then?'

'Yes.'

'Go on,' said Quinlan.

'If you or Major Hadleigh were in Nuremberg and therefore likely to appear in the Grand, I would say in my message that I could not meet Captain Spencer in the hotel that night. He would understand this to mean that the meeting was to take place at the alternative rendezvous, the Hauptbahnhof, the main passenger station almost opposite the hotel.'

'You still haven't told us whether you met others apart from Spencer,' Hadleigh reminded her.

'I do – did. It was always Captain Spencer if the meeting was inside the hotel. If outside, it could be either him or any one of two or three other men, sometimes a German, sometimes not.'

'Do you have names for these others?'

'No.'

'What does Spencer's cap badge look like?' asked Quinlan with a flash of inspiration.

She did not understand. 'His cap badge?'

'Yes. You must have seen him with his cap on at some time. What was the badge in the centre?'

Twisting her sodden handkerchief into knots, Gretl tried to remember.

'It was, I think, a sort of gun,' she managed eventually. 'A cannon on large wheels.'

'Royal Artillery,' said Quinlan, snapping his fingers. 'He's wearing the uniform of a Gunner captain. It might be an idea to check whether an RA captain by the name of Spencer has gone missing in Nuremberg in recent months. It could be a genuine name, the phoney Spencer keeping the original owner's papers in case he was ever asked for ID.'

Hadleigh questioned the validity of that theory. If it were true it would mean that the real Spencer was at the bottom of a river someplace but posted as absent without leave from his unit. Every MP in Third Army territory had a list of Allied officers and men reported AWOL. The fake Spencer would be taking a hell of a risk, walking around with the papers of a man who would be arrested on sight.

Quinlan broke into rapid English, knowing that Gretl would not be able to keep pace.

'Christ, Ben, we're not talking about minor criminals, pickpockets or car thieves. These guys are taking a risk just by being out in the open. If they've got the balls to commit a couple of murders, maybe more, have a crack at me, kidnap Willi Meissner and Hannah, they're not going to worry about a few lousy papers.'

Hadleigh accepted that. But it wasn't going to get them anywhere, knowing whether or not a Captain Spencer was listed as AWOL.

Quinlan disagreed violently.

'Ingrid said the three men who snatched Hannah were wearing British or US uniforms. They must have got them from somewhere. If we can check not only on Spencer but on how many other officers and men have gone absent in the last few months, talk to each one's CO to see if he was the type to do a vanishing act, we could get an idea what size team we're up against. Fathom that and we might be able to fathom what they're up to and where they, and Hannah, are.' Quinlan paused for breath. 'I tell you this,' he concluded, 'the thought of the SS and the BFC wandering around Nuremberg in Allied uniforms gives me a funny feeling in the pit of my stomach.'

It did not do much for Hadleigh's peace of mind, either. It was common knowledge that every one of the Tribunal judges had received crank death-threat letters since the trial opened. Maybe the guys who abducted Hannah weren't cranks. Kill the judges and their alternates and there went the trial for another year, after which the climate of public opinion would have changed, the world occupied with more pressing matters such as Joe Stalin's territorial ambitions. Defendants who would draw the death penalty in six months' time or whenever the hearing ended would just get a hefty gaol sentence in eighteen months.

But how the hell *could* anyone get at the judges, he wanted to know? They were heavily guarded where they resided, escorted by enough hardware to fight off a division to and from the Palace of Justice, which was ringed with armed troops during a sitting.

'I've no idea,' admitted Quinlan. 'But they've proved they're ruthless, they've got uniforms and at least one jeep.'

'They might also have a tank,' said Max, reminding them of one of the Most Immediate signals from Gene Masterson. The Sherman was still missing.

That clinched it for Hadleigh.

'Get on the horn to the MPs, Max. Use my name and talk to Colonel Cahn in person. Don't go into details, just ask him if he has a Captain Eric Spencer, Royal Artillery, on his wanted sheet. If he has, ask him to send over a complete breakdown of all absentees from, say, October last year. Forget about French, Russian and so on. Concentrate on British and American. Use the phone in your own office.'

'Right,' said Judd, and went out.

Hadleigh rubbed his eyes. It still didn't make any sense, he said. How did all this connect with Canaris, the fragments? What had Canaris meant about January 10? What was the BFC involvement?

'I don't see those boys going in for death-or-glory stuff.'

Neither did Quinlan. It was the same conversation he had had with Yuri Petrov before they flew to Berlin. It all hung together some way but he was damned if he could see how.

He reminded Gretl that she had been telling them how she passed on information. Had she ever met Spencer or any of the others away from the Grand or the Hauptbahnhof? In other words, did she have any idea where their base was, where they might be holding Hannah? She did not. It was always the hotel or the station.

She looked at Quinlan fearfully, aware that her life as she had known it was finished.

'Sometimes,' she said, her voice little more than a whisper, 'I had nothing for them but they wanted something of me. In that case they would call me here if it was urgent or come to my home if it was after my normal hours.'

Hadleigh shook his head in amazement. It had all taken place under his nose and he hadn't seen it.

'When did they ask you about Fräulein Wolz?' said Quinlan. 'Today? This morning?'

'No, it was last Tuesday, the day you returned from Munich. Captain Spencer telephoned me – here. I was late leaving because I had a lot to do.' She choked back a sob with difficulty. 'I had nowhere to go anyway.'

'How did they know we were back?' asked Quinlan. 'From you?'

'No. When he called he immediately suggested the station rendezvous. I got the impression he had just left the Grand.'

Where doubtless he witnessed my conversation with Petrov, thought Quinlan, trying to recall seeing a Gunner captain in the bar. He could not.

'So you met him at the Hauptbahnhof?'

'Yes.'

'And told him where Hannah was?'

The only confirmation was a tearful nod.

'You've probably killed her,' said Quinlan bitterly. 'You've probably killed her the way you killed Ilse Arndt and Angela Salvatini.'

'No!' protested Gretl, shaking her head with horror. 'That wasn't me. I couldn't have told them where Herr Arndt lived because I didn't know. I didn't even know he was dead until I came in the following day.'

'She's telling the truth, at least on that score,' said Hadleigh. 'I can check the log if you like, but I'm pretty certain she was with you in the Palace of Justice when Arndt

172

was brought in. She couldn't have given them the Humboldt-strasse address.'

'I didn't,' repeated Gretl. 'You must believe me. They sometimes have a man watching the gates, in the crowd.'

Quinlan beckoned Hadleigh to one side, where they held a rapid, whispered conversation in English. Gretl Meissner had committed no crime for which she could be punished in a court of law. She was, in any case, more victim than culprit. She had taken the soft option, but it was hard to blame her. If they could persuade her to help them, perhaps by doing so risking her son's life, there was a possibility that Hannah and Willi Meissner would come out of this alive – assuming they were not already dead.

Quinlan left it to Hadleigh to explain what was required of her.

'It's now ten minutes to six,' said the G-2 major. 'You'll use this phone to call the Grand, where you'll leave a message telling Captain Spencer you can't meet him at the hotel tonight. As we understand it, that's the code for arranging to meet him at the station at seven-thirty.'

They would have preferred to use the signal which advised the fake Spencer that the rendezvous with his contact was at the Grand, but as he presumably knew that Hadleigh, at least, was in Nuremberg, he might smell a rat and not put in an appearance at all, not now they had Hannah. There was also a possibility that the phoney Gunner captain would not turn up in person as it was an outside meeting, but that was a risk they would have to take.

'I don't think he calls on a Sunday,' said Gretl. 'He knows I don't work that day.'

'Never calls?'

'I don't know. As I've never left a message for him on a Sunday I'm not sure whether he telephones or not.'

'Let's hope he does so today,' said Hadleigh grimly.

But Gretl had still not agreed to cooperate.

'They'll kill my son,' she wept quietly, the tears starting to flow again.

Quinlan was not in the mood to indulge her.

'There's a good possibility he's already dead,' he informed her callously. 'In any event, do you really expect them to set him free when you're no longer any use to them? Your only

173

chance of seeing him alive again is to help us find their base.'

And a mighty slim chance it was at that, thought Quinlan. It was long odds against tailing whoever turned up back to where they came from, but that one would have to be played by ear. It was first things first and nothing could happen before 7.30. Nothing *at all* could happen unless Gretl agreed to work with them.

It took several more minutes to convince her where her best interests lay, but finally she nodded her head.

After making the call she was taken to the guardroom, where she would be watched over by a GI until it was time to move. She was not, they told her, under arrest.

At 6.15 Max Judd returned from his conversation with the MPs. Since the beginning of October forty-six individuals had gone AWOL. All bar nineteen had now been accounted for, taken into custody. Of those nineteen four were British, the remainder Americans. Two of the British were officers; so too were two of the Americans. One of the British officers was a Captain Eric Spencer.

'But it's going to take a hell of a long time to check with the COs of the rest, to see how many were absentee material,' Max wound up.

Quinlan said it did not matter now.

'I don't know whether it demonstrates my complete lack of faith in the modern-day soldier, but I was expecting many more than nineteen, a couple of hundred, I guess. If we're looking at this thing properly, the maximum opposition is a score and probably much less. It means they're not in Nuremberg in battalion strength so we can rule out anything that requires more than a handful of men.'

At 6.35 Quinlan was all for telephoning the Grand to see if Spencer had called in. Hadleigh gave him the thumbs down.

'They might have a man in the hotel. Christ knows, they've been running rings round us up to now. If we do anything out of the ordinary we could blow the whole ball game. We've just got to sit this one out.'

Quinlan knew he was right, but the waiting was driving him mad.

At 6.49 as they were preparing to leave, the cartography unit came through. They'd had a stroke of luck in identifying the island group. One of the team had spent some weeks

174

surveying it for use as a possible base during the time of Lend-Lease. There was no doubt the fragments depicted a volcanic archipelago in the South Atlantic, a British possession, the chief island of which was Tristan da Cunha. Only this one was inhabited; the rest were too tiny. In case they were interested and wanted to look it up on a map, Tristan da Cunha's location was 12° 30′ west, 37° 00′ south.

Although none the wiser for the information, Quinlan now saw what Butterweck had meant about Canaris's ironic sense of humour. Tristan, lover of Isolde, was a legendary Wagnerian hero.

Seventeen

Nuremberg – January 6, 1946

At 6.52 Riordan returned to the Grossreuth house after telephoning the Grand. The phone he used was in a garage a kilometre away and was one of only a couple of dozen in this area. The garage proprietor had applied to the military authorities to have it reconnected in July 1945 and, to his astonishment, the work was done the following day. The British captain used it regularly with the proprietor's full approval. The officer always paid well for the facility.

On entering the common-room Riordan inclined his head at Sternberg and thumbed over his shoulder. The former Standartenfuehrer followed Riordan into the passage, closing the door behind him.

'There was a message,' said Riordan, keeping his voice low. 'The station rendezvous.'

Had Quinlan or Hadleigh known the identity of their chief adversary they would have been amazed to witness his reaction. Sternberg's face cracked into a broad smile.

'So,' he said, 'we have guessed well. It was beginning to worry me. Not picking up the Wolz girl until today was masterly.'

'We can thank Scharper for that.'

They re-entered the common-room where Sternberg called for attention. Only Hallam was absent, taking his turn at picket duty in the grounds.

'There appears to be an unforeseen last-minute complication,' announced Sternberg. 'Comrade Riordan has just learned that the Meissner woman wishes an urgent meeting at the Hauptbahnhof. He cannot make the rendezvous personally as we still have much to discuss. Zander, you know her by sight. It will have to be you and Flisk.'

As though on cue, Riordan objected.

'You're forgetting, Zander and Flisk still have to check the weapons. They've been their responsibility all along and we can ill afford malfunctions now.'

Sternberg clicked his tongue in annoyance.

'Of course. My mind is on other matters.'

His eyes wandered around the room until they alighted on Hans-Dieter Kleemann, seated, as always, next to Anton Isken.

'You've spoken to her, Kleemann. It will have to be you. Get changed and take Isken with you. Use the jeep with the 6th Armoured Division markings.'

A rendezvous was always made in pairs, one man to drive and look after the jeep, the other to make the contact. But usually one of the Big Four went along, to take care of a chance roadblock or inquisitive MP.

Kleemann protested that neither he nor Isken spoke more than a few words of English and those with heavy accents.

Sternberg cut him short.

'This is an emergency. I need Laidlaw, Granger and Hallam here. They will be in the vanguard tomorrow and they must rehearse and rehearse again until their roles are second nature. Go now.'

176

Kleemann and Isken looked at each other and got to their feet. They had served for long enough in the SS Panzer Division Totenkopf to learn that a man didn't question twice an order from an SS colonel. Besides, these were risks they had agreed to accept and they were trivial compared with what was to come.

They left the room to change their clothes. When they returned ten minutes later Kleemann was wearing the uniform of a Third Army corporal, Isken that of a Pfc.

'The meeting is for seven-thirty,' Sternberg told them. 'Listen carefully to whatever Frau Meissner has to say and return here directly. I shall expect you no later than eight-thirty. Take no risks.'

'You may be assured of that, Herr Standartenfuehrer,' muttered Kleemann with unaccustomed humour.

Those in the common-room waited until they heard the jeep drive off. Apart from Frank Hallam patrolling the grounds, and Riordan, Zander and Flisk, who had kidnapped Hannah Wolz earlier in the day, the others were in civilian clothes. As the note of the jeep's engine died in the distance, Sternberg indicated that the time had come for the rest of them to change.

At 7.22 they gathered again in the common-room. Sternberg was dressed in the uniform of a US Infantry major, former Sturmbannfuehrer Heinrich Scharper that of a US lieutenant. Kurt Zander and Oskar Flisk were already decked out as Third Army sergeants. Tom Granger, the ex-tankman, had on a Royal Artillery bombardier's battledress that didn't quite fit, while Harry Laidlaw wore the second-best khaki of a one-time private in the Royal Army Medical Corps. All the original owners of the uniforms were dead, murdered and disposed of over the last few months by those now impersonating them.

It was a nuisance, thought Sternberg, that they presented such a motley collection, but that couldn't be helped. They'd had to take what they could where they could find it.

Zander glanced towards the ceiling, licking his lips at the prospect of what was to come.

'The girl and the Meissner brat, Herr Standartenfuehrer.'

'I leave that to you and Flisk. Bring the girl, out cold if need be. Kill the boy. We'll meet you outside.'

177

Handcuffed to the opposite end of the iron bed from Willi Meissner, Hannah listened to the heavy tread of footsteps on the stairs. Had she wanted to express her fear by screaming not a sound would have been heard, for she and Willi were gagged.

Since her abduction that afternoon she had lost all track of time. They had not harmed her. They had knocked her unconscious in the Sündersbühl house and when she recovered she was here. Wherever here was.

In a different bedroom from the one she was now in they had asked her questions. Three of them, one of whom had mauled her sexually with his big rough hands to get her to talk.

More frightened than she had ever been, even during the worst air raids, she had told them what they wanted to know. Everything. About Quinlan. Hadleigh. About Max Judd and their trip to Munich. About the photo-fragments, Bachmann and Klaus Butterweck. About her father.

They had asked her about her past and she had told them that too. About her mother, where she had lived during the war, what she had done.

She had confidently expected to be killed. Raped first, then killed. She knew these men, their sort. She had seen too many of them in the past not to know them.

The silver-haired one – the leader, it seemed – had reacted to something she said and held a hasty conference with the man in the British captain's uniform. They had started to laugh delightedly, chuckle, whisper unheard. And then they brought her here, chained her to the bed opposite the boy, left her alone.

Until now. Now, perhaps, they were going to kill her.

Flisk came in first. For a moment she didn't recognize him in his uniform. For a moment she thought the Americans were here and she was safe. Then she saw his cruel eyes, remembered him as the one who had run his hands all over her body, squeezing, probing, all the while saying it would be better if she told them what they wanted to know.

'Time to leave, Fräulein,' grinned Flisk, unlocking the handcuffs but keeping hold of her arms and not removing the gag. Again she felt him touch her, fondle her breasts, stroke her buttocks as he pushed her ahead of him.

Behind her he stood very close as they reached the door. She could feel his erection through the material of his trousers.

'Don't take all night about it, Kurt,' she heard him say over his shoulder.

Zander gazed into Willi Meissner's terrified eyes. He would have enjoyed nothing more than taking all night about it, but Sternberg wouldn't stand for that.

It was odd, he thought, increasing the pressure with his thumbs on Willi's larynx, how those who were about to die knew it long before they felt the physical presence of approaching death. It could be something in the executioner's demeanour that told the victim all hope was lost.

There, there, he murmured softly to himself as Willi's eyes started to bulge and strangled animal yelps were heard through the gag. There, there.

Eighteen

Nuremberg – January 6-7, 1946

A tiny figure in grey, Gretl Meissner stood just inside the east entrance of the Hauptbahnhof, opposite the old post office building. The reopening of road and rail communications being a major priority on the agenda of any conqueror in an occupied country, train services had long since been back to something near normal. Although the station façade still carried the scars of bomb and artillery damage, it was functioning again and crowded with civilians and military

179

personnel alike, all wearing that semi-dazed expression rail travellers everywhere have, cocking their heads for announcements, gazing anxiously at arrival and departure bulletin boards, asking questions of uncaring porters and US Army transport communications officers.

Quinlan and Hadleigh had agreed they should not go into this with half the Third Army as back-up. The objective was not to apprehend whoever made contact with Gretl but to follow him. That couldn't be done using a convoy of trucks without arousing suspicion, though if they were successful in finding the base they would call up reinforcements before making any further moves. Thus only the two of them and Max were taking any notice of Gretl Meissner, who was, they each accepted, the weak link in the chain.

They had briefed her with a phoney story. Whether she could carry it off was another matter. She was to tell her contact that American Intelligence had recovered four fragments of photograph which seemed somehow connected with the late Hauptmann Arndt. These were now in Hadleigh's office safe. She could not remove them for any length of time without the alarm being raised, but she thought she could re-photograph them if she had a suitable camera. Could her contact provide one? If he could and she gave them what they wanted, would they set her son free?

They were standing some distance from one another to cover all angles, but each of them was within thirty or forty yards of Gretl. As 7.34 became 7.35 Quinlan began to get anxious. Perhaps Spencer hadn't called the Grand.

A minute later they observed a youngish US captain approach the German woman, but it became apparent after a moment that he had mistaken her immobility for importuning, that he was trying to see if she was free for a couple of hours. When she shook her head vigorously and turned her back, he moved on.

At 7.40 Judd, who was nearest the station entrance pretending to read a newspaper, quite suddenly folded it into a roll and tapped it against his palm. Quinlan and Hadleigh scanned the crowds and simultaneously picked out the individual Max had spotted. He had on US uniform and sported corporal's chevrons, but he had never spent any time in the American military. Straight-backed, he carried himself

180

like a recent graduate from boot camp. A Marine Corps drill sergeant would have wept with joy at his carriage, but this man's alma mater was the Wehrmacht or the Waffen SS.

Kleemann took his time closing on Gretl, who had not seen him as yet. He didn't like these station meetings, but Sternberg had assured him time and time again that the safest place to hide a fake Reichsmark was in among genuine paper currency. On a platform swarming with uniforms no one was going to take any interest in one more GI corporal.

Satisfied that all was well, Kleemann went up to her. He saw she had been crying recently, probably over that brat of hers.

'Frau Meissner,' he said politely.

Her mind in another dimension, Gretl started at the interruption to her thoughts.

She recognized Kleemann, whose name she did not know, from previous meetings, but her first reaction was one of disappointment.

'I was expecting Captain Spencer,' she managed.

'The captain is otherwise occupied. Please inform me why you made the call. And smile, Frau Meissner. You look like the chief mourner at a funeral.'

Hesitantly, stumbling over her words, Gretl explained about the fragments, how they were in the office safe, how she needed a camera to photograph them.

Kleemann frowned. He had heard about these fragments, heard Sternberg, Scharper, the Englishman Riordan talking about them. But no one had ever explained to him their importance.

'Let me understand this,' he said patiently, keeping his voice soft because they were conversing in German. 'The Americans have all four fragments in the Allersbergerstrasse barracks. You can't steal them. You need a camera to photograph them.'

'Yes. It's most urgent.'

Gretl started to crack. She clutched Kleemann's sleeve.

'You must get me one at once. Then I can have my son back. He's well, isn't he? Please tell me he's alive and well.'

Kleemann tried to loosen her grip.

'Frau Meissner,' he hissed. 'You are attracting attention.'

It all happened very quickly after that.

Gretl refused to let go of his sleeve. This man, this German, was her one link with Willi, without whom she was going out of her mind.

Panicking, Kleemann attempted to prise her fingers loose and back off. From their various vantage points Hadleigh, Quinlan and Judd could see and hear some sort of argument taking place and instinctively began to move in.

Already nervous and made more so by Gretl's hysterical persistence, Kleemann sensed the jaws of a trap closing and himself caught between the steel claws.

Wrenching himself free from Gretl's grip and throwing her to the ground, he ran for the exit. In the east forecourt Isken was waiting in the jeep.

Not comprehending what had happened but knowing their quarry was trying to escape, Quinlan and the others raced after him. Suddenly they were shouting. In the space of a few seconds it had all gone wrong.

Kleemann gained the forecourt a dozen strides ahead of Judd, screaming at Isken to get moving. Isken tried to. At the second attempt the plugs sparked and the motor caught, by which time Kleemann was alongside, swinging himself aboard.

'Go! Go! For Christ's sake, go!' he bellowed.

Isken crashed into first gear. The jeep careened forward, sideswiping a stationary Mercedes. But it was gaining speed when Judd appeared abeam of the nearside hatch. Always the man to take the direct route wherever he was going, Judd wasted no time trying to wrestle for possession of the steering wheel. Grabbing the windshield stanchion with his left hand he slammed his right fist into Isken's face.

The master sergeant was off balance and thrown clear as the jeep went out of control, the semi-conscious Isken, blood pouring from his mouth, no longer able to steer it. It crashed into a line of parked vehicles, hurling Isken against the windshield and pitching Kleemann on to the forecourt. Before he could get to his feet Hadleigh slammed a size ten shoe against his temple.

Although only seconds separated them Quinlan was the last to arrive, pushing his way through a gathering throng of mystified spectators. One of the Germans was unconscious and Max was dragging the bloody driver from his berth. But

182

this was not what they had planned. Gretl had spooked her contact and that could well be as good as a signature on Hannah's death warrant.

Back at Allersbergerstrasse Quinlan was all for laying into the Germans without delay, breaking their fingers one by one if necessary in order to get them to talk. Hadleigh counselled otherwise. There were more ways of skinning a cat than with a blunt knife. Extreme measures were generally countered, at least to begin with, by extreme resistance. Besides, he wasn't sure Quinlan could carry out his threat. It was one thing to go in shooting from the hip against a man who was resisting; it was quite another to torture him in cold blood. It might work – if Quinlan could do it – but it might not. And they didn't have all the time in the world. Whoever had dispatched the Germans would be expecting them back. If they didn't reappear within a reasonable period, that could be the last they saw of Hannah. And of Willi Meissner, whose mother was under sedation in the infirmary.

'Have you a better idea?' Quinlan wanted to know.

Hadleigh thought he had. It wasn't original but it had worked in the past and might do so again. Especially with young Germans who wore their aggressive masculinity like a badge, and more especially with men who would be facing a charge of murder in the first degree.

Max Judd had supervised the strip-and-search. Apart from finding SS blood-group tattoos under each German's armpit he had relieved them of papers in the names of Corporal Jerry Thompson and Pfc Edward J. Strickland. Thompson and Strickland were on the AWOL list. There was no doubt in anyone's mind that they were dead.

In the classic manner of interrogations they had separated the two Germans, putting one, Kleemann (though they had no idea of either's real name yet), in the Trough, the larger cells, the other, Isken, in the punishment cell which had housed Ilse Arndt the night her father died. It was Judd's opinion that Kleemann was the shakier of the pair, the one most likely to break, not least because of the blow on the temple he had received from Hadleigh's size ten.

There was to be no good guy/bad guy routine. They hadn't the time. After telling Max to hunt up Privates Bennett,

Guthrie and Johnson and deposit them in the guardroom until required, Hadleigh took a near-full bottle of bourbon from his desk drawer.

'Maybe he could use a drink,' he said.

At this point Quinlan had only the faintest glimmer of the G-2 major's proposed tactics.

Kleemann looked up anxiously as the cell door opened. He was naked apart from a blanket around his shoulders and felt vulnerable. His head ached but he was ready for anything his interrogators could throw at him. A man didn't take the SS Blood Oath unless he was tough.

Quinlan took a back seat. Literally. He pulled the wooden chair to the far side of the cell and sat on it, arms folded. After a while Max reappeared and stood in the doorway.

'What division?' asked Hadleigh casually. 'Das Reich, Leibstandarte, Totenkopf?' He named the three premier Waffen SS divisions, flattering Kleemann.

'I have nothing to say,' muttered Kleemann sullenly.

'Please yourself,' said Hadleigh, 'but the only definite charge against you as of now is illegal possession of US Army property. We're too busy here in Nuremberg to bother about such matters. If that's all you're guilty of you'll be put in the pen with the others pending a formal indictment. Probably that's all it will amount to. Probably in six months' time there'll be a general amnesty. All those not guilty of war crimes will be released. On the other hand, if you were not Waffen SS maybe you were on the staff of one of the camps.'

'I was a front-line soldier,' said Kleemann. 'I had nothing to do with the camps.'

'Regrettably everyone is saying that,' murmured Hadleigh. 'The only stories we're inclined to accept are those that can be proved. I tend to believe you were a front-line soldier. You don't look the type to have served in Dachau or Mauthausen. But I need proof for my superiors. Name, rank, number and unit is all we want for the moment.'

'Balls,' sneered Kleemann. 'You know I'm no ordinary SS man on the run. You were waiting for us at the station. The Meissner woman talked and you set a trap. It's unfortunate I walked into it, but there it is.'

Quinlan tossed a glance at Judd. If this was the weaker of the two, Christ help them if they had to tackle the other one.

But Hadleigh took it all in his stride.

'You're right about the trap, of course. We did set Gretl Meissner up. We were expecting the fake Captain Spencer, however. No doubt he preferred someone else to take the risks.'

'I don't know any Captain Spencer.'

'And I don't exactly believe that.'

Hadleigh moved up a gear.

'Nor, now we're down to it, do I believe you were Waffen SS. You have, shall we say, a certain femininity about the features. Not combat material at all.'

Kleemann felt his cheeks redden at the accusation, the implication he was homosexual. That was a fucking lie, he wanted to shout. He'd had more than his fair share of women.

But he kept his rage to himself. The American was trying to goad him into doing something stupid.

'You were probably in the camps,' went on Hadleigh, not raising his voice at all. 'You're a killer anyway and what's a few more deaths. Someone murdered a woman and a young girl in Humboldtstrasse in November, though I doubt you had anything to do with raping them first. The uniform you were wearing wasn't handed over to you voluntarily. Neither were Corporal Thompson's papers. You were at Dachau or Buchenwald or Mauthausen or one of the others, and we have ways of dealing with people like you that do not involve lengthy trials. You'd better take a drink or two while I tell you about it.'

Kleemann ignored the proffered bottle. He had been willing to die before and he was willing to die now. Giving this *Ami* major his name, rank, number and unit wasn't going to help him.

'So go ahead and shoot me.'

Although he knew it to be an act, Quinlan shivered at Hadleigh's smile.

'We're not going to shoot you. We're going to hang you. But first you're going to be buggered, take it in the ass. I have a few men in my command – black men, I think you should understand – who get their kicks from sodomizing Nazis.'

In spite of himself Kleemann experienced a spasm of terror.

'I don't believe you.'

'You'll soon see. Max, get them, will you.'

185

It took but a few moments for Bennett, Guthrie and Johnson to appear. They were all black, all built like prizefighters. Quinlan had seen them around, heard them talk, knew they were as far removed from being homosexual as he was. But to the German they were the embodiment of everything he had been taught to loathe and dread.

'Take the blanket, Max,' ordered Hadleigh.

Kleemann tried to hold on to his covering, but Max back-handed him across the mouth and removed the blanket, tossing it on to the cell floor. Fear that went back a million years overtook Kleemann. He clutched his genitals with both hands and retreated on his bunk to the corner where it met the wall.

'This is not just,' he protested.

If he had not meant it, it would have been laughable.

'Take a drink,' said Hadleigh soothingly. 'It'll make it easier.'

Hadleigh watched the SS man's eyes. There would come a fraction of a second when the German would be torn between wanting the alcohol and wanting to hold on to his cock. When he judged the moment to be right, he instructed Max to hand back the blanket. Kleemann grabbed it and wrapped it around him, encasing himself in its security.

Hadleigh held out the bottle of bourbon. Kleemann took it and drank deeply, despising himself for his weakness but needing the liquor.

'Maybe now you believe I'm telling the truth,' said Hadleigh, leaving the bottle with the German. 'Let's begin with your name, rank, number and unit.'

What harm could it do? thought Kleemann. He and Isken were finished as far as the job was concerned.

He took another swig from the bottle and gabbled out the information. Hadleigh took it down in longhand on a pad and made him repeat his rank and unit.

'Scharfuehrer. SS Panzer Division Totenkopf.'

Hadleigh was not slow to make the connection between the identity of the division and the missing Sherman.

'You were a tank driver?'

'Yes.'

'And your friend, your comrade?'

'He should be telling you himself.'

'I'd rather you told me.'

Kleemann hesitated only momentarily.

'Anton Isken. Same rank, same division. I regret I don't know his number.'

'But he too drove tanks?'

'Yes.'

Hadleigh beamed, a schoolmaster giving a mental pat on the head to a bright pupil.

'Good. We progress. Now all I need to know is your business in Nuremberg and the whereabouts of Fräulein Wolz and Frau Meissner's son.'

Kleemann shook his head.

'That wasn't part of our bargain.'

'Herr Major,' prompted Hadleigh.

Hadleigh was taking his time and Quinlan's anxiety about Hannah was as strong as ever, but he had to admire the way the American was handling the whole business. He had Kleemann on the run now. By a combination of alcohol and threats he was attempting to substitute one figure of authority, himself, for another, Kleemann's commanding officer. And not once had he raised his voice.

'Herr Major,' repeated Hadleigh.

'That wasn't part of our bargain . . . . Herr Major.'

'Not part of our original bargain, agreed,' said Hadleigh cheerfully, 'but you failed to give me your name and unit until I pointed out the alternative.'

He inclined his head towards the silent Bennett, Guthrie and Johnson, who must, thought Quinlan, have played these roles before.

'Therefore our original pact is off. So, the information I require, if you please.'

Kleemann was drinking from the bottle almost without noticing it now. He had cleared, perhaps, a third of its contents, four or five good double measures, in the space of a few minutes. And it was beginning to show in his voice.

'That I can't do,' he stammered.

'Herr Major.'

'That I can't do, Herr Major. You don't understand what you're asking . . . .'

Hadleigh reached forward and took the bottle. Kleemann let it go without protest, although his eyes followed to where Hadleigh placed it on the floor beside him.

187

'I'm afraid it's you who do not understand, Scharfuehrer Kleemann,' he said. 'All right, Max. He wants to play it the hard way.'

Taking his cue Max grabbed a double handful of blanket and pulled it from Kleemann's shoulders. When the German attempted to hang on to it by squeezing himself against the wall, Max cuffed him about the head. There was little power in the blow. It was more the sort given to a recalcitrant child or over-playful dog. And all the more effective for that.

'Bennett, Johnson,' said Judd, snapping his fingers.

Like well-rehearsed actors on a stage the two black GIs came into the cell and seized Kleemann without ceremony. The German kicked out and shouted, but he was no match for their strength.

They whipped him over on to his stomach as easily as most men would a ten-year-old. While Bennett pinioned his arms and placed a huge knee in the middle of Kleemann's back, Johnson forced his legs apart in an inverted vee.

Kleemann's eyes were wide open, staring horrified at the cell door where Guthrie was very slowly unbuckling his belt, grinning as he did so.

The German began to whimper and plead. It was a sound Quinlan hoped never to hear again.

Guthrie moved out of Kleemann's eyeline, glancing anxiously at Hadleigh, who mimed him to silence. After a two-second beat he placed the bourbon bottle against the German's buttocks.

Kleemann screamed.

'All right, all right, all right! I'll tell you, I'll tell you!'

There were tears in his eyes when they sat him up, but he looked at Max with the gratitude of an infant when the master sergeant handed him back his blanket.

Hadleigh waved Bennett, Guthrie and Johnson away. They knew the routine. They would wait in the guardroom in case they were needed again. Which was unlikely.

Quinlan heard one of them say, as they disappeared along the passage: 'One day that fuckin' Major Hadleigh's gonna go too far and one of us'll end up havin' to shaft a Kraut.'

Someone else answered: 'Take it where you find it, bro'. That's as close as *you're* ever gonna get to shaftin' Mister Charlie.'

188

With shaking hands Kleemann accepted the bottle once more and drank deeply. But not too deeply; Hadleigh saw to that. The barriers were down. He wanted Kleemann compliant, not incapable.

'Let's begin at the beginning,' he said, his voice the same melodious baritone it had been throughout. 'First, I want to know if Fräulein Wolz and Willi Meissner are still alive and where they're being held.'

There was no fight left in Kleemann. It took him a moment to stammer out that they were both alive when he left and the address of the Grossreuth house, but once he was talking nothing was going to stop him. He had looked into the innermost reaches of his soul and found he was mortal. To answer the American major was a catharsis.

Max did not have to be told what his next job was. He was out of the door like a greyhound as soon as he had the address, to check it on the map and round up men for the raid. There could be no question of stealth any longer. They would hit and hit fast.

Next came the number of individuals within the house, and any others who might not be. Kleemann recited their names as though in a trance.

There was Frau Elke Niemeyer, who ostensibly owned the property and whose husband was under arrest in the Soviet Zone. She was the willing accomplice of Standartenfuehrer Sternberg, Sturmbannfuehrer Scharper, Oskar Flisk, Kurt Zander. He was not sure of the former ranks of the British Free Corps contingent, but their names were Riordan, Granger, Hallam and Laidlaw. There were two others, Kramer and Wildehopf, but they were killed. But the major knew that, of course.

'And that's the lot?' asked Hadleigh. 'An original dozen and no more?'

'Yes.' Kleemann's eyes were glazing over, part booze, part relief that his manhood was not to be violated. 'We were the last to join the battle group, Isken and myself.'

'*Battle group!*' chorused Hadleigh and Quinlan in unison.

'Yes.'

Even when they heard it they didn't believe it. The SS and the British Free Corps men, down to a total of eight now, were in Nuremberg to make an attempt on the lives of the

Tribunal judges and simultaneously try to free the defendants from the dock of the Palace of Justice. Final details were to have been worked out tonight, but the operation was to take place at 10.30 a.m. on Monday, January 7, in a little over thirteen hours from now.

'You're lying,' snapped Hadleigh, but it became obvious after a moment that Kleemann wasn't.

Spearheaded by the Sherman tank and backed up by two jeeps and automatic weapons, the Palace of Justice was to be hit as the judges were taking their seats. It was to be sudden, swift and bloody, and surprise was the key. Who would suspect a small convoy of vehicles with US markings and personnel in Allied uniforms until it was too late? He and Isken would be – would have been – driving the tank, but it made no difference that they were now in custody. One of the Englishmen, Granger, had driven tanks in the Western Desert.

'Where's the Sherman now?' asked Hadleigh. 'Grossreuth?'

'I don't know. In all truthfulness I don't,' Kleemann added plaintively when Hadleigh made a gesture of disbelief. 'Isken and I were not part of the team the night of the ambush. We were told privately by Standartenfuehrer Sternberg that we were too valuable to risk on a venture that could go wrong. He could always try for another tank but he couldn't find two more SS drivers if we were killed or captured. Let the Englishmen take the risks, the Standartenfuehrer said. Granger drove the tank to a secret location.'

'But why keep it a secret from you now?'

'You don't understand the Standartenfuehrer. Everyone was told only as much as he needed to know, in case anything went wrong.'

As indeed had happened this evening, thought Quinlan. Sternberg was obviously a cunning opponent. If Kleemann and Isken had known the location of the tank, it would no longer be a potential weapon come tomorrow.

But it transpired that the whereabouts of the Sherman was not the only item the Standartenfuehrer had kept under wraps. Quinlan tossed the names Arndt, Langenhain, Bachmann, Butterweck and Straub into the dialogue, but they meant nothing to Kleemann. He had heard the first three discussed from time to time, but did not know who they were.

Nor did he understand the significance of the photo-fragments. As for Tristan da Cunha he didn't even know it was an island in the South Atlantic.

'As I explained, we were told only what the Standarten-fuehrer wanted each of us to know.'

When they had time they would grill the other captive, Isken, but Hadleigh doubted he knew any more than Kleemann.

Backed by two GIs to stand guard over the prisoner, Max appeared in the doorway to announce that they were ready to roll.

Hadleigh had one more question. He had a lot of telephoning to do and he wanted to be sure of his facts.

'Let me get this straight. Tomorrow morning this SS colonel is going to attack the Palace of Justice. I find it hard to believe that even fanatics would contemplate such a lunatic scheme, but answer me this. If you were not in custody would you have driven the Sherman, regardless of the consequences?'

'Of course.'

'Fuck me,' said Hadleigh with feeling.

In the passage Max said he had a jeep, two armoured personnel carriers and a company of GIs in two trucks standing outside. He'd located the house, which stood in its own grounds, on a street map. They should have no difficulty finding it.

'I've got a funny feeling you're not going to find anything,' said Hadleigh. He consulted his wristwatch. 'It's now nine-twenty. From the Hauptbahnhof to Grossreuth is around a fifteen-minute drive. The meeting with Gretl was set for seven-thirty. If all had gone according to plan Kleemann and Isken should have been back by eight o'clock. Allow for a margin of error of a quarter of an hour and they're sixty-five minutes overdue. If I were this Standartenfuehrer Sternberg I'd have headed for the hills long since. Sorry, Otis, but that's the way it reads to me.'

'Then what the hell are we hanging around for,' said Quinlan.

Hadleigh held up his hand as Quinlan headed for the exit.

'We're hanging around because I'm not coming with you. You and Max can lead the operation. If I'm right and they're

191

gone, I've got to get on the horn to Gene Masterson. If Kleemann's telling the truth – and that's the way it looks – these fruitcakes are serious.'

They hit the house from all sides, but it was as Hadleigh had predicted. They found only the dead body of Willi Meissner in one of the upstairs rooms and a bewildered Frau Niemeyer in a cottage in the grounds. She could not give them the exact hour the main house was vacated. She had heard several vehicles start up some time ago, but she had paid them no attention. They were always coming and going, the occupants. She was also most indignant when Quinlan informed her she was to be taken into custody on a charge of harbouring war criminals.

There was, of course, no sign of Hannah, which left Quinlan in a state of ambivalence. If they'd wanted her dead she'd be there alongside poor Willi Meissner. But it was a two edged gift, her absence. They might have taken her to amuse themselves during the small hours before the assault.

Leaving a senior NCO to tidy up the details, he and Max raced back to Allersbergerstrasse in the jeep. Giving Hadleigh, who was still on the telephone, the thumbs down, they made for the Trough and Hans-Dieter Kleemann. The German protested that he had no knowledge of a back-up house, and they were compelled to believe him. Perhaps Isken could tell them more when they got round to him but, for the moment, they had to accept that Battle Group Sternberg had disappeared.

Isken refused to talk even when confronted with Kleemann. He raged and spat at his fellow tankman and finally had to be dragged away, yelling that he would find a way of settling accounts with Kleemann, no matter what it took.

They were in no way fazed by Isken's lack of cooperation. There was no reason to believe he knew any more than Kleemann. Besides, they had other things to think about.

Counter Intelligence Corps were in on the action now, as were Colonel Masterson and Third Army brass up to three-star general level. In accordance with their agreement, Quinlan had also left a message for Yuri Petrov to contact him soonest.

A little after midnight Gene Masterson appeared in person. The word from the brass was to play it by ear. The judges would be warned of a possible attack and security arrangements would be tripled, but there was not a chance of the trial being postponed for even a day because a handful – he emphasised 'handful' – of fanatics were threatening mayhem. If it became public knowledge that the Allies were running scared, the Tribunal would become a laughing stock.

In any case, he added, the Krauts must surely conclude that Kleemann and Isken had been taken and made to talk, and therefore call off the assault. It was a damned nuisance that they were still roaming around loose, but they wouldn't attack now.

Hadleigh wasn't so sure. Anyone nutty enough to conceive such an idea was just nutty enough to carry it through regardless. Besides, there were many aspects of the whole business that left him uneasy. Why were members of the British Free Corps involved? What was the significance of the fragments? What did they mean and why were the opposition so anxious to get hold of them? Canaris had been dead close on a year. He was incarcerated in Flossenburg and other camps for ten months before that. It was impossible for the Admiral to have known in 1944 that a potential plot existed to assassinate the Tribunal judges. Or rather, if not impossible, stretching the bounds of credulity to breaking point.

And what the devil did the reference to Tristan da Cunha mean? And the date January 10? There was more to this whole affair than met the eye and it gave him an uncomfortable feeling in his gut.

Masterson agreed that the information in their possession was far from complete but that they had to go on what they had. Hadleigh concurred.

'We'll have the Palace of Justice bottled up. If they're going to come in, they're going to go out dead.'

Nineteen

Nuremberg – January 7, 1946

Hadleigh was as good as his word. By 0900 hours a ring of steel surrounded the Palace of Justice, the forecourt jam-packed with tanks, half-tracks, armoured personnel carriers and troops on foot. Snipers were placed on the upper floors of the old Wehrmacht stores HQ opposite the Palace and on the roof of the ventilator company, Exhaustorenwerk, in Maximilianstrasse.

The entrance to the prison where the defendants were held when not in court and which backed on to the Palace was blocked by a 3-ton truck, its open rear facing Reutersbrunnenstrasse. Astride the tailboard two GIs manned a belt-fed heavy machine gun. On either side of the 3-tonner, shielded by the entrance pillars, were bazooka teams. A hundred yards further north the River Pegnitz was patrolled by gunboats.

The judges, their alternates, prosecution and defence counsel and other court officials had been contacted during the night. All had agreed to cooperate by being in the Palace by 0830. Everyone else who had business in court – stenographers, translators, radio and newspaper journalists – had their credentials closely scrutinized before being allowed in. A forgotten pass meant non-admission, with no exceptions, no matter how familiar the face.

It would have been a simple matter to block off the main road on which the Palace stood, Fürtherstrasse, for a hundred yards in either direction, and all side roads emptying into it. But with the full approval of the brass it was decided that the members of Battle Group Sternberg were to be dealt with, if possible, once and for all. If they were foolish enough to make the attempt in spite of the loss of Kleemann and Isken, Third Army did not want to scare them off before they were in the net. Otherwise they might try again tomorrow or the day after, and triple security arrangements could not be repeated without causing major logistical problems all round.

The object was, then, to let them get close but not close enough to do any damage. All tank movements within the area were frozen from 0845, armoured unit commanders being informed unceremoniously that any mobile Sherman approaching the Palace would be fired on without warning.

Hadleigh had wanted to freeze the movements of all vehicles – as the SS were known to be using jeeps – but that was vetoed on the grounds of impracticability. Apart from which it would look unnatural. No vehicle was allowed on to the Palace forecourt after 0900, however.

Since learning of the plot in the small hours, Yuri Petrov had become, in Hadleigh's classic words, 'a royal pain in the terminal excretory opening of the alimentary canal'. The Russian colonel had wanted to draft in several battalions of Soviet troops, and there was a furious row when this was turned down. But Gene Masterson knew only too well that allowing the Soviets in was a hell of a sight easier than getting them out. Petrov had finally agreed with bad grace that security matters should be left to Third Army and CIC, though he made it clear that if a disaster occurred Moscow would know at whose door to lay the blame. Masterson had the distinct impression that the Pravda print workers had already set up their linotype.

AMERICANS STAND IDLY BY WHILE SOVIET JUDGES ARE MURDERED.

By 0930 everyone who had business inside the Palace had been admitted according to the MP lieutenant whose business it was to check off names against a master list. Latecomers were to be turned away, but there were no latecomers. Although only a handful of men knew the reason for the extreme security measures, the peculiar sixth sense that journalists develop over the years had told them that Something Was Up. For the first time since before Christmas every seat in the Press gallery was occupied.

As 10 a.m. approached so did the Third Army's first headache. It began to snow, small flakes to start with but then in earnest. By 10.02 Nuremberg and its environs were in the grip of a blizzard which reduced visibility to twenty or thirty yards.

Huddled deep inside their greatcoats and taking shelter against the elements under the lee of a truck, Hadleigh, Quinlan and Judd were discussing this new problem when Colonel Masterson sought them out.

'Any ideas, Major?' asked Masterson, returning Hadleigh's salute.

'We still have thirty minutes, sir. Maybe it'll blow itself out.'

'Major Quinlan?'

'I can't see them bringing the time forward, sir,' opined Quinlan. 'The judges don't sit and the defendants aren't brought up from their cells until ten-thirty. Even if they wanted to take advantage of the cover this stuff will give them, they'd be blasting a courtroom empty of all VIPs if they tried it on now.' He grunted with disgust. 'I'm starting to believe they're going to carry it through.'

'Safer that way,' said Masterson. 'If nothing happens the men have had a useful exercise. Still, it might be an idea to double the roadside guard. The men on the rooftops won't be able to see a damned thing and a tank could be among us before we knew it.'

'I'll see to it,' offered Hadleigh.

'No, leave it to me.' Masterson winked broadly. 'The infantry are already a touch pissed off that G-2 is running the operation.' He tapped the silver eagle of rank on his shoulder. 'It could take this to get them to do as they're told.'

No sooner had Masterson vanished beyond a curtain of snow than Yuri Petrov appeared, flanked by two Mladshiy Leytenants or Junior Lieutenants. It became obvious at once that he was playing to the gallery, for the benefit of his subalterns. He was guarding his back in case anything went wrong, talking for the record.

'What do you intend doing about the snow, Major Hadleigh?' he asked in German.

Hadleigh saw that the two subalterns understood the language and felt like kicking Petrov between the legs.

'What do you expect me to do, Colonel? Give an order for it to go away?'

'That is insolence, Major, and will be reported as such to your commanding officer.'

Hadleigh gritted his teeth. He needed Yuri Petrov in this mood about as much as he needed an extra head.

'If it sounded insolent, I apologize. But, whatever the representative of the Soviet Union might think, the United States has no control over the weather. We're doubling the guards at the roadside, which is about as much as we can do with the forces available.'

'If Colonel Masterson had accepted my offer of Soviet troops, you would have more than enough men to patrol the entire length of Fürtherstrasse.'

'That's something you should take up with Colonel Masterson.'

'I intend to at the appropriate time. For the moment it is in my written report that my offer of cooperation was rejected by American security. If any harm befalls Major-General Nikitchenko or any other member of the Soviet delegation, there will be the gravest consequences.'

'Stick it in your ear.'

It did not translate well and Petrov asked Hadleigh to repeat himself. The G-2 major did so, laying it on with a trowel.

'Nothing will happen to them,' he said, trying and failing not to lose his temper. He had been up most of the night and this wasn't helping. 'A gnat couldn't get through that cordon. Nor could something the size of the brain of a Russian colonel.'

Petrov turned purple. His eyes bulged with incredulity and the veins in his temple throbbed. He tried to say something, but the words stuck in his throat. His two aides choked back laughter with difficulty.

Quinlan leapt to Hadleigh's defence. Petrov was behaving like a boor, but the American had overstepped the bounds of propriety.

'If I may have a word with you in private, Colonel Petrov.'

Petrov allowed himself to be led to one side, where he and Quinlan put their heads together and held a whispered conversation. Finally the Russian nodded and beckoned curtly to his lieutenants. The three of them disappeared through the snow.

'Thanks,' said Hadleigh. 'What did you say to him?'

'I told him you were thinking of importing a couple of girls from the French Zone and that one of them had a title. If he wanted to continue receiving invitations it might be as well if he forgot all about the last couple of minutes. You know what

197

a snob he is. I also told him he could safely leave security in your hands.'

'I wish I was that confident,' said Hadleigh moodily. 'Thanks again, but this snow is a real pain.'

'It's the same for them as it is for us.'

'Maybe so, but there's a little worm gnawing away at my guts that's warning me they're one jump ahead of us again.'

Quinlan did not reply. It wouldn't help Hadleigh's incipient ulcer by voicing his fears, but he too felt that Battle Group Sternberg had an ace up its sleeve.

The same blizzard that was whiting out central Nuremberg also blanketed the satellite town of Fürth as Sternberg, Riordan and the others left the back-up house at 10.15, slightly ahead of schedule because the snow, though useful in other respects, would slow them down.

Sternberg, Riordan, Zander and Hannah were packed into the first jeep, with Hallam at the wheel. Scharper was in command of the second vehicle, with Granger driving.

Although the most direct route to Nuremberg was Fürther strasse, this was not the road they took. Instead they crossed the River Pegnitz west of Stadt Park. From there they would drive through the suburbs of Doos and Schniegling, skirt the cemetery using Schnieglingerstrasse, and enter Nuremberg from the north.

During the last forty-eight hours Riordan and Hallam had made the run several times, simulating various kinds of hold-up. Allowing for the snow they should be at the destination within a couple of minutes either way of 10.30.

Sitting in the back between Sternberg and Zander and wearing a hooded grey cloak identical to her own, which one of her captors had produced from God knows where, Hannah listened in silence while the silver-haired SS officer repeated her part in the coming proceedings, reiterating his warning that she would be killed out of hand if she attempted to raise the alarm. She believed him. She also now understood why they hadn't harmed her in any way. But she did not expect to come out of the morning alive regardless of heavy hints that they would free her once her usefulness was at an end, and she was determined to make a run for it if the opportunity presented itself.

Riordan asked over his shoulder if Scharper and the others in the second jeep had had it impressed upon them that on no account were submachine guns to be used. There had been trouble over this earlier, Scharper and Flisk arguing that it was pointless having automatic weapons if they were to be left in the jeeps. But finally Riordan had got his way. It would be service revolvers for those in officers' uniforms and rifles for the enlisted men. The submachine guns were to remain in the care of the drivers, Hallam and Granger, to be used only in the event of an emergency.

Sternberg confirmed that Scharper and Flisk would obey orders.

'How is it going on time?' he asked.

Riordan checked his watch and peered through the windshield in an attempt to identify a landmark. He also glanced at the speedo.

'We're running a bit behind.'

'Snow's worse than I thought,' said Hallam, concentrating fiercely on what he could see of the road ahead.

'We can afford to be a little late,' said Sternberg. 'What we can't afford is going into a ditch.'

'We can't really afford either,' said Riordan. 'Let's not under-estimate the Americans. Whatever else they are, they're not fools.'

That sentiment was not shared by Ben Hadleigh as the clock ticked up to 10.30 without any sign of anything happening. It was mostly on his say-so that several hundred extra troops and a couple of million dollars' worth of hardware now surrounded the Palace of Justice. Sure, the brass and Gene Masterson had taken the final decision, but it was on his recommendation. Well, his and Quinlan's, but Quinlan had practically no official capacity here. He was virtually a freelance roped in for the occasion.

Hadleigh could visualize the entry on his service sheet. 'This officer is prone to acting hastily and on insufficient data.'

At 10.32, with the snow still falling in huge lumps, he sent Max to find Gene Masterson.

'They won't be running on schedule,' said Quinlan, reading his mind.

'They won't be running at all,' lamented Hadleigh bitterly.

199

'They've called the whole thing off, as I should have concluded last night. With Kleemann and Isken in the cooler they decided not to risk it. It was a near-hopeless scheme in the first place. It became impossible once we had two of their men. Gene Masterson's going to have my balls for doorstops. They've put it off until another day, when they think our guard's down. More likely they've shelved it for good.'

Quinlan said that there was still plenty of time and added that the sort of men they were up against were not the kind to give up without a fight.

Hadleigh disagreed.

'It's precisely because they *are* who they are that they'll back off now they suspect the odds are stacked against them. Murdering a defenceless woman and a young girl and kidnapping Hannah doesn't put them in the hero league.'

'Perhaps not, but even if we weren't ready for them they'd have suffered casualties. You heard what Kleemann said last night, that he was prepared to attack regardless of the consequences. They might have got close enough to loose off a couple of rounds from the Sherman's big gun before anyone grasped what the hell was going on, maybe even kill a few people in the courtroom, but they'd have been cut down pretty fast after that. We may call it fanaticism, even lunacy, but we've got to grant there's an element of bravery involved. Some of them would have got the chop.'

'Not if they used the tank to make the kill, then escaped in the jeeps during the confusion,' argued Hadleigh. 'They'd have been wearing Allied uniforms, don't forget, and most of the GIs around here would think twice before shooting at a friendly uniform and a tank with US markings. If we hadn't grabbed Kleemann and Isken there's a sporting chance they'd have pulled it off without a single casualty. A few quick rounds from the Sherman then away in the jeeps. If Kleemann and Isken didn't make it, that's tough titty. It's my guess they were selected for their devotion to the cause and were expendable. The whole affair would have been over in a minute.'

'You're forgetting that they were also planning to release some of the defendants.'

Hadleigh shook his head, mystified.

'That's the bit that doesn't make sense. In and out I can

understand, a swift offensive and a swifter retreat. But trying for the animals is living in cloud-cuckoo land. What the hell would they do with them? Why the hell would they want them? Goering was sacked by Hitler and discredited towards the end of the war. He was lucky not to be shot by the SS. Why would they want to save him? He might be a pretty big man in the dock, but that's only because Hitler, Himmler, Goebbels and Bormann are either dead or in hiding. Goering wouldn't rate the first team if we had the others.

'Then there's Hess. He's been a traitor in every true Nazi's eyes since he flew to England in 'forty-one. He's also a little crazy. Why would the SS want him except to put a noose around his neck? Keitel and Jodl are Army, Raeder and Dönitz Navy. Frank claims he's found Jesus and the first thing Rosenberg would need is a stiff drink, preferably from something the size of a bucket. The only man the SS could conceivably be interested in as one of their own is Kalten-brunner and....'

Hadleigh's jaw dropped a foot when he realized the full implication of what he was saying. He gaped like a gaffed salmon at Quinlan, whose expression altered from one of the bewilderment to one of horror as the penny finally dropped.

Obergruppenfuehrer Ernst Kaltenbrunner, head of the SS Reich Main Security Office and second man on the totem pole to Himmler, was not in the dock. *He wasn't even in the prison*. He was in hospital, the Hallerwiese-Klinik. Battle Group Sternberg was playing its hidden ace on the other side of the Pegnitz, a mile and a half away in Hallerwiese. The BFC involvement was still unexplained, but there was no doubt in either of their minds that they'd been duped.

Suddenly Hadleigh was yelling at the top of his voice for Max and Gene Masterson. Even as they appeared through the snowstorm Quinlan was racing for the nearest jeep.

It was a set-up. He couldn't prove it yet but it was highly likely Kleemann and Isken were not privy to the real plan. Hadleigh was right about their expendability. They'd been deliberately sacrificed by their superiors, who knew they would break under interrogation. How he and Hadleigh were out-guessed, how Sternberg had known he was sending Kleemann and Isken into a trap, would have to wait until later. But there was never a plot to hit the Palace of Justice, kill the judges. No wonder the whole scheme had seemed like lunacy. It *was* lunacy! All along they had intended going for Kaltenbrunner, who was conveniently suffering from some sort of illness, who had been in hospital once or twice before and who was now there again. It was common knowledge where he was. Although he was under guard, anyone who cared to listen to the news bulletins knew he was in the Hallerwiese-Klinik, the hospital where Hannah Wolz had worked during the war. Quinlan did not understand what that meant yet, but there was a connection between it and not finding her dead beside Willi Meissner. There had to be.

Battle Group Sternberg arrived at the Hallerwiese-Klinik at 10.42, twelve minutes adrift of their deadline owing to road conditions. Even so they did not hurry but parked the two jeeps side by side on the forecourt, as though they were just ordinary visitors.

Under the pretext of paying a call on a sick friend, in his British officer's uniform Riordan had checked out the hospital as soon as they learned Kaltenbrunner was in there. He hadn't managed to get anywhere near the former Obergruppenfuehrer, but he knew Kaltenbrunner occupied a private room on the second floor of the wing that overlooked Hallerwiese. A couple of friendly questions to a chatty houseman had elicited the information that the guard surrounding him was pitifully small; two GIs outside the door and another in the room. The Americans were less concerned about someone trying to liberate him than a suicide attempt.

It was sheer good fortune on cross-examining Hannah Wolz the previous day to discover that she had worked for the DRK in the hospital, but she was going to be an invaluable smokescreen, dressed as she was in the nurse's cloak. Less luck and more judgment was involved in convincing Scharper they couldn't walk in waving submachine guns. Someone would certainly stop them and ask what their business was, which would not do at all. It was all to be accomplished softly-softly. Up the stairs, along the corridor, deal with the external guards, inside, incapacitate the remaining guard and snatch Kaltenbrunner. There was to be no shooting except as a very last resort. Gunshots would bring people running, reduce their chances of escape. Ideally, no one should know

Kaltenbrunner was gone until the time came for his next medication or guard change.

Only four of them and Hannah were to go in; any more and they would resemble the raiding party they were.

Riordan was to go because he knew the lay-out of the hospital and had grown accustomed to being seen in public as a Royal Artillery captain. Scharper and Zander were to go because they both knew Kaltenbrunner from the old days and would be able to convince him, should he have any doubts about accompanying them, what was in his best interests. Laidlaw was to go because they needed an extra man whose native tongue was English and because he had drawn the uniform of a private in the Royal Army Medical Corps.

Hallam and Granger were staying behind as drivers of the jeeps. Flisk was remaining because he was without doubt the toughest member of the battle group. If a rearguard action had to be fought, Flisk was the man for that. It had been a toss-up whether Sternberg, who also knew Kaltenbrunner from the war years, or Scharper stayed outside. In the end Sternberg pulled rank. If it became a matter of getting out in a hurry, he knew where he wanted to be.

It was 10.43 when Riordan led the way through the entrance doors, past the row of invalid wheelchairs which would no longer be needed, one hand gripping Hannah's elbow. With an irritable gesture that was not entirely feigned he waved aside a uniformed porter who seemed about to ask if he could help them.

Also at 10.43 a small convoy of vehicles, klaxons blaring, crossed the River Pegnitz via Johanniserbrücken and swung right into Grossweidenmühlstrasse, half a mile from the hospital. In the leading jeep, with Max Judd at the wheel, were Quinlan, Hadleigh and Gene Masterson, the last furious that in all the preparations and conferences during the small hours no one had seen the wood for the trees. So convinced were they that the Palace of Justice was the target that no one had even considered Kaltenbrunner. It was the sort of oversight that had lost many a battle in the past and might do so again. He hoped the orders he had given for someone to call the hospital immediately and warn the guards that under no circumstances was *anyone* to go near Kaltenbrunner were being obeyed. He would not find out until later that the blizzard had brought down numerous telephone cables and that the hospital's number was registering as unobtainable, taking years off the life of the second lieutenant delegated with the task of getting through.

Hadleigh urged Max to go faster, but it was impossible in the conditions. Already a truckful of troops three vehicles behind had ploughed into the south side of Johanniserbrücken, blocking the bridge. Further back in his own stationary staff car, not knowing what was going on because no one had found time to tell him, Yuri Petrov was screaming at the junior lieutenant driving to do something.

Twenty

Nuremberg – January 7, 1946

On reaching the second floor unopposed, Riordan called for a momentary halt. The next couple of minutes were the most dangerous and Hannah Wolz could balls it up for them all if she failed fully to understand the consequences of any foolhardy action on her part.

'You look like a nurse,' he whispered fiercely, 'behave like one. If there's any shooting you'll be the first to die.'

Hannah nodded her acceptance of the conditions. She remembered this part of the hospital well. Nothing had changed. Unfortunately the corridors in the west wing all led away from the central staircase and lifts. There were no exits at the furthermost ends apart from fire escapes. To get at them it was necessary to open a heavy door, which would take time. But she'd try that or something else if they took their eyes off her.

The corridor containing Kaltenbrunner's room was some fifty yards long. Riordan peered through the glass partition in the swing-doors. It was as the houseman had told him. Two GIs were lounging outside a door at the far end, seemingly bored to tears. There was no other sign of life.

'Let's go,' he said over his shoulder.

The GIs, both Pfcs, glanced up as they heard the swing-doors swish open. It was a motley crew coming towards them. A British captain, a US lieutenant, a US sergeant and a British medic. And a very lovely girl whose cloak was still wet from the snow.

'Looks like the pig's got visitors,' muttered one.

'Not according to the schedule,' said the other, but he was reassured by Hannah's cloak.

Riordan caught the last sentence and knew he had to get the guards off balance and keep them that way. When he was still fifteen feet away he called: 'It's about time you challenged me, isn't it?'

Both sentries sprang to attention at his imperious tone. Neither wanted to go on report for failing to observe SOP.

'We were just about to do that, Captain,' said the first Pfc, but by then the quintet was level with them.

No one had to tell Scharper and Kurt Zander what to do next. They had rehearsed this a score of times in the Grossreuth common-room, with Hallam and Granger taking the part of the sentinels. They had to get themselves and the Americans out of the corridor without too much noise before someone appeared from an adjacent room, a nurse or a doctor.

While the two young GIs' attention was on Riordan, who was fumbling in his tunic pocket for a non-existent laissez-passer, Scharper and Zander slipped behind them, the former drawing his pistol, the latter reversing his rifle so that the butt was forward. They were all swift, clean movements occupying only fractions of seconds; so were the savage blows to the base of each skull which felled the guards. There was a muted 'Hey' from one of them before the lights went out, but that was all.

Scharper and Zander caught them before they hit the ground, but there was a clatter of dropped weapons which was only partly covered by Riordan hammering on Kaltenbrunner's door with his fist. He pushed Hannah ahead of him as he barged in.

Kaltenbrunner and his bedside guard were not alone. A doctor was examining the Obergruppenfuehrer, who was lying on the bed, naked to the waist. The three men looked up in alarm at the sudden intrusion, in time to see Scharper and Zander drag the unconscious bodies of their victims into the room and shut the door.

The bedside guard was sitting on a chair several feet from Kaltenbrunner, chewing gum and nursing his M1 carbine across his knees. It took a moment for it to register with him what was happening, but when it did he tried to get to his feet and swing the carbine into a firing position. He was several seconds too late on both counts.

As an RAMC private and therefore a non-combatant, Laidlaw was not permitted under international law to bear arms. The rifle he carried slung over his shoulder when he entered the hospital should have told an intelligent observer that all was not well, but arming him was a risk they had all accepted to take for two reasons. The first was that extra firepower might be needed at some juncture; the second because the Scot had categorically refused to be the only man in the battle group without a weapon.

In the event, before the bedside guard was even halfway out of his seat Laidlaw had slammed him across the temple with the rifle muzzle, knocking him to the floor and causing a fearful open wound. For good measure he followed up with several vicious kicks to the side of the head.

While this was going on Riordan had dealt with the doctor, pistol-whipping him into insensibility. A French civilian, part of the team which was endeavouring to ascertain what, precisely, was wrong with Kaltenbrunner, the physician was no match for Riordan's brute strength.

So far the whole action had occupied no more than forty-five seconds, and inside the room not a word had been uttered. Now Scharper decided it was time to make his voice heard. Judging by the look of horror on Kaltenbrunner's face, he thought the newcomers were an Allied assassination squad, here to settle the matter of his non-appearance in dock once and for all.

'It's Scharper, Herr Obergruppenfuehrer,' he said. 'Do you remember me? We've met many times.'

The lantern-jawed Kaltenbrunner, a giant of a man at over six and half feet tall, may have been genuinely ill but for the moment he was as mentally sound as anyone on trial for his life could be.

'Of course I remember you,' he said in his Austrian accent. 'Zander also. I don't know these other two or the woman.'

Scharper explained quickly that Riordan and Laidlaw were friends, formerly British Free Corps; they'd discussed the necessity of using such individuals last year, before the war ended. The girl was not to be trusted; she was a hostage.

Kaltenbrunner had a thousand questions, but Scharper cut them off as politely as he could.

'Later, Herr Obergruppenfuehrer. For the present we must hurry, get you out of here. Do you have street clothes?'

'No. The bastards took them away from me.'

'No matter. A dressing-gown?'

'In the cupboard.'

'Excellent. You'll be a little cold for a while, but cold is better than the alternative.'

'You have a plan?'

'It was originally to bandage your head and take you through the front entrance in an invalid chair, but the blizzard is an unforeseen bonus. We won't risk the front. We'll use the fire escape. The snow will cover our movements.'

Kaltenbrunner was on his feet now, towering above the others. There was something of the natural successor to Heydrich in his manner as he attempted to compose himself, something that chilled the blood. But his voice still held a note of incredulity when he asked if they had really come to free him.

'Of course,' answered Scharper. 'Did you ever doubt it?'

'At times. I expected someone to try when I was in hospital before.'

'We were not ready and the other place was too well guarded.'

Kaltenbrunner permitted himself a glimmer of a smile.

'And doubtless you were hoping to find all the fragments before the tenth, which would have made my rescue superfluous. It's as I thought, Scharper, precisely as I thought.'

It was also too close to the truth as far as Scharper was concerned.

'Quickly now,' he urged, handing Kaltenbrunner his robe. 'There's no time to waste.'

Nor was there, for even as Scharper was speaking they all heard the wail of klaxons several storeys below, leaving no one in doubt that the Americans had at last tumbled the Palace of Justice stratagem.

'You've left it a little late, Scharper,' said Kaltenbrunner.

'Ask him for the number,' prompted Riordan, talking as though Kaltenbrunner were not present. 'Ask him for the number contained in the fragments.'

Not bothering to don the robe and seemingly in no hurry, Kaltenbrunner shot Riordan a look that would have withered lesser men.

'You'll hear no number from my lips, whoever the hell you are. Do you think I'm a fool? The information I possess is my sole remaining bargaining counter with the Allies. I would have preferred to be free so that we could all enjoy the fruits of earlier labours, but don't underestimate my intelligence or think captivity has softened my brain. You wouldn't be here now if you had solved the Canaris riddle.'

Gesturing Zander to check the corridor, Scharper noted with dismay the use of the past tense—' I would have preferred to be free.'

'With respect, Herr Obergruppenfuehrer,' he said, 'your release is of paramount importance to those of us who served under you in the SS. As you point out, the information in your possession could be used to bargain with the Allies. Even if we had successfully recovered the fragments there would be nothing to prevent you telling your story to the *Amis* before the tenth.'

Kaltenbrunner wasn't buying it.

'You're a plausible individual, Scharper, but then you always were. I do not, however, need a crystal ball to read your mind. If you had obtained the number the documents would have disappeared. The Americans would then have thought they were listening to the ravings of a madman looking for ways to save his neck. They'd have had to take my word that what I was telling them was the truth and,' he smiled grimly, 'I do not think they're inclined to take my word on that or any other matter.'

'Corridor's clear,' called Zander from the door.

'We've no time for all this shit,' grunted Riordan, addressing Scharper. 'If he won't tell us, he won't. Let's get him to hell out of here.'

But Kaltenbrunner refused to move. Instead of putting on the robe he allowed it to fall to the floor and sat on the edge of the bed.

'You're too late. You don't stand a chance of getting me out the building alive. Do you really believe they won't have thought of the fire escapes? You've missed your opportunity by ten minutes.'

Scharper was sweating now.

'Herr Obergruppenfuehrer, you *must* come with us. The blizzard will give us cover. We have transport on the forecourt, where Standartenfuehrer Sternberg is waiting. But we must hurry.'

'So, Sternberg is still alive.'

'He is – and anxious for your safety.'

Kaltenbrunner snorted with laughter.

'The only thing Sternberg was ever anxious about is his own skin. And you mistake your man if you think he won't make a run for it as soon as he senses danger.'

He was in a different world, Kaltenbrunner, only half cognizant of where he was. His eyes were glassy and there was a fleck of spittle on his chin when he repeated that the opportunity to flee had gone.

'The Americans would like nothing better than to shoot me while trying to escape. They can't handle me, you know. I'm too quick for them, unlike those fools Hess and Goering.'

Scharper stared at Riordan, horrified. There *was* something wrong with Kaltenbrunner's mind, moments of lucidity followed by moments of insanity. It wasn't merely his own scheming that had contrived to get him into hospital. And he was planning to stay behind, sell out to the Allies in the hope of beating the gallows.

In the distance Riordan thought he could hear shouting. They had to move, Kaltenbrunner or not. But if Himmler's deputy wouldn't give them the key to the Canaris fragments he would not be giving it to anyone else either.

He cocked his revolver.

'We'll have to kill him.'

It took a moment for it to sink in, but when it did Scharper's reaction was not at all what Riordan expected.

'You can't.'

Riordan turned the Webley on him.

'What do you mean, can't? We've still got three days with him dead. Alive and talking to the Yanks it's all over now.'

Scharper was reaching for his own sidearm, a Colt .45 automatic. Kaltenbrunner was the senior SS general alive, the natural successor to the Fuehrer and Himmler. There were thousands, perhaps tens of thousands of former SS men still free, some in South America, others in Germany and elsewhere in Europe. One day, when their so-called crimes were forgotten, they would all meet again. Heinrich Scharper did not want to be known as the man who collaborated in the killing of the keeper of the flame, in spite of what was at stake. They had a few more minutes. They'd get Kaltenbrunner out somehow.

'You can't do that.'

Riordan's eyes were on the Colt, which Scharper was beginning to point in his direction. Whether the German intended using it or whether it was merely a warning, he didn't wait to find out. Christ, he thought, they're all fucking mad, and shot Scharper in the chest. The bullet's impact hurled him backwards like a discarded rag doll.

The sound of the explosion was deafening and, because it was so totally unexpected, momentarily shocked everyone into immobility. But that state of affairs did not last long.

While Scharper clutched his chest and stared with utter disbelief at the blood oozing through his fingers, Kaltenbrunner leapt from the bed and made for the door that led to the bathroom. Riordan spun round and loosed off a couple of shots in that direction, but he was too late. Half crazy or not, Kaltenbrunner was a past master in the art of self-preservation. Riordan heard the bathroom lock spring into place.

With Laidlaw temporarily frozen to the spot and a thunderstruck Zander bending over Scharper, who was moaning incoherently, the path to the corridor was now clear. Hannah made the most of it, realizing she would never get a better opportunity. While Riordan strode over to the bathroom door, intending to shoot off the lock and put paid to Kaltenbrunner once and for all, she raced for the door, slamming it behind her and running up the passage in the direction of the central staircase. Halfway there the swing-doors were thrown open and a posse of uniformed men charged through, headed by Quinlan, Hadleigh and Gene Masterson. Behind her she heard shots being fired.

'Get down!' screamed Quinlan, but when she did so it was involuntary, as she collapsed in a dead faint.

From their position on the forecourt Sternberg and the others in the two jeeps had seen the Americans arrive. They too had heard the klaxons in the distance, but the convoy was upon them before they could move. Hallam wanted them to take their chances and drive off immediately, but Sternberg counselled patience. Apart from the fact that Scharper might appear any second with Kaltenbrunner, the Americans must know they had jeeps. Any vehicle travelling against the general flow of traffic would be stopped, its occupants questioned. In a few more minutes the forecourt would be chaos. Whether Kaltenbrunner had arrived or not, with visibility still no more than twenty or thirty yards that would be the time to get out.

Neither Quinlan nor Hadleigh knew the lay-out of the hospital, but Masterson had conducted an interrogation of a dying German civilian here several months ago and recalled that there were fire escapes and at least three other exits apart from the main doors. Most of the convoy was still held up at the bridge, but they had sufficient numbers to cordon off the building.

Leaving Max to organize and deploy the ground troops, and tracked by Quinlan, Masterson and half a dozen GIs, Hadleigh led the way through the main entrance. Without breaking stride he demanded Kaltenbrunner's whereabouts from the startled porter, pulling the man along with him by the lapel when he had difficulty in finding his voice. Valuable seconds were wasted while the elderly German stammered out the required information, adding that four men in a

211

mixture of Anglo-American uniforms and a girl dressed like a nurse had entered the hospital a few minutes earlier.

They reached the second floor and pushed through the swing-doors in time to see Hannah racing towards them. As Quinlan yelled at her to get down three figures emerged one after the other from a room at the far end of the corridor, shooting wildly as they made for the fire escape exit.

Quinlan shouted not to return the shots for fear of hitting Hannah at the same moment she fell. He was crouched over her within seconds, his emotions an amalgam of anxiety and relief. But she was unhurt. Her mind had simply given up the unequal struggle with the bedlam around her. When he looked up the last of the fugitives was going through the heavy door, closing it behind him.

While Masterson went into Kaltenbrunner's room, Hadleigh ordered one of the GIs to return to the ground floor, find Max Judd and tell him that three men were making a run for it via the western fire escape. He instructed the rest of his men not to charge through yet.

'Just in case one of them's waiting for us on the other side. They're not going any place.'

That wasn't quite true. Outside, it was impossible to see for more than a few yards in any direction, but Riordan suspected, as Kaltenbrunner had done, that the Americans would have the fire escapes covered. The game was up. It was time to look after number one.

'We still stand a chance if we're fast,' he said, head bent against the snow. 'You first, Harry. Once you're on the ground make for the road and come on to the forecourt as though you've just arrived. If Sternberg didn't get out when he heard the klaxons, it's my guess he's still where we left him. If not it's every man for himself. I'll see you at the jeeps. Shake it up, for Chrissake,' he snapped when Laidlaw hesitated.

After a moment's indecision the Scot nodded and started down. Soon he was lost in the snow.

'Now you, Zander. I'll be tail-end Charlie in case they try to break through the door. Move it!'

It would have been a simple matter for Riordan to knock Zander cold, but that didn't suit his plans. He needed confusion on the ground and Laidlaw alone wouldn't create enough.

'Do you go next or do I?' he demanded, when the German seemed reluctant to move. 'If you don't want the second spot I'll take it. You guard our rear.'

But the idea of being left alone did not appeal to Zander. Besides, he wanted to report to Sternberg that Riordan had shot and perhaps killed Scharper. If the Englishman got there first the story would come out differently.

Without a word he slung his rifle over his shoulder and followed Laidlaw.

Riordan waited until he disappeared before starting upwards, using the fire escape to climb to the fourth floor. At the third he heard rifle shots followed immediately by the unmistakable sound of automatic weapons. So much for Zander and Laidlaw.

At fourth-floor level he levered up the iron bar of the fire escape door and stepped into the hospital. There was a hell of a din coming from below, but the corridor here was quite empty.

Pausing only to holster his pistol and brush as much snow as possible from his tunic, he made his way towards the central staircase. There was no one on the second-floor swing-doors but quite a commotion coming from beyond. He did not stop to investigate.

He gained the first floor without incident, but was then confronted by three GIs coming up the stairs, taking them two at a time.

'Major Hadleigh wants you to check the third-floor east wing in case they've slipped through,' he told them.

They nodded their understanding but apart from that didn't give him a second glance.

The entrance lobby was a madhouse, with more GIs – the bridge now unblocked – arriving by the minute. White-coated doctors, nurses and administrative staff were trying to ascertain just what the devil was going on. One of the doctors, a German by the looks of him, was older and seemed more senior than the others. Riordan buttonholed him.

'I need your help,' he said quietly, coolly walking the German away from the group.

Fortunately the doctor spoke good English.

'What is happening? Why are all these soldiers here?'

'There's been an attempt on the life of your most notorious guest.'

'Kaltenbrunner?'

'Kaltenbrunner. Whoever tried to kill him may still be on the premises. We have to make certain all the exits are covered. Is there a back way out?'

'Of course. Through the kitchens.'

Riordan was about to ask the doctor to show him the route when he realized he was making a mistake. Undoubtedly covered by now, anyone trying the kitchen exit was sure to arouse suspicion. It was a moment to be bold or nothing. No one was taking the least notice of him in the lobby.

'Perhaps you could show me all the exits from the outside,' he said. 'I want to be sure we've men on each and that ground-floor windows are covered. I'm sorry you're likely to get damp, but this is an emergency.'

Head down and talking total gobbledegook to the doctor about security, Riordan's egress via the main entrance was half barred by a Pfc carrying an M1. But the youngster's heart wasn't in it. This plainly wasn't the enemy he had been briefed to detain. He'd heard there was a Limey officer on the team. This must be him.

Virtually without breaking off his monologue to the doctor, Riordan grabbed the Pfc by the arm before he could ask for identification and ordered him to accompany them. There were other guards on the main doors and the Pfc allowed himself to be carried along.

Outside, pandemonium reigned, with vehicles arriving every few seconds. This reassured Riordan as he propelled the doctor and the GI towards the forecourt. If Sternberg hadn't already left before the balloon went up, he wouldn't be trying to get out now.

Although the storm was breaking slightly, visibility was still down to a hundred and fifty feet when Riordan saw the jeeps where he had left them. Telling the Pfc to go with the doctor, make sure all exits and low-level windows were covered before reporting back to the lobby, Riordan let them disappear before ambling over to Sternberg's jeep. He indicated with a movement of his hand that Granger and Flisk were to remain in their own vehicle for the present.

Sternberg looked about ready to throw a fit when Riordan loomed up and climbed inside. In as few words as it took, he told the SS colonel and Hallam that Kaltenbrunner had refused to accompany them at the last moment, refused also to reveal the number contained in the fragments. The man was undoubtedly mad. Zander, Laidlaw and Scharper were either dead or in custody. He didn't bother to point out that he had shot Scharper, nor that, if Laidlaw and Zander were dead, he was the one who had sent them to their graves.

'I was lucky to get this far myself,' he finished, all the while peering through the windshield for signs of anyone taking too close an interest in them.

'What about the girl?' asked Sternberg.

'She escaped in the confusion. I fired at her and saw her fall, but I don't know whether I hit her.'

'If she's alive she'll tell the *Amis* about the Fürth house.'

'Of course.'

'There's always the one in Zirndorf,' put in Hallam.

'I think it's a bit late in the day for that,' said Riordan. 'Kaltenbrunner left me in no doubt that he'll spill what he knows to the Americans in an attempt to save his skin.'

'You should have killed him,' grunted Sternberg, ever the realist.

Riordan debated whether to say he had tried to do just that, but eventually decided not to. It was of no consequence, not now.

'There wasn't the opportunity. Anyway, it's as we always feared, why we're here today. The question is, what to do next. In my opinion we should get out of Nuremberg and move the stuff. We'll then have to make the best deal we can, as fast as we can.'

'I'd settle for getting away from this fucking hospital,' muttered Hallam. 'The snow's thinning and before long someone's going to get curious about why we're sitting here while everyone else is running his nuts off.'

They got a break then. A couple of brighter than average MPs were trying to unsnarl the traffic jam in front of the hospital by creating a two-way stream, directing trucks off the forecourt as soon as they had disgorged their loads.

'Join the tail-end,' Riordan ordered Hallam when he saw

what was happening, signalling Granger in the adjacent jeep to follow their lead.

It was 11.06 when they turned right on to Hallerwiese. At 11.10, after feeding the now-conscious Hannah a slug of brandy from a hip-flask and getting her to answer the most important of the many questions they had, Hadleigh gave instructions to stop and search all vehicles leaving the grounds. But by then it was too late.

Twenty-one

Nuremberg – January 7, 1945

Although it would be several hours before they learned from the despondent Pfc that he had been duped by a phoney British captain, towards midday news filtered through about the two jeeps leaving the forecourt shortly after 11 a.m., vehicles that no one could account for. It still had to be proved who the occupants were, but Hadleigh was in no doubt that the surviving SS and British Free Corps men had slipped through the net.

Adding up the score in a first-floor office made available to them by the hospital's chief administrator, on the plus side Kaltenbrunner's three guards and his doctor were in no danger and would recover after treatment. Hannah Wolz was unharmed though considerably shaken after her ordeal. As her captors had not intended her to survive the raid on the hospital, they had not seen fit to blindfold her going to and from the Fürth back-up house. Being herself an old resident of Fürth she was therefore able to give Hadleigh its exact location. He had already dispatched a search team, but he didn't expect to find anything. He was right. The birds had flown.

Of the two men shot at the foot of the fire escape, one (who would later be identified as Laidlaw) had died instantly; the other (Zander) had chest and head wounds and was not expected to live through the afternoon.

The man found shot in Kaltenbrunner's room had been lucky. The bullet had richocheted off his fourth rib and passed cleanly through his body, missing the vital organs. He was in the process of being patched up and fed pain-killers, and would be available for interrogation within the hour.

The biggest plus, however, was that the rescue of Kaltenbrunner had failed. For a few anxious seconds earlier, not seeing him in his bedroom, they thought it had not. Then Quinlan heard tiny animal noises coming from the bathroom. On breaking down the door, for the man on the other side would not respond to commands to open it, they found Kaltenbrunner curled up on the floor, shivering and whimpering. When he realized his 'rescuers' had vanished and that he was not to be executed out of hand nor in any other manner mistreated, he recovered his composure with an alacrity that was truly astonishing, assuming an arrogant, dictatorial posture that would have told any psychiatrist the subject was a psychopath.

Clearing the immediate area of everyone who had no real business there took a few minutes, by which time Yuri Petrov had turned up. In the presence of the Soviet colonel, Hadleigh and Quinlan, Gene Masterson demanded a few answers, such as whether Kaltenbrunner had known that an attempt was to be made to liberate him and just what the hell was going on anyway.

Kaltenbrunner refused to tell them anything, though he hinted he had much to impart. He needed guarantees, however. He was being charged on three counts: crimes against peace, war crimes, and crimes against humanity. He made no bones about saying that he thought he could beat the first rap, that of planning, initiating and waging a war of aggression, as he was too low on the totem pole in the beginning to be privy to the higher counsel chambers of the

Third Reich. That charge could therefore remain on the indictment, but he wanted the other two dropped. In exchange (which would be tantamount to a reprieve), he would tell the Americans all they wanted to know.

The conversation was conducted in German and Petrov spluttered with indignation throughout, interrupting frequently to say that no deal could be made with war criminals without incurring the wrath of the Soviet people and government. So vehement did his objections become, ruining any chance that Kaltenbrunner could be persuaded to talk without concessions, that Masterson was compelled to pull him to one side and remind him sharply that he was in the US Zone. The United States was not in the habit of exchanging clemency for information with former Nazis, unlike the Soviet Union who interrogated every captured German of any rank at length, judging his future value to the People's cause. Ex-Nazis were only shot or hanged or turned over for trial if they proved uncooperative or useless. It was being rumoured in the French, British and American Zones that Gestapo Chief Heinrich Mueller, a known admirer of the Russian NKVD, was in Soviet hands. The word was that he was proving extremely helpful and, past sins being forgotten in this new world of *realpolitik*, in the process of becoming the number two or three man in Soviet Intelligence.

Petrov denied the allegation categorically, but conceded he might have been hasty in judging the American position. He had not meant to imply that Colonel Masterson would accede to Kaltenbrunner's terms.

Masterson did not inform the Russian that the decision was not his to take. His own reaction was to tell Kaltenbrunner to stick it in his ear, that he was going to swing with the rest of them. But he had a duty to pass on the offer, let the brass decide what to do. He had little doubt what the answer would be.

They left a guard on Kaltenbrunner, and it was on the way out that Quinlan tossed in his bombshell. In the excitement everyone had forgotten about the fragments. Now Quinlan remembered them.

'We know about Tristan da Cunha,' he said.

After seven months in captivity Kaltenbrunner's complexion was pasty enough, but if it was possible he grew paler.

'I don't know what you're talking about,' he said, but it was quite obvious he did. The trouble was, *they* didn't know what they were talking about.

It was this and the implications of Tristan da Cunha that Masterson, Hadleigh, Quinlan and Petrov were discussing in the first-floor office as the wall clock ticked up to 12.30. Masterson would have preferred Petrov to have taken a walk, but there was no earthly chance the Russian was going to do that. Neither could Masterson suggest it, for Petrov would have immediately suspected underhand dealings and cried conspiracy. Paranoia was an endemic characteristic of the Soviet Union.

The snowstorm had blown itself out for the moment and as a matter of priority Third Army engineers had traced the damaged cables connecting the hospital to the outside world and repaired them. Unwilling to leave the scene for fear Petrov would make an excuse to draft in hosts of Soviet 'advisers', Masterson had scribbled a résumé of Kaltenbrunner's proposals on a page of diary and entrusted Max Judd with its delivery to General Lucian K. Truscott. Max had returned ten minutes ago with the news that General Truscott had been in conference when he arrived but that his adjutant had promised to hand the envelope personally to the general at the first available opportunity. They should hear any time now what the reaction of Third Army brass was to Kaltenbrunner's bid for immunity.

Quinlan was repeating his assertion, with which no one was arguing, that the rescue attempt on Kaltenbrunner was because he had the information otherwise revealed by deciphering the Canaris fragments, when Max knocked and came in. He apologized for the intrusion but said that Fräulein Wolz wanted to see Major Quinlan if it was possible. After her experiences of the past twenty-four hours Hannah should, strictly speaking, have been sedated and allowed to sleep the clock round. Quinlan had persuaded her to stay awake a while longer, saying he'd talk to her as soon as they'd finished with Kaltenbrunner. She had agreed, but one of the doctors had overruled her request a couple of minutes ago, said Max, and made her swallow something.

Quinlan excused himself.

'Thanks, Max,' he said outside. 'Where is she?'

'Third floor east, the door with a guard on it. I put a man there just to be on the safe side.'

She was lying among a mountain of pillows, staring out of the window. She looked beautiful and fragile and still a little scared as he came in. Taking the chair next to the bed he resisted the temptation to reach out and touch her hands, which were lying on top of the covers. He felt awkward. Apart from this morning he hadn't seen her since taking her to the Sündersbühl house on their return from Munich, which seemed a lifetime ago.

'In England we usually bring flowers or grapes when we visit hospitals,' he said. 'I'm sorry I arrive empty-handed.'

'It doesn't matter. Is it all over now?'

'Not quite. There's still a lot we don't know. How do you feel?' he added, giving himself a mental kick for asking such a damn-fool question. How the hell did he expect her to feel?

'Sleepy.' She gave him a tiny smile. 'The doctor made me take a pill. I told him I didn't want one until I'd seen you, but he insisted. It was strange. I remembered him from the war days but he didn't remember me. He seemed quite surprised when I told him I used to work here.'

'It's lucky you did. It probably saved your life.'

'I know. It's odd, isn't it, how something that seems so trivial at the time can become so important.'

She yawned and blinked. He had only a couple of minutes to say what he had to. God knows when he'd find another opportunity or the nerve.

'Look,' he began, but she stopped him by placing one of her hands on his.

'You don't have to say anything,' she said softly. 'You weren't to blame for my father's death. He was a sick man. It could have happened at any time. He knew it, I knew it, even poor Ilse knew it.'

'I was to blame,' said Quinlan, forcing himself to look at her. 'I wish it could be different, but all the wishing in the world won't change the facts. I just don't....' He fumbled for the words, which came out in a rush. 'I just hope it won't always be something that stands between you and me.'

'It won't. I won't let it.'

Difficult though it must be for her she was trying to forgive him, and he was being churlish in not accepting what was

220

being offered without reservation. He tried to mumble his thanks, but she shook her head as vigorously as she could in her sedated condition.

'You don't have to thank me. I've had a lot of time to think in the last twenty-four hours. I thought I was going to be killed, perhaps assaulted and tortured before they finally got round to it. I was frightened, very frightened, but I kept on believing you would find a way to free me. Not Max or Major Hadleigh, but you. It stopped me from going out of my mind. Can you understand that?'

Quinlan said he thought he could.

'You'd better sleep now.'

'I think I'll have to. I can hardly keep my eyes open. Will you be here when I wake up?'

He wasn't sure but said he would anyway.

'Good,' she murmured, 'good.'

When she was breathing evenly he gently removed his hand. He wanted to remain with her, allow the peace and tranquillity of the room to wash over him, retreat into a world that was as far removed as it was possible to be from the one that awaited him outside. But he knew he was being foolish. There would be a tomorrow. With luck there always was.

He found Max waiting for him in the corridor.

'I didn't want to barge in,' said the American, 'but word came through a minute ago from the brass. We make no deals with Kaltenbrunner. Not that it's going to matter much. The other one, the one who was shot in Kaltenbrunner's room, is sitting up. He tells us his name is Scharper and he's ready to sing like a bird.'

Any loyalty Scharper might have had to Battle Group Sternberg evaporated when Riordan shot him. But more than that he remembered Kaltenbrunner saying he intended bargaining with the Americans. If that happened what he, Heinrich Scharper, had to tell them would become superfluous.

So he talked. In the presence of Masterson, Quinlan, Hadleigh, Petrov, Max Judd and a tape recorder, he told the entire incredible story as he knew it. Some of it he had witnessed personally, some was hearsay, but his audience

221

listened in stunned silence from the moment he started to speak.

Twenty-two

Flossenburg Camp: German-Czech border – April 6-9, 1945

In the beginning (said Scharper) no one was quite sure what part Canaris had played, if any, in the July Plot against Hitler's life. The little Admiral denied participation of any sort and there were those who were inclined to believe him. Had he not, after all, sent a telegram to the Fuehrer shortly after 6 p.m. on July 20, 1944, congratulating him on his providential escape? That he numbered several of the known conspirators among his close friends was not in dispute, but his arrest and detention were less due to his relationship with Claus von Stauffenberg, who planted the bomb in Hitler's conference hut, than to the SS, now that it had control of the Abwehr, paying off old scores. At least that was how it started.

Since arriving among the barbed-wire, watchtowers and endless rows of huts of Flossenburg on February 7, 1945, Canaris had received the same treatment as other 'special category' prisoners. They were permanently shackled and allowed no correspondence. They were, however, adequately fed and kept fit in order to undergo further interrogation, for, in Canaris's case, the SS was not convinced the Admiral was the friend of the regime he protested to be.

It was known to the guards that the 'special category'

inmates regularly communicated with confinees in adjacent cells by tapping on the walls, using not Morse but a simple code which reduced the alphabet to twenty-five letters, omitting J. Canaris in cell 22 was no exception. He held long if limited 'conversations' with the occupant of cell 21, Mathieson Lunding, a former Danish cavalry captain and member of Danish military intelligence.

Although they had hidden listening devices in each cell and knew the code, the SS turned a blind eye to these supposedly arcane exchanges in the hope of hearing something of value. But all they learned from Canaris's transmissions to Lunding were details of his interrogations to date, which they knew anyway, and that he expected to survive the war. Which he might well have done if his diaries, long hidden in a safe in the underground shelters of Camp Zeppelin, Zossen, had not been found on April 4 by Infantry General Walter Buhle, who passed them via Hitler's bodyguard commander to RSHA Chief Ernst Kaltenbrunner. At the midday conference in the Reich Chancellery the following day, Kaltenbrunner brandished the diaries which not only implicated Canaris with the July conspirators but also proved he had been in treasonable correspondence with the head of British MI6, Stewart Menzies, as long ago as 1942.

Hitler gave immediate orders for Canaris to be eliminated, but Kaltenbrunner was renowned for his dislike of non-judicial killing. The lawyer in him wanted everything signed and sealed before delivery. Thus it was that a drumhead court martial was to be set up at Flossenburg on April 8.

Canaris received the news of the discovery of his diaries and his impending trial (with only one possible verdict) from the camp commandant on April 6, but instead of protesting his innocence or accepting his fate he asked to be allowed to send a message to Kaltenbrunner. When informed that that was out of the question, he warned the commandant that other heads would roll if Kaltenbrunner was not told immediately that the Zossen diaries were not the only ones in existence and that he, Canaris, knew all about Alt Aussee.

Concluding that he had nothing to lose, the commandant relayed the message by phone to Berlin, expecting no reply. He was therefore astonished to receive a telegram within the hour stating that Kaltenbrunner himself and several aides would be arriving at Flossenburg on the 7th. As it happened, Allied air raids and pressing business combined to prevent their departure for twenty-four hours. It was not until early evening on the 8th that they arrived by road from Berlin.

For the number two man in the SS the motorcade was unbelievably tiny. It wasn't until much later that the camp commandant deduced that Kaltenbrunner had not wanted to trumpet his visit. Apart from a dozen motorcycle outriders he was accompanied by just four men, one of whom drove the staff car. These were introduced as Standartenfuehrer Sternberg, Sturmbannfuehrer Scharper, Oberscharfuehrer Flisk and Unterscharfuehrer Zander. The two NCOs, Flisk and Zander, were to be taken on the camp's strength with immediate effect, their presence recorded. Ever a stickler for doing things by the book, Kaltenbrunner wanted no documents turning up in the future saying that Canaris was interrogated by individuals who were not part of the Flossenburg staff. His own visit was not to be logged. Nor were the names of Sternberg and Scharper to appear.

They saw Canaris in his cell. For the time being Lunding and the occupant of cell 23 were removed to another part of the compound. Extra chairs and a table were brought in and Canaris's shackles removed. Kaltenbrunner invited him to sit.

Canaris had never been an imposing individual to look at. He was only five feet three inches tall and somewhat round-shouldered, and the months in captivity had done nothing to enhance his physical appearance. When he spoke he was inclined to lisp.

Kaltenbrunner got straight down to business.

'What's all this about Alt Aussee and other diaries?' he wanted to know.

Canaris glanced nervously at the quartet who made up Kaltenbrunner's entourage. He knew the two officers by sight and name from the days when he commanded the Abwehr, but the NCOs' faces were unfamiliar. They both looked as hard as nails, however, and he had no doubt they were there to provide the muscle if the interrogation did not go according to plan.

'I thought we would be talking in private, Herr Obergruppenfuehrer,' he said politely.

'This is as private as it's going to get, you treacherous

bastard,' snarled Kaltenbrunner. 'Say what you've got to say and let's get it over with.'

Canaris seemed faintly amused at being described as a traitor.

'I'm not sure the Fuehrer would regard your activities and those of your group as less than treasonable if he knew about them.'

'Explain yourself.'

Canaris chose his words carefully.

'The repository of looted art treasures in the Alt Aussee salt mine is what I'm talking about. They were to form the basis of the finest collection in the world after the war, in the Fuehrer's home town of Linz. Reichsminister Speer has already designed the building.

'Of course it is no longer possible for such a collection to exist because Germany has lost the war, but had we won it there would have been on display – and I mention only a few for the sake of brevity – the Ghent altarpiece by the van Eycks, the Portrait of the Artist in his Studio by Vermeer, the Dirk Bouts altarpiece from Louvain, and Michelangelo's masterpiece, the marble Madonna from the Church of Notre Dame in Bruges. There would have been Titians, Raphaels and Breughels from the Naples Museum, as well as canvases from the Rothschild, Gutmann and Mannheimer collections. There would have been works by Rubens, Reynolds, Lippi, Palma Vecchio, Frans Hals and others too numerous to catalogue here. According to my information there are almost seven thousand paintings stored in the Alt Aussee mine, of which at least five thousand could be reliably described as Old Masters. The Fuehrermuseum would have been the envy of the world.'

Canaris paused for effect, his eyes never leaving Kaltenbrunner's pock-marked face.

'Of course, only a handful of people would have known that almost three hundred of the exhibits were fakes, painted by German, French and Belgian art forgers in 1942 and 1943. The individuals concerned are no longer around to testify. I understand the SS had them executed when the work was done.'

The long silence which followed was eventually broken by Kaltenbrunner.

'You have nothing to sell, Canaris, not to the Fuehrer. He has known from the beginning what we were doing. It had his full approval. You're right about the forgeries, though I'd give a year of my life to learn how you found out. You're wrong that they would have been displayed at Linz. Had the war gone otherwise – and I do not accept for a moment that all is irrevocably lost – the real artworks would have hung in the Fuehrermuseum. Now we have different ideas.'

Canaris studied Kaltenbrunner carefully.

'Which I must assume means ransoming the originals to their rightful owners at some future date. Secretly, of course. I doubt the present political climate in the world would tolerate individuals or governments doing business with what will remain of the Third Reich. I know where the real paintings are, naturally. As head of the Abwehr I made it my business to know. You can move them – though it won't be easy at this stage of the war – but it will do you no good. Once word gets out that part of the Alt Aussee repository is faked you will find no buyers for the originals.'

'And how,' sneered Kaltenbrunner, 'will word get out?'

But Canaris refused to be hurried.

'Let me see if I have this correct. You, Sternberg, Scharper and a handful of others – the numbers necessarily small because of the secrecy needed – have stored fake paintings among real ones in Alt Aussee. I freely admit I do not know exactly how many nor the identity of the works involved, but that's neither here nor there. When Alt Aussee is overrun by the Allies and the treasures recovered by the Monuments, Fine Arts and Archives detachment, what will they find? Why, with great relief they'll find, intact, priceless works of art from all over Europe. They will have no reason to suspect that booty so carefully concealed is anything but genuine. Apart from the fact that the forgers you employed were of the highest calibre, any slight imperfections will be put down to hasty transportation or inadequate storage conditions. After examination and cataloguing the works will be returned to their owners, private collections, museums and suchlike. When that has been done, which will take time, you or one of your representatives will approach each owner individually and tell them that what they have on their walls is worthless. You will offer to return the real painting for a price. If they refuse to do business you will threaten to destroy the genuine articles. If they dare talk to the authorities it will become common knowledge overnight that what they are displaying is counterfeit. And what collector would want that known? Apart from the vast sums of money at stake there is the pride of ownership. Whether the ransom you receive is to be used for some absurd conception of a Fourth Reich or merely to line your own pockets I neither know nor care.'

Kaltenbrunner reached into his tunic pocket for a cigarette. Scharper dutifully sprang forward with a light. But within the confines of the narrow cell the smoke was overpowering, and Kaltenbrunner ground out the cigarette under his heel.

'So,' he said, trying to control his rage, 'you possess information I would rather not be made public. The fact remains that you are here, in Flossenburg, incommunicado.'

'You underestimate me, Herr Obergruppenfuehrer. My message to Berlin was that not only did I know about Alt Aussee but that other diaries existed apart from those found at Zossen. To be precise they are not diaries but several pages of notes, setting out my findings and deposited in a Geneva bank. The number of the account is known only to me.'

'And with you dead,' said Kaltenbrunner slowly, 'the account stays closed for ever.'

'I'm happy to say you're wrong.' Canaris gave the SS general a nervous smile. 'Long ago I devised a method which will enable several of my subordinates, without them presently knowing the number, to open the account should anything befall me. If I die the plan goes into operation immediately. Even if they fail for one reason or another, the bank has instructions to release the documents to the world on January 10 of the year following the war's end, which will be next year unless I am misjudging events. There was no special reason for that date other than it was on January 10, 1944 that I made my trip to Switzerland. It should also give my subordinates a few months to obtain the documents for themselves, and use them.'

'You fucking bastard!' snarled Kaltenbrunner. He back-handed Canaris across the face, knocking him to the cell floor.

Alarmed, Sternberg and Scharper stepped forward, gesturing Zander and Flisk to help Canaris to his feet. This sort of display of temper would get them nowhere.

227

'Herr Obergruppenfuehrer,' said Sternberg gently, 'perhaps we should hear what sort of bargain Admiral Canaris wishes to make.'

'I'll see him hanging from a gibbet before I strike a bargain with him!' screeched Kaltenbrunner. 'The treasonable swine has probably told Menzies and half of MI6 what he's done.'

Canaris wiped the blood from his mouth with his sleeve. Behind him, Zander and Flisk stood ready to do their master's bidding.

'Talk,' said Kaltenbrunner, calming down only after a visible effort. 'You haven't brought us all the way here to tell us how clever you've been. Let's hear your proposition.'

'It's very simple,' lisped Canaris. 'In the first place, neither Menzies nor anyone else knows what is contained in the Swiss documents. I could hardly expect the British to keep it to themselves if they knew and that would defeat my purpose. Second, no specific signature is required to withdraw the documents from the bank. Anyone giving the correct number can do so. Third, you will be given that number in exchange for my freedom and that of my family, a sum of money to be agreed, and a passage via one of the SS escape lines to South America.'

'Out of the question. The Fuehrer has ordered your execution.'

'Without a trial?'

'There will be a trial.' Kaltenbrunner looked at his watch. It was 6.35. 'Prosecutor Huppenkothen and SS Judge Thorbeck will be arriving shortly. There can, of course, be only one verdict.'

'Then I regret your little scheme becomes stillborn. On January 10 next year or earlier if my men get to Geneva before, the world at large will learn what you have done and your intentions. You will find few takers for your proposition then, even if Allied troops do not locate the cache beforehand.'

Kaltenbrunner nodded his head as if coming to a decision.

'It was a good plan, Canaris,' he said, his voice almost friendly, 'but it contains a flaw. As we know now that you are the only living soul, for the moment, who possesses the number of the account, do you think we can't force it out of you?'

They beat him up then, Zander and Flisk, slowly and methodically, while Kaltenbrunner, Sternberg and Scharper watched from the far side of the cell. Experts at their trade, Zander and Flisk kept the Admiral just this side of consciousness, though a wayward blow from Flisk broke Canaris's nose.

After five minutes of this and no sign of Canaris capitulating, Kaltenbrunner was about to sanction even harsher treatment when there was a faint rapping on the cell door. A quaking voice begged the interruption be excused but Huppenkothen and Thorbeck had arrived and wanted to know when the *Kriegsgericht*, the court martial, could commence. Judge Thorbeck had orders from the Fuehrer to report direct when the trial was over and the verdict delivered.

'We'll be a few more miutes,' said Kaltenbrunner.

Scharper opened the cell door a fraction and relayed the message.

Kaltenbrunner waved Zander and Flisk to one side. Canaris was crumpled against one wall, bleeding from the nose and mouth and holding his groin.

'Well?' demanded Kaltenbrunner.

Canaris shook his head. They would certainly kill him once they had the number. His only hope was to hang on.

'This is serious,' muttered Scharper to Sternberg, aware that Hitler would wonder what the hell was going on if he didn't hear from Thorbeck soon.

Sternberg agreed.

'If I may make a suggestion, Herr Obergruppenfuehrer.'

'You may not make a suggestion,' said Kaltenbrunner. He thought for a moment. 'Did you pass on my orders that our interrogation of Canaris was not to be recorded or even listened in to?'

Sternberg said he had. They could not see a microphone but knew there was one in the cell somewhere.

'Very well,' said Kaltenbrunner to Sternberg, 'go to the control room and see that all communications from this cell remain cut off until I instruct otherwise. Now,' he added in a tone that discouraged argument.

Sternberg went out.

Kaltenbrunner told Scharper to find Huppenkothen and Thorbeck and tell them they would not be denied much longer.

'Take Zander and Flisk with you. I want to have a quiet word alone with Canaris. Close the door behind you.'

Scharper did so. Outside he waved Zander and Flisk on ahead and hung around the passage just long enough to hear Kaltenbrunner try a different sort of threat.

'You mentioned your family, Canaris. Think of them. We know where your wife, Erika, is. Also your daughters Eva and Brigitte. Think of them and what could happen to them. Do you want them in the next cell to yours here? Or taken to Ravensbruck? Either can be arranged.'

Scharper heard a muffled sob before deciding it was too dangerous to be caught eavesdropping. He followed Zander and Flisk up the corridor.

Kaltenbrunner sought them out twenty minutes later. Sternberg looked at him expectantly.

'Herr Obergruppenfuehrer?'

'Find an officer named Langenhain, Oberstleutnant Langenhain, one of Canaris's cronies from the old days. He's the key.'

Sternberg's expression was one of bewilderment.

'But did Canaris talk, Herr Obergruppenfuehrer?'

'Too many questions, Sternberg. Do as I say. Get on the telephone and trace this man Langenhain.'

'With due respect, that can be done more easily from Berlin, using the Gestapo.'

'You're not going to Berlin, none of you, not for the moment. I must return as I'm due at a conference later tonight. But I want you four to stay here. I want to know from men I can trust that the bastard's dead. Return when it's over.'

He acknowledged their straight-arm salutes, and left.

'He's got the number,' said Sternberg after a moment. 'He's got it and he's keeping it to himself.'

Scharper shrugged his shoulders uninterestedly.

'As long as one of us has, that's all that matters.'

And at that time it really seemed as though it did.

Canaris was tried, found guilty, and sentenced to death by SS Judge Thorbeck. At 10 p.m. on the evening of April 8 the duty watchkeeper heard the Admiral tapping out a signal to Lunding, now back in his cell. For the benefit of Sternberg and the others, who did not know the code, he translated the substance of the text.

'Nose broken at last interrogation. My time is up. I was not a traitor. Did my duty as a German. If you survive remember me to my wife.'

'I think we'd better see to it that he sends no more messages,' said Sternberg eventually. 'You never know what they might comprise.'

At a little before 6 a.m. the following morning Sternberg was aroused from where he was sleeping in his clothes by the camp adjutant. Accompanied by Scharper, Zander and Flisk they went out into the courtyard.

There were five candidates for execution, among them Pastor Dietrich Bonhoeffer. All the men were naked.

They were herded across to the gallows one by one and made to mount a small pair of steps. A noose was then placed about their necks and the steps kicked away.

Canaris in particular took a long time to die, his frail body writhing for what seemed, to the witnesses, an eternity. But, at 6.14 a.m. SS physician Sturmbannfuehrer Dr Hermann Fischer pronounced life extinct.

Twenty-three

Nuremberg – January 7, 1946

We caught up with Langenhain around the middle of April last year,' Scharper said to a hushed room.

He didn't seem to care that he was implicating himself in at least several killings, for it was apparent from his tone that Langenhain was as dead as Canaris. Probably he thought that the murder of fellow Germans in wartime was not an indictable offence, or maybe that he was in so deep that holding anything back could only make things worse.

'Canaris had told him the name of the bank but not the account number. All he knew was that he had to contact Hauptmann Arndt in Nuremberg. He had seen Arndt, we established that much, but had not obtained from him the first fragment nor the name of the man who had the second.'

'Wait a minute, wait a minute,' interrupted Hadleigh. 'You're going too fast. What does that reference to the fragments mean?'

'Don't you know?' Scharper seemed surprised. 'We knew you had two and guessed you might have all four.'

'We do, but they don't mean anything.'

'They give the account number,' explained Scharper. 'When placed together, Canaris told Langenhain, they would reveal a group of islands in the Atlantic. By referring to a large-scale world map the islands would be identified. The longitude and latitude of the chief island is the number which opens the account. We knew that much but not which island group and therefore not the number. There are too many in the Atlantic to hazard a guess. The South Orkneys, the South Shetlands, the Falklands, Cape Verde, Tristan da Cunha, Ascension, the Azores, and dozens more.'

'Christ,' muttered Quinlan. It was all so simple once you had the key.

Masterson was still bemused.

'I don't understand why Canaris chose such a complicated code,' he said.

Neither did Scharper, though he was willing to make a guess.

'Complicated it may have been, but he was gambling with his life. He couldn't just give the number to Langenhain with instructions to remove the documents if anything happened to him. Langenhain might have taken them while Canaris was still alive, which would have left the Admiral with an empty safety deposit box if Kaltenbrunner had agreed to his terms. The rule was that Langenhain should only approach Arndt when he heard that Canaris was dead, but we know for a fact that Arndt was contacted way before April 9. Langenhain's explanation to us was that he believed Canaris to be dead once he was told the Admiral had been transferred to Flossenburg, but Sternberg did not consider that to be the truth. He reckoned Langenhain panicked when the war was nearing its end and wanted to get his hands on whatever was in the account before the Allies overran Germany. He did not know the contents of the documents, of course, or even that the deposit box contained documents. Perhaps he thought it held money, there's no way of telling. Anyway, Arndt refused to hand over the first fragment until he was certain the Admiral was dead because those were the instructions Canaris had given him. Shortly after that we picked up Langenhain, which left Arndt in limbo.'

It was becoming clearer now. If things had gone according to plan Canaris would have bartered the Swiss bank number for his freedom and that of his family. If he was killed and his murder became public knowledge, Langenhain would have obtained the first fragment and the second name from Arndt, which would in turn have led to the second fragment and the third name until the picture was complete. With the documents Langenhain and his friends could avenge Canaris's death by turning them over to the Allies, perhaps earning the gratitude of their conquerors but certainly putting paid to any ideas the SS might have about ransoming the paintings.

'How do members of the British Free Corps fit in?' asked Quinlan.

'Originally to act as intermediaries between ourselves and the real owners of the artworks,' answered Scharper. 'We realized that after the war it would be difficult for Germans to travel freely and for those of us who had served in the SS impossible. It would be less so for men who spoke English as their native tongue, especially if those men had nothing to lose anyway. This was before we knew about the fragments, of course. When we learned they existed and had to be found before January 10, the British Free Corps contingent became even more important. Having caught up with Langenhain we had to find Arndt. Riordan and the others were in a better position to walk the streets of Nuremberg than the rest of us.'

Petrov had a couple of questions.

'Why was it necessary to forge paintings? Why not remove two or three hundred of the more valuable works from Alt

Aussee and store them in a separate place until the time came
to ransom them?'

There were three answers to that.

'In the first place,' explained Scharper, 'all the works were
carefully catalogued. We couldn't have taken even a dozen
without someone commenting on their absence. As it was, it
took us a long time to make the switch, which we would not
have achieved without Kaltenbrunner's authority on our side.
We're talking about masterpieces, don't forget, the majority
even the man on the street would recognize. In the second
place, it is psychologically superior to approach someone who
believes he has his own property back with the news that
what he has is a fake. Thirdly, the Allies knew almost to the
last item what had been looted. Even if we could have
overcome their absence from Alt Aussee, an individual or a
gallery could not have a blank wall one minute and an Old
Master the next without someone asking where it came from.'

Petrov accepted that but still didn't understand why the
fragments were needed at all.

'Kaltenbrunner had the account number and presumably
the name of the bank in April last year. It would have been
difficult to get into Switzerland at that stage of the war, but
not impossible. Why were the papers not simply removed by
one of you?'

Scharper grimaced at what was obviously a painful
memory.

'Because Kaltenbrunner didn't tell us the number. Sternberg continued to ask him but he always made some excuse
for keeping it to himself. For that matter he said nothing of
what transpired between himself and Canaris in the cell.
Even now I don't know whether he forced Canaris to divulge
the names of the four men holding the fragments or whether
he was quite happy just to have Langenhain's name and the
account number. Shortly afterwards he dropped out of sight.
Who knows the way his mind works? None of us ever did. He
probably thought, as Canaris doubtless did, that being the
sole possessor of the account number gave him an advantage
over the remainder of us. Perhaps he would have told us
eventually or slipped into Geneva to withdraw and destroy
the documents, but the war ended and he was captured
before he could.'

'How can you possibly know that if you didn't see him from around mid-April onwards?' asked Hadleigh.

'I don't, but we had to work on the assumption that the papers still existed.'

'Which made it essential to free him before the tenth,' put in Masterson.

'Either that or find the fragments,' agreed Scharper. 'But once we knew you had Arndt's, the second option became virtually untenable. We therefore had to rescue Kaltenbrunner or at the very least get the number from him. We had few doubts that if we had not done so several days before the tenth he would try to strike a bargain with you, because after the tenth the information would be public knowledge and therefore useless to him as a means of obtaining immunity.

'Liberating him from prison or the courtroom was a pipe-dream, we all accepted that. But when we heard of his being taken in and out of hospital, we knew he was giving us a fair chance of getting to him without excessive risk.'

'What about the Sherman tank?' asked Hadleigh.

Scharper smiled faintly.

'Sternberg thought you'd be worried about that,' he said, 'but the tank was always a red herring. You'll find it at the bottom of the River Pegnitz several kilometres west of Fürth, where it was driven by ex-tank driver Granger the night it was hijacked. It was never part of Sternberg's thinking to use it against the Palace of Justice. Not that Kleemann and Isken knew that. Not that Kleemann and Isken knew anything. They were not part of the original group. We picked them up in Salzburg for just such an eventuality. They firmly believed they were going to spearhead an attack on the Palace of Justice. We knew when you took them you'd find a way to break them.'

'You couldn't possibly have known we'd be waiting for them at the station last night,' protested Quinlan.

'But we did.' Scharper seemed pleased with their cleverness. 'When we first decided to kidnap the girl, Fräulein Wolz, our only concern was to find out from her how much you knew, how close you were, if you had all the fragments. We could have abducted her several days earlier, but then we had a better notion. If we left it until yesterday, Sunday, the day before we were to try for Kaltenbrunner, it would work

235

more in our favour. We surmised you'd move heaven and earth to find out how we knew where she was being hidden. We did not underestimate you. Either you would conclude one of you had been followed to Sündersbühl – and we took great care not to follow you – or that we had someone on the inside. It was a gamble, but we thought you'd suspect Gretl Meissner sooner rather than later. If you hadn't we'd have tipped you off by telephone.

'Riordan *never* made contact with Frau Meissner on a Sunday. If on calling the Grand there was a message asking for a meeting at the Hauptbahnhof or the hotel, we'd know it was a trap. All we had to do was allow Kleemann and Isken to walk into it, following which they would reveal, under interrogation, that the Palace of Justice was to be attacked this morning. While you were there, we would be here. If there was no message at the Grand, if we were unable to inform you that Gretl Meissner was working for us or if you did not come to the logical conclusion to set a trap, we'd have sent Isken and Kleemann out on some fool's errand and informed you anonymously where they could be picked up. Either way, you would have learned from them what they believed to be true, that we were to attack the Palace this morning at 10.30. If you suspected beforehand that Kaltenbrunner was the real target you would surround him with troops. We would have seen them and known the ruse hadn't worked. However, it did work.'

'To no avail,' Masterson reminded him.

'The fortunes of war,' said Scharper in a matter-of-fact voice. 'You were too quick and Kaltenbrunner too slow. Otherwise none of us would be here now.'

'Where would you have been?' asked Quinlan.

There was still much that needed answering. Who had raped and murdered Ilse Arndt and Angela Salvatini, for example? Who had killed Helga and almost killed Ingrid? Who had disposed of Willi Meissner, the tank crew, the original owners of the uniforms Scharper and his bunch were wearing? But they could wait, as could the papers in the Geneva bank. What they all wanted to know now was where the remnants of Battle Group Sternberg had gone, the location of the real paintings, which would be one and the same place.

Scharper licked his lips nervously.

'Does everything I tell you count in my favour?'

'I'm not empowered to make deals,' said Masterson. 'The most I can say is that a transcript of the tapes will be forwarded to the competent authorities. It will be up to them to decide whether what you've told us is enough to warrant clemency should any charges be brought.'

Scharper accepted the situation without argument. If he didn't tell them everything he knew, Kaltenbrunner might. In any event, the location of the hoard was in the Canaris papers and they now had the number of the account. It would take a single phone call to one of their representatives in Geneva to pass on that information. They could have the location in an hour. It was going to take Sternberg a hell of a lot longer to move the paintings.

'The cache is in an abandoned tin mine on the road between Bayreuth and Hof, a few kilometres beyond the junction to Kulmbach. You get to the mine itself by taking a dirt road on the right of the Bayreuth-Hof highway. The entrance is boarded up with corrugated iron and wooden planks, but that's a blind. It would be simpler if I drew you a sketch. There are seven or eight tunnels inside but only one leads to the cache. At the end it looks as if there has been a heavy rockfall, but beyond the rocks is a cavern. The paintings are in there.'

'How many of them?' asked Masterson.

'Almost three hundred.'

'How do you know they're still there?' Quinlan wanted to know.

'There was a time when we thought they weren't. Kaltenbrunner made a private visit, we found out later, with half a dozen demolition experts from the SS Panzer Division Das Reich towards the end of 1944. That worried Sternberg and me so we paid a visit of our own. We thought Kaltenbrunner might have removed the rockfall with a series of controlled explosions and transferred the cache. We found no evidence to support that. Quite the reverse. If anything the rockfall was higher and deeper than previously. It took Sternberg and myself several hours to dig out a gap big enough to crawl through, but everything was as it should be on the other side. We reasoned afterwards that Kaltenbrunner had only wanted to strengthen the barrier. Perhaps he'd considered a double-cross but found it impracticable.'

'Why didn't you ask him, or ask the demolition people?'

'Because then he'd have known we were checking up on him. As for the Das Reich people they just disappeared. Presumably Kaltenbrunner had them killed on the basis that the fewer who knew about the mine, the safer we'd all be.'

'That was in 1944,' Quinlan reminded him. 'How do you know the paintings are still there now?'

'Because we've been over the mine from time to time since, the last occasion as recently as Christmas. We even watched from a distance last year while a platoon of American toops removed the battens and explored the tunnels. They came out empty-handed. The paintings are still there, I assure you, as they have been since 1943. They are stored in metal-lined packing cases to prevent corrosion or mutilation by rats. It was a carefully conceived operation.'

'The ransom money doubtless to fund the Fourth Reich, as Canaris intimated,' sneered Petrov.

'Not at all. Perhaps Kaltenbrunner had some such idea with himself as the new Fuehrer, but that did not apply to the rest of us. Even as early as 1942 some of us suspected we would lose the war now the Americans were in. If that happened the survivors would need money to escape from Europe and begin a new life elsewhere. I've read in the newspapers and heard on the radio that all SS officers have access to vast fortunes, but I assure you that isn't true. A handful of gold coins and a few Swiss francs perhaps, but not enough to live on for ever.

'It was originally Sternberg's idea. He was a policeman in prewar Berlin and personally acquainted with many of Germany's top art forgers, who in turn put him in touch with Frenchmen and Belgians in the same business. He approached Heydrich with the scheme, but that blood-thirsty fool wanted nothing to do with it, even threatened Sternberg with a firing squad. When Heydrich was assassinated and Kaltenbrunner took over the RSHA, he proved more amenable.'

'I don't believe you,' said Petrov, as always looking for a conspiracy. 'Hitler would never have agreed.'

'I regret to inform you Hitler didn't know about it, which

was one of the reasons we couldn't spend too much time interrogating Canaris, not with Judge Thorbeck under orders to report directly back to the Fuehrer. Kaltenbrunner lied to Canaris about that. Not even Himmler knew. There were only a small group of us, thirty at the most at the beginning. The majority of those are now dead.'

'How many survived?' asked Hadleigh. 'What sort of opposition are we likely to meet at this mine?'

Scharper countered that with a question of his own. How many had been killed or wounded this morning?

Hadleigh told him.

'In that case there are only five left. Sternberg, Flisk, Riordan, Hallam and Granger. Hallam is an American,' he added maliciously.

'A couple of platoons should be enough,' said Hadleigh. 'If I remember my geography of the area correctly, the Kulmbach junction is around seventy miles from Nuremberg. I'll take Major Quinlan and Max to help me round up the troops while Scharper draws his sketch,' he added to Masterson.

They left the G-2 colonel arguing with Petrov, who was already insisting on a Soviet presence on the raid. Masterson was telling him not a chance, the most he could have was himself and his two aides, take it or leave it.

'What about Kaltenbrunner?' said Quinlan in the corridor.

'We don't need him any more,' said Hadleigh, 'and I think we can safely leave Gene Masterson to pass on the good word.'

Twenty-four

It was snowing again. That and the fear of roadblocks they wouldn't see until they were on top of them had slowed them down.

They had arrived at the mine just ninety minutes earlier, and for each of those minutes they had laboured at the wall of rock using their bare hands. The knowledge that Kaltenbrunner was still alive had caused Sternberg to abandon caution. He had few doubts that the Obergruppenfuehrer would not try to make a deal, purchase clemency with information. For that reason he had not left a guard at the mine entrance, which was several hundred metres from the rockfall, nor even hidden the jeeps. They were only five; every pair of hands was needed. The snow would keep the locals indoors and, in any case, the entrance could not be seen from the main highway. All he had to fear was Kaltenbrunner striking his bargain too quickly, but he doubted that would happen. A decision regarding immunity would have to be taken at the top, written guarantees prepared, and that would take time. They had two or three hours' start, possibly a little more. He hoped it would be enough.

There could be no question of taking all the packing cases, of taking even one. They had only two jeeps and the cases were too large. Each, however, was labelled with its contents and rightful owners. They would have to open those which contained the smallest or most valuable paintings, or those belonging to men and institutions he judged most amenable to paying a ransom. If necessary, some works would be slit from their frames. The remainder would have to stay. It was a tragedy, but there it was. At least there were fewer individuals now to share the spoils. If was difficult to put a figure on the value of the cache; some of it was beyond price. But in

240

US dollars, the only currency he was inclined to accept, the entire hoard must be worth eighty or ninety million. Even forty or fifty canvases, fifteen or twenty per cent of the total, would be enough to set up five people for life.

It was back-breaking work, particularly as it had to be done in semi-darkness, the only illumination coming from strategically placed hand torches whose batteries were rapidly expiring. Beyond the rockfall, in the cavern, was a petrol-driven generator hooked up to a lighting system, and a score of full jerrycans. But it had been decided years ago that there should be no electricity in the tunnels. The mine was meant to appear derelict. It would have aroused suspicion to have sophisticated lighting outside the cavern.

Stripped to the waist like Sternberg and working next to the German, Riordan tore at the rocks at the top of the thirty-foot-high pile, wondering just how thick the fall was. He, Hallam and Granger had visited the mine on only one previous occasion and as far as they were all concerned they couldn't give a damn if they never saw it again. Sternberg heard him cursing that they were undermanned and recalled it had taken him and Scharper, the time they had been checking on Kaltenbrunner, two hours to create a gap big enough to crawl through. But then there were only the two of them. Theoretically it should have taken under an hour with five pairs of hands, but it hadn't worked out like that. Five men could expose a lateral gap one hundred and fifty per cent faster than two, but what they needed was depth across a narrow range and they kept getting in one another's way until it was decided they should work in pairs for ten minutes at a time; two at the rockface, three resting, and so on in rotation.

But it was a slow business and at the end of two hours they had still not made a breakthrough. The major problems were the suffocating dust thrown up as rocks hit the tunnel floor, and lack of oxygen which impaired efficiency. Less important but annoying were bleeding hands – and cold, when not working, occasioned by being seventy or eighty feet below ground level.

'I thought you Germans were supposed to be efficient,' Riordan grumbled once, when Granger and Flisk were at the rockfall. 'A child of ten could have figured out a better hiding place.'

Tunic over his bare shoulders to prevent his muscles seizing up, Sternberg refused to take offence. Including Hallam in his reply, he said that they'd had many different ideas as a location for the cache at the beginning.

'We thought of shipping them out of the country, storing them in Switzerland or Argentina. But that was rejected as being impracticable. It would have meant special warehousing facilities and there was no guarantee that some inquisitive individual would not start poking around, wondering what was in so many packing cases requiring such meticulous storage. Nor could we guarantee, in the instance of Argentina, that the ship or U-boat would reach its destination. Besides, we would have lost control over their physical presence, which was considered undesirable. So too was storing them in a major city such as Berlin or Hamburg, even in bank vaults. If we lost the war bank vaults would be opened by the victors. Even if we won, the big cities were going to receive a pounding from the Allied air forces. Anything that even looked like a salt mine and therefore a good place to store valuables was obviously out of the question. They would be discovered by the Allies, as they have been at Alt Aussee, Merkers, Kochendorf, Heilbron, Lauffen and the others. This was the best we could come up with. We were not to know then, of course, that Canaris, working alone as he preferred, had discovered our little secret. Or that Kaltenbrunner would be captured. When we found out about Canaris it was too late to move the stuff. In any case, there was nowhere else suitable. Neither was it considered necessary. Kaltenbrunner had the information which would unlock the Geneva numbered account. We didn't realize he would not pass it on to us or have the papers removed.'

'We should have taken a few last time we were here, as insurance,' grunted Hallam, coughing as the dust caught in his throat. 'I said all along it was dumb to trust Kaltenbrunner. He could have told the military government months ago about the cache and we'd have been none the wiser.'

Sternberg frowned distastefully at the American. They were the scum of the earth, these British Free Corps men, but he needed them. More so now than before as ransom negotiations would have to be conducted in double-quick time, from the Zirndorf back-up house.

'*I* knew he wouldn't say anything,' he said haughtily, 'not while there was a chance we could free him. Besides, you talk as though we're dealing with potatoes or apples. We're not. We're dealing with works of art, many of them hundreds of years old. If they're in less than perfect condition we shall find no buyers.'

'I don't see that bundling them into the back of a couple of jeeps and driving across Germany at zero degrees Fahrenheit is going to do much for them,' said Riordan.

'If you have a better suggestion in our present predicament I should be delighted to hear it.'

'We should have hijacked a couple of 3-tonners back in September and moved the bloody lot,' said Riordan. 'To Grossreuth or Fürth or Zirndorf. Then it wouldn't have mattered a shit whether Kaltenbrunner talked or not, whether the Americans found the fragments.'

Sternberg was tired of telling Riordan that the paintings were virtually worthless if the world's Press got to hear about and publicized the contents of Canaris's deposit box. No one would deal with them then, regardless. It would be tantamount to a painting's owner saying that he didn't give a damn what the Nazis had done; he wanted his Titian or his Rubens back at any cost.

The German was saved from having to repeat this argument by a shout from Granger from the top of the pile.

'I think we're almost through,' he called down. 'There's cold air coming from up front. Lend a hand up here.'

Riordan and Hallam scrambled up the rockfall. Before following, Sternberg checked his pocket watch by the light of the torches. It was 3.35 p.m. They had been at it almost two and a half hours but surely, by now, Kaltenbrunner would have made his deal and talked. The Americans must be on their way. He hoped they were yet to clear the Nuremberg suburbs.

Although Sternberg had no way of knowing it, it was a hope stillborn. A few minutes before 3.35 the small convoy of vehicles which had left Nuremberg just after 1 p.m. crossed the Kulmbach intersection. The leading jeep contained Hadleigh, Quinlan and Masterson, with Max Judd, as usual, doing the driving. Close behind them came Yuri Petrov's staff car, and behind that half a dozen trucks carrying two platoons of Third Army dogfaces. They had made good time for the conditions, averaging 30 mph.

Seated up front next to Judd, Quinlan had Scharper's hand-drawn sketch on his knees. The SS officer had indicated on the map that the turn-off for the mine was between three and four kilometres beyond the Kulmbach junction, on the right-hand side of the highway. The reverse side of the sheet of paper depicted the interior of the mine and its branch tunnels. Quinlan hoped to God they would have occasion to use it, the sketch, that Battle Group Sternberg had not been and gone, taking what it could carry and destroying the rest as an act of malice.

'That looks like it,' he called across to Max, who slowed down and made a signal that he was turning right. There was no sign nor any other indication that they were on the correct road, though Quinlan thought he could detect faint tyre tracks which even the heavy snowfall had not quite eliminated. They would soon know anyway. The sketch gave the mine's entrance as 400 metres up ahead.

'Let's not bowl right up in the vehicles,' suggested Hadleigh, after they had covered half that distance. 'If they've posted a guard he'll have heard us by now, but we don't have to give him a big fat target to aim at. Pull over here, Max. We'll do the rest of it on foot.'

Grumbling in the manner universal to soldiers when asked to move, the dogfaces piled out of the comparative warmth and dryness of the trucks and deployed either side of the dirt road. They were under the command of a young infantry lieutenant by the name of Joe Liddell, who came forward to find out what the next move was. Yuri Petrov and his aides remained in their staff car.

'The way it looks from the sketch,' Hadleigh told Liddell, 'there's only one way in and out. If they've left a guard on the entrance we deep-six him, quietly if possible. You can send a couple of your best men on ahead to do that right now.'

Liddell disappeared through the snow. Thirty seconds later a sergeant and a Pfc went past the jeep at a dogtrot, weaponless except for wicked-looking knives.

'Whether there's a guard or not,' went on Hadleigh when Liddell returned, 'it gets a bit tricky after that. The tunnels are narrow and unlit. We'll take torches, but if we also take

244

too many men we're going to get in one another's way. There are only five of them, so half a dozen and yourself should be enough. Plus Colonel Masterson and ourselves, of course.'

'Don't forget Petrov,' muttered Masterson.

'I wasn't,' said Hadleigh. 'I'll see what his plans are in a minute. Pick guys who can move quietly,' he added to Liddell. 'The rest can deploy themselves behind cover where they can see the mine entrance. Leave someone you can trust in command. The guys we're after are wearing British and US uniforms and three of them speak English, one with an American accent. I don't want anyone holding his fire until it's too late because he sees drab-olive or khaki, but neither do I want anyone getting trigger-happy and dusting us if we come out first. Maybe we should have a password.'

'How about Tintoretto,' suggested Masterson.

'Too much of a mouthful,' said Liddell, shaking his head. 'If you'll forgive me, Colonel, most of the guys I've got would think it's something to eat with meatballs and parmesan over on Bleeker Street. It's better to keep these things simple.'

'Okay, quiz kid, you suggest something.'

'How about cheeseburger, as we're talking of food.'

So Cheeseburger the password became.

'You can tell them to blast anyone who doesn't give the correct response,' said Hadleigh, 'though if the sketch is accurate there's no way anyone can get past us. Once we're inside we play it by ear. There's a lot of valuable stuff in there, so flinging grenades about is out. On the other hand, the guys we're up against are facing a rope if they're taken alive. They're not going to quit without a fight.'

The two-man patrol came back, looking disappointed. There was no one on the entrance but there were two jeeps parked outside. They had immobilized them by removing the rotary arms.

'Petrov,' Masterson reminded Hadleigh.

Hadleigh went across to the Soviet colonel and explained what they were about to do. To his relief the Russian did not want to accompany them. He and his aides would remain where they were.

'In your nice warm staff car,' muttered Hadleigh.

He checked the sketch again at the mine entrance. Twenty metres beyond the opening was a major tunnel which split

245

into three. The one they wanted was on the right. Fifty metres further along, this tunnel forked. They again wanted the right-hand spur. At the end of this the rockfall divided the cavern into two. The distance involved was around two hundred metres descending through some sixty or seventy feet. At no point was the roof higher than ten feet and once they reached the second spur this came down to eight. The maximum width at this point was also eight, though further on the cavern was thirty metres across by ten to twelve metres high.

They used the torches from the beginning. It was impossible to see without them once away from the entrance. They were taking a chance because the beams, though partly masked with black tape, would be observable a long way off. If anyone had had the wit to set up a machine-gun post where the spur broke out into the cavern – and it was known from Scharper that Battle Group Sternberg had automatic weapons – it would be like shooting fish in a barrel.

But there was no sign of opposition up front after they had covered the first hundred metres, though there were mid-distance noises of what sounded like ice being crushed.

Fifty metres further on, Hadleigh shuffled to a halt. They were travelling in two Indian files, hugging the tunnel walls, six feet between each man but both columns, with Joe Liddell riding point on the other, level with each other. Quinlan tracked Liddell, armed with an M1 carbine he had borrowed from one of the dogfaces outside. Max Judd was behind Quinlan while Masterson followed Hadleigh. Equally split, the six GIs were bringing up the rear.

Keeping his voice down for fear it would carry, Hadleigh beckoned everyone forward and explained that twenty metres further on the tunnel took a shallow left bend which led it into the cavern. There was no need to add that Sternberg and the others were here. They could all hear the commotion up front, muffled voices, the crushing-ice noise now obviously the sound of rocks falling. They could also feel the dust creeping into their nostrils, eyes and throats.

'They've got their minds on other things,' said Hadleigh. 'If they're still trying to get through the rockfall or if they're already through and ferrying stuff back to our side of the cavern, maybe we can rush 'em.'

246

An experienced infantry officer, Joe Liddell didn't much care for the idea of dashing along a narrow passage in pitch blackness. The defenders wouldn't have to see the attackers. All they'd have to do was shoot in the general direction of the tunnel mouth.

'If there's only one exit, maybe it would be a better idea to wait for them outside, bag 'em as they come out.'

They had discussed this on the road up from Nuremberg, Masterson, Hadleigh and Quinlan, and concluded it was unworkable. By definition, once Sternberg and his crew reached the exit they would be carrying some of the looted works of art. In the inevitable firefight which would ensue, some of them were certain to be damaged, perhaps irreversibly. As senior officer of the group, Masterson didn't want it entered on his service sheet that he was responsible for the destruction of irreplaceable paintings.

'No,' said Hadleigh, 'we've got to go in and get them.'

'Then one of us had better do a recce,' said Liddell.

Quinlan volunteered. He thought of the northern voice that had shouted 'nail the bastard' the night he was driving from Humboldtstrasse, of the men who had abducted Hannah and who doubtless would have killed her. Some of them were up front. He had a bigger stake in this than any of the others.

Hadleigh understood.

'No heroics now. Just check it out, find the score, and come back.'

'I'm not exactly a newcomer to this kind of thing,' said Quinlan irritably.

Hadleigh grinned at him.

'Why, Miss Smith, you're beautiful when you're angry.'

Quinlan elected not to take a torch in case Sternberg had posted a look-out. He asked that the others be doused until his eyes became accustomed to the darkness. When they were he moved forward slowly, edging along the wall.

He sensed rather than saw the left-hand bend but could make out nothing up ahead. He counted his paces. When he reached forty he stopped. Surely he was close to the cavern now? There was a greater feeling of space and what seemed to be a series of dim flickering lights coming from a spot twenty feet above his head and about twice that distance in front.

Later he realized that these were torch beams coming from the far side of the rockfall and shining through the gap at the apex Sternberg and the others had made. But for the moment he was puzzled.

There did not seem to be any sign of life this side of the cavern, but the darkness and the irregular configurations of the rocks made it difficult to be certain. You could hide a platoon in here and they would not be seen until you were on top of them.

Had they left anyone to keep an eye on the tunnel? Impossible to say, but the purpose of a recce was to spy out the lie of the land.

Easing the safety off the M1 and holding his breath, he continued moving forwards.

From the tunnel mouth to the base of the rockfall was, it would later be established, fifty feet. Quinlan was half way across when the stillness was shattered by the sound of the generator starting up. Simultaneously a wedge of brilliant light spilled through a fissure at the top of the rockfall. After the darkness of a moment before the cavern was suddenly as bright as day.

Although temporarily blinded by the unexpectedness of it all, Quinlan caught a glimpse of a man's head and shoulders silhouetted in the gap. Then he was diving for cover as a Thompson submachine gun opened up, kicking up dust and dirt as the marksman tried to pick him off with a long burst.

Sixty seconds earlier they had finally made the gap big enough not only to climb through but to bring out even the largest of the canvases. The torches were very weak now, but Sternberg remembered precisely where the generator was.

Ordering Hallam to remain in the opening but to keep his head down and report immediately if he saw any movement, Sternberg led the way down the rockfall and across to the generator, where he filled the tank from one of the jerrycans and pulled the cord to turn over the engine.

Due to the cold and damp and lack of regular use it needed a lot of choke and four attempts before it caught and the cavern was flooded with light. In an area measuring eighty feet across by sixty deep and thirty high were stacked dozens of packing cases, each the size of a large sea-chest. But, even as Sternberg was bending down to examine the label on the nearest, Hallam was firing and the cavern was filled with the acrid smell of cordite.

'Kill the lights!' screamed Hallam in between bursts. 'Kill the fucking lights!'

It was Sternberg obeying this exhortation almost before the words were uttered that probably saved Quinlan's life. In his panic the machine gunner had missed him, but there was no real cover in the cavern against a marksman shooting from above, and another few seconds would have seen him dead. As it was, with Hallam firing blindly into the darkness, he stumbled, heart pounding, back to where he remembered the tunnel mouth to be, almost falling on several occasions and barking his knuckles against the cavern wall but not breaking his stride until the flashes from the Thompson's muzzle disappeared behind the left-hand bend.

He collided with Hadleigh and Joe Liddell coming the other way. Catching his breath he explained what had happened.

'That's damned well torn it,' cursed Masterson when they got back to him. 'Are you hurt?'

Quinlan said he wasn't. The backs of both hands were cut and bleeding and he was surprised to find his knees trembling, but he was otherwise uninjured. He silently thanked God he'd had the presence of mind to keep a firm grip on the M1, even though he hadn't got a shot in. He'd never have lived it down if he'd dropped the bugger.

'We're going to have a hell of a job digging them out of there,' he told Masterson. 'Even if they can't see us they can hear us. All the machine gunner's got to do is aim at the noise. Under the circumstances it's a first-rate defensive position.'

'Blast the bloody paintings,' said Masterson. 'We could have them out of there or dead in two minutes with a bazooka.'

'What about tear-gas and smoke?' Liddell queried. 'There's some in the trucks and half a dozen respirators.'

'Get it all,' said Masterson curtly.

Liddell dispatched two dogfaces to do just that.

'The trouble with tear-gas,' said Quinlan, 'is that someone's got to get close enough to lob a grenade through the gap in the rockfall. Point a torch down here. Take the tape off. They know we're here now.'

Quinlan sketched in the dirt a rough outline of the position in the cavern as well as he could remember it.

'The rockfall is thirty feet or so high from the cavern floor, the gap about six by six roughly in the middle. It's fifty feet from the tunnel mouth to the base of the rocks. A man would have to expose himself for a couple of seconds to get a decent throw in. It's not a job I'd fancy, even in the dark. For that matter, if I were them I'd get the genny going again and take up better defensive positions on their side of the gap.'

As though on cue they heard the petrol engine restart and saw fingers of light illuminating the tunnel beyond the bend.

'What about the effects of carbon monoxide?' asked Max.

'Depends what sort of space they've got back there. I'm no expert,' said Quinlan, 'but I don't reckon it'll do them much harm if they're careful. It might be unpleasant, but I doubt it'll be lethal for a few hours.'

'Mexican stand-off,' said Hadleigh. 'They're not going to come out hands high because they've all got a date with the hangman and we can't get close enough to clobber them with tear-gas without taking unacceptable risks. So what the hell's the next move?'

'I've got a feeling that's coming from them,' said Liddell, cocking his head. 'Listen.'

They did so. As though from the bottom of a deep well they heard a voice calling, in English, for a parley.

A few moments after taking the decision to restart the generator and illuminate the cavern in case they were rushed, Sternberg, Riordan and Granger got their heads together. Dispatching Oskar Flisk with a second Thompson to join Hallam and giving them both orders to shoot at anything that moved, Sternberg, as realistic as ever, spelt out their predicament.

'We don't have much time. I don't know how they got here this fast, but that's neither here nor there now. There's only one way out and they're blocking it. We don't know their numbers, but I'll wager they're four or five times as great as ours. We can hold them off until the ammunition runs out, but that's only putting off the moment when we'll have to give ourselves up. And we all know what that means.'

'Keep talking,' said Riordan.

'It's my opinion they won't try to blast us out. Fragmentation grenades or rocket launchers will destroy what they've come to salvage. Nor can they rush us without suffering casualties. They can either try to starve us out or use gas. My guess would be the latter. We might kill a few of them, but sooner or later a gas grenade will get through the opening. After that we're dead.'

'If you're suggesting we give ourselves up, forget it,' said Granger. 'I'd rather take a bullet here than face the gallows in six months.'

'I wasn't suggesting unconditional surrender,' said Sternberg mildly. 'We've got something they want more than our heads; they've got something we want. We have the paintings; they have the exit.'

He walked over to the nearest packing case and tore off the label.

'We'll talk to them,' he said.

Suspecting a trick, they advanced no further than ten feet from the tunnel mouth, where, by crouching to compensate for the angle of the tunnel roof, they could see the light from the far side of the cavern spilling through the gap. They couldn't see the defenders, but they were there all right.

'What do you want?' called Hadleigh.

A disembodied English voice answered. Quinlan recognized the accent, though he had no way of knowing this man's name was Riordan.

'There's someone here wants to talk to you.'

'This is the perfect opportunity to make a pitch,' muttered Liddell, cursing his lack of foresight in not bringing tear-gas and smoke with them.

'He'll be happier speaking in German,' added Riordan.

'He can speak in Hindustani for all we care,' shouted Hadleigh. 'We're listening.'

Not showing himself, Sternberg told them what he had in mind.

'I have in my hand,' he called above the din of the generator, 'a list taken from one of the packing cases. It reads

251

that it contains two Titians, two Renoirs, a Monet, a Reynolds and several others. In total nine canvases. I am prepared to let you have these, and the rest, in exchange for an unimpeded passage out of here. Should you refuse, the aforementioned paintings will be destroyed in precisely two minutes. I will then repeat my offer with the contents of a second packing case. Should you again refuse they too will be destroyed. And so on until nothing remains here that could remotely be described as a masterpiece. I realize that at the end of it all I shall have nothing left with which to negotiate, but you will be responsible for the mutilation of a heritage. I regret I must hurry you, but the two minutes begin now.'

'The bastard means it,' said Masterson. 'Where the hell's that tear-gas and smoke?'

Liddell was way ahead of him.

'Double back to the trucks and tell the other two to get their asses out of a sling,' he ordered a third dogface, but Max stepped in.

'I'll go,' he said, tapping his chevrons. 'Let's see if these rockers mean anything.'

'Ninety seconds,' called Sternberg.

'Jesus Christ,' groaned Hadleigh. 'Titians, Renoirs, a fucking Monet. I'm no art expert, but that sounds like heavy wood. I'd lay odds the friggin' frames are worth more than I earn in a year.'

'How about lobbing a few fragmentation grenades at them,' suggested Liddell, 'just to shake the rocks around a bit?' He spoke no more than fifty words of German and most of those were concerned with bodily functions, the availability of food and booze and women, but it didn't take a linguist to deduce what was happening.

'He's right,' grunted Hadleigh. 'We may destroy a few that way, but that bastard plans to destroy the lot. Any volunteers?'

There were none.

'I guess it's up to me, then,' said Liddell, shrugging his shoulders.

Quinlan laid a restraining hand on his arm.

'Don't be a bloody fool, man. In the first place this mine looks like a rickety old structure to me. One big bang could bring the roof in. In the second place, you'd be cut down

252

before you'd covered ten feet and we'd be no further forward. Let's wait for the gas, the smoke and the respirators. We'll toss a few smoke grenades our side of the rockfall and try to get close enough under cover of that to use the tear-gas.'

'Only trouble with that,' said Masterson, peering at the luminous dial of his wristwatch, 'is that we have less than a minute left.'

Sternberg confirmed that a moment later by calling that they were now down to forty-five seconds.

'In thirty seconds we begin opening the first packing case.'

'So we lose a couple of Titians,' shrugged Quinlan. 'We'll have them before they can do any more damage.'

'Here's the gas,' said Liddell.

Max had the respirators slung over his shoulder. Each perspiring GI was struggling with an open ammunition box, the stencilled markings on one showing it contained smoke, the other tear-gas.

Grabbing a smoke canister and a respirator and keeping tight to the tunnel wall, Quinlan inched forward to the mouth. He could see no sign of life beyond the gap, but he distinctly heard a voice, apparently calling up to Sternberg, who must be tucked behind the rockfall, counting off the seconds. The voice was Riordan's, though he was speaking in German.

'There's something funny here,' he shouted. 'I've half got the lid off but there's a bunch of wires....'

The sentence was never finished. The reason why the Das Reich sappers and Kaltenbrunner had paid a visit to the mine in 1944 struck Quinlan with the suddenness of a physical blow. The demolition experts' subsequent disappearance and probable execution also became clear. The SS general had not been reinforcing the rockfall. No one was going to move or in any other way interfere with the cache unless he was present. If he couldn't share in the spoils, no one else would. Fearing a doublecross he had booby-trapped the packing case.

'*Hit the dirt!*' screamed Quinlan, diving to the floor of the tunnel and burying his head in his arms.

There was a blinding flash of light followed instantly by an ear-splitting explosion. Then another and another as the charges in the adjacent packing cases erupted, either linked in series or, more probably, set off by the first detonation.

A tongue of flame like dragon's breath leapt through the gap in the rockfall as the jerrycans of petrol caught fire and went up with the power and composition of incendiary bombs. Blasts of scorching air whipped over Quinlan's prostrate figure, tearing at his clothes, burning his hair and flesh, causing him to cry out in pain. Somewhere up front he heard screams of agony, but these were quickly silenced as the entire structure of the cavern began to collapse because of the shockwaves.

The rockfall separating the two sections of the cavern was split asunder, hurling boulders large and small and choking dust in all directions. Shrapnel-sized pieces, white hot like tracer shells, peppered the tunnel mouth, missing the supine Quinlan but killing Joe Liddell and one of the GIs who were right behind him at the moment of detonation but who were fractions of a second too late in hitting the ground. Their upright bodies took the first full force of the blast, however, and in the narrow tunnel probably saved the lives of those behind them.

Quinlan knew he had to get out, retreat. Apart from the fact that any moment now he could be killed by a flying boulder, lying as he was a few feet from the tunnel mouth there was a real danger that the disintegrating cavern would set off a chain reaction, bringing the roof down about him.

But his body refused to obey his mind. He was frozen into immobility.

A sound like a dozen artillery barrages echoed and re-echoed in his ears, slamming into his brain, turning it unwillingly to jelly. But now the explosives were spent, the gasoline fires extinguished. What he was hearing was thousands of tons of rocks imploding, filling the cavern, annihilating everything that lay beneath.

Then it was gone. Or rather, not gone but muted. He thought he had been deafened, but that couldn't be because somewhere behind him he could hear Ben Hadleigh's voice calling to him.

He had no idea how long he lay there before forcing himself to open his eyes. He could see nothing, not even the dust in the cavern, but the feeling of claustrophobia was overwhelming. Gingerly, fearing that any sudden movement would bring total destruction, he raised his head from his arms and reached forward. His fingers touched rock where, a little while ago, the tunnel mouth had been. It took him a moment to grasp what had happened, that a large boulder had blocked the entrance, sealing off the cavern, muting the inferno beyond.

A torch beam pierced the gloom and willing hands dragged him to his feet. In answer to the anxious queries regarding whether he was all right, all he could do was nod. Making a nervous joke because he too was shaking from head to foot, Hadleigh said: 'I knew you had a class act but I didn't expect it to bring the house down.'

Twenty-five

Geneva/Nuremberg – January 9-10, 1946

It was a different kind of snow in Geneva, clean, fluffy, very Swiss. They were in civilian clothes, the banker race not being too keen on men in uniform, whatever the insignia, wandering their warless streets.

After desk formalities they were shown up to a luxurious first-floor office and there given a simple form to complete. Hadleigh checked the number in his diary carefully, the longitude and latitude of Tristan da Cunha. They wanted no mistakes. Tomorrow the information in the account would be emblazoned across the world's newspapers unless properly claimed, and that was thought to be undesirable.

Hadleigh wrote: 12°30′ W 37°00′ S, and handed the form to the young male secretary, who took it gingerly between forefinger and thumb as though handling something contagious.

They waited in silence, Hadleigh, Masterson and Otis Quinlan. Their civvies had been borrowed from anyone who had such things in postwar Nuremberg, and they neither fitted properly nor matched. But that was not the only reason the male secretary had looked upon them as escapees from the workhouse. All three of them appeared to have fought a recent battle with hostile Indians.

Hadleigh and Masterson were the least injured, but both wore Band-Aids on their faces and hands where they had been struck by flying debris. As for Quinlan, beneath his ill-fitting jacket and shirt his shoulders, arms and upper back were bandaged where he had been caught by blasts of scorching air. The injuries were not serious enough to have hospitalized him, but they were distinctly uncomfortable. His hair too had been scissored away by doctors attempting to get at the burns and now, with dressings applied where unavoidable, he looked like the unfortunate victim of a shortsighted barber with a penchant for straight gin.

When the secretary appeared bearing a small steel box, apparently locked, he was preceded into the office by a tall, grey-haired man wearing a magnificently tailored morning suit and a pearl pin in his silk tie. Even Masterson, in spite of his rank, felt an urge to get to his feet, though he, like the others, remained seated. The man had Presence. His hands, the nails beautifully manicured, looked as though they had never done anything so vulgar as count money. He would have minions for that.

The secretary placed the box on the desk, gave a short bow, and went out, closing the door behind him.

The banker studied each of them in turn.

'My name is Doctor Beck,' he said in English, assessing their native tongue immediately though since entering the bank Hadleigh had conducted all conversations in German. 'I do not wish to know yours. I mean no disrespect, but it will not be necessary.'

He referred to a black leather-bound notebook he was carrying.

'You have fulfilled the conditions of the account and that is sufficient. I take it you do not have a key to the box.'

'No.' Masterson shook his head.

'I thought not, but it's of no consequence.' He took a small bunch of keys from his pocket and selected one. 'The box, you will understand, has not been opened since the account was originated. I do so now only with your permission.' He waited a moment. 'I have it, I take it?'

Masterson nodded.

Doctor Beck unlocked the box and returned the keys to his pocket.

'I will leave you now. My secretary is outside. Call him if you need me. If you choose to take the contents of the box and thus close the account, there are one or two formalities to be completed before you leave.'

The box contained half a dozen sheets of paper covered with spidery handwriting and held together by a paper-clip. As one, they experienced a sense of deflation. For so many people to have died for possession of something so commonplace seemed unbelievable.

That the words were those of Admiral Canaris appeared indisputable. Although they had never seen his handwriting the address at the top of the first sheet was Tirpitzufer 72/76 and the notes began: *From Admiral Wilhelm Canaris to whom it may concern.* If any doubt arose about the authenticity of the calligraphy it could always be checked against official documents.

They had difficulty making out some of the sentences, so cramped was the writing, but the text began thus.

'It is my fervent hope that no one will ever read this. If they do, it means I shall either be dead or have had to bargain for my life. If the former and it is you, my dear Manfred, use the contents wisely. If the latter and it is you, Kaltenbrunner, may you rot, for I am beyond your reach, one way or another.'

There then followed a résumé of the Kaltenbrunner/Sternberg plot, exactly as they had heard it from Scharper. How French, German and Belgian art forgers had faked almost three hundred Old Masters and were then executed. How the forgeries were mixed with authentic masterpieces in Alt Aussee. How the Allied recovery teams would believe the

257

fakes to be real and return them as such to their rightful owners. How the genuine paintings were hidden in the tin mine between Bayreuth and Hof.

'If you have got this far, dear friend [the notes went on] you will surely wonder why I chose such a bizarre means of getting you here, why I handed fragments of photograph to Arndt, Bachmann, Butterweck and Straub. Why also I told you only Arndt's name, the name of the bank, and the fact that all four fragments would reveal an island whose longitude and latitude become the key which opens the account. Why I did not give you the number itself. I'm sorry to say it was fear.

'Forgive me if I seem to mistrust you, old friend, though these days it's hard to know who one can trust. You will recall I asked you not to approach Arndt until you had confirmation I was dead. I also instructed Arndt not to hand you (or anyone else) the first fragment and Bachmann's name until he was sure of my demise. I know not whether you stuck to the letter of our bargain. I hope so, but I would find it hard to blame you if you anticipated events and contacted Arndt before you heard of my death. With me in prison (where I must surely be or you would not be reading this) you might have found it difficult to ascertain whether I was still in this world or entering the next. But there lies the rub. I intend bargaining with Kaltenbrunner for my life, that in exchange for the contents of these notes. If he agrees (and you must realize I am talking in the future tense here, because at the moment I am still free), you can imagine his reaction if he is informed by Doctor Beck that the account has been closed. For the same reason I cannot tell the British nor allow any single individual to possess the number of the account. If he does not agree (and you know only too well his methods of persuasion) I hope I shall be able to hold out, revealing neither your name nor the number of the account. If I fail in either respect I shall have encumbered you with an intolerable burden, but there was no other way.

'If you are reading this and the war is over, if you, Arndt and the others are alive, take these notes to the Allied military government. You will undoubtedly earn their gratitude and that, the state Germany is likely to be in, will be no small thing to have.

'If someone else (other than Kaltenbrunner) is reading this because it has become public knowledge, then I am content. His scheme will have failed and I shall take the utmost pleasure in meeting him in Hell.'

'The word from on high,' Masterson was saying, 'is that we bury this. It never happened. There was some kind of fight between troops of the Third Army and a few hard-core Nazis in the tin mine, and they were killed in an explosion. It was just a normal mopping-up operation. There were no paintings in the mine, neither real nor faked. Those that are now or will soon be hanging on the walls of galleries or private houses are the real McCoy. That's the way the brass and our various governments want it. If it ever gets out that a particular Titian or Rubens or Reynolds *could* be a phoney, the bottom will drop out of the entire art world. There's too much money at stake, thousands of billions of dollars, not to mention about five hundred years of history.'

They were sitting in Masterson's office, Hadleigh, Quinlan, Max Judd. It was, of course, snowing outside.

'Let sleeping Titians lie,' grunted Hadleigh.

'Precisely,' agreed Masterson. 'Even Canaris's notes have been destroyed. I was present when they were burned this morning. One or two of us wanted to keep them for posterity, maybe under lock and key for ever, but we were overruled. As we all know, locks and keys don't guarantee anything.'

'What about Petrov?' asked Quinlan.

'No problem. The Soviets are being remarkably cooperative. They lost stuff during the war from Leningrad, Kiev, Kharkov, the Palaces of Peterhof, Tsarskoe Selo, Pavlosk. Dozens of other places. They've now got it back. They think. The trouble is, none of us has an inventory of exactly what was in that damned mine and it's all now so much matchwood. Sternberg mentioned two Titians, two Renoirs, a Monet and a Reynolds, but which Titians and Renoirs? And what the hell else was in there? The lists were tacked to the sides of the packing cases and no longer exist. No, there's no need to worry about the Soviets. They're as anxious as everyone else to keep it under wraps. Better to display a fake that everyone thinks is genuine than rock the boat.'

'How many are in on this big secret?' Hadleigh asked.

'Apart from governments and brass and a couple of bigwigs from CIC,' answered Masterson, 'the four of us here, Petrov and those two goons he had with him. Joe Liddell might have guessed what was going on, but he's dead. The dogfaces just thought they were digging out a nest of Nazis who had some crazy plan to free Kaltenbrunner.'

'And Fräulein Wolz,' said Quinlan quietly.

They had had a blazing row about this earlier, he and Masterson. Quinlan had argued that Hannah had a right to be told after all she'd been through, especially as he had plans for her and didn't want to be forced to hold his tongue for the rest of his life.

'And Fräulein Wolz,' nodded Masterson. 'I agreed that with Major Quinlan this morning.'

'For a price,' muttered Quinlan.

He had accepted never to tell the story, nor leave behind any diary to be published on his death. They had even invoked the Official Secrets Act. The journalist in him was enraged; it was the biggest story he was ever likely to come across. But he held an ace he would play one day.

'What about Kaltenbrunner, Colonel?' asked Max.

'Back in the slammer, denying all knowledge of booby-traps. He was a touch pissed off, I can tell you, that we didn't need his help. He threatened to make a speech from the dock when it's his turn, but he won't. I made him a couple of half promises.'

'Genuine?'

'Naw.' Masterson grinned wickedly. 'No, he's going to do a jig with the rest of them only he doesn't know it yet.'

'What about Scharper?' asked Quinlan. 'Apart from the fact that he's the only one left to face charges for the killings of Angela Salvatini, Ilse Arndt, Willi Meissner and God knows how many others, he knows exactly what was in the mine. I wouldn't have thought it was a good idea to have him roaming around loose, either in prison or out of it.'

'He won't be,' said Masterson.

'How come?'

'He's dead, fell from the fourth-floor fire escape of the Hallerwiese-Klinik trying to make a run for it.'

'Christ. When?'

Masterson examined his wristwatch.

'In about an hour.'

Quinlan was shocked.

'Don't be,' said Masterson gently, reading his mind. 'You said it yourself, there's Angela Salvatini, the Arndt girl, Willi Meissner. We're just putting the score straight on their side.'

'Maybe,' said Quinlan, 'but I wish to God I was sure he was being killed for crimes he's committed and not because he might talk and put a hole in the value of the world's art collections.'

'Money, son,' said Masterson. 'It's what make it all tick over. The stories I could tell you....'

He shuffled a few papers into a neat pile to indicate the meeting was at an end. Telling Hadleigh and Judd to go on ahead and close the door behind them, he gestured Quinlan to remain where he was.

'There's just one more thing,' he said. 'I've been getting some flak from my old buddies at British Second Army HQ, wanting to know whether we still need you. I told them we did. For another couple of weeks. But I don't want to see you anywhere near the office. Ben and Max will tidy up the paperwork, such as it is. Grab yourself a decent car and take that girl of yours off to Austria or someplace for a fortnight. Anything you want in the way of gas and ration coupons is yours.'

'Thanks,' said Quinlan. 'I appreciate that.'

'Otis,' he heard Masterson mutter as he closed the door. 'Hell of a name for an Englishman.'

'What did he want?' asked Hadleigh.

Quinlan told him.

'Pity,' said Hadleigh. 'I was going to dress Max here up in a commissioned officer's uniform and suggest we all tie one on at the Grand. Later we could've found out if there's anything in this countess Petrov's always on about. Maybe she has a few ritzy friends.'

'I don't think he'd be much use to a countess or any other woman, either here or in Austria,' grinned Max. 'Not patched up the way he is.'

Quinlan returned the grin.

'I'll find a way.'

Epilogue

Needless to say, it was snowing. But now the new buildings were going up the city didn't seem as desolate as it had in 1946.

It was their first time back in over three years. It hadn't been planned that way. They had flown to Munich, to see Quinlan's German publisher, and they'd thought, why the hell not? It was only a hundred miles up the autobahn.

He was going to call his new book *Major Otis Regrets*, but his ace was that he intended telling it as fiction (for which he already had a considerable reputation), not fact, change a few names here and there. It would be the entire story of the Canaris fragments. If some clever bugger saw what he was up to and read him the Official Secrets Act, he would point out that it was just a story, no more, and one that had to be told. Hence the pun in the title.

He already had the first lines. He would begin with Sternberg and Scharper, as yet unnamed, gloating over the fake pictures. Something like:

Beautiful, beautiful.

The two SS officers walked the length of the warehouse, stopping occasionally to discuss the object of their admiration.

Something like that.

They crossed the River Pegnitz where Gretl Meissner, a few days after learning of her son's murder, had drowned herself in January 1946. The IMT verdicts had been announced later that year, and on October 16, at eleven minutes past 1 a.m., those to be hanged had mounted the scaffold. Ribbentrop, Keitel, Frank, Rosenberg, the near-idiot Streicher, Seyss-Inquart, Sauckel and Jodl. And Kaltenbrunner, who, finally, seemed genuinely amazed that this could be happening to *him*, who had run out of things with which to trade.

Goering got away with it by swallowing a cyanide capsule smuggled into his cell, Schacht, von Papen and Fritzsche were acquitted, while the remaining defendants drew hefty prison sentences.

But it wasn't the day to be remembering such things. Christmas was around the corner and they had to be back in Munich by evening. After that it was home to England where Ben Hadleigh, now a full-blown bird colonel and on the way to his first star, was joining them for the festivities. Max Judd had also promised to fly in if he could get away.

On impulse they decided to visit one of the city's biggest public galleries, where they looked long and hard at a magnificent Titian. After a moment they were joined by a middle-aged German couple, who also stood in awe before the painting and misunderstood their silence for reverence.

'A most inspiring work, is it not?' said the man eventually, recognizing their nationality by the cut of their clothes and speaking in perfect English.

'Actually,' said Hannah, digging Quinlan in the ribs but keeping a perfectly straight face, 'my husband preferred the original.'

Acknowledgements

Many individuals and organizations helped with the research for this book. Regrettably but understandably the most important individuals wish to remain anonymous. These include three former German officers, one a former member of the Waffen SS, the other two Wehrmacht. A very elderly man who once served with the British Free Corps and fought with Waffen SS detachments during the last days of Berlin gave me invaluable assistance in describing the infrastructure and training schedules of the BFC. While I made it quite clear to him that I in no way sympathized with the stance he took, I respect his wish to remain unnamed.

The major organizations whose assistance was invaluable are: The National Archives and Records Service, Washington, D.C., the Public Records Office, the Imperial War Museum, the Royal Geographical Society, and the staff of the Tiverton Library, Devon.